BETRAYALS

BY

MARY McCLEARY

ORIGINAL WRITING

© 2008 Mary McCleary

All rights reserved. No part of this publication may be reproduced
in any form or by any means—graphic, electronic or mechanical,
including photocopying, recording, taping or information storage
and retrieval systems—without the prior written permission of the
author.

This is a work of fiction. All the characters and events portrayed
in this novel are either products of the authors' imagination or are
used fictitiously

ISBN: 978-1-906018-80-1

A CIP catalogue for this book is available from the National
Library.

Published by Original Writing Ltd., Dublin, 2008.
Printed by Cahills, Dublin.

TO SEAMUS

MY ROCK.
YOU ARE ALWAYS THERE FOR ME.

ACKNOWLEDGEMENTS

I could not have completed this book without the constant encouragement from my family

Tom my eldest son was always at the end of the phone when I needed help with my computer problems.

Siobhan my granddaughter now residing in Australia was my wonderful secretary, I miss you.

The Gatehouse Writers Group and Anna Mc Cormack for bullying me to learn computers.

Darragh Mc Donald my first creative writing tutor, he saw I had potential and told me to keep at it.

John Mc Allister Armagh, my current tutor. Grace Maloney. My Editor for long hours of dedication.

Theo Mc Mahon my friend and neighbour.

My patient friends Miriam Sherry and Clare McGee.

Suzanne Toal at Zanni Photography for my portrait.

Last but not least my very talented Granddaughter Sorcha, for the book cover and putting all this together.

THANK YOU.

Foreword

Mary Mc Cleary sets her first novel in the south Ulster landscape during the "Troubles". In this story are interwoven the lives, loves, religious and political intricacies of a people and their families. The story crosses many barriers and lists the lives and loves of the main characters with all the frailties, suspicions, disappointments and joys that make it

Theo Mc Mahon

CHAPTER 1

LAURA STOMPED ACROSS THE YARD through the open door of the farmhouse, kicking it shut behind her with a loud bang. She strode through the kitchen into the big living-room, where she dropped the heavy basket of wet and muddy washing, cursing loudly all the time.

'If I could get my hands on that wee brat Beattie I would wring his neck! As if I hadn't enough to do. How anyone can be so thick. And to make matters worse the skitter's away home!'

Her father got up from his chair.

'Laura what's the matter? You know I don't like that sort of foul language.'

She could see he was angry but she didn't care. She pulled out some of the soiled washing.

'Look at this, that stupid git left the gate open again! I've just spent an hour getting all the cattle back into the field. I'd be there yet only for Seán Quinn. He was on the tractor in the top field and came down and gave me a hand but it was too late to save the washing. The animals broke the clothes-line.'

She held up the mud and dung-stained washing.

'Now I'll have to start all over again. Oh, I could kill that wee brat!'

Her father lifted the clothes back into the basket.

'Och, don't be getting annoyed. Sure it's only a bit of washing.'

The girl was furious.

'Only a bit of washing! And what would you know about it when did you ever do any? Sure you're just like all the men – you'd have the women down at the river beating the living daylights out of the clothes on the rocks if you had your way. Well, first thing tomorrow I'm going to dump that washing machine we have since the year dot and order the best automatic machine I can get. It'll do everything: wash, dry, the lot. And maybe do the ironing as well, if I'm lucky. It's not before time either... and I don't want any arguments about throwing good money away on fancy stuff.'

She picked the rest of the things up from the floor and went into the kitchen.

Some time later, when her anger had subsided, she returned to the living room. She was sorry that she had taken it out on her father. He was back in his chair reading his favourite book, *The Bible.*

'Father I'm sorry, I didn't mean to take my anger out on you, it's just...'

She turned away so he wouldn't see her tears and made a business of putting the kettle over on the range to boil.

'Look dear, it's all right, you have a right to be cross. Sure we all get angry at something. This past week has been too much for you with the shop and all. I can't do anything to help with this broken wrist but at least Myrtle and Jim will be back tomorrow and then you'll have the weekend to look forward to. Won't wee Alan be back?'

She smiled at him.

'I suppose like you I am not getting any younger and I really do miss that child... Now what would you like for your tea? You must be starving.'

After the meal, all she wanted was a long hot bath but when her father asked her to come with him on his walk, she couldn't refuse. They sat in companionable silence on the spreading roots of the big oak tree at the top of the field overlooking their farm, enjoying the early evening sunset. On the brow of the hill below, the tall farmhouse commanded an unspoilt view of rich Ulster farmland. To the east, the steeple of Tullybeg parish church jutted through the trees. Below in the valley sat Tully Lake with the mist rising above it, the Pomeroy mountains a purple haze in the distance. A man waved to them from the far field. It was Eric, the land steward, who looked after the McClean estate that bordered their farm. Laura loved the beautiful Georgian mansion set in acres of orchards, manicured lawns and well-kept rose beds. He invited them to have a look around any time and to enjoy the fruit and flowers. The place was empty, now that all the family had left. Sometimes it was rented out but rumour had it that it was going to be sold. As if reading her thoughts, her father sighed and said:

'I wonder who the new owners will be and what they'll do with the place? It's a big house to keep up nowadays, with the high cost of living. Anyway, whoever they are I just hope they are as nice a family as the McCleans were. Now give your old father a hand up and we'll head back down.'

It was late before Laura finally stood in front of the steamed-up mirror in the bathroom and surveyed her body. She cast a critical eye over it, pinching the spare skin here and there. Then she held her breasts in both hands, looked again and sighed. Laura girl, you had better get yourself in shape, for everything you have is moving southwards and you know you are well past your sell-by date. She laughed to herself and removed the bands from her long auburn hair, ran her hands through it and let it fall around her. She cleaned the steam off the mirror and watched herself in it as she tried to brush out the tangles. Och, it's no use! This will have to come off. I'm going to turn myself into a whole new woman when I get the chance. I'll even buy a brand new washing machine! She looked at herself and smiled... But what I really need is a man.

After a long bath she towelled her hair and stared at herself. Who is this woman? Where did time go? What about all my hopes, dreams and ambitions? Look at me, Laura Steenson, spinster of the parish, with a ten-year-old son. Who would want me now?

CHAPTER 2

1958

THE TWO YOUNG GIRLS sat on a low bridge overlooking an almost dry riverbed, legs dangling over the edge. They were watching the McCann children – Winnie and the twins, Johnny and Joey – and their pals playing in the water. Laura Steenson and Mary McCann were best friends.

'Well, did you ask your Da if you could go to the pictures on Saturday?'

'I couldn't Mary, sure you know what he's like, I can hear him now. "The picture house is no place for a young Christian girl, ye'd be better off reading your Bible." He makes me mad, I'm not allowed to go anywhere.'

Laura didn't tell her friend how her father raged when she did ask. He hated all Roman Catholics. He was always going on about 'them heathen papists', as he called them, how they bred like rabbits and had no morals. He had warned her just last night to 'stay away from them McCanns' but here she was with her friend as usual.

Mary shouted at one of the children.

'Winnie! How many times did I tell you not to let our wee Joey get wet. Isn't he only over a bad chest? Ma will kill both of us, for Christ's sake will you mind him!'

The young girl with a mass of untidy blonde curls looked up at her older sister and shouted:

'Well, why don't you come down and mind him yourself? I want to practice my singing beside the water. Sister Bridgid says it's good for the vocals, and she knows.'

The singing of 'The Fairy Piper' floated up to them. Winnie sang in perfect pitch, she had a wonderful voice. Laura, Mary and some of the younger children clapped. Winnie gave a low bow and smiled.

'Wasn't that great! All the nuns say that I sing like an angel. That's the song I'm singing at the concert next week. Are you coming Laura? It'll be a great night.'

She began another song till her wee brother Johnny, one of the twins, shouted at her to shut up as she was scaring the tiddlers.

'Look, I only have a couple and Joey has a jam-jar full.'

Winnie splashed her way over to him.

'If you went under the bridge like the rest of the boys, you'd catch more but you're too scared.' She began teasing him,

'Cowardy custard, cowardy custard.'

Winnie and Johnny started to push each other around until they both fell into the water. They jumped up screaming, blaming each other.

Laura and Mary were in fits of laughter at the scene below but decided to get all of them out and take them home. It was easier said than done. The river bank was very slippy and by the time they all got back to the road they were covered in muck. The girls tried to clean Winnie and Johnny and themselves but they all fell about laughing.

They looked a right sight as they strode all the way to the top of the street where the McCann family worked the farrier's yard and forge. They heard their mother before they seen her. Peggy McCann was a big stout woman and she had been talking to a neighbour in the doorway.

'In the name of Jazus, what happened to ye all? Look at the cut of yez, yer clothes are filthy.'

She looked at the two older girls.

'Have the pair of yez no sense at all, I send you to mind the wee'uns and you come back like this.'

The twins and Winnie all began talking at the one time but their mother chased them inside to get washed.

'You go on in too, Laura. Sure the tea is nearly ready and you may as well stay.'

Laura thanked her, she was delighted to stay. She looked around the kitchen at the McCann's large family of eight children: Pat the eldest, twins Mickey and Jimmy, Mary her best friend, her younger brother Peter, then Winnie and finally the second set of twins, five-year-olds, Johnny and Joey. When they were all together it was bedlam, and fun! So much different from her own quiet house.

The large kitchen was dominated by a long scrubbed white table that seated them all, with room for visitors. The older boys were always teasing her. Pat, the eldest, came into the kitchen, grabbed her at the waist and lifted her high in the air.

'Now, what about a kiss from my best girl?'

He playfully tried to kiss her, much to the delight of the younger ones.

'Pat McCann, if you kiss me you will have to marry me and you know my father won't allow it.'

Pat gave a hearty laugh.

'Then I will just have to turn and be a Protestant and join the Orangemen – I could march with your Da on the Twelfth!'

This had everyone in fits of laughter, Pat sat her into a chair beside him.

'Well, at least ye can eat with me, Ma. You've made my favourite, apple bread and soda farls.'

He jumped up and caught his mother in a huge bear-hug, and planted a kiss on her cheek. She laughed at him and shook the dishcloth at him.

'Oh, ye big soft lout, will ye behave yerself and sit down.'

She put the two plates of bread on the table with a big dish of country butter.

'Now will yez ate up, and say thanks to Laura for the butter. She churned it herself, didn't ye Laura?'

Laura went red, if they only knew how she'd had to smuggle it out without her father knowing. Laura loved eating with the McCanns, each one talking about his or her day and their father, Paddy, at the top of the table, joining in when he got the chance. You could see he was a very proud and happy man. The children helped with the clearing up while their parents went into the front room to watch the evening news on the television, a brand new addition to the house. When everything was done, Peter put on Elvis Presley's record, 'Blue Suede Shoes' and pulled Laura out to show her a new dance. Then the rest of the family joined in. Laura was having a ball until she saw the time.

'Oh my God, my father will kill me! I'll be for the high jump now. Mary, you won't be seeing me for a month, I just know it.'

'Laura, you told me that you did the milking last night and this morning. Sure it's still early, stay awhile.' Mary tried to hold her back, and went with her into the hallway. 'Wait, I'll get my bike and leave you out to the end of your lane.'

They were going out the back door when Mary's mother called her.

'Och holy God, I nearly forgot, Dr Collins left this letter for ye. I put it in my apron and never thought about it till now, here.'

Mary took the letter and tore it opened and screamed:

'Ma, Da! It's my application form for the nursing, the doctor says I just have to get you to sign, and the priest.'

She hugged her parents. The rest of the family came out to wish her well, and her mother began to cry. Her father took the letter and read it. He turned to his wife, and smiled.

'Will ye whisht, woman, sure she won't be going for months yet. She has a whole lot of stuff to do first and an entrance exam. Won't that take ages.'

Mrs McCann took the edge of her apron and dried her eyes.

'I know. It's just the thought of losing her I get it hard to believe.' She hugged her daughter, 'God bless ye love, sure I know ye'll make a great nurse.'

Mary eased herself away.

'Well, me first, eh? Then before you know it you'll be going too, won't you?' She took Laura's hand, 'You won't find a year going by till you join me. It will be great the two of us... and all them lovely young doctors!'

At the end of Steenson's lane the girls were still talking of Mary's going and how Laura would miss her.

'Mary, I don't know what I'll do when you leave. I mean the only place I visit is your house, I don't have any other friends.'

'Oh, I *am* flattered,' Mary replied in a posh voice. 'But what about your friends in the tennis club, hoity-toity Pamela and Avril? Did you see their faces when I called for you last week? Them pair nearly shit themselves when I opened the gates and joined you on the bench,' she laughed. 'The two of them jumped up like they were stung when I sat down. The sour-faced one looked at me like I was something on her shoe. And when she spoke, that voice! "You can't stay here, it's reserved for church members and we are very strict about membership. You should not have entered the gates." I mean who the hell does she think she is? Sure her Da only works in the brick yard.'

Laura was in stitches.

'I nearly died when you looked up at her and then at the gates and said in your broadest voice, "Jazus, I didn't know that his nibs up there had moved the Pearly Gates and you only need to be a member of your church. Jazus, I might just join". Sure the two of them nearly exploded with anger. Now, can you imagine me getting friendly with them... not a hope in hell!'

When they finally went their separate ways, Laura was dreading going home. Her father was coming out of the milking shed when she wheeled her bike into the yard. He glared at her.

'I don't want any of your lies girl, so don't even try. I only have to look at you to know that you were with that shower of heathens. You won't be warned again, do you hear!' he shouted.

She just nodded and left her bike against the wall, she was about to go into the house when he shouted again.

'Where do you think you're going? Get into the shed and finish the milking, then you can scour the rest of the churns for the morning.'

She was about to protest that it wasn't her turn but she knew that wasn't a very good idea.

Later, they sat at the table for supper, a meal eaten in silence as with all meals in the house. Afterwards, her father read from The Bible:

'Do not those who plot evil go astray?
But those who plan what is good find love and faithfulness
He who ignores discipline despises himself,
But whoever heeds correction gains understanding...'

Laura's mind wandered and she looked around the living room. There was little colour here apart from two bright green cushions on the brown settee. There wasn't even a wedding photograph of her parents and the two delph dogs that faced each other on the mantelpiece were the only ornaments in the house. A black-leaded range underneath them shone with continual polishing – a ritual that took place every Friday. She felt Betty give her a kick under the table as her father droned on. They were all seated at the table: her quiet and dignified mother Ruth, her dour father William, her young brother Sam, her wee sister Belle, the baby of the family and the apple of her father's eye and her older sister Betty who lived and worked in the town and only came out at the weekend. This was Laura's family who sat quietly and listened to her father as he read from The Bible every night. No wonder she craved the fun and excitement of the McCann house – it was a real home with loads of love in it. She sighed and wished she had been born a Catholic.

CHAPTER 3

THE WAR BETWEEN the different factions in Northern Ireland intensified and the changes in Tullybeg were notable. Neighbours stopped speaking to one another, only shopping in stores where the owner was of the same religion as themselves. This made things very difficult for Laura and her friendship with the McCanns became even less acceptable. After leaving school, her father got her a job in Mrs Wray's shop. It was a small newsagent and confectionery shop and the only petrol station till you reached the town five miles away. Mrs Wray was worried because her petrol sales were down badly and she told Laura that if it continued she might have to close the shop. Laura would be upset if this happened as she loved working there and she got on very well with Mrs Wray. Her husband, Robert, was often around especially in the evenings. During the day he managed a large builders' yard near the town. While he was quite pleasant to her, there was something about him that gave her the creeps. The first time she was introduced to him, she started to feel uncomfortable when he held her hand longer than necessary and recoiled when his arm tightened around her waist. He said he was delighted to have the daughter of a fellow church elder working for him and told her they should all look after each other. He followed this by spouting a proverb from The Bible.

Robert Wray was forever complaining about the Catholics that he had to employ. He said that they were shiftless and lazy and would take the eye out of your head if you didn't watch them. She knew deep down he was referring to her relationship with the McCann family. Laura didn't like him. Sometimes when they were alone he would question her about boyfriends. She hated this, especially when he stood too close to her. One evening when she wasn't busy, she began a letter to Mary. When Robert came in he wanted to know if she was writing to a boyfriend but Laura told him she didn't have one and the letter was to Mary. He put both hands on her shoulders and lectured her on how she should keep to her own kind. Then he had the nerve to ask if any of those papist McCanns had ever tried to touch her or kiss her. She was disgusted at his suggestion and told him so but he smiled at her in that strange way and told her that he was just looking out for her. She had been working at the shop for just a few weeks when he offered to run her home one evening as it was raining heavily. She didn't want to but Mrs Wray insisted and she felt she couldn't say no. They had just driven to the entrance of her lane when he stopped the car. She was about to get out when she felt him pull her arm back.

'What are you doing?' she asked.

He leaned over and smiled at her.

'Now you're not leaving without giving me a thank-you kiss, are you?'

He pulled her roughly towards him and tried to kiss her.

'Please Mr Wray, don't do that! I want to get out!'

But he only held her tighter and groped roughly at her breast as she moved to leave.

'Now, now Laura, aren't you just like all the other young ones, teasing us men till we can't help it. Come on now, no one need know.'

She felt his hand moving down her body. She caught him sharply on the mouth with the back of her hand. As she freed herself she punched him in the stomach, which took his breath away and he let her go. She pulled open the door of the car and spoke back to him:

'Don't you ever come near me again, you hear? You, a church elder! You're a disgusting auld man! If I chose to tell my father you wouldn't last long.'

As she stood on the lane, he began shouting at her that she was nothing but a Jezebel, followed by a succession of foul names. When she heard his car pull away she sat down on the grassy bank, totally shaken by the incident and wondering who she should confide in. Should she mention it to her father or not? When she got home she could tell he was in a bad temper when he shouted at her.

'Where have you been till now? With your fine papist friends no doubt! Well, I need help with the milking, come on.'

She didn't speak of it to anyone. In the next few weeks, Robert Wray totally ignored her and she was pleased that he wasn't around as much as usual. She knew that Mrs Wray had a hard time with him as she often overheard them having arguments. Laura never liked discussing him with Mrs Wray, such a gentle lady but couldn't understand how she could abide him. Since the incident in the car she'd heard rumours that he was fond of more than one of the girls in his office. She couldn't imagine what any girl could see in him. He was a weedy-looking man with receding hair and a paunchy stomach, quite short in stature. A little Napoleon, just like the other members of her church, so anti-Catholic, especially against her friends, the McCanns.

Laura was always welcome at the McCann home and called in every week to compare the letters the McCanns had got from Mary with her own. It was great to hear all the news. Winnie, Mary's young sister, had taken Laura under her wing after Mary had left and she often came into the shop for a chat on her way home from school. Mrs Wray enjoyed Winnie's humour, she had something funny to tell every time she called. Later, when Laura left her home, intending to stay for a céilí, Mrs McCann met them on the doorstep. Laura was surprised to see her looking so worried. The older woman put her hand on Laura's shoulder, and told her it would be better if she didn't call so often, she was worried that Laura might get into serious trouble being seen with them. Laura didn't understand.

'What trouble?' she asked.

'Och, the worst,' said Mrs McCann, wiping away her tears. 'A crowd of heathen rascals got young Susan McCaffrey on her way home last night. She was just off the last bus from town. They pulled her up Dixon's entry and cut off all her hair!'

'But why would they do that?' Laura asked, shocked at the news.

Mrs McCann put her arm around her.

'Just because she's goin' with a wee Protestant lad from the town. Now there's badness for ye. I wouldn't want anything like that happenin' to ye, Laura, them knowin' yer always in and out of here.'

Laura could hardly take this in.

CHAPTER 4

LAURA HEARD THE CHURCH BELLS ringing in the New Year 1965. Here she was, sitting in her bedroom writing a letter to Mary. She had expected Andy, her boyfriend, to take her out some where special. He couldn't, he said he had to stay with his father. Laura really felt so lucky to have met him. She remembered the day so well – it was just after her nineteenth birthday, July 1961.

The minister had invited the young people of the surrounding parishes to help to prepare the hall and the food for a special supper to welcome the new Moderator. This caused a lot of excitement in the congregation – they were to be 'host parish' for the first time in years. Laura was in the hall in the afternoon, trying to move a very heavy table, when this man she had never seen before rushed over to help her. She smiled at him.

'Thank you. You must be new to the parish?'

'Not really,' he said. 'I'm from the Pomeroy side. Our minister asked me to help out. After seeing you I'm glad I did!'

Laura felt herself go red as she held out her hand. He was gorgeous, tall with blond hair that kept falling in his eyes.

'I'm Laura Steenson. They put me in charge of getting these tables arranged.'

'I'm Andy Carson and I don't know a soul here but you, so you better not leave me on my own.'

He stayed with Laura all afternoon, doing whatever jobs were needed and chatting all the time. She learned that he lived with his widowed father, his sister Martha (a school teacher) and a younger brother called David and they all helped to run the family's large dairy farm. Laura found that they had a lot in common. Apart from the farm, they both liked cycling. Andy had a wonderful personality. Laura noticed that all the girls were mad about him, Pamela McKinney tried every trick she could think of to get him to pay her attention but he spent the entire evening with Laura. Her parents attended the service and before she knew it her mother invited Andy to tea the following Sunday. Afterwards Laura apologised to him, saying that he didn't have to come. Andy laughed when she told him that her parents were afraid that she would be left on the shelf.

And that's when it happened, he kissed her, it was wonderful! Laura thought she would die right there at the end of the lane. He held her in his arms and with a quirky smile he asked her if she thought he was eligible. And that's how she met Andy, the love of her life. The four years since they had met had flown and they'd had great times together. Her mother was constantly hinting about 'The Big Day' and Laura kept hoping that he would name it soon. He was so caught up in his work but she knew that he wanted everything to be perfect before they took that step. She loved him so much but where was he tonight, New Year's Eve, the biggest night of the year? Even Sam and Belle were out at parties.

But she shouldn't complain, Andy had been great. He took her to the pictures every week and he gave her her first taste of the demon drink – Laura's father would have had a blue fit if he'd found out. The only blot on the landscape was when her father insisted that they take wee Belle along - she really got on Laura's nerves at times.

A few weeks later, Andy and Laura had their first big row. He had been very attentive since deserting her on New Year's Eve but he was to take her to a special dress dance in Wilson's Hotel, and she thought she would surprise him by inviting Mary and her boyfriend to come as well. Andy had never really been in Mary's company – he always had something to do when she was visiting. Now he would be able to get to know her. But when she told him he was furious that she hadn't asked him first – Laura couldn't believe how angry he was.

'Andy,' she asked, 'are you objecting because Mary's a Catholic? I hope you're not a bigot like my father, I would hate it if you were.'

But he took her in his arms and explained why.

'Laura, times are very difficult now you know that. How many people have you heard about being attacked because their friends were of a different religion? I heard of a fellow up in Omagh who had both his legs broken because he had a Catholic girlfriend. There's crazy people out there and I don't want to get involved.'

Laura looked at him in disbelief.

'Andy, what am I going to say to my friend? I've asked her now and I was really looking forward to the evening.'

Andy held her away from him and she could see he was still cross.

'Look, you tell her whatever you like but if she has any sense she will get the message, right?'

Laura was seeing a different side to him and she didn't like it. He knew that she was going to Belfast the next day to buy a dress and was planning to meet up with her friend. What on earth would she say to her?

Mary could see that Laura had something on her mind as soon as they met. She took Laura's arm gently and said:

'Come on, what is it? Who's been standing on your toes? I know that look.'

When Laura tried to explain she laughed.

'Is that all? I thought that this famous boyfriend of yours had done a runner.'

Laura looked at her and could see that she wasn't at all upset.

'I'm really sorry Mary, I was so looking forward to it.'

Mary smiled at her.

'Don't worry, won't there be other nights?' she said. 'Now let's hit the shops.'

They had a great day out. Mary knew the all the best shops and they had great fun trying on all the latest fashion before going to the train. They decided to treat themselves to a special tea in the new Europa hotel. Waving from the window of the train, Laura knew how much she missed Mary and in her heart she hoped that her relationship with her friend would never be broken by anyone.

'I hope you're going to wear a cardigan over that, it's not at all suitable for a daughter of mine.'

Laura's father didn't approve as she paraded around the kitchen 'Oh Father,' she pleaded, 'this is my first long dress. I was ages choosing it and Mary thought it was just right. What do you think, Mother?' but her father interrupted.

'I might have known that she would have a hand in it. Sure that crowd go about half naked, so they do. If you want to go out tonight, you'll cover yourself up.'

He left the house shouting to her not to be late home, as she had to milk in the morning.

They had a great night, the music was wonderful. Laura didn't want to leave the dance floor. She was so glad that the McCanns had taught her how to dance. Andy was very impressed, not only with her dancing but with how she looked. He kept whispering in her ear how she was the loveliest girl in the room, then he tried to kiss her in front of everyone. She was so embarrassed but he just laughed and then he shocked Laura by asking her to marry him. She held on to him tightly and said 'yes'. She couldn't believe it, Andy Carson wanted to marry her! She was floating the rest of the night...

After the dance, they parked at their usual spot. Maybe it was all the gin & tonics, she didn't know but she didn't refuse him this time when he wanted to make love. Andy had taught her other ways that she could please him when they made love but they had never gone the whole way until now. (It wasn't for the want of trying on his part.) They moved into the back of the car and he was very excited. He showed her how to put on a condom – this was the first time she had seen one, never mind held one. She was all thumbs. It was all over quickly and she was very sore. Was that it? Was that what all the talk was about?

She could see that Andy was pleased. He was holding her and kissing her. She loved him so much and told him so over and over. They lay there content till she felt him get the urge again.

This time she really enjoyed it. He was very gentle and took his time to see that she was alright. Laura sighed and looked up at this lovely man who loved her when it suddenly dawned on her that she was no longer a virgin. On the way home he asked her how she felt.

'Oh Andy, so much has happened tonight, I can't wait to tell everyone. I feel so happy, I'm engaged.'But his next words brought her down to earth with a bump.

'Laura, I know you're excited but I don't want you to tell anyone yet. Let it be just for us for a while anyway.'

She stared at him.

'But why Andy? I want the world to know.'He put his arm around her and told her that he had some land deals to sort out.'Regan's farm is coming on the market soon,' he said. 'They're the only Catholics left in the townland. They've been intimidated by paramilitaries and they have to get out so I know they'll want a quick sale.'

Laura told him that it wasn't right that he would profit by another's misfortune but he said that if he didn't, someone else would.

It had been nearly three weeks since Laura had seen Andy. They had spoken on the phone but it wasn't the same. She needed him to hold her, make love to her, tell her that he loved her and that she hadn't dreamt it all.

The shop was getting busy again, there was a lot of passing trade now that spring was here. Laura and Andy were supposed to be going out that night but Mrs Wray had come down with a flu bug and Laura would have to stay late, well until Mr Wray decided to come home. He was rarely at the shop these days – Laura suspected he was still avoiding her.

What was all the racket outside? Oh my God, it's Andy and he has a new car! She rushed outside to see this brand new Ford Anglia waiting on the forecourt.

'I thought you'd decided that you were going to wait for a few more months before you bought one. Andy, it's not second hand, it's brand new!' she exclaimed.

'Of course it's new, only the best for an up-and-coming land-owner. I couldn't drive around in that old car of my father's now, could I? Come on girl, are you ready to hit the town?'

Laura looked at him, he was like a child with a new toy. She told him she'd left him a note to say that she had to work late.

'I never seen it,' he said.

Suddenly there was a voice from inside the car.

'Hi Laura, it's me, I forgot all about the note but Dad said that I could go too. Sure I'll keep Andy company for you.'

Laura looked at her young sister and didn't like what she saw. Belle smiled that little 'butter wouldn't melt' smile. She was almost eighteen, growing up much too fast and much too forward for Laura's liking.

'It's a lovely car and Andy said that he would take us to the seaside soon, didn't you Andy?'

Laura stared, open-mouthed.

'Seaside? When did you decide all this?'

Andy looked at her.

'Well, this young one said it was a long time since she was at the beach and she'd love to go and take a picnic. I think it's a great idea, don't you?'

Belle's smug little face looked out at her. Laura could have cheerfully have slapped her right then. Andy came around the car, put his arms around her, and gave her that special smile.

'Don't be cross now. Sure you know you'd love to go, wouldn't you?'

He kissed her right there, in front of the whole street.

'Now we have to move, I don't want to miss that John Wayne film. See you soon!'

He drove off down the village with Belle leaning out the window waving goodbye.

Up to now, Andy had borrowed his father's car if he needed one. The new car gave them a lot more freedom and the outings were great. They attended functions all over the country, as Andy was an up-and-coming member of the Farmers' Union. Their love-making improved as well but Laura was getting annoyed at him – he kept putting off the engagement. There was always something more important to attend to. He was buying up land at every chance he got. She joked with him that he would soon own half the farms in Tyrone but he said that having land was better than money in the bank.

'Remember this land will be yours too and you can choose which part of it you want to live on.'

Laura put her arms around his neck and smiled at him.

'Have you decided where and when this great move will take place? I'm not getting any younger you know, I'll be twenty-five next month.'

He held her tight and she could tell that he had something else on his mind. He expertly moved the position of the car seat and was on top of her before she could say another word. He whispered hoarsely:

'I wish it were tomorrow but next year we'll have a wedding the country will talk about for years.'

Afterwards, driving home, Laura asked him what he would do if she got pregnant.

'Well, if that happens we'll get married. But don't let it happen, right!'

He really annoyed her, talking like that.

She told Mary about it when they met up for a meal in town the following week but with her cheerful attitude, she just laughed.

'Will you stop worrying for God's sake. At least you know you will get engaged – you have the world at your feet by the sound of it. You've got yourself a fine man that only wants the best for you.'

'I know that but I worry about him. I think he can be too greedy and it's changed him. We used to go all over the country to dinners and dances but lately when I suggest going some place, he tells me it's only a waste of money and then he goes off and I don't see him for weeks. Then it's only for drives and when we do go some place that tinker, Belle, wants to come too.'

Mary put her hand across the table to hold Laura's.

'Listen, why don't you just tell him that you would like the ring for Christmas? And don't take no for an answer.'

She had told him and today he'd bought her a ring! It was beautiful, a small cluster of diamonds, her parents were delighted. Laura waltzed around the room showing it off but Belle had to be bitchy.

'It's very small, why didn't you pick a large diamond? That's what I am going to have when I get engaged. And look how long you had to wait for it.'

Laura wanted to hit her. She looked over at Andy but he just laughed. She let her mother try it on and watched her eyes glisten.

'It's really lovely and it suits your finger. Have you decided on a date yet?'

Laura told her they hadn't but they'd give her plenty of notice.

CHAPTER 5

1967

LAURA, HALF ASLEEP, could hear a distant ringing. It went on and on until she realised it was the telephone. She jumped out of bed and rushed out on to the landing. Her mother was halfway down the stairs, muttering to herself that there must be something wrong. Laura looked at the clock on the wall. It was nearly three in the morning. She watched as her mother went pale and screamed into the phone:

'Oh no! It can't be!'

She tried to grab the phone from her mother. Her father came downstairs with Belle following.

'What's up? What's happening?'

'What's wrong, who's on the phone?' Belle asked.

They were all talking at once. Her mother was standing, frozen to the spot, with the phone in her hand. She turned to them and said:

'It's our Sam. He's been shot!'

None of them could speak for a minute.

Finally, words came tumbling out:

'It's the sergeant at the Rosslea Barracks.'

'Dear Lord in heaven, is he badly hurt?' asked William.

Her mother began crying.

'Oh my wee Sam, my poor Sam!'

Laura took the phone from her mother's hand. She was still trying to listen to the sergeant on the other end of the line who was giving her instructions. Belle was screaming.

'Oh my poor brother. Them IRA bastards have shot him.'

William put his arms around his daughter.

'Now, my wee Belle, you can't be using that kind of language.'

Laura put the phone back and faced them all. She found it hard to get the words out.

'The sergeant says we have to get ready. There's someone coming from the barracks in town to take us to the Royal Victoria. That's where they've taken our wee Sam.'

Nobody moved for a while. Her father said nothing. Finally, he climbed the stairs like a zombie with her mother following. Belle began screaming and Laura couldn't get her to stop but she guided her up the stairs and the pair of them got dressed. Her parents returned to the kitchen in minutes, dressed and ready, and went out to the waiting car. Her father sat in the front with the driver, still not saying a word. Her mother, white-faced and still shaking, got into the back with the girls. Laura held her mother to her to try and comfort her. Belle was inconsolable. Laura thought they would never reach the hospital.

All Sam's life he had wanted to be a policeman. The day he had been accepted to train with the RUC at just eighteen, he had gone down to the village post office nearly an hour before the post was due, unable to wait for the delivery. He came flying up the lane, shouting it out to anyone within hearing. She kept remembering the last day they'd been with him, only six months ago at his passing out ceremony. The whole family had been invited to the barracks for the ceremony. Laura's parents were so proud. Her father, not given to showing his feelings, surprised everyone by hugging Sam to him and saying how well he looked in his uniform.

Betty was there with her boyfriend, Alastair Brown. That was another surprise. He could have been her father, he looked so old! He was going bald and was a lot smaller than Betty. There he was, in the flesh, so to speak. It was the first time the family had met him, they had only heard about him before, and Laura could see the shock on her mother's face. Betty had told them that he owned his own hardware shop and a house beside it and that he had one sister who was married to the minister of the Baptist church in Armagh.

Parents and friends of the new recruits were entertained to tea in the hotel. It was very enjoyable, and the first time they had all been out together as a family. Laura could see her parents loved every minute of it. They had asked Andy to accompany them, so it really was a perfect family gathering. Laura looked at them all round the table, and secretly thought that the next time they would be like this would be at her wedding to Andy. It was a lovely thought.

Betty sprang another surprise on them. Their father, normally not fond of making speeches, had begun to tell them how proud he was of Sam and how happy he was to have all the family together when Betty interrupted him. She had something to tell them. Their mother looked anxiously at her husband but he told Betty to get on with it. He was smiling,

'Mother, Father, don't be mad with me but Alastair and I were married last Friday, in the Baptist church.'

They stared at her in total silence. Belle was the first to speak.

'Betty how could you? You knew I wanted to be a bridesmaid. I'd even decided on the dress I would like.'

Betty looked at her.

'I'm sorry. I know I've shocked you all but Alastair and I thought it was for the best. He's had a lot of trouble with the shop. Last year he was burned out twice because of where it is, so his heart is not in it any more.'

She was crying now, and Alastair had his arm around her saying:

'I'm not one for fancy weddings and we both decided it would be for the best. My brother-in-law married us and we just had a family supper after.'

'I'm very pleased for you, Betty,' said Laura, getting up and going round the table to be beside her. Belle and Sam came over and put their arms around her and the four stood there hugging each other.

'Cheese!' said Andy and took their photo.

Laura would always cherish that moment. Then Alastair spoke again.

'I haven't quite finished what I began.'

They stopped and looked at him as he lifted Betty out of the chair.

'Mr and Mrs Steenson, this has been quite a surprise for all of you but please don't be angry at us. You see, we're leaving the country next Saturday for New Zealand.'

That was as far as he got. Their mother got so upset that Laura thought she was having a heart attack. Their father stood up.

'New Zealand, the other side of the world! What's got into you? Why so far away? I don't understand.'

Betty came over, putting her arms around her mother saying:

'I'm sorry but it's what we both want, there are opportunities for everyone out there, and we've both had enough of all this madness that's happening in Northern Ireland.'

Sam said he was delighted for her and he would come out for a holiday whenever he saved enough. Laura and Belle agreed that it would be great to travel that far but their parents were far from happy.

'Betty we'll never see you again, it's not like England.'

Their father was visibly upset. Before the gathering broke up, their mother insisted that Betty and Alastair come for tea next day, where they could talk in private.

Later that night, Laura and Belle were discussing the day's events. They had taken loads of photographs and Sam had introduced them to all his mates. Belle was very impressed with a few of them and even agreed to go out on a date with one.

'Did you see Andy's face,' she laughed, 'when Sam's friend Roy said he was taking me out next week? He was raging. He suggested that we go out as a foursome. I couldn't believe it! He was worse than Father when he asked the fellow all those questions. I nearly died with embarrassment, what did you think of it?'

Laura laughed.

'Och Belle, sure you're like his younger sister. He's just being protective, he didn't mean any harm. Sure isn't that Roy fellow coming up here anyway? He's a fine-looking fellow and he has his own car. At least you'll be out from under my feet. And I didn't notice Father objecting.'

At the hospital, the Steensons were shown into a small waiting room. There were four other people already there. The nurse introduced them – the family of the other policeman who'd been shot. Laura noticed that his wife was very pregnant. The woman told her it was their first baby, due in two months. Tea was brought in and the two families consoled each other while they waited for news. It was an agonising wait. They must have been there for nearly four hours. Some senior RUC officers came and went and after seven o'clock a nurse came and took the pregnant woman and her mother-in-law out. Five minutes later they heard the screaming. The young policeman didn't survive.

'What about Sam?' they asked the doctor.

He said the chances were good. Sam had been shot in the stomach and they were still working on him in the operating room. Laura looked at her parents. They had aged so much in the last four hours. Still they waited for the outcome none of them knew what else to do. Finally, at almost nine o'clock, the surgeon came to tell them that Sam would be fine. It would be a long recovery but there was no reason he shouldn't get back to normal. They were elated to hear this - tired but happy.

The next few months were taken up with visiting Sam in hospital and later at a nursing home for veterans. It was on the coast near Donaghadee and filled mostly by army and police victims of the Troubles. Sam was doing well. The awful tubes into his stomach had been removed and he was able to eat a little. He enjoyed the family visits and seemed in great form but when he and Laura were alone, she could see him crumbling. She eventually asked him if he was worried.

'Oh Laura!' he cried, 'I don't know what the future holds, I have to do a return-to-work course in the force, and I'm not certain I want to... I'll never forget when that man pointed the gun straight at me. It could have been me lying dead now, not Ivor. He pushed me and took the bullet in the head. The second one got me in the gut. I'm having nightmares all the time, I'm not sure I can face that again.'

'Och look Sam, maybe they will give you a desk job, sure they must know what you've come through.'

'I'm afraid they don't look at it like that. How many lads were shot in the past few years? And women too. Them bastards don't care who they kill. I'm losing my nerve, I know it, and I don't know how to handle it. They'll think I'm a coward if I refuse to work.'

Laura felt so helpless for her darling little brother.

'Look it has been an awful experience for you and there must be more like you.'

She said goodbye, promising to see him the next week.

Andy and Belle were waiting down on the beach for Laura. They had brought a picnic. Sam had joined them for a short while and afterwards Laura walked him to his ward. On the way back from the nursing home, she stood at the top of the grassy dunes and watched the two of them. They looked like young lovers, they were so absorbed in each other. As she came down towards them, they were laughing at some private joke. She felt like an intruder, a little jealous. Andy got up.

'Well, you were a long time, is everything alright?'

'Oh yes,' assured Laura. 'Do we have to leave now or can we wait for a while – it's lovely now, with the sun shining on the sea. I'd love to live in a place like this. Maybe you'll surprise me by buying land here too.'

'Not suitable for me at all,' he said. 'I'm only interested in farm-land. Come on, sit down here awhile and rest yourself. I'm going to help Belle collect some shells; she's fascinated by the sea.'

Laura watched as they wandered off across the beach, arm-in-arm, and she lay back to enjoy the sun. Next thing she knew, Belle was shaking her.

'Come on sleepy head, time to go. You've stayed in the sun too long, your face is all red.'

Oh no! That was all she needed.

'How long have I been asleep? You must have been gone a long time.' Laura looked at her watch, almost seven o'clock! 'Where were you two? Why didn't you wake me?'

Belle got some cream and put it on her sister's face.

'There, you will be fine, it won't blister. We went too far up the beach and the tide was turning so we had to climb up the cliff and come back by the road,' she explained.

Andy was concerned for her.

'Honestly love, we didn't realise the time it took. We'll stop at a chemist and get something for your face.'

'Och don't worry, I'll be fine tomorrow. There wouldn't be any chemist open now anyway,' Laura replied.

They packed up and went home, Laura had looked forward to this day. The weather had been lovely and she was delighted Sam had been well enough to join them but for some unknown reason she felt cheated.

Laura enjoyed reading Betty's letters. True to her word, she wrote every month. They had settled well in New Zealand and were living in a place called Papatoetoe, near Auckland. Laura laughed at the strange-sounding names of the places and the people. Alastair had bought a new shop and he had started a hardware business. They were both doing well but they worried about Sam and how he would cope in the future.

Betty wanted to ask him to come out to them, he could help with the business but she was afraid he might be offended at her suggestion. Laura knew that was the last thing her parents wanted, the thought of not seeing him every other week would be too much for them. Father always hoped that when the RUC got too much for Sam, he would return to dairy farming, marry a suitable girl and settle down. But he had already confided to Laura that farming was the last thing he wanted and he didn't want to be a policeman any more. He would love to leave Northern Ireland and work abroad - Betty's offer might be just what he needed.

CHAPTER 6

1969

THE TROUBLES IN THE NORTH were getting worse, with riots on the Belfast streets every night. Buses were burned, even ambulances were interfered with. Mary told Laura of the awful injuries they had to deal with at the hospital every day. There were frequent fires and firemen too were working flat out. Worst of all were the victims of the burning homes, cars and shops who had indescribable injuries, prompting Mary to go to England to train at a specialist burns unit. Her romance was over long ago and she knew that the hospital was her life. She had just been promoted to theatre sister, so she felt it was a good time to specialise. Laura was sorry to hear she was leaving but pleased for her. Mary really was dedicated to her profession.

Laura missed the companionship of the McCann family. The boys would wave over at her all the time and Pat always got his petrol from her. He was married now with a lovely little girl and lived just down the street. Young Winnie, now almost seventeen, kept her informed of all the news about the family. She brought Laura a lovely present from Peter on her birthday – he hadn't forgotten. He made her a pair of wrought-iron candlesticks with a delicate filigree leaf pattern. They were beautiful! He was so talented and this was just a hobby for him. Winnie said that he was attending an art class in town but still helped out in the forge.

Mrs Wray was very fond of Winnie. She was bright, she had a great personality and could mimic everyone in the village. Today she had them in fits of laughter with her tales of Mr and Mrs Kelly fighting. They got drunk every Saturday night and he accused her of flirting with Ernie Black, the barman.

'Ernie wouldn't look twice at her,' said Winnie, mimicking the way she walked with a waddle. 'Sure Mrs Kelly is like a wee duck with only three teeth and them yellow. And the black frizzed hair! That carry-on goes on every time they get drunk. Sure any man that would look at her must be half blind.'

She related more village gossip and silly bits of information. She said she would stay on and keep Mrs Wray company when Laura left.

'Sure at least we can listen to the radio in peace here, my Ma and Da are always fighting over the way the twins behave.' Winnie was talking about her brothers, Mickey and Jimmy. 'They're never at home and when they are, there's nothing but rows all the time. My Ma says they are keeping bad company. I don't understand the half of it... Sure if I was keeping bad company, I'd have to tell it in confession, that's what the nuns tell us anyway. I don't think our boys even go to Mass now. Da's worried that they'll come to a bad end and the other pair of boys are as bad. Our Johnny and Joey only fourteen and they think they're twenty.'

'Well Winnie, if I was you I wouldn't worry my head about them, sure boys do what they want anyway. Now don't forget to lock up well when you're going home,' said Laura, as she left.

CHAPTER 7

LIFE ON THE FARM was hard for her mother, she looked so tired these days. Laura was really worried about her and she had spoken to her father but he passed it off as usual with the explanation that this was how her mother would want it.

'Sure you know yourself, she has to run the dairy and look after the fowl herself or it wouldn't be done right.'

'But Father, she's not able any more. I've been watching her and I know she's living on her nerves ever since Sam's accident.'

'Sure isn't he back at work now and doing well? And the new milking machines has made life a lot easier for all of us. I don't know what you're worried about,' he said.

'I still think she's not well, sure she nearly jumps out of her skin every time the phone rings. Father, you're going to have to insist she takes it easy. She won't listen to me and I can't do any more, anyway it's time that Belle one helped out more.'

Laura was to remember her conversation with her father. A few weeks later she was standing at the kitchen sink and gazing out the window when she saw her mother coming out of the barn. She was carrying two big buckets filled with eggs she had just washed, in preparation for collection. She looked so frail. Laura was just about to go out and help her when she saw her stagger and fall. She screamed for her father to come. Her mother was deathly pale and hardly breathing. They carried her into the house and laid her on the couch. Laura rushed to the phone for the doctor. Her father was in an awful state, mopping her mother's brow with a face cloth and asking her to speak to him but she was very weak. Laura took her in her arms and tried to comfort her. She thought the doctor was never coming but he did, at last, and suggested that her mother be admitted to hospital in Dungannon so her father decided to drive them there. Laura tried phoning Belle's friends but none of them knew where she was so she left a note on the dining table for her, telling her what had happened.

They waited at the hospital for what seemed like hours. After carrying out various tests, the doctor told them that he would be keeping their mother in for a while. She had been diagnosed as being diabetic and would need a lot of nursing care. They were allowed into the ward after she was settled. She looked awful.

'Oh Mother, what a fright you gave us! I thought you were dead,' said Laura, hugging her. 'Now you will have to take it easy. Father, you'll have to get someone to help.'

'Och sure you take over now. You'd be the best one for the job and ye know what to do. We'll have to make changes when your mother comes home anyway and you'd need to be there,' he said.

'Father, I'm not going to wear myself out like Mother. Look at her! Anyway, you wouldn't listen to me and I don't want to be the unpaid help.'

'I don't know why you're complaining,' he said. 'Sure when you and Andy get married that's what you're going to be. Now I'm going to talk to your mother. You go out and phone home to tell Belle that everything's fine, she'll be worried.'

Laura laughed at that remark.

'Belle, worried! Sure she only thinks of herself, she'll not be asked to stay at home and help.'

She made her way out to the phone box in the hallway but before she reached it she saw Belle and Andy coming towards her. Startled, she asked:

'Where did you come from, how did you know about Mother?'

She thought he looked confused...

'Oh poor Belle was so upset. She phoned me to bring her here, isn't it the least I can do? How is your mother?' he asked.

'Well, she's not too great. The doctor says it's complete rest she needs now.'

Belle began to cry.

'Oh poor Mother, she really hasn't been looking well. I should have helped more.'

Andy put his arm around her.

'Now don't worry. I'm sure you did all you could, didn't she Laura?'

They made their way into the ward. Her mother was really pleased to see them. She told them not to worry, she was going to be fine. Having her mother in hospital meant quite a lot of changes, especially for Laura. Taking the bus to and from the hospital to visit took up a lot of time, so she announced to her father one evening after a long hard day, travelling and working:

'Father, I've made up my mind, we need a car, I'm fed up with all the buses and waiting around half the day.'

He began to protest about the cost and running of it but she decided not to let him dictate to her. Finally, after listening to all the reasons he agreed. She had driven their old tractor for years and Andy had been teaching her to drive his car. She knew she would manage it alright. Belle couldn't contain her excitement when she heard.

'Oh, a car of our own! When are we going to get it?'

'Tomorrow.'

'I'll be able to drive it too, won't I? Oh, I can't wait!'

'And how are you going to drive it, sure you wouldn't even get up on the tractor,' laughed Laura.

'Oh that's no problem, didn't Andy let me drive his car,' she said.

Laura looked sharply at her.

'And when did he give you driving lessons? Have you been annoying him again?'

'No, no, I haven't. It's just... When we've been waiting for you he sometimes showed me what to do, and I picked it up real fast, and Roy also let me drive when we were going out.'

Laura accepted her answer but pangs of jealousy hung over her. Och! I'm mad thinking these thoughts, sure Belle is such a child.

CHAPTER 8

LAURA FELT SO PROUD driving her car. It wasn't new but it gave her such independence. And here she was, driving to hospital to collect her mother and bring her home. They hadn't got anyone to help out yet, so she was trying to cope with the farm, house, *and* help Mrs Wray in the shop. She knew that would have to change. She hadn't been in the shop now for a few days now, and dreaded telling Mrs Wray that it looked like she wouldn't be coming back. Winnie McCann was great, she came in every day but her parents had plans for her, and Mrs Wray's shop wasn't one of them.

After getting her mother installed on the couch at the fire and making the meal for them all, Laura left Belle looking after her. Mrs Wray was delighted to see Laura. She had thought Winnie would be there as well, and asked for her. She looked at them, puzzled.

'Then you don't know? Oh Laura, I thought all the village knew, there's been awful trouble at McCann's. The army and the police were all over the house and the forge last night. They arrested Mickey and Jimmy... for terrorist activities.'

Laura looked at her, shocked.

'Arrested! Terrorists! I can't believe it. This is awful, poor Mrs McCann, I think I should go over there.'

'No, no,' said Mrs Wray, 'it's not a good idea at all. You see the boys could have been involved in your Sam's shooting. We don't know what they've been up to. Poor wee Winnie cried her eyes out here today. She doesn't know what to think. She's looking after her wee brothers till her parents come back from the barracks.'

Just at that the door opened, it was Winnie. She rushed into Mrs Wray's arms, crying. It took a long time to console her but when she was calmer, she told them what happened. They were keeping the boys in jail. They had evidence that they were involved in the IRA. Her mother and father were in an awful state. She told them she was coming over to Wray's anyway.

'And if you don't want me here I'll understand but I've nowhere else I can go to talk to someone... My Ma says we'll be an embarrassment to everybody.'

Mrs Wray held her tighter.

'You're not to worry Winnie, you'll always be welcome here, you know that.'

Laura looked at Winnie.

'Mrs Wray's right. I know it's awful about the boys but sure isn't it the times we live in. Wasn't there raids all over Dungannon and Cookstown last week. There's plenty of families feeling the same as yours – just try to help your family, and pray for them. Anyway I need you now. Your holidays are starting this week aren't they?'

Winnie looked at her.

'Yes, they're starting on Friday. I've got the whole summer off.'

'Why, that's great', said Laura, 'you see my mother's not been well as you know, and needs me at home... So I was hoping that you would be able to keep my job going here, that's if your parents agree.'

'Oh Mrs Wray, is it alright with you? I know my Ma won't mind.'

Mrs Wray smiled.

'I'll be glad to have you here, and now that I've got a man to work the petrol pumps and the yard, sure you'll only have to do the shop. Come on, the first duty today is a cup of tea for us all.'

CHAPTER 9

1970

SAM WAS HOME! His parents were overjoyed. His mother fussed over him and kept asking if he was alright. He'd just had another near miss, a firebomb, which had fatally injured two of his colleagues. He was bruised and had minor burns on his arms. Laura thought he looked awful but she knew he hated all the fussing. He hardly ever left the house but did what he could to help. Father kept telling of the plans he had to enlarge the cattle herd – he was starting on the byre next week. Laura could see that Sam wasn't interested. She knew he had something on his mind and she finally found out what, just the day before he was due to go back to work. They took a walk up to the top of the big field and to the oak tree where they used to play. Sitting down on the sprawling roots, they could survey the countryside for miles. Laura often thought she would love to have a house up here. She looked at her young brother.

'Come on, out with it. You've been dying to talk about something all week, what's wrong?'

He looked at her.

'Is it that obvious? I don't know where to begin, I have so much on my mind.'

Suddenly, he started to cry.

'Oh Laura, Father will never talk to me when I tell him.'

'Listen Sam, leaving the police force is no shame. You'll not be the only one either.'

'Laura', he said, putting his arms around her, 'you've always been there for me, ever since I can remember. You've helped me through all my problems. But maybe after today you won't want anything to do with me.'

'Sam what have you done, murdered somebody? Sure you couldn't hurt a fly,' she laughed at him. 'Come on, it can't be that bad.'

'Laura do you remember that wee nurse you liked when I was in Donaghadee, Anne Quinn? Well I've been seeing quite a lot of her. Well...' he hesitated, 'I love her.'

'Is that all? Och Sam, what are you worrying about? Sure the family are just going to have to lump it. It won't make any difference to me.'

She looked at him.

'There's more, isn't there?'

He looked away into the distance, then back to his sister, his eyes full of tears.

'Anne's pregnant... I don't know how to tell the folks, you know how Father feels about Catholics. Can you imagine what he'll say when I tell him I want to marry her? He'll have a blue fit.'

He got up and walked up and down, finally sitting on the root of the oak tree.

'Laura, how can there be so much hatred in a land so beautiful? What's wrong with people? Love thy neighbour, isn't that what we're taught in church and at school? Why can't we love each other regardless of religion? You know, I can't even tell my best mate, he wouldn't understand. And you know why? His brother was shot last year by the IRA.'

Laura got up and put her arm around him.

'Sam, I'm always going to be here for you and Anne. I'll help you in any way I can. Things will work out, you'll see. Ask for a transfer to some place further north, some where they don't know you. Sure you and Anne could settle down and no one would be any the wiser.'

'No,' said Sam. 'It wouldn't work. Anne and I have decided to emigrate to New Zealand and join Betty. I've written to her, and she is delighted to help us.'

Laura looked at him.

'Your serious, aren't you? But all that way! Oh Sam, I'm going to miss you so much. And Christmas just around the corner! When are you leaving?'

'That's just it,' he said, 'next Saturday. I'm going with Anne tomorrow to see her family. Remember she's in the same situation as I am.'

'Come on then,' Laura said, 'there's no time to waste, I'll hold your hand while you tell the folks.'

Arm-in-arm, they made their way down the hill to the gate and into the battlefield.

Later in the house, Sam paced the floor and Laura could see he was building up the courage to tell their parents. William took some papers from a pile on the table and showed them to him.

'Sam,' he said, 'I was keeping these for you to have a wee look at when you felt a bit better. And I can see you've lost the love of your job after being in that hospital.'

Sam began to protest but his father held up his hand.

'Now, now, I know you might feel a bit embarrassed about giving up the police but isn't it all for the best. Och, sure the Lord God always has a plan for us and this is what I want to show you now,' he said, handing over the papers to Sam. That's the plan for the new barn and the milking parlour, what do you think?'

Without looking at them, Sam put the papers down on the table.

'Father, I need to talk to you about...' he got no further.

His father picked up the papers again.

'Are you not even going to look at them? What's wrong with ye, boy? This is all for you. I knew you wouldn't want to go back to the force, and it's all working out fine, isn't it?'

Sam sat down at the table and looked across to his mother and Laura, who smiled encouragingly at him.

'Go on Sam, tell him your plans.'

Her mother stared at her.

'What plans, what are you talking about?'

Their father looked puzzled and then laughed.

'Och, he's going to buy the McClean place, isn't that your plan, son? And make this place the best dairy farm in Ulster.'

Sam got up from the table and stared out the window.

'No, Father, that's not my plan, or working in this place either. I'm leaving for New Zealand to join Betty and I don't...'

His father jumped up from his chair, knocking it to the floor in anger.

'You're what? Leaving? Well indeed you're not, me boyo! This is your home and your heritage and here you'll stay. That's our Betty, putting high-falutin' ideas in your head. I will...'

His father got no further. Sam turned and put his hand on William's shoulder.

'Sit down, Father, this is important to me. I'm leaving next Saturday for New Zealand and I'm getting married on Friday before I go...'

His father, red in the face, shouted.

'You're what!

His mother cried:

'No, no son, you can't! Not now.'

His father pushed Sam aside.

'What do you mean? When was all this planned? Man, but you're the sly one. Who is the girl, would it be anyone we know?' he said sarcastically.

Sam looked over to his mother and then to his sister for moral support.

'Her name's Anne Quinn. She was my nurse. I love her, Mother,' he said as he went towards her.

His mother stood up and put her arms around him, sobbing. He turned then and faced his father, who was purple with rage.

'Please try and understand, Father.'

His father raised his fist in anger and his mother cried:

'Oh William, don't!'

'You're giving up all this for a papist. Don't talk rubbish, son. Them tablets you're on has affected your brain,' William shouted louder as he raised his fist again. 'No son of mine will ever marry a papist.'

Laura jumped up and went between her father and brother. 'No Father, don't. This is not right. Sam has made his mind up, let him go.'

His father turned to her.

'So you're in this too, are you? I might have known it, you and your papist friends. Do you see where it all leads?'

Sam attempted to reach out and touch his father, who brushed his hand aside.

'Father, I knew this was how you'd be but I couldn't leave without telling you both. Please understand.'

William didn't look at him as he lifted the papers from the table, went to the range and dropped them into the flames. He lifted his cap and Bible and went towards the door shouting at Sam as he left.

'You leave this house with that woman and you're no son of mine. The devil himself is behind all this! You will burn in the flames of hell.'

The three of them watched as he went outside, slamming the door, heading towards the fields.

The shouting, screaming, rage and the tears were long over and Sam was settled in New Zealand. Laura had a letter from him. He was working with Betty and her husband – they were delighted to have him and his new bride. Sam gave a glowing description of the country that was now his homeland. But in the house you would have thought he had died. Her father had removed all the photographs of him, the big one that he had hung with pride over the fireplace in the parlour was gone. No one spoke of Sam. Her mother, who never said very much anyway, hardly spoke at all. Laura was annoyed when she discovered that the photographs had been moved. Her father had been so proud of Sam in his RUC uniform and had showed it off to any visitors who called. He seemed to have aged so much in the last few weeks and he had cancelled all the plans he had for improvements to the farm.

CHAPTER 10

TENSION WAS STILL HIGH in the village. The saddest part of all this madness was to see the children fighting and calling each other names on the way home from school. The two schools were almost opposite each other – St Martin's and the Parker Model School. Laura was tidying up at the front of the shop as they were coming out of the gates. The next thing two boys were on the ground, thumping each other and shouting names with the rest of the children egging them on.

'Come on Bobby! Beat the shit out of the slimy Papish!'

'Johnny! Kick the living daylights out of the wee Orange bastard! Go on, go on!' the children shouted.Laura ran over.

'Here stop this carry on, fighting on the street! Look at your clothes. Your mothers will kill you when you get home. Joey McCann, I'm ashamed of you, the language! And Bobby Neils, I'm going to have a word with your father when he calls for his paper tonight. What are you fighting about?'

Joey looked up at her, face and hands all grime and bleeding, shirt-tail hanging out and torn.

'It wasn't my fault! He called my brothers bad names and I wasn't going to let him get away with that.'

His twin Johnny moved over to his side, wiping his bloody nose.

'Och, they're rotten IRA jailbirds. They shoot Protestants and my father says he hopes they rot in jail,' said young Bobby.

Joey made another go at him but Johnny pulled him back.

'You wait Bobby Neils! I'll get you on your own without your Orange friends and I'll beat the living daylights out of you for you're an Orange coward!'

Laura had to hold on tight to him.

'Look Bobby, go on home and stop this fighting. Sure isn't there enough troubles here without this?'

The boys glared at each other before they and their friends reluctantly went on their way.

Mrs Wray had been watching the incident from the shop window.

'Isn't this a sad state of affairs, when school friends nearly kill each other. Sure wee youngsters shouldn't have to think of things like wars and religion. They should all be playing together, out collecting holly and trees for Christmas. Sure it's not that long ago that you and Mary McCann used to come in here selling the holly you gathered.'

'Oh don't I remember it well, getting our hands and clothes all tore, climbing up the trees. We always collected the best stuff though, didn't we? And them sixpenny bits meant so much to us. We would sit out on the bank at our lane and count every halfpenny, then come back in here to spend it on sweets for Christmas.'

'You were always the best of friends weren't you? And still are. Sure religion didn't matter to any of you. That's the way it should be. I remember Mrs McCann beating Mary down the street with the wet dishcloth and you trying to pull her back. Don't touch her Mrs McCann, it wasn't her fault, it was mine, that's what you said. It was the funniest sight!' laughed Mrs Wray, pouring Laura a cup of tea. Laura held the hot cup, amused by the memory.

'You know I remember that like it was yesterday. We went blackberry picking on the railway bank and we got our clothes in an awful state. Mary forgot she was wearing her good skirt. She was supposed to wear it for the school concert the next night, she only put it on to show it to me. She was prancing around on the step, when the Dixon girls came up with their basket to gather berries. Sure we only went with them to show them where the best ones were. I'll never forget Mrs McCann's face when she saw us coming in the door! For a big fat woman she moved like lightening out the door and down the street after Mary, and me trying to pull her apron to keep her back. She swung round with the wet dishcloth and I got the heat of it on my legs. I was red for a week! I had to wear long socks so my mother wouldn't know. God, we used to have some craic, didn't we? The things we got up to! If my father knew the half of it, I'd be dead. Especially the time I went to Mary's confirmation in St Martin's Chapel. I told my mother I had to go to Bible class. There I was sitting near Mary and her friends when the Bishop came down from the altar to speak to the children. The nun in charge had to try and hide me behind her but didn't he ask who I was and Sr Treas had to tell him. He shook my hand and said I was welcome! That nun gave me some telling off but then didn't she ask me to come back to the school for the special tea. That was a great day, no one noticed I was a Protestant.'

CHAPTER 11

NOTHING EXCITING EVER HAPPENED in the village of Tullybeg.
Life continued on its easy way, despite all the disasters in the
world. The assassinations of President Kennedy and his brother
Robert were still to the forefront of everyone's minds. They were
good men who had done so much for world peace, they would
be a great loss. If only someone could work a miracle and bring
peace to this country, thought Laura, as she read the headlines
in the daily newspaper. She loved looking at the magazines this
time of the year with the fashion pages and all the lovely ideas
for Christmas. She adored the new styles this year, they were
just fabulous! With the big event of the year just around the
corner she would have to shop for a very special dress.

The McClean family lived in a big house on an old country estate that bordered on her father's farm. Colonel McClean,
was retired from the army and spent most of his time fundrais-
ing for the Red Cross. He was throwing a Christmas ball for
his friends in the farming and business world. An invitation
had arrived a few weeks ago for herself and Andy. She was so
excited! They hadn't been anywhere special in ages so she was
going to splash out on something really terrific. She was to meet
Mary in Belfast the next day for a shopping spree. Mary said
that Anderson and McCauley had some wonderful creations.
They could spend the day and take their time and Mary wanted
Laura to meet her new doctor friend for dinner before she went
home. That evening at home, Belle was in bad form. She was
angry that she wasn't invited to the ball.

'It's not fair, why should you be invited and not me? And
anyway, Andy said it was costing far too much, he would have
to get a new suit. Now you're going shopping for a dress!'

Laura stared after her.

'That one is getting too big for her boots.'

Her mother laughed.

'Och leave her alone, she doesn't have a boyfriend now. He wasn't suitable she said.'

Andy called for Laura later that evening and she told him about the conversation.

'Well, I have mentioned something to her,' he said, 'but to be honest Laura, she has a point, you're going to spend a lot of money on a dress. We're supposed to be saving and I'll have to give a hefty donation to the charity... Maybe we'll leave it for this year.'

Laura was livid.

'Andy no, we hardly ever go anywhere! We were supposed to go to the Ulster Farmers' Convention in Portrush this summer but I had to give that up because you were entertaining some VIP secretary from the committee. We were to spend a weekend in Bangor after the Twelfth but something came up that time too. And now you want to forget about the ball? Oh Andy it's not fair. We should be married now but everything else seems to come first.'

'Och Laura, I'm sorry, sometimes I don't think. Come on, I need to get you some place quiet.'

They drove to their favourite place up near the woods overlooking the lough. It was a frosty night with a sky full of twinkling stars. They made hurried love in the back of the car. Andy held her, telling her how much he loved her and couldn't wait for their wedding. Did she feel the same? She answered him with a long and passionate kiss, exploring his body with her hands.

'Listen, let's continue this outside, I need to see all of you.'

They got out and he spread the rug on the grass between the laurels and the car, with no one to see them but the big November moon and the star-filled sky. They made love slowly, with an intensity of need.

'I feel so content,' she sighed. 'Is it always going to be like this?'

'Always,' he said, pulling her now naked body to his.

It was only after he had entered her again that she realised that he wore no protection – in the throes of their passion it had been forgotten. She wasn't worried, it was the wrong time of the month so it would be alright. And even if it wasn't, they would just bring the wedding forward. He would have to forget some of his family commitments and let his brother David help out more.

Lying now in each other's arms, warm and cosy, wrapped in the big tartan rug she had given him for his last birthday, she thought about the last visit she had made to his home.

She remembered the frosty atmosphere in the house. Martha, Andy's sister had invited her up for tea with the family. Their father had been preoccupied all evening and while Laura was helping clear the tea things in the kitchen, she couldn't help overhearing an argument between David and Andy – it was very heated. Andy was giving off to David about his behaviour, his bad debts and his gambling. Their father tried to intervene, taking his younger son's side. Andy was shouting now.

'I'm not going to hand out any more money unless you start pulling your weight around here! I'm fed up, it's time I had a life too!'

David came rushing out through the kitchen door, shouting back that:

'All he cares about is getting more land. And not for the love of it but sheer greed!'

He stopped when he saw her standing at the sink.

'Laura, you're far too good for that devil. He'll keep you hanging on for years and never marry you for he's too mean to share anything. Take my advice and find someone else.'

Laura was shocked at this revelation, she always thought that David adored his older brother. Andy came into the kitchen to stop his brother leaving but by then David was roaring down the lane on his powerful motorbike. He looked at her standing there but said nothing and never spoke of it on the way home.

CHAPTER 12

LAURA AND MARY were having a great time shopping. Laura bought a wonderful gown of midnight-blue taffeta with matching sandals. Mary insisted on buying the long blue gloves to match, as a special present – Laura was always looking after her wee sister Winnie and she wanted to thank her. They were sitting in Mary's new flat overlooking the river Lagan. Laura tried on the gown again with all the accessories. She pranced around the room, feeling wonderful.

'Oh Mary, did you ever think that I'd be going to a ball in the McClean house? Remember when we climbed up the oak tree in the top field to watch the people in fancy evening dress at the McClean's parties years ago...'

'Oh God, yes! Sure it's like yesterday. And the brass band playing on the lawn,' laughed Mary.

The friends had once gone up the avenue to watch the guests arriving at the entrance gates but realised that they could see more if they went up the hill behind the farm and climbed the oak tree. The house was ablaze with lights, waitresses in crisp white uniforms, waiters wearing white gloves with silver serving trays filled with sparkling crystal glasses. The guests were business people from the town and a few influential farmers and their wives. The dining room table was laden with elaborate plates of food and exotic fruits. But it was the ladies' gowns that girls glared at – slinky, backless and almost frontless too. They had never seen anything like them before. Mary giggled.

'Jesus, they're shameless, them women. Look, their fronts are hanging out!'

Laura watched, her mouth hanging open.

'Just as well it's summer, sure they'd catch their death, and not one of them has a cardigan.'

The two watched the dancing and decided to venture further down into the garden. They crawled under the hedge and down the bank to hide behind the laurel bushes. Some had grown quite tall, and being evergreen they hid the girls from view.

'Look!' said Mary, excitedly. 'There's the Colonel. Jesus! Look at all them medals, sure the weight of them would wear you out. And how did he get all them, I wonder?'

'Father said he made a name for himself abroad some where. Och, some famous battle in Germany I think. Father said he was one of Ulster's great heroes, didn't the Queen herself present some of those medals,' remarked Laura.

'Look at the belly he has! Can you imagine him running on a battlefield after the enemy? Sure he couldn't catch a cold!' laughed Mary.

From their secret place, they watched the dancing on a special wooden platform on the lawn. It looked like fairyland to the two young girls. Brightly coloured lanterns hung from the trees and flames leapt from two large braziers. Waiters and waitresses flitted in and out among the guests, offering drinks and food. Some guests were strolling in the garden, which looked really lush at this time of year. The girls could see Mrs Dixon holding court with her cronies, probably criticising everything about the party while enjoying the hospitality. Mary gave Laura a nudge.

'Look what the Dixon woman is wearing. It's on the prow of a ship she should be with that chest. And there's poor wee Mrs Cooke following her husband, always three steps behind.'

As the night wore on, some of the guests were looking the worse for wear as a result of all the drink they had consumed. Others were sneaking off into the bushes for a little more privacy, to do whatever they intended doing. One of those couples was getting very close to where the girls were. They held their breath, hardly daring to move.

Two people were almost beside them. The man was quite large in stature and the woman tall and slim. He began kissing her and moving his hands to more intimate parts of her body. She was groaning and making peculiar sounds. Mary and Laura looked at each other with wonderment and surprise, still hardly moving. They were relieved when the couple moved further into the bushes but they were still near enough for the girls to hear them moaning.

'Did you see who they were?' Laura whispered.

'Mrs Stuck-up Duncan and auld Councillor Corrigan! When she comes into the shop she just walks up to the counter and has to be served first. She would walk over you that one. I can't believe it!'

Mary nearly exploded, stopping her laughter.

'And auld Corrigan, what would she see in him? Sure, his belly would put any girl off. He takes Mrs Corrigan and all the wee'uns every Sunday to Mass, right up to the front seat. Jesus, he has some nerve! And he has to be first up to Holy Communion. It's people like him that make me sick.'

'What about Mrs Duncan? She teaches the juniors in Sunday school and always gives off about bad behaviour. If we ran about afterwards, remember she would say, "It's the Lord's day, we must always be respectful," in that haughty voice. Those two are just hypocrites. Is that the right word, Mary?' said Laura, looking very thoughtful.

Mary looked at her.

'Och, it's not important, whatever word we use. I know of a few I'd like to call her. Oh God, look! There's someone else coming up this way. Who is it, can you see?'

Mary leaned right over the branches.

'Oh my God Laura! That one had her legs right up in the air, and whoever's coming can't miss them.'

'Let me see,' said her friend. 'Oh no! This is going to be good, it's auld Leery Lendrum. Sure he's a dirty brute – he shakes his willie at young girls coming out of school. Look, he's stopping over there. Can you see?'

The girls could see the man just a few feet away and almost beside the courting couple. He had his back to them and they couldn't see very well but he was acting strange. He stayed there not moving. Then he began urinating into the bushes. All hell was let loose! Mrs Duncan began screaming insults at him. Mr Corrigan stood up, adjusting his clothes, red in the face. He made a grab at Leery Lendrum but the man pushed him hard and he fell back into the bushes. Mrs Duncan made to hit Lendrum but he grabbed her arm. She screamed at him:

'You old pervert, what are you doing here spying on people! I'll have to tell the Colonel about you.'

'Och, you go ahead and do that Missus and he'll tell you that I work here and I'm only following his orders, keeping the scum out. He's going to like the story I'll have for him, isn't he?' sneered the beady-eyed man.

Mr Corrigan intervened.

'Now look Lendrum, we were just having a little kiss, there's no harm in that. Now go on your way and forget all that's happened here, eh?'

'Listen to me Corrigan,' the man replied, 'first of all my name is George, as you well know. Haven't I signed enough forms for you to look at, looking for repairs to my very damp house. Sure isn't my poor mother nearly dying with bronchitis. So you just treat me with a little more respect, eh?'

'Now George, surely we can come to some arrangement? We don't want to drag this lovely lady into an embarrassing situation, do we? After all, isn't her husband in the army with the Colonel. It wouldn't look too well, would it?' smiled Mr Corrigan.

Mrs Duncan reached out her hand and tried to draw Mr Corrigan away.

'Oh don't spend time, with this... this... person! Give him a few pounds, isn't that what he's after? They're all the same. Anyway, we haven't done anything wrong,' she said haughtily.

'Well now Missus, I don't think your husband would see it that way. As for the Colonel, well I can't imagine what he will do. Isn't he always preaching family values? But sure that's up to you,' he said, moving off down the path.

Mr Corrigan moved with unbelievable speed down the path after him with Mrs Duncan trotting behind. The girls watched as another conference took place. Unfortunately they were unable to hear what was being said but their imaginations were on the boil. They climbed down from their hiding place and moved back into the safety of the hedge. They never spoke until they were back on Laura's land. Mary sat down on the mossy bank.

'Can you believe that, auld Leery Lendrum! What do you think he'll do?'

'There's a name for people like him, he's a blackmailer! He'll get a load of money from them and he'll get rich. They'll never have any peace... Maybe they'll have to kill him!' said Laura.

'Jesus but you have a wild imagination, Laura Steenson! It's all those *True Detective* books you and our Peter read. Here, don't you tell him about this or I'll be in trouble. Sure he can't hold his water, that fella, he tells Ma everything.'

'Och Mary, I won't tell anyone. Sure my father would kill me... Which reminds me, it's long after the time I was given to watch the ball. It's a wonder he hasn't come up the field looking for me.'

Mary took her arm and the two of them headed down the field:

'Och well, it was great craic, wasn't it? I'll never be able to keep my face straight when I see that auld Mr Corrigan going up the aisle next Sunday.'

CHAPTER 13

THE EVENING OF THE BALL, Laura spent a lot of time on her appearance. She had her hair swept up, with a large diamante clip holding it in place. Mrs Wray had leant her diamond earrings to match. She admired her image in the full-length mirror of the wardrobe – she knew she looked good. Surely Andy would name the wedding day this evening. Laura felt so excited. Her mother stood up as she walked into the room, her taffeta dress rustling as she moved. Her father was in his usual chair at the fire in the kitchen, reading the *Telegraph*.

'Och Laura, you look a treat. Doesn't she William?'

Her father put down his paper and glanced over.

'Well I can't deny that, you look grand. If Andy's not ready, maybe you'll meet someone who is. Sure you're not getting any younger.'

Laura looked at him. Why can't he just give me a compliment without a sting in its tail? Och well, after tonight I won't have to listen to his sarcasm much longer. Her mother fussed round her, fixing the skirt of the dress to show off the changing colours of the midnight-blue taffeta.

Time was moving on. Andy was late and she had promised Mrs Wray she would call and let her see the style. Several times she went to the window. Eventually, almost an hour late, he arrived, full of apologies – they had a sick cow and he couldn't leave. Laura accepted his excuses but somehow they didn't ring true.

'Well Andy, what do you think of your fiancé?' her mother smiled. 'Isn't she beautiful? She'll be the belle of the ball.'

Andy looked at Laura.

'Oh she certainly will, Mrs Steenson. I'll have to watch out or I could lose her. You look lovely, Laura, you make me very proud... Shall we go?'

The man at the entrance gates parked Andy's car. Sparkling stars filled the black sky as they walked up the long avenue, which was hung again with coloured lanterns. A very old Colonel McClean and his new wife, who was much younger, met them in the hallway. As usual, he was dressed in full regalia. He admired Laura and asked her to keep a waltz for him. She watched Mrs McClean, whose expression spoke volumes, 'Don't touch!' Rumour had it that he had met her in a London nightclub. He had fallen head over heels in love with her, much to the disappointment of his two sons and daughter. Laura thought that she looked really common. She wore a flimsy bright red dress that left nothing to the imagination – the neckline plunged almost to her waist! Laura noticed that Andy's eyes were glued to her bosom.

The band on the spacious landing at the top of the stairs was playing a collection of Glen Miller dance tunes. The lofty drawingroom opened into the library through panelled double-doors. A number of guests were dancing. Waiters hovered around to take their coats and serve their drinks. Andy immediately led her into the drawingroom and on to the dancefloor. They danced every dance for nearly an hour. Laura was elated! Supper was served in the dining room across the hall, the same room she remembered from all those years ago. It was a buffet, with hot and cold food and a wide variety of desserts. They found a place to sit in the plant-filled conservatory beside some farming friends of Andy's.

Laura had time to look at her fellow guests and admire the fashion the ladies wore. With Christmas just around the corner, many of the gowns had a winter look. A particular red velvet gown took her fancy. It was worn by a willowy blonde who stood with her back to them, flirting madly with the Colonel. His wife was nowhere in sight. He took her arm and led her past them, up the wide stairway. She smiled at them as she passed. It was Mrs Stuck-up Duncan, the woman from the past, looking just as good as she had been then and up to her old tricks by the looks of it.

When the dancing began again, Laura was asked out by a succession of different partners, so she didn't see Andy for ages. It was only when the charity auction started that she realised that she hadn't seen him since supper. She was embarrassed as she didn't have any money with her and couldn't bid for any of the items. She was sitting with a few of the women she knew from the Red Cross committee. Already some of the guests were staring to leave when she saw him having a conversation with a friend of his. He waved over at her. What was he playing at? He had left her alone for most of the evening and not a word about where he was going. She went over to him, furious.

'Andy where have you been, I haven't seen you for ages!'

He looked at her.

'I've been here. I could see you were not without partners, why the long face?'

'Andy I've been looking for you for nearly an hour. You weren't even here for the auction, it was so embarrassing.'

'Och stop fussing,' he said. 'I went for a few drinks with some friends I hadn't seen since the convention. We found a quiet spot upstairs. I didn't think I was that long, I'm sorry love.'

He bent down and kissed her full on the lips.

'Come on, they are playing a tune I love, Moonlight Serenade.'

He led her on to the dance floor, holding her tightly. After a few times around the floor, she had forgotten why she was worried. The rest of the evening was the happiest she ever remembered. Andy was very attentive.

CHAPTER 14

IT WAS TWO WEEKS before Christmas. The village had taken on a festive look, shops and houses had made a special effort to lighten up. Winnie was excited – she was going to be the Angel Gabriel in the school nativity play. She was helping in the shop as usual, chatting ten-to-the-dozen about how she was going to bring the house down with her performance.

'But I've got one problem,' she said. 'Is there any chance you could help?' she asked Mrs Wray.

Laura was standing on the steps arranging some chocolate boxes. Mrs Wray was handing them up. She smiled at Winnie.

'Well what's this big problem? I hope you don't want me to sing in your choir of angels. I'd clear the hall in seconds!'

'My God, Mrs Wray, I know you haven't a note in your head. Sure Robert says you'd drown out an elephant when you sing in the bath,' laughed Winnie.

Mrs Wray stopped midway in her task and looked strangely at the girl, her voice sharp.

'Since when, young lady, did my husband discuss my singing ability with you? I didn't expect it to be public knowledge.'

Winnie laughed.

'Och Mrs Wray, sure he said it in fun. He didn't mean anything by it. And sure he thinks the world of you.'

'Maybe so. It's not like Robert to be talking about me, I mean he always keeps his thoughts to himself.'

'Well,' continued Winnie, 'I was telling him about the play last week. He heard me singing in the bathroom – you were at the hairdressers. I think he came home for some papers he forgot. Why, is there anything wrong? Sure we talk all the time. He says he'll buy me a special Christmas present because I'm helping you so much.'

'Och well, he likes young people, it's just that he never talks very much. I'll see that you get something you'll really like.

Now what was that wee problem you wanted help with? Come on into the kitchen and tell me all about it.'

With that, Mrs Wray turned and went into the kitchen, forgetting that she had been helping Laura. From her perch on the ladder, Laura could see that the woman was worried. She remembered the pass Robert had made at her. Christ, she thought, surely that dirty auld brute wouldn't touch Winnie, she's just a child. The memory of that evening when he tried to touch her came back. Should she have a word with Winnie? Laura watched Winnie going about her job, looking like she hadn't a care in the world. Indeed, the girl had done some growing up these past few months. She had developed quite a large bust and was wearing lipstick when she got the chance. Och, there was no way she'd look at Mr Robert Wray. She probably had a secret boyfriend that she didn't want to talk about yet. Eventually she would tell her and they'd laugh at the outrageous idea of her being interested in Robert. Oh God, she prayed, let me be right!

A few days later, Laura was busy with a customer when she glanced out the shop window. She thought she saw Andy's car going past, driving very fast. Was there someone with him? She couldn't see properly. Where was he going in such a hurry? She had only seen him once since the ball and he had seemed very preoccupied. When she asked him why, he told her he had a lot on his mind. His brother, David, was in trouble again – he had crashed his bike into someone's car and Andy had paid a large amount of money to the owner to keep him from the courts. When they kissed goodnight, she sensed his thoughts were not with her but she put it down to the trouble with David.

Laura parked the car outside the house. She was so tired... It had been a long day and she had stayed even longer than usual to sort out some invoices. As she was leaving, Mrs Wray told her to take it easy and have a rest until dinnertime the next day. Laura welcomed that advice as she had a lot of Christmas preparations to finish. Her mother was still not able to do much around the house. The woman who helped out wasn't too bad with rough work but when it came to cooking she was useless. And as for Belle! One would think she didn't live at home at all – she was never there these days, away here, there and everywhere with her friend, Freda. Ever since the ball it looked like she had been avoiding Laura.

Laura walked into the kitchen. Her parents were in their usual chairs at the fire but just sitting, not reading or knitting. She put the shopping away, talking about her day. Her parents didn't speak. She looked over at them. Things don't change, she thought. As she prepared the evening meal they sat there, still not speaking, not moving. The kitchen table was already set, so she put the plates of dinner down. It was then she noticed that her mother was crying. Laura ran to her.

'Mother what's the matter, are you sick again?'

But there was no reply, just more tears. She looked at her father.

'What is it?'

She saw a letter in his hand.

'Oh no it's Sam, what's wrong Father, tell me.'

She was almost in tears herself. Her father handed her the letter but there was no stamp on the envelope and it was addressed simply, 'Laura'. She tore the letter open, a quick glance was enough.

'No! No!' she screamed. 'It can't be, he couldn't do this to me, he just couldn't! It's that bitch Belle, it's all her fault. Oh my God, why? Why?' and then she remembered no more.

The blackness swallowed her up as the kitchen floor came to meet her. She was on the couch when she came to, worried. She looked up at her mother who was mopping her brow with a cold face-cloth.

'There, there, dear. You've had a bad shock, you'll be alright. I'll get you a cup of sweet tea, just be still.'

Her father was standing over her.

'I knew there was something about that Andy Carson that I didn't like. Now he runs off with our wee Belle... a bad rascal, a bad rascal...'

Laura came too very quickly. She eased herself up to sitting position and looked up at her father in disbelief.

'I don't believe I'm hearing this! "Our wee Belle", is that all you have to say? You're worried about that wee bitch, no word about what he's done to me?'

Her father stared at her with a disapproving look.

'Now listen Madam, I won't have any bad language in my house. Watch what you say, aren't you old enough to know better? Sure you must have noticed something. Wasn't Andy always taking Belle out with you wherever you were going?'

'Oh yes Father. From the very start, since I was a child, all I listened to was, "Sure you can't leave your wee sister on her own" and "won't she be no bother". We didn't have a choice, take her here, take her there. Sure, Andy, we'll give Belle a lift home from town. Even when we went away for a few days you had her primed to go with us.'

'That was different, sure it wasn't right, the pair of you going off on your own. You know the church wouldn't approve of that type of carry on, it would make you look cheap,' he said, going back to his chair.

Furious, Laura fumed:

'Make me look cheap! Will you listen to yourself. And what do you think your precious Belle has done? She has been after him from the start, and you knew it, Father.'

'Look don't have any rows, we have enough to cope with,' said her mother, putting the tea tray on the table. 'Here Laura, drink that hot tea, you'll feel a lot better,' she added, handing her daughter a cup of the steaming liquid.

'Mother I don't want to upset you any more but I'll never feel better again. My fiancé has run off with my young sister and he hadn't the guts to face me. Everyone is going to know I've been made a fool of, jilted at nearly twenty-six years of age. She's just nineteen, Andy the bastard, is thirty-three, and he's just jilted me. How will the church elders look at this? Oh, that slimy no-good bastard, may he rot in hell!'

'Look Laura, I've told you not to use that language. Indeed, I was thinking of asking the Reverend Whylie to come up and speak with you. He will know what to tell the congregation next Sunday.'

As he spoke, her father made to go towards the hallway and the phone but Laura screamed.

'Father are you mad? Do you not think I've been humiliated enough? And you want the minister to tell all those Holy Joe's the gritty details. Well, don't bother. The way gossip spreads around this village, they'll know all about it soon enough.'

'Look Laura, you're not thinking straight, sure how would you be? It's been a bad shock, and you'll need guidance from someone who understands. We'll have to face the neighbours. Who better than the minister? He will give out the story that maybe you understood and wanted Belle to leave with Andy, so that you wouldn't be too embarrassed when you heard they got married.'

'Married?'

Laura looked at her father.

'How long have you been conjuring this up? And what makes you think he'll marry her? Do you know more than you're saying?'

Her father got up from his chair and came towards her.

'Laura, you know how close Belle and I were. Well, I did discuss this with her and she wanted my blessing, so I insisted that she get married before they left. The Reverend Whylie arranged it with a friend of his in Portadown this morning.'

Her mother, who had been very quiet during all this, spoke.

'William Steenson, I can't believe you could be so devious to your own daughter, how could you? All that sneaking behind her back, how long have you known? Tell me! Tell me!'

She was shouting now.

'Och calm yourself down, don't get in a state. It was the day after that fancy ball Laura insisted Andy take her to. Sure Belle told me he tried to get out of it but Laura, you were that stubborn he couldn't. He came down here to see her while the dancing was going on and Belle wanted him to take her away then but he wouldn't. She was that upset when she told me.'

Laura was dumbfounded.

'The lying bastard! And wasn't he the considerate one not letting me down for the ball! And you Father, how could you take her part, knowing what they planned? Oh he's the dirty coward, he couldn't face me himself. He knew how Belle has you wrapped around her finger and you would do the dirty work for her. But why the letter?'

'Well, I thought it would look better for your mother and you to have something wrote down like.'

'Huh, so that's the reason? That's supposed to make it easy for me, is it Father?'

'Och stop going on, sure you must have known the way things were, that he would never marry you. He's kept you going for too long with his promises, "Maybe next year". Och well, maybe never, isn't that right? Isn't that why I told wee Belle, she'd be better with a wedding ring on her finger before she went off with him?'

It was getting worse. Her own father, such a traitor.

'Well I hope you're satisfied now Father, you have managed to get rid of all of us.'

Laura threw out her arms.

'This is all of your own making. First Betty, she couldn't tell you about her relationship and got married on the quiet. Then Sam, you talked him into joining the RUC, never stopped going on about it since he was a wee child and then when he finally did, he was scared. He was afraid to tell you he wanted out but he fell in love with a wee papist, well that nearly finished you. As far as you're concerned he's dead. And all because of your bigotry! Now you have a lovely grandchild you will never hold in your arms. And Belle… but I know she'll be welcomed back into the fold, isn't she your favourite? How long is she staying away? Long enough for me to leave, I hope.'

Laura's mother was crying.

'William, William, what have you done to my lovely family? But maybe it's part my fault. Didn't I know the man I married, he always gets his own way.'

Laura put her arms around her mother.

'Don't upset yourself, enough has been said. It's over now, I'm getting out.'

'No Laura, maybe I didn't say enough. Maybe it's my fault because I let your father dictate my life since the day I married him.'

They sat quiet for a while, nobody speaking, then to Laura's surprise her mother continued:

'You wouldn't think it now but I was once a vibrant young girl with dreams just like every girl has. But my darling mother died when I was just sixteen so my father – he was very stern – thought it would be better if I got a suitable husband. I didn't want a husband, I wanted to stay on our farm, I loved it there. It was just over the border, Scotstown, in County Monaghan. I had plenty of friends and a good schooling. I was happy. Then out of the blue one Sunday after church, my father introduced me to William and told me that he was the man he had chosen for me to marry. I stood there in the churchyard looking at this stranger. I couldn't take it in! We went back to our house and while I was making the tea my father and William had shook hands on the deal. I was sold like one of the animals. I wasn't given a choice. I just knew his name and that he had a dairy farm like ours. My father said I wouldn't know the difference, it was just like moving house. I wasn't even seventeen, I knew nothing of the world. We were married within the month. There was no way you went against your father. William promised me the earth, moon and stars, a big farmhouse.'

'He forgot to tell me he had a witch of a mother who even looked like one. I haven't talked to you much before about her. She was a wee dumpy woman with a tongue like a viper and she never shut up, always complaining. She hated the sight of me from the start. A dirty lazy woman who spent most of the day in her bed and had to be waited on. I was the new unpaid slave. Well, I got plenty of earth, digging it. The moon and stars too every night because they were well out before I was finished my chores. Then William, a typical man, demanded his rights, tired and all as I was. His mother had very dirty habits and didn't believe in washing too often. She took to her bed when I was expecting our Betty and had me up and down them stairs running after her. She wore me out. Sometimes she wouldn't make it to the toilet in time, said it was her bad legs, so you can imagine the cleaning. Ugh, it still makes me feel sick!'

She stopped speaking and put her head in her hands. Laura's tears and anger had left her and she was spellbound listening to her usually gentle mother. She could see the suppressed anger in her tear-filled eyes as she lifted her head and looked over at her husband. He was sitting in his chair again with his face in his Bible.

'William, what did you do? Help me? "Oh no, it's no job for a man," you said but you never minded all the manual jobs I had to do. Every time I spoke out, I was told to remember my place. So after all the years of hardship I just got on with it and kept my mouth shut... Sure I didn't have any choice!'

It was the longest speech Laura had ever heard her mother make. She went to her and held her tight.

'All these years and you never spoke of your family or where you lived, why?'

Her mother looked at her.

'Why? I've just said. After a few years here I lost my identity. I was that tired sometimes I even forgot my own name.'

'But my grandfather, didn't he come to visit you? Or did you ever go back to Monaghan? You never talked about your home to us,' Laura asked.

'No. I didn't,' she said. 'I was only married a few weeks when my father took a new wife. Och, a young one, just a few years older than me. When I wrote to him to tell him how unhappy I was, I got a very sharp reply that he had a life of his own now and I had to get on with mine and that was the end of it. I didn't write again. Just five years later the minister, Reverend Harper, wrote and told me that Father had died, a massive heart attack. His young wife got everything, the house and all the land. I had Betty and you – you were just a month old – and Esther, your grandmother, to look after and this place. What could I do anyway? I had no claim on the farm or the house, his new wife saw to that. So here I stayed. But you mustn't give up your life to this. You're free now to do whatever you like. And remember, there's still time to be a nurse. You always wanted that, didn't you?'

Laura smiled but looking at her mother with a new insight. She had learned more about her mother's past in these few minutes than in her whole lifetime. She looked across at her father, slumped on his chair, head in his hands. She stood up and went over to him, putting her arms around him as she had never done before.

'Father, I won't hold what's happened against you. It's not your fault, sure Belle has had you in the palm of her hand since the day she was born. It's up to you now to look after Mother. As she's just said, I'm free. I don't know about the nursing, I think maybe I'm too old to learn but I might travel.'

Her father looked up at her.

'You're a great daughter, Laura. Maybe I didn't give you credit sometimes but it's the way I am. Sure your right, you're free and if you want to travel, well, it's your life.'

'Don't make plans yet, dear. Take your time and don't travel too far away. Now I'll make us a fresh pot of tea – we all need it now, don't we?' said her mother, going into the kitchen.

Laura sat down heavily on the chair at the table staring at the spoiled meal. She looked at the clock over the fireplace. Was it just under an hour ago that her life had changed so dramatically? What would she do? Where would she go? To Mary's? Abroad to New Zealand to Betty and Sam? What would they think of all this? She would have to write to them soon. The village would go to town on this juicy bit of gossip. Och, she thought, what do I care what they think? But she did, she didn't want to be the centre of attention. Oh damn that Andy Carson! How could he lie to her like that? The night of the ball, he made love to her. They had gone into the rarely-used parlour in the early hours of the morning after they got back from the dance. How could he? Knowing he planned to run off with Belle? Where were they? Where were they having their honeymoon? Was it in Dublin where Laura and Andy had planned to go on theirs? Do I care, Laura thought? Yes I do, I love him. She looked up and saw her father watching her and for the first time she saw tears in his eyes.

'Father don't, it's over. I'll get over it. I'll go away for a short while and then maybe it will be easier when I return.'

Her father said nothing for a while, and then he mumbled something.

'What did you say, Father? I couldn't hear.'

He stared at her with tears flowing from his eyes into his gnarled old hands.

'The pair of them have gone to Canada.'

He barely whispered the words.

'Canada? How? It takes time to organise a trip like that, I mean, passports and stuff. Jesus! How long has that bastard been planning this? Father, have you known for long?'

Her father wiped his eyes dry and looked at her.

'No, it's what Belle told me yesterday. Andy arranged everything. Now you know as much about it as I do.'

Laura looked at him.

'So there's no more surprises then. Just as well, I don't think I can cope with anything else.'

Laura cleared the uneaten meal away and helped her mother with the tea things.

CHAPTER 15

CHRISTMAS CAME AND WENT. Laura remembered it in a sort of haze. Mary wanted her to come to Belfast to stay with her but Laura knew that she had arranged a holiday in the sun with her doctor boyfriend and wasn't going to spoil it for her. Anyway, she couldn't let Mrs Wray down and if she went to Belfast the villagers would miss their field-day with the news that she was jilted. The shop did more trade that Christmas than Mrs Wray ever remembered – Laura was a nine-day-wonder. Some of the nosy old biddies from the church tried to get her to talk, saying that talking things out was good for the soul, so she stopped helping out with her regular duties, flower arranging and cleaning the vestry. Her excuse was that she was much too busy with the shop.

'How dare they, the old hypocrites, all they want is news. Some of them women thrive on it. They parade up the road every Sunday with a stack of bibles under their arms that would build a house,' Mrs Wray fumed. 'And they're in and out of here under every pretext you could imagine. Listen Laura,' she said, 'don't let them do-gooders get under your skin.'

The McCanns were shocked, hugging her, offering her all sorts of kindness. Mrs McCann sat on the settee with her arms around Laura, who allowed herself to cry until she thought there were no tears left. She never cried in front of her parents, who had the house to themselves for a change. Laura couldn't imagine it empty. After the tears and a wee badly-needed brandy, she did feel a lot better. When the boys returned they made light of it with jokes and shy Peter even suggested that maybe there was a chance for him now. The way he looked at her with such compassion, made her wonder. Young Winnie surprised her, always ready with the quick remark, just hugged Laura and ran upstairs. Laura heard her crying. She had wanted to go up and console Winnie but Mrs McCann said not to worry, she

71

was behaving strangely these last few days, she thought it was boyfriend trouble.

'She'll be back to herself soon and drive us all up the wall with her wisecracks, you'll see.'

After a week Winnie was still very quiet. She did her job in the shop but rushed away as soon as she was free, no chat, no laughter. Laura missed her endless chatter, she would have enjoyed her right now, the way she was feeling. She dreaded going into the house every night with her parents watching her, their eyes filled with sympathy, her mother asking:

'Did anyone say anything to you?'

She usually made the excuse that she was far to busy to answer their questions.

Christmas came and went and Laura was delighted it was all over. She had done all the cooking and after the church service she couldn't get away quick enough. She was annoyed with her father for lingering on talking to the minister and his wife, as she sat in the car waiting. She saw the people leaving the church looking at her and she knew she was the topic of conversation. Finally, her parents got into the car and on the drive home her father spoke of the kindness of the Reverend Whylie and how she should be grateful he was taking such an interest in her problems. Then he surprised Laura by saying that the minister's wife was calling on her tomorrow to discuss an idea she had. He told them that Mrs Whylie had suggested that Laura spend some time with her invalid sister who lived in Ballyclare in County Antrim. She would make a wonderful companion – they were both so intelligent and would have a lot in common.

Laura was quiet on the way home, so her parents took her silence as an agreement to the plan. Dinner was again eaten with very little conversation. Laura hardly touched a bite. Her stomach was very upset these days, indeed the cooking of it didn't help. Her parents ate heartily and complimented her on the meal. She was clearing up when her mother broached the subject of the invitation from Mrs Whylie again.

'You know Laura,' she said, 'it will be good for you to get away from here for a while, especially to someone that we know. And who knows, you might like it enough to stay.'

Laura took an unusually long time drying the plates before answering her.

'Mother, you reminded me last week that I was free now. Do you honestly think I want to go and be an unpaid servant to Mrs Whylie's invalid sister? From what I've heard of her, she goes through servants and companions like water through a sieve. And don't I know one or two of them. What about Emily Brown, old Dr Brown's spinster daughter? When he died they decided it was the best thing for her. She left here a happy smiling lady and returned a year later a broken old woman, sure we hardly recognised her. Didn't she tell Mrs Wray that she was on the go morning, noon and night and no matter what she did, there was no pleasing the woman. There was nothing that serious wrong with her, apart from arthritis in one of her knees but she insisted on being taken everywhere in a wheelchair. Could you see me coping with that? Anyway, why can't she get someone from her own part of the world?'

'Mrs Whylie explained,' said her mother, ' that she needs to know that the person she gets is of very good character. She didn't want anyone local. Who better than her own sister to give her a reference? She thought it would suit you even for a short while. Why don't you think about it, dear?'

Laura was worn out.

'Mother please, I know you want what's best for me but I'll decide. I'm certainly not going to wet-nurse a cranky old woman who has nothing to do with her time but complain. You should know all about that. Don't worry Mother, I'm alright, honestly. I'll wait until the New Year and then I'll make a fresh start for myself, a whole new beginning. I want you to promise me that you'll take care of yourself when I'm not here, won't you?'

Her mother smiled at her.

'Laura, you've always been a good daughter and you're not to worry, your father and I will be fine. You do what you feel is right.'

'Oh, I can see that a lot of things have changed. He even brings you breakfast in bed and you don't let him dictate any more. You're the boss now, eh?'

Laura was glad to get back to normal. She sat a the table enjoying tea with Mrs Wray. The shop was quiet except for the regulars and Winnie was having some time off before she went back to school.

'Well Laura, are things any better for you? I hope you don't mind me saying this but you don't look well at all, are you sleeping alright?'

Laura could see that she was concerned.

'Och, I'm fine Mrs Wray but you're right, I'm not sleeping well. I'll get over it, don't worry.'

'I can't help worrying. You have come through an awful lot of heartache and I'm sure you've lost weight. I think you need a long holiday.'

'Well,' Laura replied, 'I was offered something, a change of scenery and to be a companion.'

'I don't believe it, Mrs Whylie's sister. So you're the next charity case?' interrupted Mrs Wray.

Laura nodded.

'Yes, she thinks I'd make a cultured companion. What do you think?'

'You're not thinking of taking it, are you?' she asked. 'Not after what I told you about Emily Brown. And do you know someone else who went?'

Laura shook her head.

'No, who?'

Mrs Wray poured out another fresh cup of tea.

'Do you remember wee Sadie Wilson, you know, the oldest of the butcher's girls? She got into trouble with that Catholic fellow from the town and she was sent to a home for wayward girls, up in Derry some where. I think the baby was adopted.'

'Of course I remember her,' Laura said. 'She was a lovely girl, and wasn't she mad about that fellow. Sure I gave her a lift into town a few times. I saw him, you know, a fine big fellow, he was waiting for her at the corner. You could see he was daft about her, I thought she had eloped or something.'

'No, no, nothing like that. Her father was Grand Master of the Lodge. He couldn't let a daughter of his marry a Catholic, wouldn't he be booted out if that happened?'

Mrs Wray looked so sad.

'Such a pity she couldn't live her own life.'

Laura looked angry.

'There we go again with this awful bigotry, why can't people be allowed to follow their heart, without being branded? Things must have been terrible for that wee girl. At least I haven't that problem. Anyway, what happened to her, is she with Mrs Whylie's sister?'

'No not any more, she accepted the job, though I don't think that would be the right word for it. Her father took the minister's advice, and after her child was born she was taken by the minister's wife to her sister.'

'And how did she get on there?' asked Laura.

'Not very well, I'm afraid,' said her friend. 'She stayed nearly a year, didn't her poor mother tell me herself. Sadie wrote to her after her father sent her away and said he didn't want her back here again. The poor woman was devastated. He's one rough brute, you see him at the Twelfth in all his regalia, smiling and waving at everyone. You'd think butter wouldn't melt in his mouth. Och, he's one hard man. Is it any wonder the older ones all left home? That woman has an awful life with him. I've often asked my Robert what he sees in him, they're very friendly but he passes it off and tells me it's Lodge business or the church. That's men for you.'

Laura looked at Mrs Wray.

'I've never got to know that man well. I let my father do business at his butcher's shop but I've heard him shouting at the family sometimes.'

Mrs Wray looked at her.

'Maybe it's just as well you don't know him. He rules that family with a whip. There was six of them but as they got older they couldn't get away quick enough. Sure that oldest boy of his treats his wife just the same, didn't he give her a bad hiding only last year and she lost the baby? She can't have any more you know. She told people she fell down the stairs. You wonder why the rest of them left home. Isn't there only one wee girl left now, God help her.'

Laura thought about her own family and their life, when at home. Were all men the same? Did they all want to rule? Mrs Wray brought her back to the present.

'You were asking what happened to Sadie, weren't you? Well she's in New York now and doing well and her boyfriend went out to join her last year. Her mother said she was very depressed after her time in Ballyclare. Didn't that sister of Mrs Whylie's beat her with her walking stick and call her awful names. And not only that but she locked the kitchen up after she had eaten, so Sadie was half-starved as well. But she saved every penny she earned to get enough to leave and her mother managed to help her... without her father knowing of course.'

'Can you imagine Mrs Wray, that my family would want me to go there? If she got my temper up sure I'd kill her! I would never stand to be treated like that,' laughed Laura.

'Now you know what you're missing, don't you?' said Mrs Wray laughing. 'Anyway have you any idea what you want to do?'

'I'm not sure yet. I haven't told Betty or Sam and they make life in New Zealand sound great. I would love to visit them but it's a long way off, isn't it? And I worry about my mother. I'd never forgive myself if anything happened while I was on the other side of the world.'

Mrs Wray reached out and placed her hand on Laura's.

'Listen, you have a chance now to do what you want. You're young and healthy, will you stop worrying about what may never happen? Go out into the world and live a little. I wish I had the chance but it never happened, I've been in this house and shop since I was born.'

'Didn't you ever leave it when you were younger?' asked Laura.

'No, I never had the chance. Oh, I had dreams too, just like every other girl but I was an only child and I had to help out here when I was still at school. Then my father joined the army and was injured. He never recovered. By then I had met Robert. My only regret was that we couldn't have children.'

Laura put her arms around the woman.

'Right, you have made up my mind for me. I'll write to Betty next week. The first of January, 1969, a whole new beginning for Laura Steenson.'

Laura didn't put her plan into action. Life took quite a dramatic change. It was New Year's Eve and snow had been falling all day. It was freezing now and getting about was proving to be very dangerous. This was to be Laura's last week at the shop. She was going to tidy up her affairs there before leaving. She wanted to get away early in the New Year and there was a lot to do yet. Winnie wasn't coming into work, she had flu just when Laura needed her. Her parents were not surprised when she told them she was going, they were expecting it. But when they heard she wanted to visit New Zealand it was a different story, her father was raging.

'Do you have to go to that heathen country? Surely there's places closer to home. What's wrong with Scotland or England, and they're not too far away?'

Laura laughed.

'New Zealand, a heathen country. Father, take a look around at this wee country of ours. We have bigotry, badness, bombs, shooting, families against each other, all in the name of religion. How more heathen could you get? In New Zealand no one cares what religion you are. They follow Christ in their own way and still manage to get on with each other. Why can't it be the same here? You know why? Because there's too much brutality and greed and the church ruling your life.'

'Now Laura, don't bring the church into this, it's not the church's fault that Andy walked out on you. You must stop the bitterness. Surely travel wherever you want but don't be bitter over what has happened. In a few months you'll wonder why you felt this way and you will meet someone else. Sure you're a lovely girl, aren't you my daughter?'

He smiled at her. Her father's speech surprised her and Laura went over and hugged him.

'Father, of course I'm your daughter, I've got your strength, haven't I?'

She didn't see her father's tears as she moved away. Her mother came into the room – she had been upstairs resting.

'Don't tell me you two are rowing again. Did we not have all this out before? I don't want her leaving this house under a cloud. This is always her home, no matter where she goes, do you hear me William Steenson?'

Laura and her father both stared at her.

'Alright Ruth, I know who the boss is from now on.'

Laura smiled at the pair of them. She knew that things would be fine with them, whatever about her problems. She left them to it, not even waiting to have lunch as her stomach was playing up. She decided that she would write that very evening to Betty and Sam.

Laura stood outside the house, the snow was quite deep in places and she could see light drifts on the corners of the fields. She would never manage the car in this. Her father, in one of his good moods, offered to drive her down in the tractor but she declined, preferring to walk. She loved the snow, remembering the snow when she was young, flying down the high field on anything that would move freely. Sam pulled out the big tin bath from the shed, slid down the hill and finished up in the ditch with two broken teeth. Their father slid down the hill after him when he heard him crying. Laura smiled to herself. As a family they'd had some good times as children. She stood at the top of the lane surveying the scene before her. The valley below was covered in a blanket of snow and the sun was shining, causing the overnight frost to sparkle like millions of tiny stars dancing in the distance. She sighed, thinking that this was the loveliest place in the world. If only things could be different.

The McClean home stood silent and empty - there was no movement of animal or human. The Colonel and his young wife had gone to live abroad – her father had told her just last night that the estate had been sold. It was ironic really, for that to happen now. Andy always had his eye on that place. Tears started again. That could have been her home... She walked on till she came to the corner. The lough was visible, shimmering in morning light. As she watched a flock of wild geese, flying V-shaped, landed gracefully on the water. They looked so beautiful and free. And that's what I am, free like the birds, she thought.

By the time she reached the village Laura was warm as toast, her face tingling. Her stomach was much better. Mrs Wray was surprised to see her.

'What on earth are you doing coming out in this weather? Come in here to the kitchen, I have the kettle boiling.'

Laura smiled.

'I'm fine. I loved the walk, even if it did take an hour but I loved it. Everything looks so clean and crisp, isn't it a great start to the New Year?'

'Och it's hard to believe it's 1969, where has this year gone?' She looked at Laura. 'You do look better you know, it must be the snow.'

Laura laughed.

'Maybe it is... I'm going to stay here for a couple of hours, then I have to get the bus into town. I've got to visit the bank, then I'm going to see about a passport, so if you want to get the hair done do it now while I'm here. Is Winnie still off?'

Mrs Wray poured out two mugs of tea.

'Here drink this, do you want some toast?' She handed Laura the plate of hot-buttered toast. 'You know, I'm worried about that child. I've hardly got two words out of her this week and she's not looking well at all. She came in here the other evening as white as a sheet. I told her to go back home but she said she wanted to stay. God love her, she looked lost. I asked her to tell me what was the matter but she just looked at me and cried, "I can't tell you Mrs Wray, don't ask me."'

'It must be boyfriend trouble,' said Laura. 'I don't think there's anything wrong at home. I was talking to her mother yesterday. They're fine, with the exception of the boys. Och, it's hard for the family having them in prison. That house was like a morgue at Christmas. When I think of the craic we used to have....'

'Are them boys still in Long Kesh? I though they were going to be moved. They say it's only the real dangerous ones that gets put in there. God Bless us but it's hard to believe that it's the same wee boys that used to come in here, with their pennies in their hand and a big smile on their wee faces. "Two three-penny bags of sweets, please," they used to ask me. Then I had to count the sweets into the bags in case one got a sweet more than the other. I still can't believe that they are terrorists.'

Laura looked at her employer's sad face.

'You know something, I think it was the bad company they got involved with, and those big-shot leaders talking about a free Ireland. You notice none of those boys got arrested. Isn't it the same with our side, all they want is a Protestant-run Ulster. They're living in a dream-world, aren't they? Here, come on you, get into your coat and over to the hairdressers and make yourself beautiful for Robert.'

Mrs Wray smiled at her and did as she was told.

Laura left the bank and stood mesmerised near the doorway. She moved as in a dream up the street towards the town square. What should she do now? There was no point in going to the post office for her passport forms. She got to the bus stop to discover that there was only one bus leaving that evening because of the snow. She had nearly two hours to wait. She needed to be by herself to think. She didn't fancy the café near the end of the street it was always busy. The hotel was the only place. She entered the big double-glass doors, the heat hitting her like a wave as she did so. There were very few people about, it suited her fine. She choose a corner table by the window and ordered coffee and a sandwich though she knew she could never eat it. She hardly noticed the other customers in the room, travellers like herself, in from the cold. Only they wouldn't have her problems would they? The food arrived and she sipped at the hot coffee. She could still see the face of the bank manager, Mr McBennett.

'I'm afraid, Miss Steenson, you must be mistaken, that account has been closed.'

Laura stared at him, shocked.

'Cleared, it can't be! There must be a mistake! When? Please check again. That was our joint account, we never touched it, that was for saving, we've been saving for nearly five years. Oh my goodness! What's happened?'

Mr McBennett came around the desk to comfort her.

'I'm so sorry but the cashier didn't make any mistake. Look, I'll call Miss Lucas in and she can explain.'

He went to the door and was gone only a minute. He returned with the lady she had already spoken to.

'Now, Miss Lucas, let's get this problem sorted. When was the account closed and who authorised it?'

The tall woman looked at Laura very suspiciously.

'I have the documents here, Sir, you can see for yourself. The account was closed on the 16th of December.'

'Yes but by whom?' said Laura, impatiently.

'Oh, by Mr Andrew Carson and his fiancé.'

'His fiancée! But I'm his fiancé,' said Laura. 'I'm the only one who can sign. How did this happen? What did she...?'

But she already knew what she looked like didn't she... Belle, her darling sister.

'Can I see the withdrawal document, please?'

Miss Lucas handed the document over to Laura, who looked closely at the two signatures. Belle really is a good forger, I wonder how long they were planning this? Years, maybe. She handed the papers back to the disconcerted woman.

'Thank you. Don't worry, I'm not blaming you. You never met me before, did you?'

'No, no, of course not. He also closed his other account. He had all the right papers and bank books. I even asked him if he needed any help to transfer such a large amount.'

'Yes,' said Mr McBennet, 'you see it's policy at this bank to offer to transfer funds when someone is moving abroad. We like to help our customers as much as we can but Mr Carson preferred to withdraw all the funds in cash. Indeed, I was worried that he should be carrying such a large sum of money on his person but he assured us that is was no problem for him.'

The man was in an agitated state, wringing his hands.

'This is a big worry for the bank, as you have proved that you are indeed the second signatory on the accounts. We must do something. We'll have to call the police – these transactions were fraudulent.'

Laura put her hand up.

'No, no, Mr McBennet, no police. I don't want them involved at all. I'll have to deal with this myself. Anyway, I know what's happened now, it will be alright.'

But the bank manager wasn't satisfied.

'I'm afraid that won't do at all, Miss Steenson. You see, I'm responsible for all transactions here and a fraud has clearly taken place. There can be no doubt about that. It's a major offence, I'll have to follow it through. You understand, don't you?'

But Laura surprised him by saying:

'I don't want the police. I'm not making a complaint so without it there's no cause for them, is there? My wish is to go home and forget all about it.'

'Forget all about it, madam? There are thousands of pounds involved, do you realise that? I can't let you do that, it happened in my bank.'

The manager was nearly having a heart attack.

'Please, Mr McBennet, I don't want you to worry. Half of the money was mine but far as I'm concerned it's a family matter now.'

Laura couldn't wait to get out of the stuffy office, she needed to be in the fresh air. She stood, put on her warm gloves and held out her hand to the bewildered manager. Miss Lucas still hovered in the background. She shook hands and thanked them both, saying she would be in touch. The manager followed her and opened the outer door for her, wishing her a Happy New Year. How ironic, she thought as he did so, he was probably biting his tongue now.

She sat in the lounge of the hotel, not wanting to leave the warm turf fire. She loved the smell of the glowing embers. She ordered another coffee, still an hour to wait. The 16th of December, the day after the McClean ball! How could he? After what they had been to each other. She was glad to be sitting on her own. No one could see her blushes when she thought of that last night of lovemaking in her front parlour. They were out of their clothes in seconds and on the floor, not caring that her parents were sleeping just overhead, all caution forgotten in their extreme passion. Now she felt like a real slut when she thought of what they did. She was sorry she started on the coffee, she should have had hot sweet tea. The very thought of what had occurred was making her ill. So much for her freedom, he couldn't even leave her that. Andy took her dignity, her hard-earned savings and now her freedom. For without money, where was it, this so-called freedom? It's gone with everything else, now what will I do? I can't follow my dream and travel. I'm stuck here, whether I like it or not. At least I've still got a job. Laura hadn't felt this low since Andy had left. She had thought she was getting over it, especially when she'd started making plans for the future. The thought of that devious couple really annoyed her. All the time they were planning this. He had used her. Did Belle realise that he was having sex with her at every opportunity and telling her all those lies? How much he loved her, what would they do when they were married, where they would live. Now everything was gone. What should she do about the forgery? She hadn't a clue where to start, should she ask someone for advice? Who? A solicitor? Not her minister, anyway. She didn't want pity, especially from him. He would probably bring his washed-out do-gooder wife with him, maybe they would find a workhouse for her.

She was still upset but she couldn't help but smile to herself at the thought of the minister and his wife running around the country looking for a suitable home for her. Laura couldn't believe how gullible she had been regarding the money. They had decided to open an account in the local bank nearly five years ago and start saving. Andy had come up with the idea of the joint account – it made sense after all.

'What's the point of having two accounts, it's all going to be ours isn't it?' he said.

She protested that she couldn't save as much as he could but he laughed it off, telling her how silly she was and to stop being so independent. They agreed that if either of them needed money at any time, they could withdraw whatever was needed, providing they put it back. It worked quite well. Andy would sometimes need money in a hurry, she would sign the withdrawal form for him, he would then show her in a few weeks that he had put it back. Because he'd be doing more business then she ever would, he thought it best that he should keep the lodgement book – it did make sense after all. Suddenly she remembered the incident before the ball at McClean's. When they'd decided to go, she knew she needed a new dress and a few things. Andy was reluctant at first but finally agreed to her going on a shopping trip. She'd asked him for the lodgement book or that he take her to the bank the next day to withdraw some money but she remembered that his mood changed very quickly. Now she knew why – he didn't want her to go anywhere near the bank. Instead he opened his wallet and took out two crisp fifty pound notes. She looked at him amazed. He had an awful lot of money there, she could see the wallet was bulging. When she protested that it was too much, he laughed at her and said to stop worrying.

'Won't it save you having to go to the bank?'

She looked at the notes.

'It's too much, one of these will do.'

She handed the other back but he refused to take it.

'Look, Christmas is almost here and you'll be needing some spending money. I tell you what, take this one as my present buy something nice for yourself,' he said.

The incident was very fresh in her mind. She raged. The two-faced bastard, he knew all along what was coming. I must have 'Fool' printed on my forehead, she thought. As she stood up, anger raced through her. She put on her coat and gloves, grabbed her bag and headed out for the bus and home. She would have to explain it to her parents and she certainly wasn't looking forward to that.

CHAPTER 16

A WEEK HAD PASSED and Laura's mind was in turmoil. Her life was stretched out before her. She couldn't see any hope now of leaving to start anew. Her mother asked her if she had made any plans yet but Laura told her she was going to wait a while. Ruth Steenson was delighted that her daughter was going to be with them. Secretly she hoped that Laura would never leave. It was too much to take in. She didn't discuss how she felt with William. He would just grunt as usual and say, 'Maybe it was all for the best, but Ruth still couldn't get over the deceit of it all, Belle behaving like that behind her sister's back. She knew that Belle was always flirting and loved attention but that she would go that far! It was hard to think badly of one's own daughter.

Ever since she had been a small child she'd always managed to get her own way, from insisting on winning any game she played to manipulating her father into giving her anything she wanted. Belle would plead with William and he'd smile at her and off she'd go, winning again. Ruth remembered an incident that happened when Laura had asked for a bicycle for her birthday. She had been talking about it for weeks, a big blue Raleigh that had everything, including a lovely big basket at the front. She had saved and worked hard around the house and farm and hadn't refused a single job, no matter how difficult. When she first asked her father he refused but she offered to help pay for it by working. Laura was nearly ten and getting very tall. Her old bike was much too small for her. She came home from school one day, all excited. It was going to be her birthday in two months and she had seen the bike in town, in the window of Irwin's shop. Every Saturday after that when they went into town, she made her way to the shop just to stand and gaze at it. One day she plucked up the courage to go in and ask about it. The man in the shop let her sit on it. She was over the moon with joy at the thought of owning it, so William agreed that if she worked hard and saved her money, he would see.

When Belle heard about the new bike she had one of her tantrums. She was just five years old and when she started acting up, there was no stopping her. Ruth remembered giving her a good slap on the legs for her bad behaviour but Belle ran to William out in the farm, telling him between her sobs how her mother had beaten her, making it sound like she was whipped. Belle insisted that she should have a new bike too, a red one. They tried telling her that it was Laura's birthday present and she needed it for school but it didn't make any difference. She wanted a red bike and no one was going to change her little mind. William laughed at Belle's antics but Ruth wasn't too pleased with her. They agreed to get Laura her bike. Money wasn't too plentiful but Ruth said that it was necessary. Didn't she deliver the eggs every week to the store? Her old bike wasn't strong enough and maybe she would clean it up and paint it for Belle... And it was left at that.

The Saturday before her birthday, Laura couldn't contain her excitement. She planned on taking the bus to town with her friend, Mary. She had left her old bike at a friend's house the day before, so that they could cycle the four miles home together. William knew that his daughter was anxious to get off into town to get her bike. But he deliberately kept her at home as long as he could, insisting she finish her chores. As usual, he was blaming Mary's family for leading Laura astray.

'That papist family,' he called them. 'What do you see in them? They will only bring you down to their level.'

Ruth remembered when Laura finally got to leave and catch the bus into town. She flew down the lane, jacket flying behind her and one of her blue hair-ribbons trailing down her back. Later that evening when they were watching out for her return, Sam began calling excitedly:

'Come on quick, it's our Laura! Do you hear her ringing her bell?'

As he ran down the lane to meet Laura, Ruth noticed Belle sulking by the gate.

'Come on Belle,' she called, 'your sister's home.'

But the child refused to move, shouting:

'It's not fair! I don't want to see her auld bike! Why can't I get one?'

Ruth told her they were going to clean and paint Laura's old bike but it didn't make any difference, Belle still made a fuss. Her father wasn't there to console her – he had gone off with a friend on some job but hadn't said where. Ruth watched Laura push her new blue Raleigh bike up the lane, ringing the bell, her face showing the happiness she felt. Betty, who had been baking a sponge for the birthday tea, came out of the house covered in flour. She ran down the lane and hugged her sister.

'Och, it's lovely Laura,' she said, admiring all the different accessories. 'Can I have a go?'

She tried the bike out around the street.

'Come on Belle,' called Laura. 'You next. I'll hold it for you, try it out.'

'I don't want to ride your rotten old bike, I want one of my own! Anyway, it's awful looking... and I hope you fall off and break your neck!' Belle screamed, as she ran into the house.

Ruth was annoyed at her behaviour and called after her:

'You go straight upstairs this minute madam, until your manners improve.'

They heard the kitchen door slam loudly...

Sam was next to admire the bike.

'Here, you ride it Sam,' said Laura, handing him her prized possession.

'I'm not getting up on a girl's bike. Sure the fellas would laugh at me. It's a grand bike alright but I'm going to save for a motorbike. When I'm older I'm going to get a Harley Davidson, it's the best.'

Betty teased him.

'Well you weren't too proud to ride Mother's bike when I was teaching you and it's a really old-fashioned one, look at the shape of it!' she laughed.

Ruth looked at her rusty old bike lying against the barn door.

'Och indeed, and weren't you all taught to ride on it? And I am not one bit ashamed of it either. I remember getting that bike from my father for my sixteenth birthday and I was every bit as proud as you are, Laura. Indeed, it has served me well. I rode into town twice a week on it after I was married, to sell the eggs at the market and sometimes a few chickens. And I carried a load of stuff home on it as well. Sure you young ones have it all too easy now. Come on, Laura let me see you ride your fancy bike. Maybe we should find out how many chickens that new basket will hold, eh?'

The Steenson children laughed, apart from Belle who was still sulking inside, and joked about what they could carry on the bike. They were still out on the street when they heard their father and his friend Bobby Clarke coming up the lane in the truck. They moved out of the way for the truck to turn. Their father got down from the cab and invited Bobby to stay for a cup of tea but he refused, saying he had to get home. William went to the back of the lorry and let the security side down. Turning to the children he asked:

'Where's Belle?'

They told him she had been sent inside, because she was bold.

'Och sure she's only a child, why are you always teasing her? Well, I see you got your new bike, Laura. Mind you look after it, it cost quite a penny.'

Laura wheeled the bike over for his inspection.

'Well Father, isn't it lovely? Do you like the colour? Thank you, thank you, I really will look after it, I promise that I...'

Laura didn't finish her sentence. She was looking into the truck. Her father was lifting a spanking new red child's bike with stabilisers out of the truck. Ruth remembered the look on Laura's face.

'William, what are you thinking of? This is not right, you shouldn't have given in to her. The others never get what they ask for by throwing tantrums. You're showing her she can do what she likes. I know what I'd like to do to her.'

'Och will you stop woman, can I not do as I like for my own child? You're always whinging. Where is she? Belle, Belle, come on out!' he called.

He hardly had the words out when Belle flew through the door and into his arms, crying:

'Mama is going to beat me and I was good.' Then she saw the bike. 'Oh, Dada, my new red bike, you *did* get it!'

She ran over and tried to ride it.

'It's no gooood!' she howled. 'It's too big, I can't reach the pedals!'

'Now, now child, stop that. Sure the seat just needs moving down a bit.'

He adjusted the seat and sat Belle on her new bike. The crying stopped immediately. He held the bike till she felt she could control it herself, then she cycled proudly round the street.

'Look everyone, look at me! This is *mine* and no one is touching it!'

Just then there was a shout from Betty inside the house:

'Oh no! What happened my lovely cake and the buns?'

Ruth got to the kitchen first. Betty was standing crying at the table. She had made a sponge cake and iced it for Laura. It was in bits on the floor, surrounded by buns, all squashed up. When Laura and Sam came in they saw the mess.

'Oh Mother!' cried Betty. 'That spoilt wee brat, it was her! And I worked all day for a nice surprise for Laura. She's that jealous of everyone getting more than her. I'll kill her when I get my hands on her! How could she do this?'

Betty was really angry and Laura was in tears. Ruth stood there looking at the lovely surprise, ruined.

'Och Betty, it was a lovely thought, thank you. But I can't believe that Belle could be that wilful. What am I going to do with her at all?'

Just then the culprit came in, holding her father's hand.

'What's happened in here? That's an awful mess, did you knock the baking over, Betty?'

Betty fumed.

'No, I did not knock it over. That spiteful wee brat did, didn't you?'

She went to grab her younger sister but Belle backed away behind her father, crying:

'She's going to hit me and I didn't do anything wrong!'

'What do you mean didn't do anything wrong? You were the only one in the house, weren't you?'

Betty went for her again.

'It wasn't me, it wasn't! It must have been the dog – he was lying at the fire. Dada, don't let her blame me!'

William put his protecting arm around her.

'Sure we know you wouldn't do something like that. Get that dog out on the street Sam. He shouldn't be in here anyway, the useless auld thing. And keep him out, he's nothing but trouble.'

'Father,' protested Sam, 'Jack wouldn't. It was that one there, she's telling lies, I know it!'

'Do as you are told and take that dog out, do you hear me? And we will have no more blaming anyone, it's done now. Anyway, fancy cakes we can do without. Betty can make us some of her special pancakes. Sure they go down well, don't they?'

With that he went and sat on his favourite chair with Belle on his knee. She had won again. Ruth sighed, remembering. And she's still winning.

Laura drove her car into the yard of the farmhouse. The light from the kitchen window reflected on the wet cobbled street. She reversed into the barn and sat thinking of everything that had happened in these last few weeks. The humiliation she had endured was the worst. Everywhere she went people looked at her with pity. She knew that many more were talking and laughing at her behind her back. Last Sunday she thought the service would never end. Reverend Whylie's irritating voice droned on and on and she felt the walls of the small church closing in on her. She wanted to leave but she knew that would only cause more gossip. On the way out, she saw her friend, Mrs Wray, and the two left together. She told her parents she would only be a minute.

She had just made it down into the yard at the side of the house when she vomited all over the hedge. Cold sweat clung to her hair and she felt she was going to pass out but she made it indoors with the help of her friend.

'Look Laura, you're in no state to drive home. Stay here and I'll make some excuse to your father. Give me the keys of your car – he can come for you later.'

Without speaking, Laura handed her the keys. She stumbled up to the bathroom just in time for another bout of vomiting. After some time she cleaned herself up and went to lie down on the couch in the sittingroom. Mrs Wray found her there and handed her a mug of hot sweet tea.

'Now, sip at that and you'll be fine. Did you eat something that disagreed with you?'

'Well, I didn't like the taste of the omelette last night. I thought it was the mushrooms I put in. Mother didn't like them either but I don't think she was ill.'

Mrs Wray looked at her.

'Well the colour's coming back to your face. That's probably what it was – sometimes mushrooms can be dodgy enough. Were they wild or did you buy them?'

'My father got them from the low field when he was bringing in the cows yesterday. They looked great. I ate some after I washed them. I love them raw but maybe there were a few wrong ones. I'll not be eating any more, I can tell you.'

'You know Laura, you haven't been looking great for a few days now, indeed since you came back from the town last week. You didn't say how you got on. Did you get the form for your passport? Was everything alright?'

Laura turned her head and looked out the window. There were a few stragglers on the street. She could see Mr Dillon knocking on Devlin's pub door and the barman opening it to let him in, looking up and down the street before going back in. Men, she thought. Nothing to worry them, one looking for more customers and the rest looking to get drunk. They always had it easy – didn't they call the tune? She turned back to a worried Mrs Wray.

'I'm fine now, don't worry. I was just thinking how men had it so easy.'

'Haven't they just! I expect Robert Wray is over there in Black's pub with the rest of the Holy Joes, putting the world to rights. And he'll come back here carrying his bibles and hymn books, expecting me to think he was delayed on church business. Isn't he just like all the rest of them, they only think of themselves. Indeed that's all he has been doing lately. Sure he's never at home these days. If it's not church business it's the lodge. I don't bother asking any more... Here, would you like more tea? I'll make some fresh.'

Laura protested:

'No, no, I'm fine, I'll have to get home and help with the dinner. What did you tell my parents? I don't want them worrying.'

'I told them I had a problem with an order for tomorrow morning and you were the only one who could deal with it. Can't we all tell a wee lie when we need to?' Mrs Wray laughed. 'I'm glad to see you looking better. You were green, you know. Are you sure you're alright?'

Laura nodded and smiled.

'I don't know what I would do without someone like you to talk to, you are so understanding. I'd normally phone my friend Mary but she's away in Spain with her boyfriend. I'll go up to Belfast for a wee visit when she comes back. I'm going to need some sound advice and she's great.'

Laura turned her head away again, tears welling up in her eyes. Her friend put her arms around her.

'Cry all you want love, it helps relieves the tension. You're bound to feel a lot of emotion, sure it's only natural. But isn't time a great healer, sure in a few months you will have got him and her out of your system. You know what I would do if I were in your shoes? I'd plan a visit to New Zealand. Sure what's stopping you, aren't you free as the wind?'

But the tears seemed unstoppable now and it took some time before Laura could speak. Finally, she dried her eyes.

'You may as well hear the rest of it. I went into the town the other day. I was determined to get over this and I'd planned my freedom. I wanted to see Betty and Sam, I even started a letter to them but the bank manager brought me down to earth with quite a bump. I didn't think Andy could do any more to me. Boy, was I wrong.'

She proceeded to tell Mrs Wray her story.

'You can't let them get away with this! Them pair could go to jail, do you know that? Oh the rascal! He must have been planning it for some time. How could your sister do that to you, what sort of a girl is she?'

Laura looked at her.

'A very spoiled one, always was, from she was able to talk. But you know I blame myself too, sure didn't she come every-where with us? You know that. I had to take her with me every-where we went. Didn't I have all this out with Father. Wasn't he the one who pushed her with us – cinema, dances. Sure wasn't I delighted to see her getting boyfriends of her own, though none of them lasted very long. I still can't believe the deceit of it all, I never expected to loose all my savings. Now I could hardly spend a weekend in Portrush – so much for my big plan to go to New Zealand.'

'Now look, Laura, you are not to worry about money. If you want to go to New Zealand, that's no problem, won't I give you the money. You need a break, girl, and I'm going to see that you get it. And I won't hear any excuses.'

'Well, I'm still not making any plans yet... You're far too generous but I might just take you up on it.'

'There's no might about it. You're going to plan that trip, even if I have to go and get the passport form myself. A couple of months away will do you the world of good. Anyway, what did your family say? I'm sure they were annoyed.'

'Well, I didn't get around to telling them yet. Mother wasn't looking that good these past few days and I don't want to add more worry for them.'

'Laura, they've got to be told, it's an offence. Mr McBennet will have to tell the police, after all it's his duty as a manager.

Then all hell will be let loose. You'll have to tell your parents yourself, they can't hear it from the police.'

'I know it's an offence but I don't want the police involved. I already told Mr McBennett that I'm not bringing any charges. Sure it would kill my mother, not to mention what it would do to my father. Doesn't he think the sun shines out of Belle's eyes. I'd never forgive myself if anything happened to them because of something I said.'

'Och, and knowing that young tinker of a sister of yours, isn't that what she is banking on? She knows you won't do anything to hurt them. You're far too good-natured for your own good. But it's your family Laura, and you know best.'

'Yes, Mrs Wray, I understand all that but there's nothing I can do. I will tell them about the money. But not now, sometime... Now I'm going to phone my father to come in for me. I don't fancy walking home in these shoes. I'll be in after lunch tomorrow. Are you still going into town?'

'Och that's great, Laura. I'm going to tell Robert I need the car, I hate waiting around for the bus. That's going to cause a few words as well. You know, I've only been in that car twice this month, he's always using it... But he will just have to do without it tomorrow.'

CHAPTER 17

LAURA TOOK HER SHOPPING from the car and walked towards the house. She looked in the kitchen window as she passed. Her mother was knitting as usual and her father was reading his Bible, no change there. What's going to happen when I tell them my plan? As she watched, her father glanced up at the clock. It was half past nine. He put his Bible carefully on the shelf, regular as clockwork. He nodded at her mother who put away her knitting and went into the back kitchen. It was time for the Ovaltine and the two digestive biscuits – same thing every night. Laura stood there silently, watching her parents. She wondered if they would be alright if she did leave them. Looking through the window at them now, she felt like she was spying into their lives. Did all old couples end up like them, with nothing to say to each other? What way would she end up? Would she meet anyone else? Her life was so uneasy now, she couldn't make decisions about her future.

She opened the outer door and called out:

'Sorry I'm a bit late Mother but I had a lot to do.'

Her mother came out of the back kitchen holding a tray of cups and biscuits, smiling at her.

'I was just wondering about you, what kept you tonight?'

'Och, Charlie the petrol attendant didn't come in today. He has flu, so we were run off our feet and I was ages finishing up.'

Her mother poured hot Ovaltine from the big jug into the cups.

'Here, come on over to the fire and drink this, you look frozen. What about wee Winnie, is she not helping at the shop these days?'

'No, she's not in either. She can't seem to shake this flu bug, it seems to be taking over. I hope she's better by the weekend,'

Laura said, putting the shopping away. 'I'm going to need her, we're really busy these days.'

She joined her parents at the fire, removing her shoes and warming her feet. Ruth handed her a warm cup, asking her husband:

'Is yours alright William? Do you want anything else?'

'No,' he said, 'this is fine, thanks. What about you Laura, are you feeling better?'

She stared at him.

'Better Father, what do you mean?'

'Well, I thought you were looking a bit pale this morning and you're still not sleeping well. Oh don't look at me like that, didn't I hear you walking the floor of your room many a night? I know all this must be hard for you.'

Laura was totally surprised by this revelation from her father, it wasn't like him.

'No Father, I haven't been sleeping too well but I'm alright, really I am. I expect it will take time but I've made a decision about my future.'

Her mother looked anxiously at her.

'You're going away aren't you? Well, maybe it's for the best... As long as you come back again.'

Her father poked at the embers of the fire. He added some more turf from the basket beside the hearth before he spoke.

'Where are you going lass, is it far?'

'Yes Father, I've decided to visit Betty and Sam in New Zealand.'

She looked at him, his brow deeply furrowed in a worried frown.

'Please Father, don't get upset again. I'm not leaving you. I'm coming back, I promise.'

Her mother's eyes were brimming with tears.

'Did you tell them that you were going to visit them? What do they think?'

'No Mother, I didn't write yet. I have a letter started and tonight I'm going to finish it.'

'They seem to be doing well. Sam's letter at Christmas was full of the new store that Betty and her husband were starting. The photos of their houses are all so grand. It's a far cry from the farm and Tullybeg, isn't it? Did you read it yet, William? There's a lovely photo of their wee child. She's just beautiful, isn't she Laura?'

'Och, she's just a wee pet, I'm dying to see her. Father, will you write a letter and I'll take it with me? And I'm going to take some photos of the farm and you and Mother.'

'Don't bother with all that nonsense, I'm sure they remember what we look like and I'll not be writing any letter. Your mother can do that, doesn't she do all the writing anyway?'

'Oh Father, let bygones be bygones. Sure if things are going so well, maybe they'll be able to visit us soon. Would you still not talk to Sam?'

Her father was finished his Ovaltine. He stood up and lifted his cup and plate and went into the back kitchen. Her mother looked over at her, shaking her head.

'Look child it's no use, he'll never change, Sam hurt him too much. Leave it for now. Maybe before you leave things might be different but knowing how stubborn he is, I doubt it very much.'

Her father returned to the fireplace and lifted a bunch of keys down from the hook.

'I'm going out to lock up and see to the animals. Damp down that fire before you go to bed, Laura.'

Laura knew by the sound of his voice that no more would be said on the subject of Sam. She looked over at her mother who was staring with her sad eyes into the dying embers of the fire.

'Oh God, why can't we be a normal family like everyone else!'

Her father's behaviour was making her feel guilty about leaving them. Tomorrow or the next day, she was going into town and sort out her passport. Laura was worried about accepting the money from Mrs Wray but she would take it on condition that she would pay it back. She could always work it off anyway. She joined her mother, who was washing up the supper things.

'Go on up to bed, Mother. I'll finish up here, I can see you're tired... And don't worry about me, I'll be alright. I've always wanted to travel. I'm already looking forward to it – imagine all that way and I've never even been on an aeroplane before.'

Her mother hugged her tightly.

'I know you will, didn't you always have your head screwed on? It's just that I'm going to miss you so much.'

After her parents had gone to bed, Laura sat down. From her handbag she took out an unopened letter. She looked at the postmark again, 'Cookstown' it read. She wondered why anyone would get in touch with her from that family. She knew it was from Martha, Andy's sister. She opened it. Inside there was just one page.

High Road Farm
Gortnacarn
Pomeroy

My dearest Laura,

This is the most difficult letter I have ever had to write, and that is
why it has taken so long to reach you. My Father and I are still in
a state of shock about Andy's elopement with your sister. Indeed
he has been quite ill, I thought he was going to have a stroke.
I had no idea that anything was wrong, he behaved just the same
going about the farm business as usual. Then he told Father his
plans the evening before he left. My Father thought he was joking until he read the letter he left next morning. I telephoned
and spoke to your Father, I expect he told you, but he assured me that they had left and also that they had got married.
I expect you must still be reeling at the speed of it all. I am very
worried as he has left my young brother David in total charge
of the farm and dairy, a stupid mistake for I know that he will
run it into the ground, and Father can't do very much any more.
Laura. I was so looking forward to having you as a sister and
coming to live here in the family home. I knew my Father felt the
same. He was very fond of you and always said you would make
a fine wife for Andy. Coming from farming stock was so important. How he has ruined all our lives. I had planned to get married this summer to the Reverend Walter Brooke and to do some
missionary work in Africa but now I'm not sure if I can because
of Father. Andy has telephoned from Canada he is living in
Ontario. He rented some property until he finds some place he
can buy but I expect you already know all this from your sister.
I don't know what your future plans are but I sincerely hope that there are no bad feelings between us and
I am very sorry for the way that things have turned out.
I don't expect an answer to this but I just want you to know that I
will always think very highly of you.

Yours sincerely,

Martha Carson

Laura read the letter once again to let it sink in. She was fuming – that cold calculating bastard! So he was already taking her for granted. He and his father had it all planned. She was going to be housekeeper and nursemaid to the farm and his father, Richard. She held the letter in her hand turning over the pages. Then for no reason, she started to laugh. She went over to the sideboard and lifted a framed photo of the family including a smiling Belle. Looking at her young happy-go-lucky sister, still laughing, she said:

'Belle, my darling spoiled sister, you are welcome to that self-contained bugger! And I hope you get all that you deserve because he never intended carrying out the plans we made. You saved me from a fate I didn't expect. Maybe you can twist him around your little finger, like you did Father but somehow I doubt it, for the two of you are too much alike, both selfish bastards. I'm well rid of both of you, now I can really get on with my life. I may not have any money but I still have my freedom.'

CHAPTER 18

LAURA ENJOYED HER TRIP to Dungannon. She collected the passport form from the post office, posted the letters to Betty and Sam and made a few personal purchases. Then she treated herself to tea in the hotel. She looked around at the rest of the customers – it was very busy today. She sat at the same table beside the fire, thinking of last week when she got the news from the bank. Right now she felt nothing for Andy. One day, I don't know how but I will get my own back. The waitress came and took her order. She was feeling hungry. She hadn't been eating too well but today she ordered a small steak with all the trimmings. Except the mushrooms, she still felt they had caused her sickness. She decided to have a drink while she waited for her food. She was reading a magazine when the drink was put down in front of her.

'Now, I don't think that's how a lady should drown her sorrows.'

Startled, she smiled at the waiter. It was Peter McCann.

'Peter! What are you doing here? So you've found out that I'm a secret drinker – I'll never live it down in Tullybeg! Come on, sit down here, what would you like?'

She waved the waitress over.

'Maybe we should get drunk together!' Peter laughed. 'But I'm only in for a sandwich before I get the bus. I was at art class in the Tech.'

When the waitress came, Laura insisted that Peter had something to eat. The food was great and like two old friends they enjoyed each other's company. Peter was always easy to get on with and Laura confided some of her problems, as well as her plans for New Zealand. He was taken aback at that.

'Laura, I hope you're only going for a holiday. I'd miss you and so would our Winnie, she idolizes you.'

'Winnie's a great child. I'm really very fond of her and I couldn't go to New Zealand if I didn't have her filling in for me. She could run that shop on her own.'

'Sure that's all she talks about at home, you and the shop and Mrs Wray. But you know, lately I notice that she's just not at herself, you know, the way she's always joking and taking the mickey out of us. She seems to have changed and she can't take a joke any more. Just last week Pat was kidding her about Seán McMahon, Barney's son. He's always hanging around the forge, says he has an interest in the horses but when we tell Winnie he fancies her, well, she went mad and shouted and raved at the pair of us to mind our own business. It wasn't like her at all.'

Laura laughed.

'Men, sure you know nothing about women. Did you ever think that maybe you were too close to the mark. She might just fancy him. She won't want any interference from her watchful brothers.'

'Och, I've a lot to learn haven't I? But then I always put my foot in it when it came to girls, I never know what to say.'

Laura looked at this tall good-looking young man.

'Well, you're never been stuck for words with me. You and Pat always had plenty of chat and cheek. And what about the girls at this art class you go to, what are they like? Sure a fellow like you must be having to chase them off.'

Peter went red in the face.

'Och Laura, don't you start. Sure some of the girls there are mad in the head. I know a few of them alright but I don't have time to get too involved. I've got exams next month and I have to have this portfolio finished.'

He pointed to a large black carrying case.

'This, Laura, is my life. It's all I ever wanted to do.'

Laura leaned down, lifted the case on to the table and opened it, to Peter's protests. She was amazed at what she saw – photographs, paintings and drawings. They were wonderful and she told him so. He was totally embarrassed and tried to explain some of them. He moved to near the back of the portfolio and showed her some wonderful scroll-work and one of the candle-sticks he had given her for her birthday.

'Peter, they are just great. I don't know much about art but I know what I like. That scroll-work on the staircase design, I've never seen anything like it. Have you made that too?'

'Yes, I've got it in the forge along with a lot of other stuff. I'm lucky I've got my Da's place to work in. Laura, that's what I'd like to do, wrought ironwork in my own designs. But I'm going to need some place of my own for that. God knows when that will be.'

'What about your father, he must be proud of you. You're very talented. Is there no room in the forge for your work?'

Laura continued turning the pages.

'These are just great,' she said.

'My Da agreed to let me go to art class on condition that I finish the course. I'm interested in making bigger pieces now, so there won't be any room in Da's place. I've a long way to go before I'm finished.'

They continued talking about the possibilities of his creative art, and how he would eventually like a workroom and show-place. The rest of the time flew by. Laura realised that she hadn't enjoyed such good company in a long time. Even with Andy – he was so predictable. She always knew in advance what they were going to do, especially when it came to sex. The evening always ended with sex. She blushed again when she thought about it. She saw Peter looking at her, she thought, my goodness, I hope he doesn't get the wrong idea and think I'm blushing because of him. Peter carried her shopping to the car and she let him drive her home – she was glad of the company. It had started to snow again and by the time they reached the village it was coming down very hard. She decided to stay at Mrs Wray's for a while, 'til it settled.

Peter drove the car into the yard behind the shop.
'Is this alright for you,' he asked. 'Do you want any help with the bags?' He got out and raced round to open the door for her.

'Thanks Peter, the shopping is fine. I really enjoyed this afternoon, you were great company.'

At the door she turned and kissed him, then fled inside. Peter stood for a while, touching his cheek and smiling.

The two women sat talking over a cup of tea, all about Laura's day in town and meeting Peter. Laura went into the shop to attend a customer. The snow had stopped, so she told Mrs Wray that she would tidy the place up before she locked the door. She was clearing the window of some stock when she noticed Nurse Boyd racing up the street. There must be something wrong some where. While she watched, the nurse went into McCann's. Oh goodness, someone must be ill! Maybe it's Winnie, her flu must be worse. Just then the doctor's car pulled up. There *is* something wrong, maybe it's Mrs McCann. She went into the back where Mrs Wray was cleaning up the kitchen. She turned when she heard Laura.

'What's wrong, are you sick again? You're as white as a sheet!'

Laura grabbed her coat.

'I'm going over to McCann's, there's something wrong. The nurse and doctor have just gone in. I hope it's not something serious.'

She went back into the shop with Mrs Wray on her heels.

'Go on over Laura. Let me know if there's anything I can do. I'll lock up here. And now call me, won't you?'

Laura promised to do so and started across the wide street but before she got to McCann's an ambulance came racing up and the attendants jumped out, carrying a stretcher. What on earth has happened, thought Laura. She went into the hallway to see Mr & Mrs McCann standing, arms around each other, crying. Peter and Pat were standing on the lower stair and the younger twins, Johnny and Joey, stood in the kitchen doorway, wide-eyed, questioning the goings-on. Just then one of the ambulance men came down the narrow stairway carrying someone wrapped in a blanket. He was followed by the doctor and the nurse. There was blood dripping from the blanket. Laura stood there, unable to speak. Peter saw her and came over.

'It's our wee Winnie, there's something the matter with her. Ma found her screaming. There was blood everywhere! Oh Laura, what's wrong with her?'

She put out her arms to comfort him.

'Did she cut herself? What has the doctor said?'

The McCanns followed the doctor out to the ambulance where the attendants had taken Winnie. Pat talked to the doctor and the nurse. He looked very worried as he came over to Laura and Peter.

'Doctor McConnell said Winnie has lost a lot of blood. She's had a haemorrhage. They're taking her to the hospital for a transfusion. Laura, it's best that Peter and I go too. Could you look after Johnny and Joey till we get back? I don't want to ask my Sheila with the baby coming soon, do you mind?'

'Of course not,' Laura answered. 'Go on and look after your parents, they need you. The twins and I will be fine.'

She went over to where the twins were standing crying and put her arms around them.

'Come on you two, inside. Winnie will be alright. Sure the doctors in the hospital are great. Wave goodbye to them all.'

The ambulance pulled away with the boys following in their car. Laura and the twins stood watching the lights on the ambulance until it disappeared down the hill. Then she brought them inside out of the cold. She didn't want them seeing the bloodstains in the virgin-white snow. She would come out and throw boiling water over it, after she had settled them.

It seemed like hours before the ten-year-olds, Johnny and Joey, would calm down. They were inconsolable and kept asking all sorts of questions. Would the doctors operate on Winnie and open her with a knife? Would it hurt her? Why was there so much blood? Laura tried her best to answer them. She reminded them of the time Joe had been in hospital having his appendix removed and how kind the doctors and nurses were. All the presents he got and how they made him better. After she had read them their favourite stories, she put them to bed and they both fell asleep. She sat watching the two boys for a few minutes, covered them over and put the small night-light on. She left the room, quietly closing the door behind her.

On the landing, she had to pass the girls' bedroom. She peeped in to the darkened interior. The only light in the room was from a small night candle in front of the statue of the Virgin Mary. Laura smiled to herself, remembering the times she spent in here listening to Mary, her telling her of all the novenas she made to the statue when she needed help with her exams and special intentions, explaining why she had to say all the prayers. Indeed there was many a time Laura knelt with her. This is where all their girlish secrets were discussed, especially the boys they fancied. They used to chase wee Winnie out in case she would tell her mother. Winnie, she thought, dear God, please help her now.

Laura went over to the end of the bed and knelt down in front of the Virgin and cried, thinking of them carrying her out with the blood flowing from her. She prayed quietly for a few minutes, then spread her hands out in front of her on the bed. They felt wet. Puzzled she got up and switched on the light. The sight before her caused waves of nausea to flow through her. The bed was totally soaked in Winnie's blood. Pillows and sheets reddened and black with congealed clots. She ran for the bathroom next door and made it just in time. Afterwards she sat there, unable to move, cold sweats causing shivers down her spine. Finally she was able to make it down the stairs and to put the kettle on for some hot tea. She looked around the big comfortable kitchen, the big white-scrubbed table filling the centre of it, the remains of the evening meal, most of it uneaten, staring back at her. She knew she had to go back upstairs again and face that bedroom – she couldn't let the family return to all that mess.

Cleaning up took nearly an hour. She put the soiled linen in a rubbish sack as it would have to be burned, remade the bed with fresh sheets and covers, and left everything tidy. Her stomach was in bits by the time she was finished.

She was sitting at the big range with another cup of tea when she remembered Mrs Wray. She looked at the clock and couldn't believe it, almost one thirty. What was happening, why didn't they phone? She couldn't phone the hospital, it wouldn't be right. She went out to the front door. The street was silent and deserted, apart from the light from Mrs Wray's sittingroom – she was waiting for news. Laura dialled the number but it was Robert who answered.

'Oh sorry, Mr Wray, I thought it was your wife. Is she still awake? It's Laura here.'

'I know who it is,' he answered sharply. 'I'm not senile. What do you want my wife for at this hour? Do you need to cry on her shoulder again? Well you can't, she's been asleep for hours and you'll have to wait until morning.'

The phone was slammed down. Laura was raging. The sarcastic brute, who does he think he is? She fixed up the fire in the big range and filled the kettle. They would be glad of tea when they returned. After clearing the table she made some sandwiches, then curled up on the couch under a rug.

She must have fallen asleep, for the next thing she heard crying. The boys were helping their parents into the kitchen, they were hysterical. Laura jumped up quickly, asking:

'Winnie, is she worse? Oh God, what's happened?'

None of them could speak for ages, they just looked so lost. When Pat found his voice, it was cracked with emotion.

'Winnie's gone Laura, our wee Winnie's dead. The doctors did what they could but it was too late, she lost too much blood.'

He almost fainted. Laura held him, unable to take it all in. She looked at Peter who was still holding on to his parents. His face showed anger and rage. She couldn't understand.

'Peter, I'm sure the doctors did everything they could, don't be angry at them.'

'Laura, I'm not angry at the doctors. I want to kill the bugger who caused this, the bastard that got her pregnant and took her for an abortion. Jesus, and her just a child!'

He went to pieces then and hurried out of the room. She wanted to follow but Pat stopped her.

'No don't, he needs to be on his own. None of us can take this in, how could this have happened? Look at Ma, she hadn't a clue.'

Laura didn't know what to do to comfort them. Paddy and Peggy McCann sat wrapped in each other's arms in a trance and Pat put his head in his hands and cried again. What should she do, what could she do to help them? The only thing she knew was to make fresh tea. She sat the mugs on the table and uncovered the sandwiches. Pat and his father sat down and began to eat.

Later Peter returned, soaking wet. She helped him to remove his sweater and put a rug around him. He took the tea she offered with a quiet 'thanks'.

It was sometime before anyone spoke. Peggy McCann broke the silence.

'Winnie wasn't herself these last few weeks. Sure I thought it was just teenage stuff, ye know how they are. The boys here was jokin' her about boyfriends but she didn't give any of her usual back cheek, she just flew upstairs to the bedroom. There was no talkin' to her at all. She didn't go over to the shop the other day. She said she had a dose of the flu an' didn't I believe her. Sweet Jesus, if I only knew!'

Mrs McCann broke down again.

'Och Mrs McCann, don't talk. Why don't you go and rest? There'll be plenty of time to talk.'

Laura held her as she wept.

'Och my wee Winnie, what'll I do without her wee smilin' face? Who would do this to her? I thought she was stayin' in the bed today but she came down the stairs this mornin', all dressed. She was wearin' her good coat. I asked her where she was goin'. She said she wanted to get out of the house for a while and she was goin' into town to meet her friend, Bridgin. Do ye know, I don't think that child ever told me a lie before.'

The crying started again. Paddy hadn't spoken at all until now, he had been staring into the fire. Now he stood up.

'Pat, Peter, we'll have to find the bastard that did this. We can't sit here doin' nothin'. The doctors said that the police would be callin' in the mornin' but there must be something we can do. Who was she seein', was it that young Brannigan boy? Jesus, I'll kill the wee shite when I get my hands on him!'

Pat went over to him.

'Da don't, we can't do anythin' yet. Anyway, we don't know yet who the boy was. Nurse Boyd said she wanted to talk to us but she said she'd wait until tomorrow. Maybe she knows somethin' we don't. Wasn't she talkin' to Winnie for a while before the ambulance came. Maybe Winnie told her somethin?"

'Och maybe yer right son but not knowin' is just awful. Anyway have the police to do with it? Sure what happened to my Winnie has nothin' to do with them fellows. I don't want them hangin' round our house, they only bring bad news. Wasn't there enough nosy parkers here when the buggers lifted my boys?'

Mrs McCann looked at her husband, her eyes swollen with crying.

'Och Paddy, were ye not listenin' to that doctor at the hospital? Didn't he say that because Winnie had an abortion the police will have to investigate. And if they find out who did it, it's jail for them. Dear God in heaven, I hope they find them, soon. I know what I'd like to do to people that butcher wee children. Jail's too good for them. Sure didn't they murder our child?'

Again floods of tears. Laura made an excuse and left the room to go and see the twins. Peter began to clear away the tea things. Turning from the sink, he asked:

'Pat, what about Winnie's friend, Bridgin? She might know something. I'll call her tomorrow. Didn't she say she was going to meet her today? Do you think someone in Dungannon did that abortion? Jazus, somebody knows something and I mean to find out.'

'Look, Peter, there's nothing any of us can do and it's getting late. We're all going to be busy tomorrow – it's time we got some sleep. Come on Da, I'll help you up,' said Pat, going over to his father.

'Och yer right son, c'mon. What about Laura? Will ye stay here, Laura, or do ye want Pat to drive ye home?'

'Look, I'll drive Laura home if she wants me to,' said Peter. 'I'm sure Pat here is anxious about Sheila and I don't feel like sleeping anyway. Is that alright Laura?'

She smiled at this big fellow with such sad eyes.

'Thanks Peter I'd like to go. I did phone home and I told them about Winnie earlier tonight. They'll be wondering if I'm not home when they get up.'

Laura went over and hugged Paddy and Pat and said good-bye. She knew that Mrs McCann would be sound asleep by now.

The cold air hit them when they went into the yard to get the car. It had stopped snowing. There was very little on the ground as Peter drove out the short distance to her home and turned the car on the street outside her house.

'Laura, thanks for being there tonight, you're a true friend as always. I just wish you were at the hospital as well. It was terrible, the screams of my wee sister and watching Ma and Da, none of us able to do anything. Apart from losing a lot of blood, she had an infection. The doctor told us that dirty instruments were used at the abortion, that's what caused her death. Jesus, what sort of people could do this? And how many times has this happened to other girls?'

Laura put her arm around him.

'Don't Peter, I know it's hard for you all. We're all going to miss her. Imagine, you and I were sitting today in the hotel talking about her and she was lying in agony – I just can't take it in. I could see the change in her too but I thought it was some boy she fancied. For some strange reason she wouldn't talk about it. She was always full of craic and quick with a smart answer. Oh God Peter, I'm going to miss her so much! And I promised Mary that I would watch over her – it must have been a terrible shock when you told her.'

'Pat and I phoned her tonight. The police were great, they organised the phone call to Morocco for us. That's Africa, you know. I could hear her like she was in the room with us, it was unreal. But Laura, to hear Mary crying, it was awful. She's calling back in the morning when she gets her flight times.'

Laura put her hand on his.

'Do you want me to meet her plane? It's no trouble and it's not that far.'

'No thanks,' he said. 'It will give me something to do. You feel so helpless at a time like this. I don't know how my Ma and Da are going to get through this.'

He broke down again and cried bitterly. She put her arms around him and held him. Finally he looked at her and before she knew what was happening, he kissed her full on the lips. They broke apart abruptly – he must have seen how shocked she was.

'Laura, I'm not going to apologise for kissing you, I've been wanting to do it for ages. I was jealous of that Andy fellow every time I saw you together. I'm glad he's out of your life, you're far too good for him. But don't be mad at me, I want to be here for you... always.'

'Peter, I could never be mad at you. Sure you're like a brother to me and always were. I think the world of you and all your family.'

Peter grabbed her two hands in his.

'Laura that wasn't a brotherly kiss. I think I love you and I always have, do you understand?'

She lifted her hands and held his face.

'Peter, don't say any more, you're confused. Too much has happened today and maybe you'll regret it tomorrow. Don't worry, you didn't offend me. As a matter of fact, I enjoyed it.'

She leaned over and kissed him.

'Now that's both of us making fools of ourselves.'

She got out of the car and leaned on the door.

'Now get yourself home and try to get some sleep. I'll see you tomorrow. Goodnight, or should I say good morning? It's nearly three o'clock.'

He watched until she was inside and the light was on, then turned the car and went homewards. He knew that life would never be the same again, for him or the rest of the family.

CHAPTER 20

St Martin's Chapel was crammed to capacity. The nuns from the convent had done a wonderful job. They had white flowers with rich green foliage everywhere – on the altar, at the entrance, and cascading around the tall pillars that stood like sentinels down each side of the church. Winnie's coffin was covered with white roses... Laura was overwhelmed by it all and found the heavy perfume of the blooms too powerful for her weak stomach. She kept near the back so that she could make an easy exit if it was necessary. The McCann family filled the two front pews. The funeral had been held up an extra day, as Mary and her fiancé had problems getting home.

To Laura, it was the longest three days she had ever spent and it must have been a living nightmare for the family. Now they had to face the biggest challenge... seeing Winnie laid to rest. At least it wasn't raining. It was a sunny January day but very frosty. The whole village had turned out. Those who couldn't fit inside the little chapel were lined up outside, all around the adjoining graveyard. There were representatives from all of the local churches and a large congregation from Laura's own church. Looking at some of them Laura was surprised, for most of them were hardened bigots. Even her father was there. Her mother said she couldn't bear to see a child laid to rest but she really felt for the family. As the ceremony ended, Winnie's school friends lined up for a guard of honour. The cortège made it's way slowly down the path to the open grave under a big hawthorn tree. Once again, waves of nausea swept over Laura and she would have fallen but a steady arm caught her – it was Mrs Wray. She guided Laura in silence to the little gate at the far corner of the graveyard that led out into the road at the back of the village. Laura tried to protest but her friend shook her head.

'No, you have been through enough lately. You haven't slept. You'll be next if you don't stop – you can only do so much. Come on, I'm frozen. I'll make us both some tea.'

Laura turned to take one more look at the coffin. They had almost reached the grave. It was the saddest sight she had ever witnessed. The coffin was carried by the four boys – Pat, Peter and the elder McCann twins, Mickey and Jimmy. They had been released from prison for the funeral but armed guards walked alongside them. Could they not let them alone till they buried their little sister? There were enough policemen around the graveyard to guard the country. Where did they think the boys could run to? Had they no hearts at all?

Laura saw Mary standing with her arms around her parents. Her boyfriend Yusef was looking after young Johnny and Joey, who were totally mesmerised by it all. Laura felt Mrs Wray tug gently on her arm.

'Don't Laura, there's nothing more we can do and they know that you're here for them.'

The two women entered the house and the warmth from the big cooker enveloped them. Laura's feet were frozen. She removed her new court shoes. She should have worn her fur-lined boots but she thought they weren't dressy enough. Tea was ready in minutes and they sat in comfortable silence, warming themselves at the fire. It was ages before they spoke, each feeling there was nothing more to say. There was such finality about a funeral. Just for something to say, Laura asked where Robert was – she hadn't seen him at the church or the graveside. Mrs Wray looked worried.

'That man's been like a hen on a hot griddle these past few days. I've hardly got a word out of him. He said he couldn't attend the service because of all the work he had to do but he's been like that for ages. We had a row the other day about the car. He knew I wanted it but at the last minute he went off in it, not a word of explanation to me. I was to go into town that day and he was to take over in the shop for a while. When he finally got home, him and I had words and he stormed out again. He didn't even wait for his dinner.'

Mrs Wray turned to Laura, tears welling up in her eyes.

'That's the day that child died. My God, I still can't take it in! We'll never hear that wee voice again, no more singing at the top of her voice, no more wild stories. I'm going to miss her so much...'

The woman totally went to pieces, she was distraught. She left the room to wash her face, telling Laura she would be alright in a minute. When she returned she was looking better and asked Laura if there was any news regarding what had happened.

'The police are all over the place, asking all kinds of questions,' Laura sighed. 'I don't think there's any news yet but somebody must know something. I mean, someone performed an operation on her. I've heard that there were places in Belfast where women could go if they wanted to get rid of an unwanted child but how could anyone do that to a young girl? I hope they find them, and soon. They should be put away for life. But where would Winnie find out about someone like that, Mrs Wray?'

'Och, there's a lot of speculation at the moment and some stupid women in the village here making the most outrageous suggestions. I had to chase that nosy-parker, Isobel Wright, out of the shop when she told me that Winnie used a hot poker on herself or maybe a bread-knife. Did you ever here such nonsense? People will make up stories if they can't find the right answer. Do you remember, just a few weeks ago we were joking her about boyfriends. Didn't she get very upset? I wonder who made her pregnant?'

Laura went around the table and put her arms around the crying woman. She was shaking with her sobs.

'This has been too much for all of us. Why don't you go and lie down? I'll stay and sort out the evening papers, then I'll close the shop. Maybe Mr Wray will be home by then and he can take over?'

'Och, maybe your right. Sure I'll feel better when I've had a wee rest. Are you going back over to the McCanns?'

'Yes, I'll call home first for I know I'm going to be late. I don't know how long Mary's staying and I want to spend a bit of time with her. What did you think of her fiancé, he's lovely isn't he?'

Mrs Wray smiled.

'Well at least it took some of the sadness away. Did you see the faces of the neighbours when he got out of the car last night? I'd say he was the first black man any of them has seen. Wee Charlie Dillon looked up at him and asked him if he was one of the black babies that they gave their pennies to help. Sure his mother didn't know where to look, isn't he a consultant or something like that?'

'Yes,' answered Laura. 'Mary met him in London when she went to train at the burns' unit – he specializes in severe burns and he's here at the Royal for six months. Mary and him get on great. He's daft about her and her family are the same about him. She worried about telling them about him because he's black but she needn't have. That's one thing about the McCanns, colour or creed doesn't matter, he's like one of the family.'

Laura handed Mrs Wray a fresh cup of tea.

'Now, take that up to bed with you and I'll see you tomorrow.'

CHAPTER 21

LAURA FOUND MARY at her house surrounded by a host of relatives and friends. They had only just returned from the funeral. The nuns and some of the village women had prepared a hot meal in the hall for anyone who called and on such a cold day it went down well. After that they made their way to the house. Peter saw her arrive and came over.

'Are you alright? I saw Mrs Wray take you out of the graveyard. I was worried about you.'

Laura looked at him, worried about her at a time like this.

'Peter, I'm fine. Like everyone else, I was overcome with emotion. I can't imagine how you and the family must feel.'

His arm came round her back and he guided her towards members of the family she hadn't seen for years – some aunts and uncles that she knew well. One of them, Peter's Auntie Alice from Armagh, was delighted to see her and soon had the room-full of people actually laughing. Auntie Alice recalled a holiday Mary and Laura had with them.

Alice and her family owned apple orchards so at harvest time it they were grateful for any help they could get. The girls loved it and worked well but they were not familiar with the boundaries and wandered all through the orchards gathering fruit. It was when they got on a trailer to return to their aunt's that they made their mistake. Sitting in the trailer, they realised that the drive back was taking longer than before. Finally, they stopped at a strange farm and didn't recognise anyone – they knew they were at the wrong place. Then one of the women harvesters called them to pick up their day's wages, all of three shillings. Only then did it dawn on them that they were on the wrong farm. Not only that but it was on the far side of Portadown, miles from where they should be. The girls couldn't understand it for everything had appeared quite normal and they had even been included in the workers' midday lunch. Mary laughed as she remembered the woman with the food looking at her strangely when they said they hadn't brought any food or drink with them. But they didn't go hungry as everyone had shared.

Things were soon sorted out when the owner of the orchard, Sammy Brown had telephoned a worried Auntie Alice and told her what had happened. He said he would drive them home himself. Indeed, he was full of praise for his two new workers and wanted to know what time he should collect them the next day. Their aunt declined his offer. Mary remembered it all vividly, pleading with Auntie Alice not to tell her parents or they wouldn't let her back again. Laura remembered that they had been invited back for the Harvest Social but she couldn't ask her parents as she knew they would refuse.

Later, when things got quiet at the house, the two friends went out for a walk in the cold frosty evening. Mary's fiancé Yusef had returned to Belfast by train. Mary spoke lovingly of him and how caring he was. His older brother was also a doctor and his younger sister was studying medicine in New York – she had worked extremely hard to win a scholarship. His parents lived and worked in Africa-Senegal to be precise. He and Mary intended going out to visit them next autumn. She laughed when she told Laura of the looks he'd got from some of the older villagers.

'Did you see Maisey Donnelly in the church? I thought she would fall out of her seat. She leaned that far out to look at him I thought she'd fall over, and the mouth wide open! Well, for one thing, they can't say that the McCanns are an ordinary family, can they? Two boys in jail for terrorism and a young girl dead from an abortion at sixteen. Oh God Laura, what are we going to do without her?'

Mary fell apart, sobbing, her body shaking. It was a long time before she was calm again.

'Laura, I've got to find out who this bastard is and I'm not going to leave here till I do. I know the police are doing their best but it's not enough. Will you come with me into town tomorrow? I need to see Winnie's friend, Bridgin. I know her mother said she's in shock but I've got a feeling she's afraid to talk about what happened. What do you think?'

'You could be right, the child's afraid but of who?' said Laura. 'I've gone over and over it all. Winnie hardly ever left the village – she went to school on the bus and home again, then it was to the pictures in Dungannon to meet her friends. Sure you know your father never let her out late and the bus stops almost at your own door. For the life of me, I can't think of anyone she was friendly with.'

Mary leaned over the bridge. She picked up some stones and threw them into the flowing river. It was a beautiful sight but they didn't see it. The frost had made wonderful patterns on the foliage along the riverbank and the branches were shimmering in the early moonlight – everything looked so crisp and clean. If only the world could be the same. Mary sighed.

'Why didn't she confide in me? Jesus, Laura, I would have done anything to help her. I could have looked after her and she could have kept her child if she wanted, stayed with us in Belfast till she was ready to return home. But to go down that road, sure she wouldn't know where to start. Someone knew exactly what to do and how to go about it and I'm convinced that it wasn't any young boy. What do you think Laura? Sure you knew all the young fellas in the village. Is there anyone likely?'

'Not that I know of. Sure we were always joking her in the shop about boys. She enjoyed the craic and always had a smart answer. She said that the boys were of no interest to her, that she was going to look for a rich auld man and soap the stairs the night they got married. Mrs Wray and I used to split our sides laughing at some of the things she would come out with. But lately, as I told you, she didn't joke at all. When I told her about Andy and Belle, I was expecting her to come out with some smart answer or funny wisecrack but she looked at me strangely and ran upstairs. Your mother found her in her room, crying but she thought that she was upset for me. It's an awful nightmare and a mystery to us all, Mary but I know that we will get to the bottom of it. Hopefully sooner rather than later, for your family's sake.'

'You know Laura, I've never got the time to ask you how you are coping with all that. The nosy-parkers in the village must have had a field day. You must have been gutted and I wasn't there for you. I've been watching you, you aren't looking too well. Are you sure you are alright? What you need is a holiday, what about New Zealand?'

'Och, it's a long story Mary. Maybe I only thought I loved Andy. Right now, if he came begging on his knees I wouldn't take him back. Belle's welcome to him! I've only just discovered how unfeeling he was, and how greedy.'

'Greedy? What do you mean?'

Laura then related the incident at the bank and how humiliated she had been.

'The no-good bastard. Jesus, I'd shoot him and her! She was one convincing little bitch wasn't she? Knowing all along and saying nothing. Och, they'll never have luck and I know that you will get over this – you're the strong one, Laura.'

CHAPTER 22

THEY FOUND BRIDGIN'S HOUSE. A very worried-looking woman opened the door to them and invited them in. You could see that she had shed many tears. Mary had met Mr and Mrs Donnelly, Bridgin's parents, when they called at the McCanns' house to offer their sympathy to the family. They enquired after Bridgin but her mother said that there was no change – she was just lying there hardly saying a word. The doctor was worried that she wasn't eating and when she did, she immediately got sick.

'You know Mary, Winnie was like one of my own. We thought the world of her. She was always laughing and joking. My wee Seán, he's just seven, adored her. She joked that she'd wait for him till he grew up and maybe they'd get married. Didn't he spend ages making her a special Christmas card. She was delighted with it. She hugged him and told him it was the first card she'd got from a boy and would always keep it. You know, he was ten foot tall with pride.'

Mrs Donnelly burst into tears again and it was a while before she could speak. She offered them a cup of tea, telling Laura:

'Winnie was always praising you – she looked up to you so much. I still can't understand why she didn't confide in you. She was here the Saturday before and I noticed that she had got very quiet. Bridgin and her planned to go to the cinema but later she said that she was getting the six o'clock bus back as she had to help in the shop. Bridgin went with her to the bus stop. That's the last time we saw her. Then when we heard what happened – sure we just couldn't take it in. And then I had to tell our Bridgin. Dear God, I'll never forget her wee face. She went hysterical. We couldn't get her settled. Her Daddy went across the street to get Dr Collins and that's the way she's been since. We asked her if she wanted to see Winnie before the funeral but she just went to pieces. We don't know what to do for the best – we feel so helpless.'

Mary put her arms around the crying woman to comfort her.

'Can we go up and see her? She knows us. Sure wasn't it only a few months ago that the pair of them came up to Belfast and we took them to the zoo. We got on great – they loved Yusef. They had great craic and teased him about the pennies for the black babies. Yusef enjoyed the craic with them that day. He would be here now but he had to return to the hospital. He'll be here in a few days and I'll take him up to see her, if that's alright with you.'

The woman shook her head in grateful thanks.

'Sure I'll agree to anything that will make her right again.'

She brought the girls up to the bedroom where Bridgin lay facing the wall. She looked so small and helpless lying there. She turned to them when her mother spoke to her. Dark circles rimmed her eyes, her skin almost transparent. She gave a feeble smile when she saw them. Mary went to her and they clung together, not speaking. Bridgin's mother excused herself and left the room.

'I'm so sorry, Mary, I didn't want to go to the funeral, I just couldn't.'

Mary comforted Bridgin, telling her that everything would be alright. She asked Laura how they were going to manage at the shop without Winnie. Her concern was touching.

'She loved that job you know, she was always talking about it. I wished that I could get a job there too but I have to help Daddy in our own shop. He wants me to be a watchmaker just like him.'

'Well, that's great. Someone always needs a watchmaker, you'll never be out of a job,' said Mary.

'Do you want to be a watchmaker, Bridgin?' asked Laura.

'Well, Daddy says I've a flair for it because I've got small hands and I know I can do it but I'll have to leave home to go to college.'

'Sure isn't that the best of it, getting away from home and meeting new friends. I'm sure when the time comes you'll love it,' said Laura.

Bridgin began crying again.

'No, no, it'll never be the same again! We always planned this together, you know. Winnie was going to do business studies and we were going to share a flat. It was going to be great – now it's all over! I don't know what I'll do without her, she was my best friend.'

Mary sat on the bed beside her and held her hand.

'Bridgin, we need to know who Winnie was seeing. She must have mentioned boys. Who was it, you must have some idea?'

Bridgin turned back to the wall again and stayed that way for ages without moving. Finally, without looking at the girls, she spoke. She said it was all her fault and that Winnie and her had a row a few weeks ago. They used to go to the pictures nearly every Saturday but sometimes Winnie wouldn't turn up. Then at school on Monday she would make an excuse that she had to work at the last minute. Then they would be friends again till the next time. She said Winnie was moody and sometimes she would cry for no reason. They didn't have any special boyfriends. They were friends with boys but none of them interested Winnie. Boys would ask them out but they never went.

'Please think hard, Bridgin,' said Mary. 'There must have been someone, or something she said. You were the only one she would tell. Did she say anything, anything at all?'

Still with her head to the wall, she told them that they had been talking about boys one day when Winnie said something strange – she wondered if Bridgin would ever go out with an older man. They talked about it for ages. Bridgin said someone about twenty would be alright. Her sister Eileen's boyfriend was that age and he was lovely but Winnie said she meant a lot older than that.

'I laughed at her and asked her did she mean someone her Daddy's age but she didn't laugh, she looked dead serious. She said that someone older liked her and he bought her a lovely necklace for Christmas. She had to hide it because her mother wouldn't understand and she wouldn't like her to take presents. But Winnie couldn't see any harm in it, she said he was just being friendly. I asked her who it was but she just said "that's for me to know and you to find out". She wouldn't talk about it again, even though I tried to get her to tell me.'

Mary and Laura looked at each other. Who? They stayed for a while, trying to cheer Bridgin up – they didn't want to leave her crying. Then Bridgin asked Mary:

'What exactly happened to Winnie, what made her die?'

'Didn't your mother explain to you?' Mary wondered.

The girl shook her head.

'Not really. She said I didn't need to know the details because I'm too young but that Winnie got pregnant and died because she was too young. But there's more than that isn't there? I heard my Mammy and Daddy talking and it's something awful isn't it? And it's all my fault, I know it is.'

Bridgin began sobbing again. Mary tried to explain what happened as best she could and to get her to understand that none of it was her fault. She didn't feel right explaining the abortion to her but this child shouldn't live in ignorance. Maybe that was the problem, that children need more education on these subjects.

Laura felt helpless and she was feeling sick again. The room was very stuffy as all the bars on the electric fire were lit. She excused herself and just made it to the bathroom in time. Luckily it was just across the landing. Green bile filled the basin. She felt terrible, very weak. It was a while before she could return to the bedroom. She could see that Mary had explained in detail what had happened to Winnie. Bridgin was getting sick into a bowl. Laura wanted to run out but forced herself to stay and help clean the girl up. Bridgin was still insisting that it was all her fault:

'You weren't there,' she said. 'Winnie and I had a terrible row last Saturday. She broke her promise again and I said awful things to her. She said she had something to tell me but I didn't listen. I said she was always telling lies and I had enough. I left her standing there crying, half-way up the street. She called to me to come back but I walked away.'

Bridgin couldn't be comforted. Mary held on to her, trying to tell her it didn't matter.

'Mary, I didn't leave her to the bus like I told Mammy – I didn't even look back. So you see it is all my fault! If I had just listened, all those awful things wouldn't have happened, she would still be alive. She was my best friend, I should have listened.'

She lay in Mary's arms. You would have thought she was asleep but all at once she lifted her head sharply to ask them a question.

'Mary, will I have to tell all this in confession next week, is this a mortal sin? And I'll have to tell Mam. Oh God Mary, I'm so sorry, it's all *my* fault, *my* fault!'

Mary's heart went out to the girl.

'Now look pet, none of what happened is your fault. It was a man that did this to her, it's *his* fault. If we only had a clue as to who he is. Now just put it out of your mind and get yourself downstairs to your family. They're worried about you and you must start eating proper food to get strong again. Look, you don't know any more than we do, so try to stop worrying and concentrate on getting well, won't you, Bridgin?'

Suddenly she sat upright in bed.

'Mary, I think your Daddy knows the man.'

The girls stared at her in disbelief.

'What, my father knows him? Why do you say that?' asked Mary.

'Well, it's just something I remember. When I asked Winnie who her admirer was, she laughed and said that if her Daddy found out he would kill him. He called him a black bastard and he said he hated having to do business with him at the yard for he never liked Catholics. She said "my Da's wrong isn't he, for he likes me". That's all she said, I forgot about it until now.'

Mary hugged her.

'It doesn't mean anything, I mean it could be anyone. Sure my Da's always saying things he doesn't mean. Look we'll have to go now but when I bring Yusef to see you next week I want to see you up and smiling, yes?'

Bridgin agreed:

'I will, I promise.'

Then she had a worried look again.

'Will I have to tell the police all this? Mammy says they want to talk to me.'

'Yes,' said Mary, 'you tell them everything. Bridgin, don't be afraid, you didn't do anything wrong. It's not your fault that this happened to Winnie, you have nothing to hide.'

They said their goodbyes and went downstairs to Mrs Donnelly. She was pressing them to stay & eat with the family but they declined as they had a lot to do. Mary told Mrs Donnelly she was bringing Yusef next week and to take Bridgin out some where, if that was alright. The woman was delighted. They had made such progress with Bridgin and she was content to know that Mary had explained things to her. She saw them to the side-door and out on to the street. The cold January wind was biting into them as they braved the hilly climb and into the market square, hardly able to say a word. Mary held on to her friend's arm.

'I know what we need, especially you – two large brandies,' she declared.

They crossed the square and into the hotel. Seated at the blazing turf fire with the drinks in front of them, they discussed in detail everything that had taken place.

'What do you think, Laura, you know everyone in the village? Have you any ideas? And I wouldn't mind anything she said about my Da. Sure it's just his way, and isn't yours the same? Aren't they always name-calling?'

Laura said nothing – her mind was racing with awful thoughts. Mary continued.

'Like when she mentioned the yard... it could be any yard. I mean, behind our house where the horses wait to be shod we call "the yard", then there's the butcher's yard, where he kills the animals. Oh my God, it's not that auld butcher Wilson? Oh no, please God, it couldn't be him? Who else has a yard that my Da would have to visit?'

She stared at her friend and saw the change in her.

'Jesus, you *know* something, don't you? Who? Tell me!'

She grabbed her friend's arms. Laura was in a daze. Her face was like death and she was shaking all over. Mary held the brandy glass to her lips and made her sip it. When the colour began returning, she looked at Laura, pleading:

'Tell me all you know, please!'

Slowly she related the incident in the car and other odd things that had happened with Robert Wray, and the way he used to look at her. Then how some of Winnie's remarks had made her wonder and how she had put them out of her mind because Winnie was just a child. Now it all came back to her. But surely he couldn't do such a thing, bad and all as he was? Winnie was just fifteen. Didn't he always claim he detested Catholics, wasn't he a Church Elder? No, it couldn't be him. But the more Laura thought about it, a lot of other little details came to mind. She remembered Winnie saying that Robert was getting her a present. When she asked why would he do that? Winnie got confused and that wasn't like her. But then she said it was for helping Mrs Wray.

The girls discussed at length what they should do. They were close to the police barracks, maybe they should go up and ask for the sergeant in charge of the case and tell him all they knew. If they were wrong, then what? They would be in awful trouble, Robert Wray would never forgive them and he could sue them. They thought over their dilemma for ages – Laura was worried about Mrs Wray and what all this could do to her. After two more brandies they were no further on. They decided on some food but when it was served Laura knew she could never eat it so she ordered tea and toast instead. Mary was hungry and ate heartily but she cast a worried eye at her friend who was nibbling on a piece of bread.

'There's something wrong with you, isn't there Laura? You were sick down in Donnelly's. I thought it was just the heat in the room. Have you been feeling like this before? You haven't been looking too well either.'

'No, no, I'm fine, don't fuss,' replied Laura.

Mary sighed.

'I know this hasn't been easy for you and you have had a lot to cope with lately, especially with that bastard Andy. But your health is important you know. When did you last see a doctor?'

'A doctor, for me? Och, don't be daft.'

'Yes Laura, I mean it, you must see a doctor if you aren't well. You've been under a lot of stress, remember.

'Look I'm fine, I just didn't fancy any dinner. Anyway, I've been putting on weight, I need to diet.'

'Well, look after yourself. And as for dieting, don't – if anything you've lost weight. Now what about this holiday? You mustn't put it out of your mind. Have you any plans?'

'No not yet Mary. As you say, I've had a lot on my mind but I will think about it. Right now I have my suspicions about Robert. He was always sneaking around and looking at me when he thought I didn't notice. After I had been out with Andy, he would try to question me about what we got up to. He said what he would like to do if he was in Andy's shoes. He was horrible.'

'I hope you didn't let him away with talk like that. I know what I would like to do to that boyo.'

Laura sighed.

'Well, I just put up with it for the sake of Mrs Wray. She's a lovely lady and I couldn't hurt her feelings.'

'Well, she's about to get an awful let-down when we tell the police. What do you think?'

'Mary, do you feel that maybe we should talk to your family first and let them know what we have discovered?'

'Are you mad Laura? Sure you know our boys and my Da. They would just go and find the dirty auld bugger and beat the hell out of him. I know that's what would happen and we still haven't enough to go on. No, the police must be told.'

Laura agreed with her – she knew only too well how the boys and their father would react. They would kill Robert, given the chance. They left the warmth of the hotel lounge and went out again into the biting wind.

The police station was at the top of the square, commanding a view over the whole town. Sergeant Hall's office was on the top floor and the view was far from the girls mind's as they told him everything they knew. He listened intently to everything, interrupting only to ask valid questions and taking note of them, especially dates and times that Laura was able to help with. He talked to them about the case and reminded both of them not to discuss what they had spoken of to anyone, even the family. The girls agreed and he escorted them down to the front door, saying goodbye to them with a concerned expression on his face.

CHAPTER 23

IT WAS A WEEK AFTER the funeral that the news broke. Several men and boys had been taken to the police station for questioning. The village was heaving with gossip. Some people had the suspects tried and convicted.

The McCanns were in an awful state, not knowing what to think. Mary was worried about her parents, especially her mother. Peggy McCann just sat there most of the day in a daze, holding a Fairisle cardigan of Winnie's – it was a present she had bought her for Christmas. Winnie had worn it on that last fateful day, she loved all the colours. Paddy McCann and his sons had their work and indeed they were very busy. Peter told Laura that they had farmers coming to the forge that never had done any business with them before, including quite a few Protestants. The tragedy seemed to bring the village together, everyone was genuinely concerned for the family.

Laura had missed church the previous Sunday. Ironically, after the regular service Robert had led the congregation in prayers for the family and said that the culprit would soon be brought to justice – so Mrs Wray told her. Laura couldn't wait to tell Mary. They met every day to discuss the latest news. Laura was keeping a close eye on Robert; he seemed to have changed. Mrs Wray told her he was reading his Bible every night and hardly left the house except for work. When she asked if he was alright he told her he was getting fed up with his job. He felt he needed a change and said he was going to see his brother in Scotland. She was upset at this, for he had been with that firm for years.

'Winnie's death has affected him more than I realised. I told him that I didn't want to leave here and start some where else. He said he was only thinking about it but if he did go he wouldn't expect me to come and that Scotland was only a few hours away. Now what do you think of that? And he wouldn't even discuss it any more, just picked up his Bible and left the room. I don't know what to think.'

Laura knew that she was very upset and tried to comfort her but she was afraid of her own emotions regarding Robert Wray. She couldn't let her know how she felt about that man.

When she finished in the shop she went across the street to see Mary and told her what she had heard. Mary was dumfounded.

'That auld devil is going to run away to Scotland? Not a bit of it. Take my word, he's planning on going a lot farther than that. I think we should tell Sergeant Hall. We can't let him slip away that easily. And as for reading his Bible every night, he has a guilty conscience. You mark my words, he's as guilty as sin.'

Laura had given Mary the use of her car, so Mary drove her home. They sat in the car now on the hill overlooking the lough. Sergeant Hall had been very interested in what they had to say and told them that they were just waiting for confirmation from their colleagues in Belfast and they could complete their investigation.

'Did you see our Peter? He knows we're up to something. Sure every time he comes into the room we stop talking. I feel awful keeping him in the dark.'

'I know,' Laura sighed, 'he was trying to quiz me too. I told him it was just girl-talk but I don't think he believed me.'

'You know Laura, I've had my eye on him and I think he fancies you. I see him watching you and he has all the symptoms.'

'Peter and I always got on well. Sure he's like a brother to me, don't talk nonsense.'

'Well somehow I don't think his looks say he wants to be you're brother. Now that Andy's out of the picture you'd never know, eh?'

The evening sun was sparkling on the lough and a few swans were gliding homewards. It looked so peaceful, it was hard to imagine that there was so much heartbreak happening. Mary told her of her visit back to see Bridgin – she had been delighted to see Yusef. They took her out for a drive and ate fish and chips before they left her home. Bridgin had made a great recovery and ate all her food. She was going back to school next week. They talked for a while about other things. Mary said she was anxious to get back to work. The new burns ward was full and there was talk of opening a second one. Mary sighed.

'We really need an aftercare centre. Families are finding it hard to manage when patients go home. If there was some place where they could stay for a few weeks to learn how to cope. But like everything else, it all takes money. Maybe the government will see sense soon. Come on, let's get you home.'

As they drove up to the house, Laura's father came out into the street waving at them, he seemed agitated. Laura jumped out of the car.

'Father what's wrong, is Mother sick?'

'No, no,' said her father, 'but Mary's brother phoned, they need you at home. There have been some developments, the police are there now.'

Mary went white.

'Come on, Laura, come back with me. Thanks Mr Steenson.'

They drove quickly back down to the village. A police car was just pulling away from McCann's and Peter was in the doorway.

'Thank God you're here,' he said. 'Come in, quick.'

Mary's father was sitting on the couch with her mother whose face was white. Her father looked up when they entered and in broken words he told them that the police had the man that caused Winnie's death. There were no doubts they had the right man. Mary sat down heavily on the chair at the table she looked at Laura tears, filling her eyes.

'Oh thank God, thank God.'

Peter looked at her.

'You know, don't you? You know who it is. Pat and I have been feeling so helpless and you pair know who the bugger is. Well, tell us now.'

He was going red with anger. Laura took hold of his arm.

'Peter, we made a promise to the police. I'll tell you tomorrow whatever happens, I promise, but we can't tonight.'

Peter wasn't satisfied, his father Paddy said nothing. Pat came back into the room, he had put the twins upstairs when the police came.

'I couldn't help overhearing. So you two have known all along and you didn't see fit to tell us! Why Mary, why?'

Mary looked up at her older brother, still filled with tears.

'Pat we couldn't. Please understand. I knew how you two would react, you would have spoiled the arrest. Please understand, we did for the best. Let the police deal with it.'

Laura looked up at the man she used to idolise as a child, a big gentle giant.

'Pat, we did it for the best and if he was the one who did it he will get justice.'

Peter prepared the supper for everyone and the twins were allowed down again. They were full of questions as to why the police called. Their father took them, one on each knee, and told them the truth, that the police had caught the man responsible for Winnie's death. They understood. Their mother Peggy still didn't speak. Mary saw her up to bed and Laura said goodnight to everyone. She went out to get into the car and wondered about Mrs Wray – how did she take the news? Should she call and find out if she was alright?

There was a light on in the Wray's upstairs sittingroom and the yard lights were still on. Laura decided that she would go and check before she went home. She drove her car into the yard, used her key to open the side door and called out but received no answer. She went towards the stairs and called again. The sittingroom door was partly open and the only light came from a table lamp at the window. Mrs Wray was lying over the armchair in a very awkward position, as Laura touched her she slumped forward and almost fell on to the floor. Laura caught her and sat her upright.

'Mrs Wray, Mrs Wray! It's me, Laura, answer me.'

The woman mumbled something unintelligible, her breathing was very light. The telephone was lying on the floor where she must have dropped it after hearing news of Robert's arrest.

Laura picked it up and dialled for an ambulance, then she called Mary.

Mary and Peter arrived almost at once. Mary confirmed that the woman was having or had had a heart attack, and looked like she'd had a slight stroke as well.

'I can't understand why the police didn't send someone out to tell her, a woman alone in the house receiving news like this.'

Peter stared at Mrs Wray, his mouth open, unable to take in what he was hearing.

'Was it? Was it *him*?'

'Yes,' said Laura. 'He was the one we suspected and the police must have done the rest.'

'Oh my God! And he shook hands with us at the funeral, consoling us on our terrible loss. The dirty auld hypocrite! Jesus, if only I'd known, he wouldn't be in a cushy police barracks tonight, he'd be at the bottom of the lough.'

'And that's why we didn't tell you, he must be brought to justice. Your way wouldn't have accomplished anything and you know it, don't you?'

Laura looked at Peter.

'Mary's right, Peter, this way we will prove his guilt. Your way would only have brought more trouble for your family.'

'How long have you pair known? I knew you were keeping something from us. All the secrecy, why didn't you tell us?'

Peter sat, face in his hands. Mary was exasperated.

'And that's why we didn't speak of it. We promised the police we wouldn't and we have only suspected him for a few days.'

But Peter wouldn't be put off.

'You should have told us, it's not right.'

Mary, holding Mrs Wray to keep her head straight, was getting annoyed with her younger brother.

'Do you not listen Peter? If you had your way you'd be in jail tonight keeping your brothers company. Do you not think that Ma and Da's had enough trouble in their lives: a daughter dead, two sons in jail and one more heading that way. Will you grow up!'

Then she burst into tears. Peter held her, telling her he was sorry, that he didn't want any more hurt. Just then they heard the ambulance arrive. Peter agreed to take the keys and look after the house and business while the girls accompanied Mrs Wray in the ambulance to the hospital in Dungannon. He promised to phone Laura's parents with the news.

They stayed nearly all night, waiting for news of the sick woman but it was early morning before the doctor told them the prognosis was good. It was just as well she was found in time, another hour and she would have died. He praised Mary for her nursing and smiled at her.

'I new the day I signed your application that you would go far and now you're running the burns unit. Keep up the good work, I'll be back to see your friend shortly. She has had a slight stroke but with care she'll recover and we have a monitor on her heart. What she needs now is rest and no upsets. What about her family?'

Mary and Laura looked at each other. Mary introduced Laura and told the doctor that she was the closest family she had right now. They went on to explain about the situation and how they had found Mrs Wray. Doctor Williams was also surprised that the police had sent no one out to break the news to the woman. He enquired if there were any other relatives. Laura told him about Robert's brother in Scotland. Robert hadn't spoken of his brother before as they hadn't seen each other in years. Mrs Wray had an old uncle in Fermanagh and a spinster cousin but she hadn't seen them since her father died nearly fifteen years ago.

'Well,' said the doctor, 'it looks like it's you I'll have to report to. Are you agreeable to that?'

Laura said she had no problem helping in any way she could. He advised them to get some food and plenty of rest as Mrs Wray would not be having any visitors until next day. The girls thanked him and made their way to the canteen.

Sitting at the table with the food in front of her, Laura knew she couldn't face it. Nausea filled her again and she rushed to the toilet. When she returned, Mary stared at her with concern and handed her a cup of tea.

'Now drink, it's sweet and it's good for you, especially now. And take this piece of dry toast, no buts.'

Laura accepted both and none of them spoke until she had almost finished the toast.

'Your colour is coming back. Do you feel any better? Hot sweet tea and dry toast is the best cure I know for morning sickness.'

Laura stared at her open mouthed in total shock. Mary smiled at her friend.

'You mean you didn't suspect anything, even with all this sickness? I wondered about you when you got sick at the Donnelly's last week.'

Laura, still in shock, could hardly find words.

'No, Mary, no! I can't be, not now. I would know. Oh Lord, no!'

Mary laughed.

'Laura from what you told me about you and randy Andy you're not a virgin, so why not? You mustn't have taken precautions. Don't look like that, it's not the end of the world.'

They discussed symptoms and compared dates and Mary asked when her sickness had started. Laura told her about the last time she and Andy had had sex and how they had got carried away. How could she have been so foolish? At her age too!

'Listen girl,' said Mary, 'it happens, it's natural. At the time you thought you loved him, what is more natural than to make spontaneous love with the right person? How could that be foolish?'

'But I do feel foolish. Look at the pickle I'm in now! Oh my God, this will finish Father. Another scandal in the family. Me with an illegitimate child, I'll be banished forever!'

'Don't talk nonsense. You're not the first or the last for this to happen to.'

'Oh, I think I'm unique. After all I'm nearly thirty, I've got no money to my name and soon no home. Now that's all Tullybeg needs.'

Mary laughed.

'It might be that way now but things change. You're still the same Laura. More importantly, you're still my friend, my best friend, and I will do whatever it takes to see you through this.'

Laura gave her a weak smile.

'Och, and I'm going to need all the friends I can find when this news gets out.'

'I know it's too soon to get your head around this now but you'll have to visit a doctor to get it confirmed.'

Laura inhaled and held her hands to her tummy. She was glad they were in a quiet corner of the canteen.

'Sweet Lord, me with a baby! I still can't take it in. Imagine... fat, pregnant, Protestant, nearly thirty and not a man in sight. Our church and the whole of Tullybeg will have a field day.'

'Look girl, stop worrying about what other people think. That causes more stress and heartache than anything else.'

'Yes Mary but I can't put my family through that. Sure they would never live it down and it could kill my mother, what on earth am I going to do?'

'Do? The first thing is to see a doctor. I'll take you to a friend of mine at the hospital if you like.'

'Maybe I'm worrying about nothing, maybe I'm not pregnant. As you say, stress can cause all sorts of medical problems. Lately I've had my fill. And now Mrs Wray. She only has me and a few women friends from the church group.'

'There you go again, thinking of someone else. You'll have to have a check-up anyway. What about your family doctor?'

Laura stared at her.

'Our doctor? I couldn't go to him, sure I've known him nearly all my life. I'll go to one here in town, what do you think?'

Mary took her friend's hand.

'Whatever you decide. It's early days yet anyway but it's best to have these things done now and you'll have plenty of time to make plans.'

As they talked about the future and 'what if', they saw Peter come into the canteen looking for them.

'Well, any news. How's the patient? I thought I'd come and bring you pair home. I got Mrs Moore to look after the shop. She called to see how things were. She helps out now and again, doesn't she?'

'Och, you're great, Peter. There's no change in Mrs Wray and we can't see her yet, so it's best that we go home. I'm dying for a bath. Come on Mary, a few hours rest will do us both good.'

CHAPTER 24

IT WAS THE TELEPHONE that wakened Laura from a deep sleep. Her mother came into her bedroom and told her that Mary had called and for her to come down to the village when she was ready as there were some developments. But there was no change in Mrs Wray. She thanked her mother, telling that she would have a bath before she left. She filled the bath-tub, added her favourite essence, then some bath bubbles. As the warm foam spread over her firm body, she thought of everything that had taken place in the last few days, the fact that she could be pregnant and the change it would make in her life. How would she cope? Should she just disappear? Maybe she should go to New Zealand. No, she couldn't burden her family with her problems. And what about Mrs Wray, she couldn't leave her, not now. And the police, would they find enough evidence to convict Robert? Dear Lord, so much was happening all at once.

She moved her hands sensually down her wet body, nipples hardening at her touch. Then to her stomach and strong thighs, letting them linger at her most sensual spot, the core of her womanhood. A strong yearning was growing inside her. This was the first time she had felt like this since she had made love with Andy. The craving grew stronger. She lay there remembering their last long and erotic lovemaking and all the empty promises. It was in the parlour after the ball. She laughed when he insisted on putting a chair under the door-handle, saying that they had to be careful, so that her parents wouldn't hear anything – their room was at the back of the house. They removed each other's clothes in a frenzy of excitement at the prospect of their lovemaking, scattering their finery all over the floor. Andy was demanding with her body, bringing her to new heights. They whispered to each other their most secret thoughts and needs. Andy was so experienced in making her feel good.

Suddenly, she was brought back to reality, remembering the nightmare she was in. The fact that Belle's bedroom was directly overhead as they made love and knowing that he had spent a long time with Belle that same evening, made Laura's stomach begin to churn and all notions of sex quickly disappeared. She finished her bath feeling ashamed for her thoughts. She dressed, anger burning a searing pain in her body. Maybe she would write and tell Belle that Andy was going to be a Dad. Would it make any difference to them? Probably not.

CHAPTER 25

LAURA WATCHED THE WOMAN she loved like her own mother. She was so weak. She looked so vulnerable lying propped up by pillows, tubes coming out of her arms and nose, heart monitors at the side of her bed. How was she going to tell this gentle soul the disastrous news about her husband? The doctors had said any more shocks could kill her. The responsibility was too much but there wasn't anyone else and she knew Mrs Wray would be asking for Robert as soon as she awoke. She had been at her bedside now for nearly an hour. The Reverend Whylie had called to see her and said he would be back later when she was able to talk. He spoke to Laura briefly of Robert's arrest. He was still in shock at the news but felt that maybe Laura was the best person to tell Mrs Wray, as she was the closest to her.

'I don't know how the elders and the congregation are going to take this awful news. I mean he was one of the members that we all looked up to, always a strong pillar of the church. He must have been led astray by the girl – they are so precocious these days. Maybe the poor man was ill.'

Astray? Ill? Laura wanted to scream, the audacity of the man!

'I can't believe I'm hearing this! You a minister, making excuses for that vile man. How could you? And trying to lay blame on an innocent child. You were at the police station when they listed the charges.'

'Now, now, Laura,' he almost whispered, 'we mustn't judge, it's for the Lord above to do that. I must do what I can, he begged me to help him. I can't turn my back on one of my flock when they need me, you must understand.'

'That's up to you. As far as I'm concerned that murderer can rot in hell and that's where he belongs. Now if you don't mind Reverend Whylie, I think you should leave.'

Laura moved her chair closer to the bed and turned away from the stunned vicar. He stood for a few minutes looking straight at her but she didn't turn round. Then he left quietly, closing the door behind him. Laura saw a movement in Mrs Wray's fingers. She reached over and held them. The woman's left hand lay lifeless on the covers. She looked up at the monitor but there was no change, just a steady beat. As she watched, the woman's eyes opened and a weak smile creased her face. Her fingers gripped Laura's hand tighter.

'Laura,' her voice slurred, 'it's good to see you.'

'Don't try to talk Mrs Wray I'm just happy that you're going to make it, you had us all worried,' said Laura, tears filling her eyes.

'No, don't worry about me, I need to talk,' Mrs Wray spoke slowly. 'I heard you and the Minster talking.'

Laura was dumbfounded.

'Oh I'm sorry, Mrs Wray I thought you were asleep. I didn't want you to find out this way.'

The woman smiled at her.

'Look Laura, the first thing you must do is call me Violet, this missus thing must stop.'

'I've always called you Mrs, it's a sign of respect and I don't think I'd ever get used to calling you Violet. It's a lovely name though.'

'Well you will just have to as I will only answer to my name, and don't worry about me, I'm stronger than I look.'

Laura smiled at her.

'You certainly are, you have surprised me, and the doctors too I suppose.'

Violet told her about the telephone call from the police but her suspicions had already been aroused because of the way her husband was acting. Then she began to think of different incidents when she saw Robert and Winnie together. She thought he began taking an interest in the girl last summer. She would catch him looking at her and they were always joking together. She didn't worry as she just thought Robert was delighted to have Winnie around. Sometimes he would leave her into town when she was going to meet her friends for the cinema. Violet never worried about it but lately he had changed and he and Winnie become secretive. Just last night she had confronted him about his actions. Laura could hardly take this all in. She told Violet that she didn't need to talk any more if she didn't want to but the woman looked up, her eyes pleading.

'Please Laura, I need to talk. I've been keeping it all to myself for too long. I'm as much to blame for that child's death as Robert.'

She said Robert was livid when she questioned him and he stood there protesting his innocence saying that Winnie was a little slut and led him on and that she had loads of boyfriends. Violet told him that she didn't trust him and he should go to the police and tell them the truth. She reminded him that this wasn't the first time, but Winnie was just a child. The other girl he had trouble with was much older. She was a typist in the firm and Violet had to give her a lot of money to keep quiet. Now she wondered how many others there were.

Laura listened in disbelief at the astonishing confession from this quiet lady lying before her. Violet continued her story, telling Laura that Robert had begun to pack his suitcase. He had asked her for the cheque-book as he needed money but she refused to let him have it. He then went searching for money in the shop. She told him that she had been in the bank that very day depositing money. He didn't believe her and began to shake her demanding that she tell him where she kept money, he then pushed her about, calling her filthy names, telling her that she kept him down and he hated her. He grabbed her and struck her hard in the chest saying that she was never any use to him in or out of bed . He said a lot more hurtful things that totally shocked her. She was seeing a side to him she never knew existed. Violet pleaded with him too. He was ugly in looks and in manner. As he was about to go, he turned at the doorway.

'I don't need your money, you lousy bitch! There's plenty in my office safe. I hope I never see your hateful, whinging face again!'

She told Laura that she didn't remember how long she had sat there. She began feeling numb and couldn't get up for ages but she finally managed to get to the telephone and called the police station, telling them where to find Robert. After that everything was a blur until she'd woken up last night in hospital. Laura couldn't believe what she was hearing. So it was Violet who had called the police, not the other way round! Laura filled in the gaps for Violet, telling her how she had called over and found her slumped on the chair with the telephone beside her on the floor but it was Mary who had saved her life with her quick thinking. Violet began to cry, saying that maybe it would have been better if she had never been saved and when Mary knew the full story she might regret helping her. Laura told her that was nonsense, that neither Mary nor her family would hold anything that happened against her. Laura stayed until the doctor came on his rounds. As he was telling Violet how pleased he was with her progress, Mary appeared at the door.

'Well you certainly look a lot better than when I last saw you.'

She went over to the bed to hold Violet's hand and Violet smiled at her.

'I believe I owe my life to you, how do I thank you for that? I always knew that you would make a great nurse, thanks Mary.'

The doctor agreed with her. He asked the girls to wait outside while he attended to Violet.

The two girls sat outside discussing Violet's progress and Laura repeated everything that Violet had told her. Mary couldn't believe her.

'You mean, she called the police for him? Well, fair play to her. It must have been awful informing on her own husband. I hope he never finds out it was her.'

Laura asked her about the police, how they had come up with the final evidence. Mary explained that the police in Belfast had been suspicious of certain women in the city and when they brought them in, one of them was able to describe Robert Wray and his car. These women had been running illegal abortion clinics for ages but police couldn't find anything when they raided them. They had been watching one of them in particular and noticed three different women going in the back lane to her house late at night. Then they pounced – the woman had given them enough evidence for an arrest. Sergeant Hall told Laura that Robert was still protesting his innocence when they put him in the cells. The sergeant said they hoped to have the trial soon to save the McCanns any more heartache. Mary sighed.

'Well, maybe my family will be able to sleep better now. Ma paces the floors every night and it breaks my heart to see her.'

Dr Williams came out to them. He said that Mrs Wray was improving but because of the stroke she would have to stay in hospital for some time. Her left side was paralysed but with care there was no reason why she shouldn't recover. He told them they could visit now, just for a few minutes though, as she was very tired. The strain of it all was visible in Violet's eyes. Laura gave her an update on the shop and told her how Peter and Sandra Moore were keeping things going. Things were shipshape and she shouldn't worry. Laura said she would move in until Violet was ready to return. They left after that as they wanted to let Violet get some rest but as they closed the door, tears filled the woman's eyes.

CHAPTER 26

TWO DAYS LATER Laura left her friend to the little train station at the end of the village. Mary had to go back to work but not before she had made Laura promise to visit a doctor. They arranged to meet in a few week's time. After the train pulled out for the city, Laura drove out to the far side of the lough. It was very quiet except for a few inquisitive cattle. She got out and walked along the winding path, trying to concentrate for she had an awful lot to think about. Deep down she knew she was pregnant. She didn't need any doctor's confirmation but for her health's sake she would make an appointment. Her biggest worry was her parents. How was she going to tell them? They were still in a state of shock with the news of Robert Wray. Her father, like the minister, was going on about how good men could be led astray especially with young Catholic girls who would encourage men like Robert if they needed money, they were all sluts. Laura was so enraged she felt like hitting her father and then she shut him up when she told him that Robert had come after her too and the incident in the car and how she'd had to fight him off.

'So Father,' she said, 'am I to be called a slut too? Is that what you think of me?'

Her father was speechless.

'I was old enough and threatened to tell you and the Reverend Whylie but Winnie was just a child, she had no defence for a devil like Robert. How dare you call that innocent child a slut, I'm ashamed of you even thinking like that.'

As usual, her mother tried to intervene.

'Laura, please, your father didn't mean it like that. We're all finding it very hard to accept what has taken place. I mean Robert Wray was a very upright man, everyone looked up to him.'

'Mother, I don't want to upset you but Robert Wray was the devil incarnate. I know that now and I could have been a victim too but I was too clever for him.'

'Now Laura, we must keep our heads and not go making more accusations. After all, we don't know all the facts yet,' said her father.

Laura was fit to be tied.

'Father, you're not listening, didn't you hear me? I could have been a victim. Do you think I'm telling lies? Anyway, Winnie wasn't the first girl, there was another one before that, someone from his office.'

Her father was getting angry.

'Laura, you haven't been yourself lately with all that's happened. Sure Robert didn't mean anything by it, you took it the wrong way. I find it hard to blame him. Something must have happened to him. I know he wasn't himself lately, maybe he was on some kind of tablets that didn't agree with him. There must be some other explanation for all this.'

'Father, there's no point talking to you. Why don't you visit Winnie's grave? Maybe then you will open your eyes to your so-called friend.'

Laura sat remembering all this. How could she confront them now with the news that she was pregnant? Where did she go from here? How long could she manage to hide her condition?

She sat on one of the big rocks at the side of the lough. It was so peaceful. The only sound came from the birds nesting overhead and the lowing of the cattle in the field as they made their way up towards the farm for milking. In the distance she saw Barney McGuigan and his dog coming down the field towards them. He shouted 'hello' over to her, enquiring after Mrs Wray. She watched him as he guided the last of the stray animals through the gate. She stayed there for some time, not wanting to go home. Dusk was falling and it was getting quite chilly. The mist was rising over the lough. Laura made her way back to the car. She couldn't face going back to her parents' house. Her problems with them would have to wait for another day. She had too many other things on her mind right now. At the end of the lane she turned the car back towards the village and the shop.

CHAPTER 27

MARY AND LAURA sat in the familiar window seat of the flat, looking out on a wonderful view of the River Lagan. Three weeks had passed since Laura had sat in Dr Collins' surgery to be told that she was definitely pregnant. The baby was due around August 10th. She decided that she would take up Mary's offer and spend a few days in the city. Mrs Wray was in a convalescent home near Omagh. She would be there for some time until she felt able to cope and return home. Peter was helping to convert the big storeroom into a bed-sittingroom for her. Violet had remembered that it had been the family parlour when she was younger but her mother had used it for storage after she had opened the shop. They had to call in a builder to remodel the old back kitchen and install a toilet and shower stall, as Violet would be unable to climb the stairs. The work was well underway and it would be complete when she returned. Laura was using this time to buy some new curtains and bedding to make it more cheerful. Peter had used his artistic talent to divide the bedroom from the sitting area with wrought-iron and wood panelling. It was looking really good. Violet could sit at the big bay window and watch the goings-on in the village. Mary looked at her, flushed with excitement with all her plans.

'Well, you have settled Mrs Wray and the shop, have you given any thought to your own plans?'

'Och, there's time enough for that. It's my family I have to think about first and I don't know where to start. I've been that busy lately I didn't want to think about it. I mean I won't be showing for a while yet, will I? And with my mother's health not so good I'm really worried what this news will do to her.'

'Laura, there's no easy way out. Sooner or later they are bound to find out unless, and I really don't like talking about it but you have a choice you know. As it's early yet you could have an abortion or have it adopted. God knows there are a lot of childless couples would only be glad to give a baby a home but Laura, the choice must be yours. No one else can decide, you understand that, don't you?'

Laura sighed.

'Of course I understand but there is no big decision, Mary. Whatever the future holds I'm keeping the baby and remember, you're going to be involved too. Won't I need you as godmother?'

'Well, I hope so. Sure I would want you as well when it's my turn.'

'Now, tell me all your news. When is Yusef going to make an honest woman out of you? I hope it won't be until I have regained my figure.'

Mary laughed.

'We're not making any plans yet, we're quite happy to leave things as they are at the moment. Yusef is fighting with the committee at the hospital for a larger burns unit. The one in use at the minute is much too small and to make matters worse we have to use part of it for recuperation. Those poor people should have a place away from the hospital, out in the country some where with plenty of fresh air where they can be really rehabilitated, helped to go back to work, mix with people and maybe learn new skills. Oh there I go again and I promised I wouldn't talk about work. I'm sorry Laura, now let's hit the shops.'

Laura stood up and smoothed down her skirt.

'Do you think this looks too tight? Maybe I'll look for something more suitable. I don't want any of those awful smocks.'

'Och they're terrible. God, that's all I ever remember my mother wearing, big flowery ones and wide dirndl skirts. They always looked a sight and wee Mrs Jackson down the street, she was always pregnant at the same time, God love her. Sure she wasn't the size of two turf and her skirts always swept the floor. She must have worn the same ones every time - you could see where the flower pattern in the front had almost faded. No, that style wouldn't suit you at all. I think we'll get you a few baggy shirts and maybe trousers, they always look smart. Come on, before you grow any bigger!' laughed Mary.

CHAPTER 28

LAURA CAME DOWNSTAIRS carrying a suitcase. She was hoping to get it out to the car before her mother saw it but just as she reached the hall door her mother came out of the kitchen.

'Laura where are you going, why the suitcase? Sure your only back from Belfast. Oh dear, are you leaving now for good? Please Laura, don't go yet, I couldn't bear it, just wait a few weeks. Och, so much has happened I couldn't bear it if you weren't here.'

Her mother began to cry.

'Och Mother, don't get upset. I'm not leaving not really, didn't I tell you I would stay down at Mrs Wray's for a few weeks. She's coming home today and I don't want her to be on her own, especially at night. Mrs Moore couldn't stay – she has her family of wee'uns, and there's no one else. Sure I'll be up every day.'

She looked at her mother.

'Are you alright Mother? You don't look well, come on.'

Laura guided her into the sittingroom and on to the couch.

'Mother, will I call the doctor? Oh Mother, I'm sorry for up-setting you. Why didn't you tell me you weren't feeling well?'

'No, no, Laura, no doctor. I'm alright, please don't worry about me and I'm not sick – I have been taking my medicine. It's just that, seeing you with your suitcase I thought that you were leaving us. Och I'm just a silly old woman and I expect a selfish one, if the truth be known.'

Laura hugged her, then dried her mother's tears.

'Mother, if I could tear myself in two I would but you know that Mrs Wray will need me for a while. Lord knows how she will cope when they bring that beast of a husband of hers to trial. It's going to be very hard on her and she'll need all her friends.'

'Och I do understand, and sure as you said we'll see you every day, won't we?'

'Of course Mother. Sure I'm only down the road you know. I'm just thinking, why don't you come down and visit her? I know she would love to see you.'

'I don't think so. Sure you know I never go anywhere and she might think that I'm only after news, and the way your father feels about Robert Wray he may not approve of me visiting. He still can't come to terms with all that's happened. He was telling me that after the church meeting last week, he thought that the Reverend Whylie was going to have a heart attack.'

'Och well, everyone is feeling the effects. The McCanns will never be the same, yet there's Peter doing all he can for Mrs Wray. He's such a good-natured man. He feels no ill will. It's a pity that there aren't more people like him. I didn't notice many members of the church rushing to help.'

'Now don't start jumping to conclusions. A lot of them people may not know what to say to the woman, I mean I don't know what to say to her. Your father has been to the hospital to visit her and he's very concerned. It's going to take time to re-alise the awful crime that Robert has committed. Do you think Violet will visit him in jail?'

'No Mother, I don't think she will be rushing to visit him. He did a dreadful thing. I don't expect that she will ever forgive him and I wouldn't blame her. Now what about a wee cuppa and one of your scones before I go?'

Violet Wray and Laura sat together on the couch looking out on to the village street. A few people were passing and some of them waved in.

'It's great to be home, it's like years since that night. Some-times I wish I had died but now I'm glad that I didn't. You've been a true friend, Laura,' said Violet, holding out her good hand.

'Och now, don't start that all over again. I only did what any-one would do and it's great to see you so well. Now what about these changes. You didn't say much, are you pleased?'

Violet looked around the warm cosy and bright sittingroom with the glowing fire.

'Not pleased? Sure I'm speechless! I can't believe that this was my storeroom. And the new bathroom, hasn't Peter worked a real miracle? He has such good taste – I'd never have thought of using these colours.'

Laura got up, added more coal to the fire and looked around the newly-decorated room. Yes, it was lovely. Peter had suggested the colours. At first she was worried that Violet wouldn't like it but the rich plums and creams worked really well. Violet had given her full consent to change anything and to buy whatever was needed. She saw the cream Chesterfield suite and it was a good contrast against the plum-coloured carpet. Velvet curtains were added to complete the décor. The bedroom behind the wrought-iron divider was tastefully decorated to match. Peter had indeed showed his artistic skills – no wonder Violet was speechless.

Laura had moved her things to a spare bedroom. She told Violet that she would stay with her until she felt strong enough to stay by herself. Deep down Laura didn't feel very secure herself. What was in store for her? She had been kept that busy lately she didn't have time to think about herself but she knew that she couldn't leave her plans any longer. And what about her parents, when was the best time to break the news of her pregnancy? After the episode with her mother this afternoon, as far as she could see, the best time was never. Laura finished preparing the evening meal for the two of them and brought it back into the sittingroom. After they had eaten, she made Violet comfortable on the couch.

'Now look, if you have anything to do or maybe go out somewhere go on and don't worry about me. Mrs Moore will close up the shop. I must say you are looking very well, Laura. All this activity seems to have done you good.'

'I don't know about that... Anyway, I'm here to keep an eye on you, whether you want my company or not. Now is there anything you need?'

'Yes there is, actually. I said you were looking a lot better but I know you have something on your mind. Is it this holiday you have been thinking about? Have I spoiled your plans?'

Laura looked at her and laughed.

'Och don't be daft, a holiday is the last thing I need now.'

Violet sighed.

'Laura, I have known you long enough to know that you have something on your mind. I saw you sitting by my bedside in the hospital and when you thought I was sleeping I saw you cry. I didn't say anything but I can see that you still have that faraway look... Now what's the matter? And remember, after all that's happened to me lately, nothing you can say will shock me.'

Laura looked at the frail little woman who had survived her husband's vile actions. She was going to have to know sometime so why not now? Violet was right, nothing shocked her, she sat and listened to Laura's news and held her hand.

'Are you disgusted with me, I'll understand if you are?'

Violet squeezed her hand tighter.

'Och Laura, don't say that. You're not the first girl it's happened to and you won't be the last. I don't know what you intend doing but whatever you decide I'm here for you. There will always be a home for your baby and all.'

'Thanks Laura,' she replied. 'You're a good friend. I may have to take you up on your offer because I don't know how my parents will take the news. I'll probably have to leave the country.'

'Well, that could be arranged as well if that's what you want but I can't see your mother letting you go. You'll find the right time, Laura, I know you will and remember, whatever happens, it will be a nine-day-wonder, I mean, look at me.'

Laura stood up and went over to the window. Looking out at the familiar sight of the street, she smiled to herself. Nine-day-wonder! It wasn't just nine days, nine months!! What did it matter how long. Her parents would see it as a lifetime of shame, especially her father. She thought of the litany of events that happened in the last few years to her family: Betty, gone to a new life in New Zealand with an older man for a husband;

then Sam leaving the RUC and running off with a Catholic girl, banished because of their religion; then Andy jilting her and running off to Canada with her younger sister; now the biggest shame of all, pregnant and no husband. It was bad enough when they had wanted to get her away to the minister's sister-in-law when the news got around that she was jilted and left on the shelf at twenty-nine. But now, they are about to discover that she was pregnant, Lord only knows what they would suggest, some nine-day wonder! She turned to look at Violet who was staring anxiously at her.

'Laura, for God's sake don't worry, you'll only make yourself ill. You will have to watch your health now. I know it's not going to be easy to tell your family but you can't leave it much longer, can you?'

Laura paced the room, unable to express how she was feeling about her father and mother.

'How do I tell them?' She moved back and sat down beside Violet. 'I love them so much, I can't bear to hurt them any more. Mother's health hasn't been that good and I can't see a good time to give them news like this, can you?'

Violet held her hand.

'You're in quite a pickle, aren't you? I'm not sure how to help you, I wish I could. If there's anything you need you only have to ask.'

'I know, but right now let's concentrate on getting you well. I'm going into the shop to let Mrs Moore home. Will you be alright here by yourself?'

'Of course I will. In a few days I'll be able to go into the shop as well and I don't want any arguments. Now go on, see you later.'

Violet watched as Laura walked across the room and into the hallway. Such a sweet-natured girl, she sighed to herself, and with her new short hairstyle and the blue trouser suit, she looked just great. Maybe it was being pregnant but she seemed to have blossomed in these last few weeks. There was a bloom on her cheeks and her eyes sparkled. She would make some man a wonderful wife – that Andy hasn't realised what he has lost.

She didn't deserve to be left in this predicament, not her. And how would her parents react to her news? Knowing how strict her father was, it wasn't going to be easy. He was also a very silly man, letting all his family leave him because of his stupid pride.

Dear Lord, if only she had been lucky enough to have a family, nothing they did would ever make her ashamed of them. Now here Laura's parent were, about to make the same mistake. Violet thought about Robert lying in Crumlin Road Jail, would it have been different if she had kept her child? She thought back to her younger carefree days but were they really carefree? No, not like today's young people.

Violet's family had been even stricter than Laura's. Her mother, just like Violet, had been an only child, always surrounded by adults. Like her daughter, she had worked day-in and day-out for her father's fuel business. Violet had never had the chance to mix with young people of her own age except at church and the choice there wasn't great. So when Seán Downey entered her life, everything changed. He was a handsome young lad and he drove one of her father's coal trucks and she had got to know him as he came into the office to hand in his worksheet at the end of every day. He would always find excuses to stay that little bit longer and chat with her. When he began to pay her attention, she was so excited. She was crazy about him but of course they had to keep their meetings secret. He was a Catholic from Mill Row, a street of poor run-down cottages at the far end of the village by the river bank. All of the six families residing there were Catholic, so socially there was no way her family would entertain him. But they found ways and carried on a relationship for over a year. Then the inevitable happened, she got pregnant.

Seán decided that they would run away to England – his sister lived in Manchester. So they sat out by the lough one evening planning their future but a nosy neighbour saw them and told Violet's father. He had nearly killed Seán with the handle of a shovel and told him to leave that very night or he would finish him. They didn't even get to say goodbye to each other and she was packed off to a clinic in Belfast. The pregnancy was terminated, she had no say in the matter.

Later, when Violet's mother was dying, she told her that Seán had written her many letters but they had kept them from her and burned them all. It was after Violet's father had been killed in the war that she heard that Seán had been killed around the same time. He had joined up shortly after leaving Ireland.

The following year, she had been introduced to Robert Wray. Of course he had no idea about her past and they were married in a few months. They had a quiet relationship, nothing very exciting. He was kind to her in a cold way but she had never felt the warmth or the passion she'd had with Seán. She couldn't believe that Robert had found out about her affair with Seán and about her pregnancy and hadn't said anything. Instead he took his revenge by having affairs with any young girl who took his fancy and was easy prey. Now look where he was. This time he had gone too far – she never wanted to see him again, she didn't feel anything for him.

She thought again of Laura and how different her situation was, or was it? She was young, her parents didn't give her a choice but Laura knew her own mind and she did have a choice. She chose to keep her baby, whatever the outcome. She was a wonderful strong girl who didn't want to hurt the people she loved but she had to. Would they banish her too? But fate has a habit of stepping in and it certainly did this time for Laura.

It was April and spring was showing everywhere. The flowers had never looked so good – daffodils lined the laneway up to the farmhouse like tall soldiers and the smell of apple-blossom from the orchard wafted into the house. Laura was helping out with the egg-collecting, then she had to visit the far field and bring down the cattle for evening milking. A neighbour woman who helped out around the house and farm, was off today at a wedding. Her father was at the market in town, so she offered to help out. They could have got someone else but with the milking machines there was no real heavy work. She promised Violet that she would do no lifting or carrying. She was starting to show now, into her fifth month but she managed to wear clothes that covered her little bump. The doctor was pleased with her progress and she had never felt so well.

She had spent the previous weekend in Belfast with Mary. They'd had a great time. She bought some new clothes, mostly shirts and slacks, and Mary made her buy a lemon duster coat for when she got bigger. They had a meal in her favourite restaurant and she came home by train. Again they discussed her future. Mary had arranged for her to visit the hospital obstetrician and book her confinement.

Coming down from the milking shed, Jake, the sheepdog, was playing about in front of her. As she came towards the door of the house he jumped up to play with her and she lost her balance and fell backwards over the flower-tub. Her scream brought her mother out. She couldn't get up and knew that she had done something awful to her leg. It was then she felt a wetness between her legs – it was blood. Her mother couldn't lift her and panicked. Laura knew that to move was very unwise. She told her mother to phone an ambulance. While they were waiting, Ruth made her comfortable with pillows and a blanket – there was nothing else to do. Laura was worried, was she losing the baby? This was still not a good time to tell her mother, she thought, another shock could kill her. So she just lay there hoping help would come soon.

The pain was almost unbearable, she hardly remembered the journey to the hospital. The doctors and nurses were fussing over her. She was able to tell the doctor she was five months pregnant so he said he would give her a local anaesthetic. She told the nurses that her mother might need attention. They told her not to worry and they agreed that they would contact her father. She saw the worried look on the doctor's face as she began drifting on a snowy soft cloud. Well, she thought, I'm glad I'm drifting, for all hell will soon be let loose.

CHAPTER 29

It was 1977. Laura was up with the birds. She had most of the chores done by the time her father came down for breakfast and she was singing when he came into the kitchen.

'Well we don't need a radio when you're here, do we? It's a long time since I heard you so happy in yourself, and I suppose I don't need to ask the reason why. What time is he expected?'

'I'm not sure,' she answered. 'Pat McCann said he would be here if he had any news of the arrival time. Oh Father, I have missed him so much. I can't wait to see him.'

'Are you bringing him up here or do you have to go to the shop first?'

She looked at her father.

'Well, I don't know until he arrives. Are you still going into town with Ernie Smith?'

'Och, I said he could call here for me. I want to go to the mart but sure I'll be back before four o'clock.'

'Don't worry Father, I'll be bringing him up here for his tea anyway. Myrtle Brooks will be back soon and I'll get her to make one of her specials, he'll like that.'

As they ate their breakfast she looked over at her father. He was looking very well for his age – he would be seventy-six next birthday. He had mellowed so much in the last few years from the grumpy old man that he used to be. It was awful the first year after her mother died. Several times she thought that he would follow her, he was so depressed. Only for circumstances he probably would have but it was great to see him looking well. She knew that she would have to keep an eye on him because of his heart. She would have a word with Ernie when he called. She didn't want him wandering around the mart on his own – if he fell again it would finish him. When they phoned her at the shop a fortnight ago to say he was found lying in the yard she thought he would never recover but he surprised them all and now he was the picture of health.

Laura had the house spic and span by the time Myrtle Brooks, who helped out, arrived. She had seen her father off and had gone upstairs and changed her clothes. She wanted to look her best. She chose white cotton slacks and a pink sleeveless blouse and brushed her hair till it was shining. She liked the reflection that smiled back at her, a big change from last night.

She went downstairs and out into the August sunshine. The country looked great, the honeysuckle was in full bloom and the perfume was competing with her mother's roses. They had never looked so good. A large bunch of buds and blooms would look great on the kitchen table for the tea. She could smell Myrtle's baking – if she was not mistaken that was chocolate cake she was making, his favourite cake, for his birthday tomorrow. Myrtle called her to say the bus would arrive in an hour. Laura stood in the shop doorway looking down the village street. Pat McCann came towards her with his twins, Moira and Monica, they were almost eight years old. The girls ran to her.

'Laura, Laura, we were talking on the phone to Auntie Mary today. She's coming up tomorrow, isn't that great?'

They said nearly everything in unison. Laura took them by the hand.

'Come on, I'm sure you two would like a lolly, what flavour do you want?'

Here they differed, Moira wanted orange and Monica raspberry. They waved to Mrs Wray who was at the sitting-room window. She smiled at them and asked if they would call and see her later.

'Well,' said Pat, 'no need to ask if you missed him, you're like a hen on hot bricks.'

She punched him playfully on the arm.

'What do you think? I hate it when we're apart, I can't wait.'

'Well you needn't wait any longer,' he said. 'Look.'

A blue mini-bus was coming up the street. She peered in as it stopped. Where is he? She couldn't see him. Passengers were unloading their bags. There was no sign of him. She was about to go over to the driver when two arms grabbed her from behind in a tight hug and a voice she loved called out.

'Hello Mum, I'm back.'

She turned around and the biggest smile she ever witnessed spread over her son Alan's face. Arms around each other, they hugged tightly until Alan pulled away.

'Stop Mum!' he said. 'The boys will see me and they'll think I'm a sissy.'

'Well I don't care what they think. I want another hug, come here.'

She playfully tried to pull him to her but he got away and bumped into Moira and Monica. They were pulling at their brother Niall's bag, shouting:

'Niall, did you bring us anything from the seaside?'

'Yes I did but you'll have to wait till I get home. Give me my bag.'

As Niall tried to get it, the bag opened and out spilled a pile of wet dirty clothes. Pat came to the rescue.

'I see you brought something nice for your Mam as well. Did they not teach you at scout camp to wash your own?'

'They did,' said Niall, surprised, 'sure they *are* washed, they're just a bit wet.'

He hurriedly pushed some mysterious paper bags back into the bag. Laura looked at Alan.

'I suppose you washed all your clothes as well, did you?'

'Yes Mum. The camp was brilliant, we had great fun and Niall and I won two badges, one for swimming and one for nature trail. Do you want to see them, wait a second and I'll...'

He was about to tumble everything out of his bag but she stopped him.

'No Alan, we'll wait till we get home, then I'll hear all about your camp. I can't believe how you have grown in three weeks – you'll soon be as tall as me. Come on, we have to go over to see Mrs Wray for a few minutes.'

They said goodbye to Pat and his family but not before Laura reminded them about Alan's birthday party next day.

'Maybe you will get your mother to come up as well, she might enjoy it.'

'Well, you never know,' said Pat. 'Mary is coming up and she might get her out of the house for a while. Now come on you lot, your Ma will have your tea ready.'

Laura watched as the twins were still trying to pull at Niall to show them the presents. Arm around her son's neck they walked across to the shop and Violet Wray met them at the door.

'I was watching for my wee fella to get off the bus but I couldn't see him and then I spotted this tall blond young man. Oh Alan, I didn't realise how handsome you had grown. Come here and give an old woman a big hug.'

She held out her frail skinny arms and Alan flew into them.

'Och Auntie Vi, you're just an auld charmer,' he said, laughing, as they all went down the hallway into the kitchen. In minutes Laura had a pot of tea on the table but Alan preferred a mineral and a bun.

'Now that's all,' said Laura. 'I have to get dinner for everyone later and I don't want you to spoil your appetite.'

After quickly drinking and eating he asked if he could go into the shop and look at the comics. Permission was granted and he fled.

'Och Laura,' said Violet, 'he's lovely and he's growing up so fast. Sure it's just like yesterday when he was in the pram and suddenly he is almost a man.'

'I know,' said Laura, 'and tomorrow he'll be ten, sure I can't believe it myself. I missed him these last three weeks.'

Violet smiled.

'And you know that's only the start of it. This was his first time away from you. I know you weren't sure about letting him go but isn't it great to give him his independence, sure it will be the making of him.'

'I suppose so but somehow I begrudged him growing up he's not my baby any more, is he?'

'No he's not,' said Violet. 'And that's a good thing. Sure joining that scout troop was the best thing you ever let him do.'

'Och I know. Do you remember my father ranting on? He didn't want any of it, I think he thought that they would convert him to the Catholic church and no matter what I said he wouldn't change his mind. Sure he'll be at Alan tonight, wait and see. He'll be questioning him about what prayers he said and if he went to Mass. He reads a passage from The Bible every night and asks the child questions later, just like he did when we were small.'

Laura had been delighted when Pat McCann had told her of the troop. The headmaster in the school had been involved in scouting before getting the job in Tullybeg and decided to form a scout troop for the young boys of the village. He announced that religion would make no difference so a few of the more outward Protestant families allowed their boys to join. Niall and Alan were best friends so it was only natural that they joined together but when the camp was mentioned she was worried. The headmaster was Jim Gallagher, a native of Gweedore in Donegal, so he planned his camp in a field next to his family home and just over the hill was the sea. It sounded great and Alan never stopped talking about it. Laura went to the first meeting with two other Protestant families to find out more about it and was satisfied that they would be looked after well. Jim Gallagher said his younger brother and sister would be helping out. The Protestant minister of the area was Reverend Hugo Macmillan – he would take the three Protestant boys to Sunday school while the other seven went to Mass. It all seemed very satisfactory but not for Laura's father, nothing would convince him:

'They will get instructions in the Catholic religion, I just know it, and they will come home speaking in a foreign language and you're mad if you let him go.'

But Laura saw how much Alan wanted to go so she agreed and now she was glad. He looked great, and the one thing she didn't want for him was growing up a bigot like Andy and his grandfather. She had to remind him so often about things he said about Catholics in front of Alan but there were times there was no stopping him. So she gently explained to Alan that he wasn't to pay any attention to the ravings of old men and to always remember that all people were created equal in the eyes of God and she hoped he would understand. She went into the shop to call him but Jill, who was helping out, told her that he had gone down to see Peter.

She went to the side door and into the yard. Violet Wray had allowed Peter to use the old coal sheds for his welding. He had really changed the place in the last few years and his wrought iron-work was in great demand. He created some wonderful art work – buyers were coming from all over the country and he was even getting orders from Scotland and England. Laura had persuaded him to exhibit at an art fair in Belfast nearly four years ago and he had never looked back. She stood watching now as he was explaining a new design to Alan – they were great friends. Since he'd been born Peter had taken a great interest in him and of course the gossips had a field day even though Alan looked totally different. Peter, like all the McCann family, was dark-haired with sallow skin whereas Alan was the spitting image of Andy – no one who knew him could deny it – he was almost Andy's double, tall and very fair. She stood looking at the contrast in the two heads bent close together. Had she done wrong in not letting Peter be a father to him?

Every year at Easter Peter proposed to her and every year she turned him down. Oh, she had a variety of excuses, the most obvious one being her father. Sometimes she thought she loved him. He accompanied her to any event or social outing she wanted to attend so everyone saw them as a couple. She wouldn't agree to marrying him but they were the best of friends. Alan turned to her.

'Mum, look at the new designs Peter has, aren't they great? And he has a big job for that new hotel in town. Look, come and see,' he was as excited as Peter.

The plans were laid out on the workbench – a collection of drawings for a long winding staircase for the hotel – he had incorporated the owner's name into the design. Also iron frames for the large mirrors that would hang on the wall. Laura was very impressed at his talent.

'These are wonderful Peter! You have surpassed yourself this time.'

Peter was pleased with her comments and showed her the hand-painted shells that Alan had given him.

'What do you think of them Mum?' said Alan. 'Aren't they lovely? I have some for everyone and a special one sitting on a stone for you, Mum, and I painted your name on it. Wait till I get it for you, it's in my bag.'

Laura smiled at him looking at the painted shells.

'Well, it looks like you have some competition Peter, you aren't the only artist in town, eh? You'd better watch out or you'll be on the street,' she laughed. 'Come on Alan, it's near dinnertime. Your Granda will be worrying about us, I'll see my present when we get home.'

They said goodbye and Alan asked him if Peter was coming up to his birthday party. He ruffled Alan's blond hair and said he wouldn't miss it. They packed all Alan's gear into the back of the new station-wagon Laura was now driving. It was big enough to take Alan and his friends on their outings but it was a tight squeeze sometimes.

William Steenson had been in and out of the house this past hour watching for their return. When he heard the familiar sound of the car he made his way back into the house, picked up the paper and sat on his usual chair. Alan came bouncing in.

'Granda, Granda I'm back! Did you miss me? How's your arm? I missed you, and the cattle, are they alright, is Daisy still milking well?' He rushed over and knelt at William's feet.

'Oh, so you're back,' replied William, putting down the paper. 'You know, there was so much peace and quiet in this house I thought I was living some place else. Even the dog was quiet.'

He reached down and pulled the child up.

'My goodness are you sure that you are Alan Steenson. Sure he was only a wee small runt of a fellow when he left here, is it you?' he smiled.

'Och Granda, I couldn't be anyone else, could I? Do you think I've grown a lot?' Alan stood up and reached his full height. 'Look at me, haven't I grown big?'

William smiled proudly.

'Och dear me, you're man big now alright. I suppose you're much too big to hug your auld Granda, are you?'

Alan didn't wait he was in his Granda's arms with William ruffling his overgrown hair. That's how Laura found them as she stood in the doorway.

'Well excuse me, am I the lackey here? I thought that in the scouts you were taught to look after your own bags not leave your tired old mother to do it all. Look at me, I'm wore out.'

Alan ran to her and took the bags from her.

'Sorry Mum but I had to see Granda first, and we were taught to look after our things, didn't I wash all my clothes in the river. Sure they just need to hang on the line. I'm great, so I am.'

Just at that Myrtle Brooks came in, she had been up collecting the eggs.

'Well, well, a sight for sore eyes and that's what you are Alan Steenson, come here till I kiss you.'

'No, no, Myrtle, I'm a big boy now, I'll just shake hands.'

As he did so, Laura and her father had to stop their laughter.

'Well now,' said Myrtle, 'seeing you are a big boy you can help me set the table for the dinner. Come on, I cooked some lovely lamb chops, your Granda's favourite, and something special for afters.'

Alan smiled at her.

'Well I suppose I missed your cooking too, Myrtle.'

She laughed.

'Oh you! Come on, you wee charmer.'

The evening meal was a success – William was in great form and Alan hardly stopped chatting. They heard all about the camping field and being shown how to light a safe fire and how to put it out.

'But the best thing was cooking the sausages and beans and Mum, they tasted great! I can't wait till Niall and I make our own camp. You can help Granda but we'll wait till your arm is better, then I'll show you how to cook great sausages, won't that be great Mum?'

'Of course it will, providing you don't set fire to yourself. Remember you're not to do anything like that unless Granda or I know about it first, right?'

'Alright,' he answered. 'Now Granda we need to go and see if everything on the farm is doing well, are ye coming?'

Laura watched the pair of them heading up to the top field, Alan holding his grandfather's injured arm very protectively. She smiled as she watched them disappear.

The sun was still shining and after she finished in the kitchen, she went out to rose garden, it was so peaceful here and the perfume was at its best at this time of the evening. Laura and her mother had created this little heaven from what used to be the vegetable garden. It was situated at the side of the house and captured the evening sun. Peter had made a lovely ornamental gate with 'Ruth's Garden' scrolled at the top and two archways for the climbers – right now they were a blaze of colour with several varieties of roses all fighting to reach the sun. The other beds were designed in circles and diamonds and Laura had planted miniature lavenders for their colour and perfume. Her mother loved the garden and would sit for ages with her knitting under the shade of the big pear tree in the corner. Her father, of course, was against it from the start.

'What's the point of taking up good ground for stupid flowers? You can't eat them for your dinner,' he grumbled but her mother pointed out:

'The vegetables could still been grown in part of the big potato field – we don't use half of them anyway.'

Finally, he consented for one of the men to dig it for them. When he saw Laura with the grape and spade one day, he asked her what she was doing. When she told him that she intended digging in readiness for planting the roses, he grumpily replied that it was no job for a woman. It was nearly two years before he agreed that as usual they were right, the finished garden was wonderful. On most evenings they would take their tea out there but it was a nuisance when they had to move table and chairs as well. So it was a big surprise when he came home from the mart one day with his friend, Ernie Smith. From the back of the trailer they had lifted a wooden table and matching chairs. Laura's mother was delighted and couldn't wait to use them for tea that evening. Laura had made matching cushions for the garden suite – they looked great. Sitting in one of the chairs with a cup of coffee, Laura thought of that awful time when her parents discovered that she was pregnant – it was a living nightmare at the time. If it hadn't been for her mother, things would have been so different. After the fall that fateful evening when she thought that it was all over and she bled so much, that it was the end of the baby, she always remembered seeing the face of her poor mother. She must have overheard the doctor – she came rushing in crying, holding on to her daughter tightly. Laura had lost a lot of blood and it was touch and go. She needed several transfusions before she responded. She was drifting in and out of consciousness, not aware of what was happening to her. She heard voices, some angry, her father's? Then she was gone again, to that lovely floaty place. It wasn't till she finally came round that she discovered that the fall had happened two days ago and it would be some time before she was out of danger. The doctor was telling her this when her mother arrived. Laura could see by her face that she knew everything – Ruth came over to the bed and held her.

'Oh my Laura,' she cried. 'I thought you were going to die. I was sure we were losing you, I never prayed so much. 'Oh, thank the Lord!'

'Och Mother don't, sure it's hard to kill a bad thing don't you know that, and I'm very bad, as you know.'

'Laura love, sure nothing matters as long as you're alright. I couldn't care less if you are pregnant, as long as you're still here. Nothing in the world is more important this minute. Now, all I want is for you to get better, do you hear me?'

'Mother I'm sorry, I don't want to hurt you and Father and as soon as I'm able I'll leave – Mary said I could go and stay with her.'

'Leave!!' said Ruth. 'After putting me through this, I wouldn't let you out of my sight. Do you think I want my grandchild born with strangers?'

'Och Mother,' sighed Laura. 'The shame would be too much for Father. You know what he's like, he wouldn't be able to face the neighbours.'

'Och neighbours be dammed!' declared Ruth.

Laura was speechless at her mother cursing.

'Don't look at me like that, I'm human too you know. Haven't I lived with your father for nearly thirty-five years? You just let me deal with him. He'll rant and rave but remember, his bark is worse than his bite.'

Laura smiled.

'You certainly have got stronger these past few years. You know Mother, coming out with everything that night was the best thing you ever did.'

'Och, I suppose I kept quiet too long, always afraid of speaking my mind. But it was you, Laura, that I got my courage from. I listened to you tell your father a few home truths that night and I knew that it was time for me to speak out. Sure it *was* the best thing I ever did, your father and I get on much better now. You can see that too, can't you?'

Laura tried to move but the effort was too much. Her mother was concerned.

'Are you in pain love, will I call the nurse? She's just down the ward.'

'No, no I'm fine, it's just that I can't move this side too well. I'm still very stiff and I don't think there's much more they can do. They've put my leg in plaster, right up my thigh. Look at the state of me!' she said, pulling back the bedcover to reveal her well-plastered leg.

Laura's mother hurriedly tidied the cover back again.

'Now you must be careful love, I don't want you to catch a chill on top of everything else.'

Laura sighed deeply.

'If I did catch a chill it might lead to something worse. Maybe that would end my wee problem, eh?'

'Och, don't talk stupid now, I'm worried sick as it is. That fall could have done untold damage. I'm going to see that doctor that's attending you to find out more. I mean, that broken leg is going to cause you problems, I'm sure of it.'

'I don't want to be a burden to anyone either and it looks like I'm going to be here till they give me the all-clear but what happens when it's time to go home?'

Ruth propped up her daughter's pillows.

'We'll worry about that when the time comes, you just do everything your told, young lady.'

Laura laughed.

'Mother that's a wonderful turn of phrase, for someone in my position isn't it? "Young lady", I can't see many people calling me a lady, never mind young, can you?'

Ruth took her daughter's hand.

'Well at least if I have done nothing else for you, I've cheered you up – it's good to hear you laughing.'

'Och I'm just thinking, me walking around the village and some of the church elders meeting me with, "Good morning young lady", that would be funny, wouldn't it? Especially when my bump will be very noticeable.'

'Laura, you're terrible really but I'm glad you're like this. What do we care what people say? The only important person is you and this wee baby you're carrying.'

'Thanks Mother, I'm glad to have you on my side but now I've got to meet Father and I'm not looking forward to that. Did he drive you in? Where is he?'

'Your father's been just as worried as I have. Sometimes he may not show it as you know but when he stood at your bedside the other night you should have seen the look on his face, Laura. You were at death's door lying there, hardly breathing, it was awful! He just sat with me, looking so lost… Don't worry about him, he won't reject you or the child, I know it. Sure we didn't sleep a wink that night.'

'Och Mother, I know I've let you down but I got a big shock too. Sure it was Mary who made me face up to it. I couldn't believe it – just goes to show you how naïve I am. Imagine, nearly thirty years old and didn't know I was pregnant.'

Ruth looked very uncomfortable.

'You don't have to talk about it, that's your private business. I mean, you and Andy, sure it was only natural, after all, you were together a long time. Things have changed since my day – then it was marriage or nothing.'

Laura's expression changed, tears appeared.

'No Mother, things haven't changed. It's bad behaviour that's the same, and the woman always pays the highest price. That bastard used me and left me to face the consequences. And as for our Belle...' Laura paused, 'she's welcome to his arrogant ways, for I don't think he'll ever change.

Ruth sighed.

'Are you really over him Laura? I don't want you eaten up with jealousy, it wouldn't do you any good. There's a better life for you, I'm sure of it.'

'Oh Mother, I can just see the queues of men waiting to propose to me! I'm a fallen woman now, just like Sadie Carr from the mill cottage. Hasn't she three children now?'

'Och stop talking nonsense child. You are not the first girl to fall but you have breeding and character. Sure God help some of them girls, they got no start in life at all.'

'Have I Mother, even after all this? What about the church? I'm sure the Reverend Whylie will organise his sermon next Sunday to suit the parable of Mary Magdalene, the fallen woman of the Gospel. He doesn't like me very much anyway. As I said before, I didn't want to hurt you or Father and I will go away to have this child if that's what he wants.'

Ruth by now was visibly upset.

'Hush child, there will be no talk of you leaving, enough of my family have gone and that's the end of it. Now I'm going out to find your father or he'll think that they have admitted me too.'

'Who's getting admitted now?'

William was standing at the end of the bed. Ruth turned towards him.

'William, I'm sorry, I meant to call you in sooner but Laura and I had a lot to talk about.'

'Och, no difference there. Sure isn't that what you women do all the time. Now how's the patient?'

He came over and took Laura's hand.

'I'm fine Father, or I will be in a few weeks when I'm walking again.'

There was an embarrassed silence between them, broken when the nurse arrived with the medicine trolley. She told William and Ruth that it was time for Laura to rest. Laura could see the relief on her father's face. Her mother asked if she could speak to the doctor and was advised to wait until the next day as the doctor was busy in the labour ward. They said goodbye to her, her mother lingering on with a worried look on her face. Laura waved them both out with a bright smile. She didn't want her mother to know that she was very concerned for this unborn child she was carrying. The irritable feeling in her abdomen was still gnawing away at her. She prayed a silent prayer for God to forgive her and let this baby within her have a healthy life.

CHAPTER 30

THE NEXT FEW WEEKS flew by, tests and more tests. The doctor was worried about Laura's continual blood loss and she was losing weight. Finally, in her sixth month of the pregnancy, she was declared to be over the crisis but she was still very delicate. Every time her parents came to see her, she could feel their concern and she saw their delight when they were told she was out of danger. All she needed now was plenty of rest and the right diet. Her friend Mary was great as usual, as were all the McCanns. Laura was worried about leaving Violet Wray in the lurch but she needn't have, as Peter proved a wonderful nurse as well as sharing the running of the shop with Sandra Moore. Violet was progressing well and moving around. Laura received a vast collection of 'get well' cards, messages and flowers and was thrilled. Because of her weakness, she was only allowed visits from her family and close friends. She was glad of the reprieve – it gave her time to think more about her future and what she should do. She wasn't going to run away she decided, now that the baby was confirmed safe. She would have it here in the hospital. The doctor attending her had been wonderful and introduced her to the staff of the maternity unit. She would have to attend it now every week but she had made her decision. Laura would miss having Mary at the birth but she knew it was for the best.

'But remember my girl, I'm first for godmother, whether you want me or not. Did they tell you what you were going to have?'

'Oh Mary, I don't want to know. Whatever it is, I'm going to love it to bits. I just wish it were coming now, I'm getting fed up in here. I know they're doing their best but I'd love to be able to climb into my own bed.'

'Well you won't be climbing anywhere for a while,' said Mary. 'That plaster won't be coming off for a few weeks yet, so stairs are out of the question. Where do you intend sleeping?'

'My mother has already arranged all that, she's had one of the farm hands bring down a bed from upstairs and put it up in the sitting room. Knowing Mother, everything will be just perfect.'

'Och, I was talking to her at Wray's shop yesterday. I can't believe the change in her, she looks great, no sign of the invalid now. I know your predicament isn't what you would have wanted but you need attention – she's in her element! She was in getting your favourite magazines.'

'Yes she is looking great,' replied Laura. 'Maybe I was keeping her down too much but I was worried that she would overdo it.'

'Well it's nice that she feels needed. You know she looks years younger as well, I like her new hairdo and I told her so. She was telling me she has it the same way for years. Now with that new cut you can see how beautiful and natural it is. God I'd love natural curls like that. Look at mine, dead straight, I can't do anything with it.'

'Och, she has lovely hair. Do you know her secret? She collects the rainwater from the barrel at the side of the house uses it for rinsing, it gives it a lovely shine, doesn't it? Look at the state of mine, it's so dry, I can't wait till I get to the hairdresser's.'

'Now that's what I like to hear, you taking an interest in yourself. Oh, you're really on the mend girl. If you're like this in the hospital, God help the men when you get out.'

'Well, chance would be a fine thing regarding the men. They're the last thing on my mind,' Laura laughed.

'Well I have to go, I'll call in tomorrow before I leave. I'm taking the twins and wee Bridgin to the pictures tonight. She wants to come and see you when you are allowed visitors, will that be alright?'

'Of course Mary. And tell Peter thanks for the lovely flowers, I'm looking forward to seeing him.'

The next three weeks were full of anxiety for Laura and her parents. Several times she thought she was losing the baby, she felt drained. The doctors and nurses were kindness itself. Being in hospital so long made her realise just how hard they worked, and such long hours. Today she was seeing a gynaecologist about her problems. She'd hardly slept a wink last night with the worry. She began to think that this was God's punishment and if she lost the baby that maybe it was for the best. But she prayed for God's mercy and asked for his forgiveness and promised that she would be the best mother that ever give birth. It was another two days before she knew that God had answered her – she was given the all clear by her doctor. Laura reacted by bursting into tears. Her mother was delighted. Her father just stood at the bottom of the bed unable to speak. How did he feel? Was he pleased that everything was fine or was he still embarrassed? A few weeks later she found out.

Laura had been home for two days and things were working out fine. Her bedroom was lovely, newly decorated with white wallpaper with tiny rosebuds all over it and new pink curtains to match her bedspread. Some of the heavy furniture had been moved out and stored in the barn. She was going to have the plaster on her leg for another few weeks, so stairs would be out of the question. Her back was still very tender so she was fortunate that they still had an outside toilet. She looked around her cosy bedroom – her mother had worked wonders! She could imagine the arguments it must have caused with her father, who hated change, but it was great that her mother was now more assertive – she looked a new woman.

Laura was just finishing dressing when she heard a car pull up on the street and her father's voice welcoming the Reverend Whylie and his wife. This was all she needed! Of all the visitors she'd had while in hospital, they were the worst, with their patronising smiles and their bunch of limp daffodils. They had called one day while Peter was there. She really enjoyed his visits, he made her laugh, keeping her up-to-date with the goings-on in the village. He'd been telling her about Big John O'Brien getting stuck in the door of the outside privy and putting his foot through it. The pair of them, heads close together were in stitches laughing when the Reverend and his wife appeared, giving Peter a very disapproving stare. Peter offered Mrs Whylie his chair and then left, saying he would call again soon. Mrs Whylie forced a smile, nearly cracking her face. She said she didn't think it very advisable for Peter to be seen visiting, in the circumstances.

'Some people will come to the wrong conclusion. You know how gossip starts, my dear.'

Laura didn't feel like an argument but felt an answer was called for.

'I'm quite sure the gossips are enjoying all this but then you'd wonder where they get their information from, wouldn't you?'

That shut her up. The Whylies had stayed for about fifteen minutes, which was still too long. They said they were bringing good wishes from the whole congregation and if there was anything she needed, she only had to ask. After that, they tried to make polite conversation – Laura had been exhausted by the time they left.

Now here they were again! Laura supposed they meant well but they just got on her nerves. Her mother came in to ask if she was coming out or would she rather that the Whylies came in to her. Laura was up and dressed, so they sat in the kitchen while her mother prepared tea for them all. Laura felt terrible, unable to help. The talk finally came round to her plans for the future. Daphne Whylie put her hand on Laura's and asked where she intended having the baby.

'I don't expect you will want to stay around here when it's near your time.'

Laura's father looked sheepishly over at his wife, who was handing out the tea things. Ruth put down the plate with the fruit cake on it.

'Well now Mrs Whylie, that's for Laura to decide', she said and, looking directly at her husband she added, 'William and I agree that whatever she wants to do it will be fine with us, isn't that right William?'

'Och, whatever she wants to do,' he replied. 'Sure doesn't she do it anyway, always very headstrong.'

The Reverend Whylie put his cup and saucer down on the table and addressed William.

'Yes, yes, that's all very well but we must remember that we have a duty to the Church not to cause any more gossip than necessary,' and turning to Laura, he continued, 'I'm quite sure, Laura, that you don't want to hurt your parents by flaunting yourself around the village. It would be better if you stayed quiet until your confinement, don't you agree?'

Laura avoided his gaze as she slowly finished her tea and put the empty cup back on it's saucer. There was an awkward silence and Laura could see Daphne Whylie looking at her husband anxiously.

'Laura dear, don't take this the wrong way but we have a solution to your delicate problem, now if you just listen we'll...'

Daphne didn't get to finish. Ruth, who was usually so reserved and quiet, surprised the company by interrupting.

'Mrs Whylie, I expect you mean well but it's not your problem. Can't you see Laura prefers to make her own plans, after all she is a grown woman. After what we have gone through in this family, nothing anyone can say will hurt our feelings. If the gossips are annoying you I'm sorry, there's nothing we can do about it.'

Laura had never loved her mother more than she did just then but the look of surprise on the faces of the other three made her want to laugh. The next shock was her father's statement.

'Reverend and Mrs Whylie, I know you mean well and as you know I've always respected you and tried to live up to the Church's teachings but this matter with Laura is her concern. Ruth and I will respect her wishes, whatever they are. I do hope you understand, we wouldn't like to offend you.'

Flustered, Reverend Whylie put his cup and saucer down.

'William, as I said before we don't want to intrude on family maters but this,' he began to get very red in the face, 'this is somewhat different as I'm sure you'll agree. I... I mean we, thought our suggestion would be of valuable help to you. As I said, you are an upstanding family and so very well respected by all our congregation.'

Everyone could see he was struggling. Daphne, as ever the faithful wife, came to the rescue.

'Laura dear, what we have in mind is a wonderful idea and it would solve all your problems. Why don't you just listen?'

All this time Laura never said a word, her mother giving her the odd anxious glance. Now she put on her best smile, looked directly at the minister and asked.

'So, tell us, what exactly is this great idea that you have designed for me? Not another companion's job for your dear sister, I trust. I don't think I'm the right client for that job, especially now,' she said, patting her swelling stomach. 'I wouldn't be able to run up and down the stairs to answer her every need. I hope we are agreed on that.'

Daphne was getting embarrassed.

'Now there is no need to bring that up. I realise that I was wrong to suggest it but this is different.'

Ruth began to clear away some of the tea things. She smiled at Daphne as she removed a plate from in front of her.

'Aren't you great, always thinking of someone else when you have enough troubles of your own. And sure doesn't every family have them? None of us get off scot-free, not even you'

William and Laura stared at this usually quiet woman. The two guests looked aghast at each other. There was another prolonged silence. Reverend Whylie smiled weakly.

'Oh, er, yes, you must mean our Simon. There have been rumours I expect, not always the right ones. Yes, well, he is taking some time off from his studies. He found it wasn't what he wanted so he will probably change his direction. You know how young people are.'

Ruth looked directly at him.

'Well, you know what the gossips are like, especially in this place. I heard that his mind was made up for him by the dean of the college – he didn't approve of Simon's behaviour. You know what young boys are like, too fond of the girls and the drinking and not enough time for the study, isn't that right? Sure it must be an awful worry to both of you. And here you are trying to sort our Laura's life out, sure you're great, the both of you.'

The Reverend tried to placate matters.

'Ruth, I'm surprised at you listening to gossips, it's not like you. And as you say we are only trying to do our duty by offering our help and knowledge to your family.'

Ruth smiled at him again.

'I know that, and of course we are grateful to you but as we said before, it's Laura's choice where she wants to have her child and that's an end to it. Now if you don't mind I think it's time for her to lie down again. Nurse Conlon is calling shortly to check on her.'

She helped her daughter to her feet and guided her back to the safety of the bedroom. Their guests stood up and said it was time they were leaving as they had other parish calls to make. But before they left, Daphne gave William a letter saying that maybe when they'd had time to think it all through this would be of some help. William took the letter and saw them to the door and out to the yard where their car was parked. He stood for a long time looking down the lane after they had driven off.

Ruth and Laura were sitting on the bed in fits of laughter, neither of them could speak for ages. Finally, Laura looked at her mother.

'Well you're the dark horse, aren't you? How did you find out about *our Simon*?'

Her mother, still laughing, told her that she had been down in Wray's shop when Violet asked her to come in for a cuppa.

'I was waiting for your father anyway, so I did. While we were there she left the door open so she could speak to Sandra Moore if she needed anything, so we couldn't help overhearing Sandra talking to her friend Lucy Boyd. You know Lucy, she works a few days a week in the vicarage. Well, Lucy was telling her all about Simon Whylie being 'sent down', as they say. Why don't they say expelled, isn't it the same? Anyway the Reverend and Daphne were rowing all day with him. Apparently he's very fond of the drink and the dean discovered that he brought girls to his room for parties. The church is paying a fortune for his education. He had been warned several times but he never heeded it. So there you have it, they're just the same as the rest of us.'

Laura laughed with her.

'Yes, human!'

They were still discussing it when her father came in and handed her the letter.

'Here, they gave me that for you, I don't know what's in it.'

She took the letter and opened it. Her parents were about to leave but she asked them to stay till she read it, it was from the matron of a private clinic in Rostrevor, Co. Down, and run by the church. They look after sick and retired clergy and offered a home for girls like herself who were awaiting confinement. There was a house on the grounds for delivery and after-care. They offered adoption and fostering services and she could help pay for her keep by working at the clinic. The letter told of a waiting list of good families looking to adopt and many more offering foster-care while the mother decided on her future. If she would like to visit, there was counselling available but it was advisable that intending visitors should book early for a place. After reading it aloud, she handed the letter back to her father.

'Here, maybe you could return this when you see the Whylie's again, I don't have need of it.'

Ruth put her arms around her.

'Don't worry love, as we said, whatever you decide.'

Laura told them that she didn't want to embarrass them any further.

'We never talked about this but I never stopped thinking about it and I know it must be hard for you both, especially you Father, with your commitment to the church. Regardless of what you just said to Reverend Whylie, I'll do whatever you want. I can go to Belfast as soon as my leg is better. Mary had offered me a home with her for as long as I need it and I can have the child in the hospital where she is. I don't mind. I honestly don't know what I'm going to do after it's born but I will never give it up for adoption, I know that.'

Ruth's arm tightened around her.

'Laura, we don't want you to leave, we need you here and I know that we will love that wee baby when it arrives. There will always be a home here, sure it will be great having a wee'un around the place again, won't it William?'

Laura looked over at her father. He sat holding the letter, not answering for a while. Then she saw tears flowing from his eyes. He pulled out his handkerchief and wiped them dry. Then he stood up and holding the letter aloft, he tore it to pieces.

'This is not for us. This is where you should be, here at home. Maybe it will be a boy and sure I could always do with another man around here, couldn't I?'

CHAPTER 31

THE NEXT FEW MONTHS flew by and Laura was on the mend. She was off the crutches and driving again. She felt great and the doctor was pleased with her. It was a wonderful summer, the weather was at it's best. She walked down to the river most days and watched the children playing in the shallow water, she loved the sound of their excitement. The McCann twins were always there – sometimes she would take them back to the shop with her and treat them to lollies or ice-cream. Violet Wray continued her recovery. She was now walking without any aid and was able to use her left hand a little. Her speech was slurred but she was greatly improved. There wasn't much work to do in the shop now, just the books and goods invoices and some other minor chores. Laura helped out in the shop to cover lunch breaks and such. Sandra Moore was an excellent worker and Laura had found another young woman to work part-time. Peter's ironwork was becoming very sought-after and he was now taking orders for fences and gates. In his spare time, he was still creating some wonderful pieces of art, forever on the look-out for exhibitions. He was a wonderful friend, and had called most evenings while she was recuperating. When Laura was well enough, he would take her out for drives. He used to laugh, telling her that he loved giving the gossips something to talk about.

Mary came up from Belfast often – she was still worried about her parents. Her mother was terribly failed and there was no any laughter in the house. Her father never went out to the pub any more. He walked the roads on his own most evenings, his wife unable to join him. Winnie's loss was felt very strongly and they had to contend with the impending trial of Robert Wray and the two Belfast women who had performed the awful abortion. The one good thing about it was that this dreadful death had made the law clamp down on the illegal houses where abortions were performed – as a result there were a lot of arrests. Violet Wray refused to contact Robert in any way, even though he sent her a letter every week – they were sent back unopened and she applied for a divorce.

Today Laura was taking her mother and Violet out to the seaside, they were in great spirits. Ruth had packed a picnic and Violet provided the cool drinks and the cakes. Laura gave them a choice of places to visit. Her mother suggested Portrush or Bangor, two places she had always wanted to visit but had never got the chance.

'I remember when the children were small there was a trip to Bangor organised by the church, I was looking forward to it for weeks. I made you and Betty matching gingham sun-dresses in red and myself a navy dirndl skirt and a white sleeveless blouse. Sam got new shorts and your father bought you all new white sandals. Belle was just a baby and we were leaving her with Mrs Boyd, who used to live at the end of our lane. Her husband was working for us then. You know, it's like yesterday.'

Laura stopped preparing the food and looked at her,

'What happened? Why didn't you go?'

'Och, didn't Belle develop tonsillitis during the night. Her throat swelled up we had to get the doctor. Sure I couldn't leave her and that was that.'

Laura thought to herself, Belle again, always ready to throw a spanner into the works. She looked back to her mother, she was in a thoughtful mood.

'You know I remember those gingham dresses, they were lovely. We had a great time that day. I think it was the very first time that we had been to the seaside and we gathered big shells for you and Belle. Sam got sick all over Father on the way home in the bus. Were there no more trips after that, I don't remember'

Ruth packed the food in the big wicker basket and added the cups and glasses.

'No, there weren't any more trips organised by this parish. The bishop put a stop to outings after that.'

Laura stopped what she was doing,

'Surely the bishop couldn't find anything wrong with families enjoying a day out at the seaside. What did the minister do?'

Her mother went very quiet, finally saying:

'There was nothing he could do. He left the parish shortly after that. I never knew what happened and of course your father would never discuss church business with me.'

'So there were no more outings, that was mean wasn't it? All those children never getting to the sea. I remember us all going by train to Belfast to visit the zoo and Belle screaming when she saw the lions. That's the only family outing I can remember. But sure we will make up for it now, we'll have a great day tomorrow in Bangor. The weather forecast is good so get out your swimming suit, Mother,' she laughed as she patted her swollen belly.

'Wouldn't I look well in a swimsuit, that would surely cause talk,' Ruth smiled at her.

'That's plenty of food, sure you have enough there for an army. It's a pity Father wouldn't come with us.'

'You know I've never been out with your father for a day, not even a picnic by the lake, isn't that something? All these years and we never went anywhere together.'

'I suppose he was always busy on the farm, he didn't have the time,' said Laura, trying to make excuses for him.

'I think it was the way he was brought up. As far as his auld mother was concerned, an outing would only be a waste of time and money. Sure we never even went to town together like most farmers' wives did. He went on the tractor to the market and I went on my bike, we didn't even meet up. I'd see him there, of course but he was always with the men and once I had my eggs and chickens sold I had to hurry home again. Sure didn't I have you lot to see to? I can tell you now but I used to envy you and Andy going away together for the day, wishing I could go too, just to get away from here for a few hours.'

Ruth sighed, looking into the distance. Laura watched her mother with a feeling of sadness as she covered the filled basket with a new tea towel.

'There, all ready.'

'Mother, I promise you I will make up for all your lost outings. By the time were finished, you'll be exhausted. Right, I'm away to have a bath, then bed. Remember, we're starting out early tomorrow.'

A hazy early-morning sun welcomed Laura as she drew open the bedroom curtains and gazed out at the scene before her. Her father, always an early riser, was herding the cattle up to the top field helped by their dog, Shep. She watched till he was out of sight beyond the trees. Mother's flowers were in full bloom in the yard below, their perfume wafting into the bedroom. Through the trees she could just see part of the lake. As she watched, some swans flew over and landed one after the other. They were a sight to see with their wide wingspan, long necks and feet tucked up behind. A mist lay over the water and the graceful birds disappeared into it. Looking at this peaceful scene, she wondered how anyone could live in a big city with the constant noise of heavy traffic and all the soot and smog. Looking up at the sky with the sun getting stronger, she thanked God for her life.

She reached out to close the window a little when she suddenly felt a strong movement. Her baby gave such a kick she nearly fell backwards. She sat on the bed, with both hands feeling its movements. She had felt slight sensations before but this was different, this was her own flesh and blood telling her it was alive! She wrapped her arms around her stomach, feeling she was already cuddling it. Another strong kick nearly took her breath away. My own darling baby, I can't wait until you are born, you will be the best loved baby ever. Oh Andy, you don't know what you're missing. She wondered then what would it look like, blonde and blue-eyed like Andy or dark like herself. Sitting there holding herself she thought, did my mother feel like this when we were coming? Or had she time to sit and dream like this? Knowing her mother's gentle nature, she felt that she would have found the time. She spoke to her own baby now, told him what she hoped for him in his life and other endearments. She was brought out of her dreaming by the sound of her mother's voice telling her that breakfast was on the table.

The day in Bangor was a great success. She sun was shining, the town was crowded with holiday-makers and day-trippers like themselves but Laura quickly found a place to park, while Violet and Ruth looked at the shops. Later on they moved up to Ballyholm and found a place for their picnic. The two older women had a great time and they got along well. They were sitting under the shade of the trees in their folding chairs and Violet was telling them of previous visits she had made here. Once when she and Robert were courting, they came for the day and he spent most of it persuading her to let him book into a hotel for a few hours but she held her ground and steadfastly refused. She had loved Robert then but they had never ventured further than kissing. She knew he wanted more than that. When he asked her that day, sitting on the rocks, she was tempted but afraid of the consequences. What would her mother think of her if she got pregnant? It would kill her. Suddenly she realised what she had said.

'Oh Laura forgive me, I wouldn't for all the world hurt your feelings and I'm sorry Ruth, it's just came out. Oh, me and my big mouth!'

'Will you stop, how could you hurt my feelings, don't be daft. Anyway, I was enjoying your story. So Robert didn't seduce you and he married a virgin, eh?'

Violet smiled.

'Yes, that's the way it was in those days. My mother always told me, "Don't blot your copybook". Sure I didn't even understand what she meant until I got older but if you pardon me for repeating it, she said that well brought-up girls never blotted their copybooks. I suppose it was her way of giving me a quick lesson in sex education because nobody talked of things like sex in my day. It wasn't only the girls that needed talking to, sure didn't well brought up boys behave badly too. Do you remember the outings the church used to have? I think the last one was to Portrush.'

Ruth nodded.

'I was just telling Laura about that very outing last night.'

'Did you tell her why there wasn't any more? It was an awful embarrassment then, wasn't it?' said Violet.

Laura saw the two women looking at each other.

'I didn't even know the whole story,' said Ruth. 'Remember, I wasn't even on that outing and, of course, William would never talk about it.'

'Will you for goodness sake put me out of my misery and tell me what happened that was so awful,' smiled Laura.

'Well, we had a new curate young, very good-looking. The girls were all mad about him but he was engaged to the Bishop's niece and planning to get married in autumn. I saw her once when she was visiting. She played the organ for the choir, nice girl but very plain, hadn't much to say for herself if I remember.'

'Oh I do remember her,' said Ruth, 'she helped out at the church sale. The old minister introduced her to me. You're right, she hadn't much to say, I think she just nodded.'

'Will you pair please get to the point, you're driving me crazy waiting to hear what happened,' said Laura.

'Alright,' smiled Violet, 'just wait, I'm coming to it. I'm trying to remember her name, what's this she was called, do you remember, Ruth?'

Ruth thought for a while then she laughed:

'I do, a strange name, didn't it remind me of our dog, Brownie. Her name was Bronwyn Boyd, it was a name I never heard before, a nice name though, wasn't it?'

Laura was totally exasperated at this stage.

'Well,' continued Violet, looking at Laura, 'Bronwyn came along that day to help with the children and gave the parents some time to enjoy themselves. We had arranged to have a picnic on the beach at a certain time but no one could find Bronwyn or the new school-teacher, Richard Beatty. Everyone searched for ages, it was very worrying.'

Laura couldn't wait.

'Did they fall into the sea, where were they? Who found them?'

'Will you wait, I'm coming to that! Well, one of the older children was very quiet and didn't help with the search. Finally his father got him to talk. He said he'd been with the missing pair earlier but they had chased him back when he wanted to go over to the rocks with them. He was annoyed, that's why he wouldn't tell. After a long search and with the help of the police, they found them in one of the small caves – the tide had come in and cut them off!'

'So they were found. Sure there's no harm then, that could happen to anyone when they go exploring,' said Laura.

'Och but that wasn't the end of it,' said Violet with a sly smile.

'You mean there's more, well come on, tell me, don't keep me in any more suspense,' said Laura.

'As I said, the police were called in to help. Next thing there was an ambulance as well. Some of us women went over to see if we could help. Weren't the police carrying the bold Bronwyn out, covered in a small blanket, she hadn't another stitch of clothes on her! You should have seen the minister's face, not to mention the young curate. After her came Richard Beatty, trying to cover himself with a hankie and him blue with the cold.'

Laura nearly exploded.

'Oh my God, they were naked! What about their clothes, why didn't they have them?'

'Where do you think they were, the tide washed them away. They had other things on their mind. I suppose they just didn't realise how fast the tide moves.'

Ruth sat watching Violet, her face cracking up in smiles.

'So *that's* why William wouldn't tell me! Wasn't he always praising young Richard Beatty and how proud his family were of him. Didn't he even say that he was an example to all young men,' she burst out laughing. 'I can't believe it. What happened to the pair of them after that episode?'

'Well, naturally they didn't travel back with us. I'm not sure how they went but we were told by old Reverend Patton that we must not speak of it to anyone and he would come down very heavily on anyone that did. You remember Reverend Patton,

Ruth, he was a strong man where the church was concerned. Goodness knows what he would have done to anyone who broke his word. So no one did, that I recall.'

'What about Bronwyn and Richard, what happened to them, did she marry him?' enquired Laura.

'Well, Richard didn't even stay another night in the village. His parents were devastated, and him an only child. I think he went to England and his family moved over there too. As for Bronwyn, she was never seen around here after that and the new curate was sent to another parish some where. I never heard of him again. But there was no more outings ever allowed again. The only thing we have now is the parish picnics and they're always held near the village, no travelling anywhere.'

Laura looked at her mother.

'Can you imagine what the Reverend Patton would think of me? I'd probably be banished forever to a workhouse some where. Isn't that what they used to do to girls like me years ago?'

'Och that's right,' answered her mother, 'women had it very hard years ago. Indeed some are still suffering the stigma of illegitimacy and they're not always, as you say Violet, from very poor families. Sure anyone can slip, can't they Violet?'

Laura watched the two wise women and then broke the silence, joking:

'I'm glad, that you aren't going to send me to a workhouse, Mother, sure wouldn't I miss all this,' she said, spreading her arms wide and breathing in the sea air. 'Come on let's pack up and go back to the beach, I want to cool these swollen feet in the water.'

They paddled in the water, waves lapping around their feet. She could see her mother was really having a great time. They gathered shells, Ruth wanted some to put around her garden, and they watched the children running in and out of the water, screaming when a big cold wave washed over them. Finally, they had another look around the shops and bought some silly souvenirs. Before heading for home, they sat on the wall at the Pickie Pool eating large cones of ice-cream. Laura had never seen her mother look so well. The seaside had brought her colour up and her curly auburn hair was tossed by the breeze. She was wearing the new lilac short-sleeved suit that Laura had made her buy and it really suited her, she looked years younger! Violet was like a teenager in a lemon shirt-waister dress and white sandals. It was hard to tell her age but Laura knew that she was forty-eight, ten years younger than her mother. The only difference lately was that Violet's stroke had caused her lovely jet black hair to turn almost white but somehow it suited her. No one was in a hurry to leave and Laura promised that it was only the beginning of many trips out. They were just heading into the village as the dark red sun was setting over the spire of the church.

The birth of her son was almost too sudden, for he had decided to arrive early. He was due late in August and Laura was getting more and more excited. She was feeling great but her doctor insisted that she report every week for her check-up. She had given up driving and her father would take her into town if she needed to go. They had been in that morning for things she needed for her confinement and she had put all the necessary items in her suitcase. Everything else was being stored in Robinson's shop – she didn't want them around until the baby came. They went to the shop to see the cot and pram she had chosen and was delighted and surprised to find that her father had them both paid for. She had only left a deposit but he insisted on getting them for her.

Laura was making the evening meal. Her mother was out in the garden and her father was in the back kitchen washing his hands when he heard the crash. He rushed in and Laura was trying to sit on the couch, the tray with plates and food all lying on the floor. She told him to call the ambulance, as the pain she was having was very severe. While he was on the phone her waters broke. She couldn't believe it, it was too soon, too soon! Her mother came rushing in when she heard her husband's anxious shout. She managed to help Laura to lie down. She tried to get comfortable but the pain kept coming, she knew then it was time and told her parents. The next pain she had her son popped out, bawling his little head off. Her father took charge. Calmly, he cut her umbilical cord – he'd had the presence of mind to put the knife into the kettle of boiling water on the range and had washed his hands. Her mother was crying as she wrapped her new grandson in a fresh towel and handed him to Laura. She knew she was a mess, as the placenta from the birth was still coming but with the state of euphoria she was in, she couldn't care less. She was holding her son. A perfect specimen. He was beautiful still bawling and she was so emotional. A mother can never explain that moment to anyone, only she can experience it. Her father's tears fell on her as he bent over to kiss this little wonder. You could see he was bursting with pride. Her mother sat beside her, wiping the sweat from her forehead and patting her cheeks.

'Oh Laura, I just can't believe it, a lovely wee boy and delivered by us. Och William, isn't he just lovely.'

Her father nodded in agreement, unable to speak. Ruth got busy and began cleaning up the mess. Afterwards she emerged from the kitchen with a tray of tea for them all. Laura's father cleaned up the spilt food and went upstairs and brought down a rug to cover her. They were sitting enjoying the tea when the ambulance arrived.

She only stayed in hospital for two days. She was in great form and was shown how to bath and feed the baby. Now here she was back at home. The amount of baby things her mother produced overwhelmed her. She had new baby clothes, blankets, everything she would need. Standing proudly in the corner was a magnificent Silver Cross pram – silver chrome and navy with large wheels and dressed all in blue, covers and pillows to match.

'Father,' she cried, 'what have you done? This is not the one we left over, it's too much! Thank you both, I'm delighted.'

Her father went over and wheeled the pram towards her.

'There's nothing good enough for my grandson and it was your mother that chose it.'

Laura smiled her thanks to her mother. Ruth was laughing:

'Would you look at him, he never wheeled a pram in his life before and you would think he was doing it for years, he's a real natural isn't he?'

Laura looked at the baby lying peacefully in her arms.

'By the way, Father,' she said, 'the doctor at the hospital had great praise for your expertise on cutting the cord. He said you did an excellent job and he didn't have anything more to do.'

'And sure why wouldn't I?' he said. 'Haven't I been doing the same all my life with the cattle, it's just the same. Now I think it's time you took a wee rest, I'm away out. By the way, I've got two cattle about to calve soon, do you want to come and help me?' Laughing, he went out into the yard and back to his chores.

Laura had another surprise when she went up to the bedroom, it was completely redecorated with curtains, bedspread, and a lovely new rug on the floor, all in shades of blue. But the biggest surprise was the cot, not the one she chose but a magnificent white wood on detachable rockers with a pale blue chiffon canopy, and all the bedding she would require.

'Och Mother, it's lovely but you are too good to me, I don't deserve it. It's just beautiful,' she said. 'What about the name, do you like it?'

Her mother looked down at the baby.

'We are both thrilled! William Alan Steenson, it sounds great doesn't it, something very regal about it.'

Laura smiled and looked at her sleeping son and reached over and kissed him.

'Yes, it sounds just right. Welcome home, William Alan.'

The next few weeks flew by with most of the McCann family calling or sending her presents for the baby. Mary arrived the weekend after he was born. She walked around carrying the baby, cooing and singing to him.

'Oh you are so beautiful and so content. You know that you have a lovely mother, don't you? I'm your Auntie Mary and I'm going to be your fairy godmother because anytime in the future, when your mother says no, you just come to me and I'll say yes.'

She laid him back in his pram again and pushed it gently to and fro.

'I can't believe he's here and he came into the world without a bit of bother. How did you do it? Seven and a half pounds of human being. Oh he's gorgeous, he really is and your parents can't stop talking about him. Didn't I tell you things would work out alright?'

'I know you did and they have been great. Father keeps looking into the pram at him when he's asleep and my mother, sure she can't do enough for me, they have me spoiled.'

Mary was still staring at the baby.

'I called in to see Patrick's new baby on the way here. Och, he's lovely too but so tiny. God love Sheila, she had a hard time delivering, nearly two days in labour. She was ill a lot of the time during her pregnancy. Little Niall is still only five and a half pounds. They have to feed him every two hours on a special formula but I was holding him and he's very sturdy. He's coming on fine but Patrick and Sheila are that worried.'

'I was talking to your mother last week, the baby was still in hospital. It will be great for them, their first grandchild and he is just two weeks older then mine. Maybe they will be friends like we were, eh? How long are you staying? We have to arrange the christening soon and I want to know when it would suit you. I know by the sound of things that you are kept very busy – is there no end to these troubles at all?'

Mary sat at the table beside her while Laura poured out fresh tea.

'I can't see it, every night there's at least four badly burned. Last Saturday night I had eight admissions all with bad burns. Yusef has asked for more help for our unit we are all overworked as it is. The big problem is still there, not enough room to nurse the victims and to let them recuperate so we just make do. It's great to get away from the smell if nothing else but maybe someday we'll get something bigger. Now, are we going out for that walk? I want to wheel this lovely pram.'

Baby Alan was thriving. The weather kept up that summer which meant that Laura was able to take him outside a lot, but today was going to be his first visit into the village. Laura had arranged to meet with Reverend Whylie to finalise the christening. She had decided on a quiet service next Sunday afternoon. She had taken the baby for walks as far as the pathway to the lake, the opposite direction from the village but she decided that she would walk as far as the vicarage today. She might leave the pram and get her father to pick her up afterwards at Wray's. It was a good two miles and she knew she wouldn't be able for the return journey as it was mostly uphill. It was just as well that the pram was well sprung, for she realised after that first walk with Mary the laneway was not the easiest place to wheel it. The rains last winter had left tracks nearly a foot deep in places but it was great once she was on the main road – about a mile from town the footpath began. She smiled into the depths of this luxurious pram at her darling son. He really was well-behaved. Lying in his little blue smocked romper suit and bootees knitted by his grandma, he looked adorable. She had almost reached the footpath and was delighted that there wasn't much traffic, when this little bright green two-seater car raced by, driven by a young fair-haired man. Suddenly it screeched to a stop and reversed back to where she was. She nearly died when the driver hopped out over the door and came over to her – it was David Carson, Andy's young brother.

'Laura, Laura!' he cried, 'I thought it was you, how are you? But I shouldn't ask, you look great. I know I should have called to see you but I didn't know if I would be welcome or not.'

Laura flustered, didn't know what to say.

'Er... I'm fine David, as you can see, and yourself? You're looking great as well. I like the car better then the bike, eh. You must have got sense.'

'Yes, maybe I did. Dad didn't like me on the motorbike so I talked him into getting me this little beauty, an MG sports, great isn't it? Andy always wanted one like this, in red.'

'Och, it's really nifty. How are your father and Martha keeping? Well, I hope, like yourself. I didn't like to phone because I wasn't sure how I would be accepted, I hope he understands,' she said, wheeling the pram backwards and forwards.

'Laura you know my Dad and Martha liked you a lot, same as me. I always said you were far too good for that selfish bugger, didn't I?'

David sat on the bonnet of the car. He did look well, more grown up.

'Dad is doing well, we're running things together and getting on great. I suppose it's because I don't have big brother telling me what to do and Martha is about to get married to her minister so she's happy but what about you? It was terrible what he did. We never knew a thing. Dad was devastated for ages but now, as I said, he's great. But you must have suffered something awful from the shock, how did you cope at all?'

'Well David, as you said it was an awful shock. I had no idea, especially with my own sister but life goes on. I had my parents to think about as well. Like your father, they were devastated.'

'Well I expect your family hear from Belle and how they are doing, especially with her being pregnant. I believe it's expected next month. They seem to like Ontario, he's in the property business buying all around him.'

Laura hadn't enquired about Belle though she knew that her mother had received a few letters. She was saved from having to answer by David's next question but again unable to reply when he asked her if she was baby-minding. He looked into the pram and smiled at the baby, not realising that Alan was his nephew.

'He's a lovely wee fellow isn't he? But that's something that you won't catch me worrying about. Them wee babies are time enough when you are well over thirty, aren't they? Now I have to rush, heavy date in the city tonight with a lovely wee nurse. Maybe I'll see you sometime, I'll tell my Dad and Martha I met you. Bye.'

She had no time to talk and she was glad as she watched David jump into the car and speed off. The meeting left her very flustered. Seeing David like that took her unawares because she really hadn't thought out how she would approach the subject of the baby. Should she tell them or not and she didn't ask her mother if she had told Belle yet. It was something that she didn't bring up but knowing her mother she would want to talk about it soon. And the news that Belle was expecting, was she pregnant when she left? Laura wouldn't be surprised if she had been, sure they must have been having sex as well. The baby moved around and she adjusted the light cover and the sun canopy. Looking in at him, knowing he was the spitting image of his father, she stroked his cheek gently and whispered:

'It doesn't matter if he owns all Canada, he will never own you You're mine and mine alone till you're old enough to make up your own mind,' she smiled. 'My beautiful Alan.'

She had decided that she would call him Alan rather than William. Her father agreed. Yes, he said, keep it simple.

The reception she received at the vicarage was cool but efficient. Daphne Whylie didn't appear at all and Laura was delighted. Reverend Whylie showed her the text of the service and asked if she wanted anything else included. She did, Laura had chosen prayers to incorporate her parents. When asked about godparents, she informed him that Violet Wray and Mary were her choice – she could see that he wasn't very pleased when she mentioned Mary.

'I hope your friend understands what being a godparent entails,' he said, 'that they must undertake to see that the child is brought up in the true faith. This might prove difficult as your friend is of a different persuasion.'

'I don't think that will be a problem. Mary is a very good Christian, surely that's the most important factor. Aren't we all equal in the eyes of God?' she said.

'Yes, yes, that's true of course but having your friend as godparent may not be a very sensible thing to do,' he said, rubbing his hands as if worried.

'Not having her as a godparent? Is there some where in our teaching that tells us that because she is a Roman Catholic she can't be? I never heard of it.'

'No, not really, it's usually left to the discretion of the minister like myself, you understand.'

Laura was getting angry.

'Are you telling me that you don't approve of her because of her religion, I can't believe I'm hearing this.'

Laura began to wheel the pram towards the door of the study but she was halted by the minister.

'No, I didn't say that.'

Laura looked at him, he was red in the face.

'Well what do you mean? I'm getting tired of all this pussy-footing and interference in my life, if you don't want to christen my baby just say so. I can go elsewhere, you know. Are you still annoyed at me for not leaving and having my baby some where you have chosen?'

'No, I'm just trying to do what's best for everyone,' he answered.

'Best for you and the bigoted members of the church you mean? I've had enough, I'm going.'

She pulled open the door just as Daphne was crossing the hall carrying the remains of tea things on a tray.

'Oh Laura, hello how are you? The baby is well, I trust.'

Laura had the pram in the hall. Neither Reverend Whylie or his wife looked at the baby. He came up behind her putting his hand on her arm to detain her.

'Laura please don't go like this. I'm sorry if I upset you, I didn't mean to but I did have my reasons.'

'Reasons?' said Laura, 'What reason could you possible have to refuse to christen my baby because of my choice of godmother?'

'It's her morals, I....'

He didn't get any further, Laura turned on him.

'Morals, Mary! How can you talk of her like that?'

'Please,' he said pleading, 'Listen to me, she is living in sin with that African doctor. How could she give any child an example of a good standing in life, living like that? I'm surprised that your parents are agreeing to it. Remember, we must think of the welfare of the child.'

Laura tried hard to keep her anger under control.

'I think you have a very selective memory, what about the big christening party not too long ago for a certain church elder's baby grandaughter? Everyone knowing there's no way that her husband could be the father after his dreadful accident? You couldn't miss the baby's lovely red hair. He's the spitting image of a certain councillor she was having an affair with and he's a Catholic I believe.'

'Oh dear me, Laura, you really surprise me. I didn't think that you would mention horrible gossip like that. I don't know what to say, I really don't.'

His face was getting redder by the minute. Laura stared at him.

'I didn't think that I would repeat that sort of gossip either but you have driven me to it with this holier-than-thou attitude.'

She had the pram out on the avenue but again he stopped her and surprised her with his next words.

'Laura I'm very sorry if I upset you but I thought I should bring the subject up. Please forgive me but I must follow my Christian duty. Of course I'll christen the baby, now let's discuss your plans.'

Reluctantly Laura listened to him explaining how the service would go and what she had to do. She managed to get away as quickly as she could but she was still fuming when she crossed the wide street and went into Wray's sitting room.

It was time for the baby's feed. Violet propped the cushions up around her while she fed him and was amazed at how Laura took to all this mothering.

'I can't believe I'm watching you feeding your baby. You really amaze me and I'm going to tell you something else. I've never in all my life saw a woman breast-feed. You look so content sitting there, it's times like this that I wish I was able to have children. He's a lovely little fellow and now he's about to be christened.'

'Aye, and only just. That minister really made me angry with his high-and-mighty attitude.'

'Why,' said Violet, 'what did he say, was he being awkward?'

Laura then related all that took place between them to a shocked Violet.

'Well isn't he the right hypocrite after that sham that took place a few months ago over Elder Simpson's daughter? Sure the whole village knew who the child's real father was and then he took over the church hall for a celebration! I thought that was totally uncalled for. And the style of the people that was invited, sure I sat here in the window watching them arrive, you would have thought that they were going to a fancy wedding.'

'I remember you telling me about Mrs Simpson's hat with all the feathers. You would have thought that an auld black crow had landed on her head and died, that's what you said! Didn't I tell my mother about it. Violet, she laughed that loud you would have heard her all the way over here!'

Laura changed the baby to her other breast.

'You know,' she said, 'he really annoyed me when he spoke of Mary that way. Sure there's not a better Christian walking this earth than her and she's totally dedicated to her patients. And he doesn't like her morals! I should have told him to mind his own bloody business, after all Mary's private life is none of his concern, is it?'

'No, you're right, it's not. Now are you nearly ready for a wee cup of tea?' said Violet. 'Anyway, maybe you got the Reverend on a bad day, last Sunday gave him a lot of annoyance.'

'Why,' said Laura, 'What happened? Mother and I didn't go but Father said nothing when he came home but then he wouldn't anyway.'

'Well,' said Violet, 'I suppose to some of us it was very funny but not to the Reverend. As you know, it was Communion Sunday and the church was packed. I was sitting up near the front beside the choir stall, so I saw it all,' she began to smile.

'Well,' said Laura, rubbing the baby's back to bring up his wind, 'what did happen?'

'You know Davy Scott the wee cobbler, him with the club foot?' asked Violet.

'Of course,' said Laura. 'Sure isn't he always drunk. I'm waiting months to get my shoes off him.'

'Well,' said Violet, 'he only goes to church now and again and he's always boggin'. I'll swear he must be wearing the same clothes since his poor mother died. Last Sunday he didn't look too bad. Some of the church ladies gave him some clean clothes but then he rarely washes himself so it was a waste of time. He had the hair all plastered down and the shirt was white. Anyway, wasn't the minister always at him to attend church more often but he said he wouldn't like to embarrass him because his clothes wasn't suitable. That's why the Women's Circle got him good ones. Anyway, he was sitting across from me with his face washed and his greasy hair plastered across one side of his head, smiling at anyone who would look at him. And him with only three teeth! I tried to avoid him but it wasn't easy.'

'That's good isn't it? At least he went to church,' said Laura. 'Why was the minister angry, was he not pleased that he went at all?'

Violet laughed again.

'No, no, it wasn't that but when it came to communion time he was first up for the sacred wine and after he got it he pulled at the Reverend's vestments. You won't believe what he said. "Och, will ye fill it up again, sure I love my Jesus," that's what he said! Well, you should have seen the Reverend's face, he was purple with rage.'

'Oh Lord above,' said Laura, 'it must have been great to see the look on some of the faces. Father never said a word and he must have been sitting in his usual pew near wee Davy. What happened after that?'

'Oh it was awful, most of the congregation saw the whole thing. Sure they couldn't keep their faces straight but you could see most of the older ones were disgusted. Then the verger and one of the elders took the poor wee man out into the vestry.'

Laura laughed.

'I expect he won't be allowed back into the church again. Did the minister say anything about it?'

'Yes, of course he did,' said Violet. 'He went up unto the pulpit after communion and spoke for ages on the evils of drink and how it can reduce you to something like we had just witnessed. I never saw him so angry. He asked us all to pray for

Davy that he would be converted away from alcohol forever and that we shouldn't discuss what had happened ever again.'

'That must have caused a bit of a stir, I expect that's all the people talked about outside the church,' Laura laughed.

'Well now, you know why he wasn't in great form. When you saw him today, sure he hardly spoke to anyone after the service. He made his excuses and took Daphne's arm and flew over to the vicarage,' said Violet. 'Now come on, the kettle's ready, I'm sure your dying for tea.'

Laura changed the baby and let Violet nurse him while she freshened up. Afterwards they took a walk out in the village. Violet wanted to wheel the pram. They were met by a lot of inquisitive stares but most of the people that knew Laura from the shop were genuine in their good wishes for her and the baby. They went down as far as the bridge and rested there for a while, enjoying the cool breeze under the shade of the trees. There were a few children playing at the water's edge. The younger McCann twins, Johnny and Joey, and their friends came up the bank to look at the baby, the little girls wanting a chance to wheel the lovely pram. Violet was surprised when Laura told them that the baby's name was Alan.

'I thought you were going to call him William,' said Johnny.

'I was but I liked the name Alan better, anyway one William in my family is quite enough,' said Laura.

On the way back they called to McCann's and Peggy came out to see the baby. Laura looked at this frail little woman – she must have lost over two stone in weight, she had aged so much since Winnie's death.

'Well, God love him, isn't he just lovely,' said Peggy. 'The size o' him, wouldn' he make two of our Pat's wee Niall. How's he keepin'? Mary said he wasn't feedin' too well but that wee child's the picture o' health. Ye look great yerself, Laura.'

'He's doing great now, it just took a bit of time for me to get used to feeding him. He's a great wee fellow. What about your new grandson, he's a lot better now, isn't he?'

Mrs McCann smiled.

'Och he's doin' the best and puttin' on plenty o' weight. An' yer wee man is bein' christened on Sunday? Our Mary's that excited ye would think it was her own. I'm lookin' forward to the day when she's a mother but God knows when that'll be.'

The three of them chatted for a few minutes. Laura asked if she would like to come up on Sunday for tea with the rest of them. Peggy thanked her but told her she wasn't ready to go out yet. They were just arriving at the shop when Laura's father pulled up to take her and the baby home.

CHAPTER 32

LAURA, WITH ALAN IN HER ARMS, waved goodbye to her guests. It had been a lovely day, the christening went well. There were a few busybodys still sitting in the church after the regular service was over but she knew when she saw them that they were only there to look for gossip and it didn't bother her. One or two of them came over to speak to her father. Mary proudly carried William Alan in his beautiful christening robe, a family heirloom. Ironically, the last one to wear it had been Belle. The baby looked so content. Violet Wray was beaming fit to burst – it was the first time anyone had ever asked her to be a godparent and she looked great in a pale blue linen suit and matching hat. Laura's mother wore her best navy suit, standing with her arm linked into her husband's. They were smiling proudly at their lovely grandson.

Yusef, Mary's fiancé, brought more colour to the occasion, wearing traditional robes from Senegal, blues and a vivid orange. He looked so handsome standing beside Peter and the twins, Johnny and Joey, who were staring around them in wonderment. They had never been inside a Protestant church before and were asking Peter in loud whispers where were the statues and why weren't there any candles. Peter hushed them to be quiet. Mary wore a lovely floral dress of pale pastels and a big straw hat. Laura had chosen a cream linen suit with a full-length skirt and a little lace confection for her hair. She looked around her guests and smiled a big 'thank you' to them all. Just then the Reverend Whylie entered, accompanied by his wife Daphne. It surprised Laura to see her there, after Daphne's coldness when she had visited the manse.

As expected, Alan roared the place down when the cold water was generously poured over him. Laura wondered if the Reverend Whylie's generosity was designed to make sure that the baby was well and truly christened. The ceremony was short and the party followed the minister out of the church into the wonderful warm September sunshine. A few people had gathered to wish the new baby well and indeed some came with lovely presents – this surprised and delighted Laura. Some of them were children who were customers in the shop. She showed the baby off and thanked them for their kindness. Yusef had a camera and took some pictures with the grandparents and then Laura with the godparents. Her father invited Reverend Whylie to stand in for one with them. Laura noticed that Daphne had left the happy scene, no doubt disgusted at the goings-on and frivolity at an illegitimate's christening.

Myrtle and Jim Brooks had prepared everything during their absence at church. The big kitchen table was laid outside and every chair available placed here and there in the yard. Laura laid the baby in his pram and helped serve the wonderful meal and the festivities went on well into the evening. She noticed her father engaged in a long conversation with Yusef. The twins ate everything in sight but were generally well-behaved. Myrtle had worked wonders, the christening cake was a marvel of white with blue icing spelling out 'William Alan' and the date. Of course her desserts were something else and there was high praise for her skills.

Now they were all gone and Laura was exhilarated but exhausted. Mary had helped Myrtle and Jim clear up so there was nothing left to do. Laura's parents were inspecting the wonderful presents the baby had received, not just the lovely clothes but the more lasting ones. Violet Wray had opened a bank account in his name and her card said that every birthday would be remembered with more. Mary had done something similar, a bursary for his education. Her parents' present was the two large fields adjoining the McClean estate. Laura was speechless, claiming it was too much but her father told her:

'Wasn't it all going to be his anyway and he may as well start to be a landowner now.'

Laura thanked them both. Yes, a landowner, just like his father, she thought to herself. She looked at the peaceful sleeping baby. He would never know the despair he had caused her, the worries about her health and her parents' acceptance of him. She need not have worried, her health was great and her parents were both thrilled with this little wonder. She could see he would be spoiled if she didn't keep a firm hand, which she intended to do.

CHAPTER 33

LAURA KEPT HER WORD. She could hardly believe it, Alan was ten today. He was a wonderful, well-adjusted boy and very loving. He had his moments like most children and would try every trick in the book to get his own way when he wanted something. But generally he listened and was almost always well-behaved. She sat in their haven of a garden that had matured into a glorious collection of colours and textures. Now in early September, the roses were at their best. Her mother had carefully designed three diamond-shaped rose-beds in reds, pinks, white and yellows. Underneath she had planted shrubs of lavender. Laura sighed.

'Oh Mother, I do miss you so much. I feel so close to you, here in this place you loved.'

She walked around, touching and smelling the plants and flowers, remembering when they were chosen and the craic when they had planted them, her father's sarcastic remarks. She knew deep down he really enjoyed the finished result. Laura had loved to see the two of them sitting there on a good evening, in silent companionship when the sun was high. Her mother would sit knitting under the trees while watching Alan asleep in his pram. When he was older, they fenced of a portion of the lawn for him to play on. Ruth and William took care of him when Laura had to work at the shop.

Before she knew it, it was his first day at school. Her mother insisted on coming with her and Laura was surprised when she heard Ruth asking various questions from the young teacher. The Model School wasn't very big, only four classrooms. It was at the back of the church, surrounded by a stone wall. Her mother was worried that the gate didn't close properly, maybe some of the little children would find it easy to get out. She was assured by this young girl that it couldn't happen as the children were watched all the time. They needn't have worried about Alan, he left them standing there and was already playing with the other children he knew from Sunday School. He brought over a little girl called Alice and a boy called Derek to introduce them. Laura and her mother stood at the gate with other anxious mothers, a bit longer than necessary just in case. When they met him that afternoon he was full of the joys of his first day and asked could he call at his friends Niall's house to see if he enjoyed his first day as well? Niall was Pat McCann's son and they had been best friends since they could talk. And so they got into a routine. She would leave him into school every morning and after school he would come into the shop and sometimes stay there or go and play with Niall at his house until it was time to go home. On special days, her father would take him into town to the cattle fair. They were great friends. In the evening they would tramp the fields together and sometimes they would walk as far as the lough. At weekends Niall would come with them. Laura was glad that Alan and her father got on so well, it made her mother's death easier for William.

Ruth's death was so sudden that none of them could come to terms with it for ages. It was just after Christmas. Alan was seven. The house had been full of people and laughter on Christmas day when Violet joined them for the traditional fare. They'd had a big Christmas dinner every year since Alan was born and on Boxing Day they invited their special friends. Mary and Yusef were married now but they didn't have any children but his younger brother and sister, who had been living with them since their father had died, were there. They were both studying medicine at the College of Surgeons in Dublin, two wonderful young people. Peter was there with young Niall, his nephew, and Myrtle and Jim Brooks.

Laura's mother was in great form. She loved having guests and had never looked so well. They played games and for the first time there was dancing in her house. Just a few old time waltzes and the Hokey Cokey and some Irish jigs played by Peter on his accordion but there never was a happier group. Mary invited Laura up to Belfast to celebrate the New Year with them and she was excited at the thought of it. She had bought a new dress and was looking forward to wearing it. She was going to stay for a few days and to go to the New Year sales in the big stores. Alan was content to stay at home with his loving grandparents and to help his Auntie Violet in the shop. It was early on the morning before New Year's Eve. She had planned to travel up the next day to the city so she had a lot of preparation to do before she left and she was busy in the kitchen. Her father was already out at the milking. Laura put on her last wash in the washing machine and had the breakfast ready when her father came in with Jim Brooks. She called Alan and he came running downstairs, shouting excitedly:

'Mum, Mum, I can't waken Grandma!'

Laura took the stairs two at a time with her father following. Ruth was lying as if asleep but Laura knew she was dead. The cup of tea which her father had brought up to her sat untouched. She was so peaceful-looking. Her father stood beside Laura, numb with shock. Finally he moved over to hold his dead wife's face in his hands, tears flowing from his tired eyes. Alan held on to his mother.

'Mum, is Grandma dead? I couldn't get her to answer me, will she go to heaven now? Miss Burton at Sunday School told us that last week.'

Laura was secretly glad that Miss Burton had taken that particular burden off her shoulders, she held her son tightly.

'Yes love, Grandma is going to heaven.'

The three of them stood there silently for a few minutes, looking at this gentle woman. Jim and Myrtle came quietly into the room.

'I've taken the liberty of phoning for the doctor, I hope I did right?' asked Jim.

'Yes, thank you Jim,' Laura answered, 'it had to be done. It's just the shock, she was in such good form lately. Her health seemed to be fine, she never complained of anything being wrong.'

Myrtle stood sobbing quietly at the doorway and they were still there when Dr Lawson arrived. None of them knew what to do. The next two days went quickly with friends and neighbours calling day and night. Laura wanted Alan to stay at Niall's house but he cried and refused to leave his Mum and his Granda. He never left William's side, sitting with him and holding his hand. Now and again Laura caught him staring at her father with a concerned look. He seemed to think that if he let his grandfather out of his sight, he would die too. Her heart went out to her little son. He was so confused when the undertakers were carrying her mother's coffin out to the church. Loudly he enquired why couldn't they put Grandma out in the garden beside the roses, she would like it much better there. He cried bitter tears at the graveyard, he didn't want his Grandma left in the ground all by herself. Laura had quite a job persuading him to come home. He did but only because she promised that they would come back before bedtime.

Later that evening, just as it was getting dark, the three of them stood at the graveside and looked at the mountain of flowers. Alan pulled his favourite teddy bear, Tufty, out from his coat and gently placed it on the grave.

'Now Tufty, I want you to look after Grandma and don't let her be lonely.'

Laura held on tightly to her father, they were overcome with emotion.

CHAPER 34

LIFE AROUND THE HOUSE and farm went back to its regular routine. Chores had to be done and the animals had to be seen to but it wasn't the same, there was too much silence. Out of respect, the radio and television were not used. Laura only spent a few hours at the shop in the mornings when she left Alan to school and before he left home he called over to the graveyard to talk to his Grandma and Tufty. Laura was worried about her father. He seemed to have lost interest in everything and he wasn't eating, so she insisted that the doctor look at him. It had been over a month since her mother's death. It so happened that Alan was up in the fields with Jim Brooks and another farm hand when Dr Lawson called but he saw the car turning in the yard from the top of the field. Jim told her afterwards that Alan flew down the hill as if he had wings, shouting:

'Granda, Granda!'

He ran into the house. His Granda was being examined by the doctor and he flew into William's arms crying:

'Oh don't you die too Granda, Mum and I need you!'

It nearly broke Laura's heart watching him. She went over and gently took him back, explaining that the doctor only wanted to check his Granda's heart, that he was fine. She was delighted when the doctor assured them that he really was fine and would live for a long time yet.

'Providing that he eats properly and takes his walks.'

Dr Lawson talked to Alan.

'Now young man, the eating has to be your Granda's problem but the walking will be yours. You will see that he walks with you every day when it's fine. We wouldn't want the pair of you to get wet and end up with colds, now would we?'

Alan nodded in agreement.

'Oh don't worry Doctor, I'll look after him, I'm a big boy now.'

Laura was so proud of him, he looked so manly and she felt so guilty that she hadn't explained properly about the doctor's visit. He was growing up so fast.

She saw the doctor out and watched her two men settle down to watch television. She had a mountain of letters to answer, they were piled up on the table in the sittingroom. Right on top were the letters and telegrams from Betty and Sam, so she decided that they were top of the list. As Betty and Sam were living in different parts of the country, she sent them both telegrams announcing their mother's death. She didn't send one to Belle as she expected her father to do that. The replies from New Zealand were there next day but none of them were returning home. She didn't expect them to either. They had made good lives for themselves and by the news in their regular letters they were doing well.

Sam and Anne had two little girls now and he was a partner now in the hardware business with his sister Betty and her husband. They had opened two more branches of their hardware shops and managing them took up a lot of time with all the travelling they had to do. When Laura had cancelled her original plans to travel and told them why, they had both been wonderful with their love and support. They wanted her to come and make a new life for herself and the child in New Zealand, money was no problem. She was very grateful to them both and told them so but when news of her pregnancy had been happily accepted by her family, she knew she had done the right thing in staying at home. Betty and Sam were very generous with gifts for herself and Alan. She didn't want to accept anything but they insisted, they sent Christmas and birthday gifts, some wonderful Maori artwork and two massive sheepskin rugs last year. Betty told her that there was a cure for back pain in the rugs, so she kept them on her parents' armchairs. In the last letter from Sam, he was asking her if she fancied a holiday with them. He painted a glorious picture of Auckland and sent photos of them all having a Christmas picnic on the beach beside their spacious home. She was very tempted but said that she would wait until Alan was a little older before she would travel. Betty's last letter was asking for them all to come out – she saw no reason why her father wouldn't visit if his health was up to it. Laura read the letter again and looked at the photos she had sent with it. Betty was looking years younger, very tanned, wearing white shorts and a strappy top, holding Sam's baby girl, Tara, her husband Alastair beside her with his arms around her. They looked so well and Sam and his pretty wife Anne with their eldest child, Graine, sitting in the garden at the barbecue.

CHAPTER 35

LAURA STOOD AT THE BEDROOM window watching Jim and Myrtle Brooks walk hand-in-hand down the lane to their cottage. Such a godsend they had been to the family, coming into their lives just when they were most needed. They had come from Belfast in answer to an advertisement in the papers for the job of caretaker at the McClean estate. Laura had met them when they were looking for directions. She showed them where the entrance was, expecting Sam McKee, the land-steward, to be waiting for them but instead there was a young boy there to tell them that Sam had been delayed for an hour or more and that they were to wait. Laura could see that they were tired, so she invited them up to the farmhouse for tea. Her mother made them welcome and invited them to come back whenever they needed eggs or milk. They introduced themselves and said how much they were looking forward to living and working in the country. Jim had been working in a tyre factory where he had developed chest problems but he had a love of gardening and wanted to work outdoors. Myrtle had worked in a small, family-run bakery. They were both in their early forties and had no family. Over the next few weeks Laura got to know them very well. Myrtle proved not only to be a good friend but a great worker. They came to an arrangement that she would give them a few hours when they weren't working at the big house. There wasn't much to do there anyway, as it was occupied by a lawyer and his wife who only came at the weekends. They discovered that Myrtle was an excellent cook and her baking was top class – she spoiled them with her tarts and cakes. William was in his element, he loved sweet things, so life fell into a pattern and everyone was satisfied, Laura especially, with the baby coming. She knew that day wasn't for off – this child had her stomach kicked sideways.

All that was over ten years ago and Myrtle and Jim were almost part of the family now, Laura couldn't picture life without them. They were there for her parents and when she was ill, doing everything that was needed around the farm and house and when she took Alan home for the first time, sure they spoiled them rotten. Indeed there were times she felt very guilty with all the attention, it didn't seem right somehow. There she was, treated like a queen, despite having just produced an illegitimate child. But she never held her head in shame as she supposed she might have done, or behaved like the church would expect her to. At least it got the Reverend Whylie and his wife out of her life. They didn't come calling, not once since Alan was christened, and if her father was annoyed he never said. They visited when her mother died but they were very quiet and didn't talk much. There was a new young minister in the parish now, as the Whylies had retired to England.

She looked around the garden. The evening sun was just about to set, giving the whole countryside a gown of orangey-red, time to go in. As she rose, she saw her father and son returning from the fields. Alan, as usual, was full of chat. She watched him walking beside William, the two of them with stout sticks. Alan saw her and shouted excitedly.

'Mum, Mum! Big Daisy is almost ready for calving, can I stay up and help Granda and Jim? Can I, can I? Sure I don't have school tomorrow.'

Laura saw her father nodding in agreement. She smiled and ruffled her son's blond curls as he pulled away.

'Mum, can I help, please?'

Laura smiled.

'Of course you can, if your grandfather says yes. I suppose you'll have to learn sometime, didn't you tell us you want to be a vet?'

Alan looked up at her with a very serious face.

'Well, I want to be a vet, yes, but I want to have my own farm as well. So how do you think I'm going to manage that?'

She laughed.

'Well, you have great ambition, haven't you? But I imagine that with hard work you will get one thing or another. Now come on, it's supper time, then a wee rest and Granda will call you if Daisy starts, alright?'

They removed their Wellingtons at the door, with her father asking if there was any of Myrtle's apple tart left for supper.

Laura assured him there was plenty.

'I was just sitting there in the garden, Father, thinking of the first time we met Jim and Myrtle. You know it was just a month before Alan was born.'

'Och, sure the time has flew. Look at him now, a big ten-year-old and thinks he knows it all!' he laughed. 'Just like you were when you were his age, just the same.'

After supper Alan lay down on the couch and Laura covered him with a blanket and before she finished clearing the table, he was sound asleep. Her father said he would call him when the time came. She said goodnight and left to have a bath. She promised Mary she would spend next weekend in Belfast – she hadn't been now for nearly a month. As she lay in her aromatic bath, she thought of her bleak social life. It was almost non-existent now but whose fault was that? No one but hers. She did have her chances these last few years, she had to admit that but she had her responsibilities as well. She smiled to herself now as she remembered her last big love, Ian.

CHAPTER 36

1968

LAURA HAD MET IAN nearly five years ago. She had been at one of the hospital dances with Mary, Yusef and some new friends she'd made through Mary. They were all connected in some way to the Royal Victoria Hospital. Mary introduced them. Ian was new to the crowd and had been working in England these last few years. Now he was head laboratory technician. He was interested in the effects of burns on the skin and was hoping to develop a safe medication to help the unfortunate victims of severe burning. She found him fascinating. Ian was very handsome, tall with dark hair peppered with grey, which gave him a very distinguished look. He paid her a lot of attention and was a very skilled dancer. At the end of the evening he joined Laura. He had already asked if she would stay on for a while but she didn't feel that she should. He pleaded with her so she compromised. She had to go home the following day but she agreed she would go out to dinner with him the week after.

So began her relationship with Ian Telford. They met every month after that, going to the theatre, the cinema, or just walking. She loved going up to Cave Hill to sit looking down at the lights of busy Belfast. They would usually end the outing with a few drinks in one of their favourite little pubs.

It was on their third date that she finally agreed to stay over at his flat. They had been out for a meal at a new restaurant down by the river. It was all very romantic, he chose a table with a waterside view and gave her a single red rose. She felt loved and protected by this wonderful man. She had no secrets from him, on their second date she told him about her son Alan and her parents. He said he was divorced from his wife, June. They had no children. It was by mutual agreement and she was now married to someone who had been in the background for sometime. He blamed himself for the split – in the early days of the marriage he was struggling to achieve something special in his work, so it meant he had to work very unsociable hours. He would insist that she still go out with her friends and she did. Eventually they were only meeting at odd weekends and so the inevitable happened.

'Now,' said Ian, 'that's all about me, the rest is an open book.'

She did enjoy his company, he had a great sense of humour as well. She told him she didn't want any commitments as she had to let her family come first. He agreed, he told her he felt the same about his work, so it worked out fine for both of them. Tonight he was very attentive and as they danced to Glen Miller's 'Moonlight Serenade', she knew she needed more. She felt quite sexually aroused dancing cheek-to-cheek with Ian. When the music ended he held her tightly and kissed her but they said nothing. She was unaware of the looks they were getting from the other dancers. She collected her bag, he paid the bill and they left. Outside he was able to get a waiting taxi for the short drive to his flat, kissing her all the way home.

Inside her apartment still no words were spoken, they just devoured each other. The first time the sex was animalist and hurried, the second was exciting as he made love to her in a way she never though possible. He explored every inch of her and when she did the same to him, she didn't feel in any way ashamed. Sex with Andy had never been like this, it was always *his* need, hardly any foreplay, more like, 'Brace yourself Laura, I'm coming!'

This man lying beside her was strong but she felt his touch so tender and caring. She lay now content, his strong arms enfolding her. She traced the outline of his face and moved down to his chest, hairless and smooth. He moved gently towards her, smiling, and began kissing her tenderly on every part of her face, his hands exploring her firm and wanting body. The lovemaking was slow, sensual and fulfilling. She awoke in the morning to the smell of fresh coffee. This was the first time she'd had breakfast with her lover. After that it was a regular occurrence, meeting once a month and keeping up a great friendship in between times.

After the first time with Ian, he had dropped Laura off at Mary's apartment. Mary hugged her with a welcome.

'Well girl, you look like the cat that's just finished all the cream. You don't have to say a word, it's written all over your face!'

Laura smiled at her.

'Good, I'm glad you don't want the details, it would take too long. Come on, I'm dying for tea and toast,' she laughed, as she made her way to the kitchen.

Her mother had noticed a change in her. They were folding the bed sheets, just off the washing line, and Laura was humming a popular tune. Ruth handed her the folded sheet.

'I've never seen you look so well, Laura. The past few months has put a great bloom in your cheeks, those wee trips you take to see your friend in the city are doing you the world of good. Even your father has noticed it and we think you have a secret boyfriend, have you?'

Laura looked at her.

'I can see that nothing escapes you and yes, I *am* feeling good. You're right, I have a boyfriend but that's just what he is, a friend. We like each other, he's very nice.'

Ruth smiled at her.

'Well, is that all your going to tell me?'

'Mother, there is nothing else to tell, no special romance. We go out places, sometimes on our own and sometimes with Mary and husband.'

Ruth wouldn't be put off.

'Well, do you think it will get serious? Maybe you should ask him to come up here to visit us.'

'No mother, that's out of the question. I don't think I'll be inviting him home.'

'Why? Don't tell me he is a big-shot doctor and you are ashamed of us,' her mother turned away, hurt.

Laura held her.

'No mother, I would never be ashamed of my family or home. Ian is a lab technician and a good friend of Mary's, that's all.'

She went back to folding the laundry.

'Laura, he's not married is he?' asked Ruth, tentatively, ' Is that the reason?'

Laura was beginning to feel sorry for telling her mother anything.

'No Mother, he is not married. He was but now he is divorced, no family, no commitments, only his work. Are you satisfied? There's no romance, I just like him. Remember, Alan is my life, he always comes first.'

Ruth stopped folding and put the laundry down.

'Laura I'm sorry, I don't mean to be nosy but you are a lovely young girl and I don't want what has happened in the past putting you off finding a nice man. You weren't meant to live your life alone, don't shut yourself off.'

'Mother, I'm not shutting myself off. I go out with my friends, I'm always meeting new people, Mary sees to that. And Ian just happens to be one of them. You mustn't worry about my social life, I'm enjoying every minute of it. I don't need a man full-time in it.'

'Well, as long as you know what your doing. I hope someday you'll meet someone that's worthy of you. Alan is over five now and he won't be a little boy forever.'

Laura repeated the whole scenario to Mary the following weekend. The sun was just setting as they sat in her picture window, which overlooked the Lagan.

'You know Laura, your mother's right, you need a man in your life. You get on so well with Ian, you could do worse, you know.'

'So now you're in the matchmaking business, are you?' laughed Laura. 'Look, Ian and I understand each other. We do get on great, I'm very fond of him and we both meet each other's needs but it can't go any further.'

'But why?' asked Mary. 'You can't live like a nun just because of Alan.'

'Mary, you should know, I'm certainly not living like a nun. I'm having a great time and so is Ian, and that's all there is. I don't know how long it's going to last.'

'Well, as long as you're happy and you know what you're doing. Come on,' said Mary, heading for the door, 'it's time for some serious retail therapy.'

The affair with Ian continued for almost ten months, they even managed a romantic weekend on the continent. He had heard it was her birthday and surprised her by asking her to come with him to Paris. When he told her, she was dumbfounded, there was no way she could go. She didn't even have a passport she told him and what about her parents? Ian held her to him.

'Now you're finding obstacles. Think this through before you decide.'

She looked at him.

'How? I can't go, Ian, and that's that.'

'About the passport,' he said, 'you told me you got one when you first decided to take a holiday. Even if it's out of date you can go to the office in the morning and ask for a cover note. The weekend is not for three weeks, so you will have a new one anyway in plenty of time.'

'I thought it took weeks for a passport to come back, are you sure?'

'Yes, I'm sure. Your parents know that you are seeing me, don't they?'

'Yes,' said Laura, 'they know we meet but that's all. I don't know how they will react when I tell them I want to go off for a weekend.'

'Just tell them the truth, that I'm taking you to Paris as a birthday treat. I don't see that they would object. From what you tell me, they sound a wonderful couple.'

'Oh Ian, they are, and so very understanding.'

'Well then, just ask them if they would look after Alan for the weekend. I can't imagine them saying no, not to you.'

They had been out for a lovely long lunch and were sitting curled up on his couch. It was springtime and the evenings were getting longer, so she was driving home later. She felt so content beside him, his fingers entwined with hers. She hadn't seen him for nearly a month and when she'd arrived at his apartment this morning, he was so pleased to see her. Within ten minutes they were in his bedroom making love. He was his usual attentive self, seeing to her every need. She explained she couldn't stay over and he said he understood. That's when he told her he had a surprise for her birthday but he would need her undivided attention for a whole weekend. Paris, she thought, I've always wanted to see that wonderful city but how will my parents take it? It was fine when she was just going to Belfast now and again and staying over sometimes but a full weekend, *and* flying to Paris? Oh she would love it! Ian moved towards her and, taking her face in his hands, he kissed her.

'Where were you? You were miles away, I hope your were thinking of me.'

Laura cuddled up to him,

'Have you been there before?' she asked.

'Yes, in my student days. I worked in a hospital there for the summer before I graduated. We had a wonderful time and I'll enjoy it even more showing it to you.'

Laura loved Paris and visiting all the tourist attractions. Ian was a great guide, he knew all the best restaurants and clubs. They walked hand-in-hand down the Champs Elysees, like all the other young lovers. It was the best birthday she ever had. They went shopping before they left and she bought presents for the family: Myrtle, Mary and Violet and, of course, something very special for Alan. She was surprised at how well her parents reacted – her mother was delighted when she told her.

'Oh, imagine you going to Paris! I've only read about it and seen pictures. It looks a grand place, don't forget to take your camera.'

'What's this about a camera?' said her father coming into the room.

Ruth turned.

'Och William, our Laura's is going to visit Paris with her friend Ian. What do you think of that?'

'Well I don't know, sure you can't speak French, how will you get on? I don't know why people want to visit a foreign country.'

Laura looked at her father.

'Look, if you don't want me to go I'll understand, it was just an idea.'

'Not want you to go, where did you get that notion? I'm just wondering how you're going to get on without knowing how to converse, that's all.'

Ruth held her hands up.

'Will you whisht man! Don't you watch television, don't you see them programs about France and other places? Sure they all speak English now. That won't be a problem for our Laura.'

'Och, I suppose you're right. He must be a very good friend to take you to some place like that. Is it serious between the pair of you or maybe I shouldn't ask?'

Laura looked across at her mother who was smiling behind her father's back.

'No father, it's not serious, he is just a good friend, I already told mother,' she laughed, 'maybe you want to get rid of me, do you?'

'Now we won't talk like that, you go and enjoy yourself.'

He left the room, muttering about these high fallutin' places. Ruth and Laura fell on the couch laughing.

Ian and Laura continued to see each other all summer and then the inevitable happened. Laura knew something was coming and that she wouldn't like it. They had been out that evening to the theatre, a wonderful musical at the Opera House. Ian was unusually quiet all evening. They came back to the apartment and he made coffee. When she asked him what was wrong, he took her in his arms and began to make love to her, coffee forgotten about. Afterwards he held her and told her how much he loved her and asked if she felt the same. For a long time she didn't reply. When he asked her again, she turned to him.

'Ian we agreed, we don't talk about love, don't ask me, please.'

He kissed her very tenderly.

'Laura, do you love me, I need to know?'

'Why Ian? This has been great, why spoil it? You know I can't answer you.'

'Laura please, tell me. I got some news last week, it's about my appointment, something I've worked for a long time. I'm leaving Belfast, I need you to come with me, please, please,' he pleaded.

Laura looked at him, shocked.

'No Ian, no, I don't want you to go! When?'

'At the beginning of next month, it's a job in Austria. I'll be leading a team of technicians and developing a new drug to treat burns. I've been working on it for months, I told you about it.'

'Oh Ian, I'm so happy for you! I know it's what you wanted.'

She put her arms around him.

'You're going to be very famous some day and I can always claim I was your friend, but Ian, I can't come with you. We went into this relationship with our eyes wide open and we both knew it would have to end.'

He held her and pleaded with her again.

'It won't be the same without you. I love you, Laura.'

For hours they debated on the whys and wherefores but she knew deep down it could never be. Laura turned away. She didn't want Ian to see her tears.

Mary and their friends had arranged an outing to the Europa Hotel, a meal together and then on to a nightclub. Laura and her friend had talked into the wee small hours the week before, about Laura's feelings. Mary knew how she felt about Ian – Laura admitted that she did love him and would miss him very much. She knew it wasn't to be but she was going to make the most of the farewell night. Yusef had explained to them how Ian was going to really be tied up with this new job, he wasn't going to have a lot of spare time.

'Laura, Ian has asked you to come over for a visit, why don't you do that? He doesn't want to break with you but he knows that he won't have a lot of time to himself in the first few months. Surely you understand how he's fixed.'

'I do Yusef, of course I do, but I've already told him it's better a clean break. I've no right to tie him down. I don't know when I'll be free, if ever.'

Mary sighed:

'You know something, you sound like a real martyr. I'll be taking out me fiddle next.'

'Och, will you stop slagging. I do feel bad but I can't help it. Do you not think I feel bad about missing him? I'm going to miss him more than he will miss me. Ah, and in more ways than one, if you know what I mean,' said Laura, laughing.

Mary hit her playfully with a cushion.

'Well, at least you won't die wondering.'

The weekend of the dinner arrived. All week she had been a bag of nerves. Her mother noticed that she wasn't herself. Violet was up at the house visiting. Her mother and Violet were planning on attending a Harvest Tea in the hall the following evening. They were joking with William and asking him if he would accompany them.

'Wouldn't we be the proudest women in the parish, sailing into the hall, one on each arm? We'd look great, wouldn't we?' laughed Ruth.

'Och, we'd be the envy of all the women there,' said Violet.

'Well, you're just going to have to want, aren't you, and find some other eejit. I'm away out to find Alan and Niall. I need some men to support me, there's too many women in this house.'

William left, shaking his head, with the women laughing in his wake. The two women continued discussing the plans for the harvest until they noticed that Laura's thoughts were elsewhere.

'Are you alright, Laura? You're miles away. I suppose you're looking forward to your party tomorrow night,' said Violet.

Laura had told them that there was a special celebration dinner in Belfast and she would be staying over.

'Is it for something special, did you buy a new dress?' enquired Violet.

'Bring your dress down and show it to Violet,' urged Ruth, 'it's really lovely. Why don't you try it on?'

'No mother, I won't try it on but I'll show it to you, Violet.'

She went up to her room and got the dress. She was glad to leave the kitchen for a while, she was feeling really down and wasn't in the mood tonight for any craic. Several times she wondered if she was doing the right thing, would she ever meet anyone like Ian? She didn't think so. Violet admired the black sheath dress cut with a plunging V-neckline, which Laura hoped wasn't too revealing. Mary had assured her it wasn't. She was holding the dress against her to show it off, when Violet produced a package with colourful wrapping.

'I was hoping you would be showing a wee bit of cleavage because this little birthday trinket needs that. Here love, Happy Birthday!'

Violet kissed her and gave her the package.

'Violet, what are you doing?'

Laura opened the package, tearing away the wrapping to reveal a long velvet-lined jewellery box containing a gold chain with wide links and a T-bar with a tiny garnet on the corner.

'Oh my goodness, Violet, it's beautiful!'

She put the necklace on, the gold feeling cool against her warm skin.

'Look mother, isn't it lovely? Violet, you're too good. Thank you, I love it!'

She kissed her friend and gave her a gentle hug. Her mother fingered the chain.

'It's really beautiful, looks good on you, Laura. Maybe it'll cheer you up, you've been looking very down.'

'I'm fine Mother, it's just,' she hesitated, 'it's just my friend Ian is leaving and I'm going to miss him. That's what the dinner is for. Ian is going to Austria to work in a special clinic, he has been waiting for this for ages. We're all very happy for him.'

Ruth gave Violet a very worried look.

'I'm sorry he's going, he has been a real tonic for you but sure maybe he will be home for a holiday.'

Ruth could see that Laura was upset. She didn't know what to say to her and was afraid to say the wrong thing.

Laura was glad when the tea was finally over and she took Alan up for his bath. He was full of chat tonight, he had been at Niall's after school. They were making masks for Hallowe'en and Niall's father, Pat, had helped them. Alan told Laura all about it.

'You know, Mum, Uncle Pat's great. He got us lovely coloured paper and he helped us use the glue. Mine is a monster and Niall's is the devil. His wee sister wanted a blue one and when we made her one she screamed the place down. Uncle Pat tried all sorts to keep her quiet. Was I like that when I was a baby, did I scream the house down?'

'You were the best baby there, sure you never cried.'

'Did I not, was I really good?' he asked.

'Yes, you were, once you had your teddy you never moved,' she said.

He looked at her with those big innocent blue eyes.

'Well, it's just as well I was quiet, wasn't it? Because I didn't have a Dad like Niall's sister has to walk me up and down when I did cry. Why didn't I?'

Laura had known that this would come one day but not today.

'Well Alan, it's a long story and when you're older I will tell you.'

'Oh Mum, why don't you tell me now instead of my bedtime story? Please, please, Mum, then I can tell Niall why.'

'Why do you want to tell Niall, did he ask you?'

'Not just Niall, some of my friends from school ask me and I don't know what to say. I do have a Dad, don't I?'

Laura lifted her son and brought him into his bedroom. While she was dressing him in his pyjamas, he continued to ask questions. She had contemplated the idea of telling him some story about his father being killed in a car crash but now it was time, what would she say? She had discussed this with her father and he said to tell no far-fetched tales, tell Alan the truth. She looked at Alan now, he was more like Andy every day. She got her hair-dryer and used it on his hair for just a minute. Normally she would take him downstairs to the fire and dry his hair there but then there was the problem of getting him to bed again. She put him into bed with Teddy Tucker beside him and covered him with his big blue quilt. It was patchwork with cars and horses on it. Then she lay down and took him in her arms.

'Are you going to tell me about my Dad?' he asked.

Maybe she could put him off for another few years, she thought. She lay holding this armful of sheer joy to her breast and thinking of how to begin. He snuggled in closer to her and held his face up to her with questioning eyes.

'I'm ready Mum, tell me about my Dad. Was he a soldier or what did he do, Mum?'

She told her son that they had been very much in love, one time but something happened, then he didn't love her any more and one day he just went away and never came back.

'But Mum, what about me, why didn't he take me? I'd like to travel, did he forget?'

'No Alan, he didn't forget, he didn't know about you. I didn't tell him, you see I didn't want to lose you.'

'Was I born then?' he asked.

'No, you weren't born, I didn't tell him that you were coming,' she hugged him lightly, 'I wanted you all to myself.'

'But will he come and see me sometime? What's his name?'

'His name is Andy or Andrew but he has his own family now. I don't want him to come and see you.'

'Did he not love me, is that why he went away?'

Laura's eyes were filling with tears, she could hardly find her voice to answer her.

'Alan, the reason you don't have a Dad is my fault. You see, your aunties and uncles had just left here to live far away and your Grandma and Granda were very lonely, so I couldn't leave them, so when your Dad left I stayed. I didn't tell him you were coming. I knew he wanted leave, do you understand?'

Alan's hand went up to her face and wiped her tears.

'Don't cry Mum, I don't want to make you cry. I don't need a Dad, don't I have Granda. Isn't he great, he told me about the time you and Auntie Mary got caught stealing apples from McClean's orchard. What did Granda do, was he cross?'

Laura sighed. Well that's that, and here was I, worried about what he would say! She began to tell him about her escapades with Mary and made him laugh. Before long he was sound asleep.

CHAPTER 37

THE CELEBRATION DINNER was a great success. Everyone was enjoying themselves, everyone, that is everyone but Ian and Laura. They were pretending, and both of them knew it. As the evening wore on, the crowd got merry. Earlier in the evening, Mary had told Laura that she and Yusef had booked a suite in the hotel for them so they could have a last evening of romance. Laura looked at her friends, embarrassed.

'Are you serious, a suite no less! Does Ian know?'

'Yes, I told him this morning. He acted the same as you, all embarrassed.'

'Well I am,' said Laura. 'I know that he had to give up his flat and he was staying with one of his friends. I thought that I would be staying with you tonight.'

Mary smiled.

'Sure I knew that you would need a bit more privacy than our flat. And it's a farewell present for Ian, he can have it for the next two nights before he leaves.'

'Well it's a lovely idea, thanks. I'll enjoy a night of luxury in this fabulous place,' said Laura.

'Is that all you will enjoy, what about dishy Ian? You are bad, you know, to let him slip through your hands. He'll have some big blonde Austrian girl in weeks, you'll see,' she laughed.

Laura sighed.

'You know, Mary, we had all this out before. I'd love to go with him, he knows that but it's not possible. Anyway, he is going to be very busy for the next few months.'

'Well, as long as you know what you're doing. Anyway, I hope you enjoy the evening,' said Mary.

Enjoy she did. They ate and danced the night away. She had great fun and a lot of teasing from Ian's friends but she took it all in good fun. Soon everyone was saying 'goodnight' and most of them 'goodbye' to Ian. He took her hand and led her into the bedroom, one of the most luxurious rooms she had ever seen. A large four-poster bed commanded the centre of the room, decorated in shades of blue and cream with rich tapestry curtains and wall-hangings. A deep pale-cream carpet covered the floor and all the furniture was in Queen Anne style. An ice-bucket with two bottles of champagne was on the coffee table, complete with delicate fluted glasses. Large candles burning in silver candlesticks created just the right ambience. A sittingroom and a very spacious bathroom completed the suite. Laura turned to Ian smiling:

'This is just perfect.'

He put his arms around her, holding her close.

'If this was a honeymoon suite it would be even better, wouldn't it?'

Laura looked up at him, puzzled.

'Ian don't do this to me, you know how I feel and I know it's the drink talking. If I was to say yes, we would both regret it tomorrow.'

He kissed her with a passion and whispered:

'Laura I love you, I've never felt like this before.'

She put her fingers up to his mouth.

'Shush, don't let's talk about it now.'

Their lovemaking was wonderful. He brought her to heights she never knew existed and afterwards they lay in each other's arms, drinking the champagne, feeling contented and sleepy. She was just dozing off when the building shuddered and the empty glasses fell to the floor. They were both out of bed and grabbing clothes. Laura quickly pulled on Ian's shirt, it was the first thing she found. Grabbing her bag and a sheet from the bed, he took her hand and led her out into the corridor. Alarms were going off and other guests were going in the same direction. Ian warned them away from the lifts and towards the stairs. They were on the sixth floor and by the time they reached the first landing another bigger tremor shook. As they watched, a large crack appeared in the wall opposite the stairway. People were rushing and screaming:

'Bomb! Bomb!'

Smoke was coming up the staircase to meet them, everyone was spluttering and coughing. Then a new hazard, dust, great clouds of it coming from everywhere. Ian and Laura and some other guests reached the third floor when they found two elderly people crouched in the corner. The woman was very distressed and trying to hold the man in an upright position. Other guests were rushing past, ignoring them. Ian ran to the man – you could see he was having a heart attack. Ian looked at Laura, who was consoling the woman.

'Laura we need to get him out fast, can you help? I'll take his head and shoulders if you could manage his feet.'

Laura did as she was asked. She had to forget her modesty and take off the sheet so that she could help to carry the man. His poor wife followed, carrying Laura's bag. It was slow going. Finally, near the lobby, one man stopped to help. They were soon met by firemen, who took over. There was total chaos outside, crowds of bewildered guests in various states of dress and undress were being helped by nurses and firemen. Ian put the elderly couple into one of the waiting ambulances and it sped off towards the hospital, then he went to see if anyone else needed help. Laura had inhaled a lot of smoke and was asked to sit by the back of an ambulance. As she was sitting there coughing, she heard a familiar voice. It was Mary.

'Oh my God, Laura, I'm so sorry! Are you alright, it's all my fault?'

The two friends held on to each other, both crying. Laura assured her she was fine, while still coughing, then laughed as she said:

'Well, you certainly know how to give a chap a good send-off, everything's gone up in smoke.'

'Oh, I'm glad you can still laugh,' said Mary. 'Look, I can't stay, we were all called in and I nearly had a heart attack when I heard it was your hotel.'

'What was it, a car bomb?' asked Laura.

'Yes, not one but two. One was in the underground garage, the other one was just outside. The whole back of the building is gone.'

'Was anyone badly hurt?'

'Well, we won't be sure how many for a while but I know two firemen were badly burned. The car exploded when they went to get the underground staff out.'

'Well, thank God we were lucky. Now you get along, I know you're going to be very busy.'

Mary handed her a set of keys.

'I'm going. Now you take a taxi and get to the flat. I phoned Peter so he'll let your family know you're safe, you can call them yourself later. Are you sure you're alright?'

Mary hugged her and left. Then Laura realised that she had no bag and no money. People were getting into the ambulance now and she felt in the way. There was smoke and dust everywhere. Firemen were anxious to get people away from the building. There might be another bomb and the structure could be unsafe. Laura stood there, totally bewildered, not sure what to do. Then two strong arms were holding her.

'Laura love, are you alright? I was so worried but I couldn't leave that old couple. Here, I brought your bag and the sheet.'

Ian gently put the smoke-stained sheet around her and led her down the street where there were plenty of taxis waiting. He put her into the first one and told her he had to get back to the hospital to help but he would call her.

'I'm afraid your car was wrecked, the firemen told me. I wanted to get your overnight bag, can you manage without it?'

Laura thanked him and told him she had plenty of Mary's things to wear. She kissed him goodbye and when the taxi pulled away, tears filled her eyes. She let herself into the flat. Tiredness overtook her and she fell into the bed in the guest room, exhausted.

CHAPTER 38

THE SMELL OF FRESH COFFEE filled her nostrils as she awoke from a deep but troubled sleep.

'Och, the sleeping beauty is awake.'

She looked up. Peter was sitting on the edge of the bed.

'Here, I brought you some toast too.'

Laura leaned up on one elbow.

'Where did you come from, what time is it?'

Peter looked at his watch.

'It's nearly one o'clock. I saw your father and told him what happened, then I just got into the car and drove here. I knew you would need a lift home. I was talking to Mary, she phoned here and said your car was ruined. Are you alright? I heard you coughing a lot.'

'I'm fine, really. There was a lot of smoke but I'll be alright. Thank you for seeing my father. He would have heard the early news this morning and worried. You're a great friend, Peter.'

She was sitting up in bed now.

'I must look a right sight, I need a good scrub.' She looked down at the shirt, and then at Peter, feeling totally embarrassed.

Peter smiled.

'I like the fancy nightshirt, smoke and all.'

'It was the first thing I grabbed,' she explained.

Peter didn't ask her any more questions. She finished her coffee and Peter had the shower running for her, with a pile of fresh towels. She stood and let the hot water wash away the smoke and grime. Using Mary's expensive shampoo, she washed her hair and thought of last night. She would never see Ian again? She was really going to miss him. Did she love him? She didn't know. Then she realised that today was the fifth anniversary of Andy's leaving. What was it, about December? Men, she would

232

forget all about them for now and concentrate on Christmas and on thanking God that she had been spared to enjoy it.

CHAPTER 39

THINGS WENT ALONG at their usual pace. Alan was so excited about the birth of the new calves – Daisy had two – Alan and had helped his Granda and Jim deliver them. He came racing into Laura's bedroom at five o'clock to announce that Daisy had become a mother again. He began going into detail about the birth, something that she could well do without at that time of the morning. Alan was even more sure now that he was going to be a vet.

'Just think Mum, I'll be able to help Granda all the time. He won't have to pay any more money to Mr Richardson, the vet. I'll do it all, won't it be great!'

She agreed with him, that indeed it would be great, having a vet in the family.

'Now,' she said, 'it's still early, please let me get back to sleep.'

'Don't you want any breakfast? Myrtle is making a big fry for us men, we were working all night,' he said proudly, leaving the room.

Down at the shop later she was telling Violet about it.

'You should have seen him, Violet, he was so full of himself. You would have thought he'd delivered the calves himself.'

'Well, at least he is still convinced he wants to be a vet after all that blood and gore. Most boys would run a mile from it,' laughed Violet. 'Laura, when you get a break later, I need to talk to you.'

Laura looked at her.

'It sounds serious. You're not sick, are you Violet?'

'No, I'm fine,' she said, 'I'll see you in an hour or so, right?'

For the next two hours Laura was busy. Lorna, who regularly helped out in the shop, was going to be late today so Laura didn't have much time to think of what Violet wanted.

Almost 1975, things were changing in the world, even in the village. The council were cutting down the big trees that lined the centre of the village because of the new power lines that were being installed. They were leaving the big oak at the top of the street. At least that was something, thought Laura. She loved that tree, it brought back memories of her childhood. The green that surrounded it was big enough for the children to play on and have picnics and such. In the evening, some of the older residents would sit underneath it and discuss politics and world affairs. Of course, there was not much traffic then. Things had changed, the speed of traffic through the street was dangerous now. The council had to put some of the new zebra-crossings outside the schools and traffic wardens on duty when the children were coming out.

As she looked out the window now, she saw Mary's mother sitting there under the tree, lost in her thoughts. Mary had told her last week that her brothers, the elder McCann twins, were going to be released from prison but that they hoped to find work with their uncle in New York. The whole family was upset but they knew that it was for the best, there was no future for Mickey and Jimmy here now. Mary's mother was feeling bad. They had been there for nearly twelve years now for alleged terrorist activities, convicted when they were nineteen. It was nearly too much to ask a mother to bear. Laura watched her now. She must call on her before she went home. She finally got time to sit down for a cup of tea with Violet.

'Now, what's your news?' she asked, looking at her friend, when Violet suddenly burst into tears.

Laura ran round the table to her. Holding her, she asked what had happened. Through her tears, Violet pulled a letter from her pocket and told Laura to read it – it was postmarked 'Crumlin Road Prison'. What was that vile man looking for now, she wondered, as she began to read it. But it wasn't from him, it was from the governor, informing Violet that Robert had had a heart attack and wanted to see her. In the envelope was a security pass to the hospital wing for two o'clock the next day.

'What do you think Laura? I said I never want to see him again and I meant it but now I don't know what to do.'

'Violet, I can't tell you what to do but I know that whatever it is, I'll go along with it, you know that.'

Violet took the letter from her and read it again.

'I've thought of nothing else since it arrived this morning, I was going to talk to the minister about it but how? I don't know, I don't have any feelings for him, you know that.'

'Yes I do, and it was very hard for you, wiping him out of your life like that. But you didn't need to put blame on yourself the way you did, you were very brave, Violet, and still are.'

Violet sat down heavily again.

'I don't know that I'm very brave. I couldn't have managed without you and your family. But what should I do about this?' she said, waving the letter.

'What does your heart say, or should I say your conscience?' asked Laura.

'My Christian duty says I should visit him but I'm afraid to. It's a long time since I've seen him, remember, and I don't want him shouting at me.'

'Oh Violet, I don't think that will happen. As the letter says, he's had a heart attack. He won't be in much form for shouting. Maybe he wants to see you before he dies, to ask your forgiveness.'

'Och Laura, do you think so? If I thought that, I would go. But I don't want to go on my own.'

Laura didn't let her finish.

'Violet would you like me to go with you? I'd be happy to, if you want.'

'You really are a good friend Laura, thanks.'

'Right, that's settled then, I'll drive you. I'll find out where it is from the police station in town.'

'What time will we leave? I'll need to tell Lorna to get her daughter in to help, just in case.'

So the next day they left early on the pretence of shopping in the city – they didn't want Lorna to ask any questions. Laura told her father the real reason, she knew he would understand.

They arrived at the prison just before two in the afternoon. They were met by a prison guard who told them to go straight to the Royal Hospital, as her husband had suffered a massive heart attack that morning. At the hospital, they were shown directly to the intensive care ward. A kindly nurse brought Violet to the bed. Laura had been holding her hand so she pulled away but Violet refused to let go, she looked at her pleading:

'Please Laura, don't leave me, not now.'

At the bedside they both were shocked when they saw what used to be Robert, lying there, tubes coming from all parts of his body. He was just skin and bones. The skin had tightened over his cheek bones, giving him an awful skeletal appearance, dark circles where his eyes should be. The hair that remained was pure white and his long bony fingers were lying useless on the bedspread. The doctor in charge came over and spoke to them, explaining that his patient had had a stroke immediately after his second heart attack. He understood what was happening but couldn't speak. Robert's eyelids fluttered excitedly when he saw Violet and for the rest of the visit he just stared at her. They stood there helpless, not knowing what to say or do. After a few very silent minutes, a prison officer came over to her and took her arm gently.

'Mrs Wray, would you like to come with me. I have some things of your husband's he wanted you to have.'

Violet looked kindly at him.

'Maybe you don't realise sir, that Robert and I were divorced nearly nine years ago. I didn't want any more to do with him and I don't want anything that belongs to him. I'm only here because he's dying – I still don't have any respect for him,'

The man looked at her.

'I understand Ma'am but maybe you should have a word with the minister who has been his confidant these last few years. He's waiting in the relatives' room, it's this way.'

They were brought down a long corridor and into a comfortable furnished room with plenty of armchairs and a coffee table laden with magazines. A man was staring out of the window with his back to them. When he heard them enter, he turned round. It was a very old Reverend Whylie. He came towards Violet and took her hands in his.

'Violet, it's good to see you. I'm glad you found the time to come and visit Robert. He has been talking of you and your life together these last few months.'

Violet looked at this man who had also changed so much since she last saw him.

'Reverend Whylie, how unexpected! I thought you had retired to the south of England. How long have you been working at the prison?'

He smiled at her.

'It's a long story but I didn't feel retirement was right for me. I wanted to do something to help others in a more practical way, so here I am. They needed someone at the prison and I felt unfulfilled with nothing to do.'

'I'm glad to see you. And you remember Laura, I'm sure,' said Violet, removing her hands from his and turning to Laura who had remained at the doorway, unsure whether or not to stay.

'Of course I remember Laura and it's good to see you, how is everyone in the family?'

They exchanged some information and Laura excused herself, telling Violet she would go and see Mary and would be back for her in half an hour. A young nurse showed her into Mary's office. She had to wait until Mary was free. Mary showed enormous surprise at Laura sitting there.

'Hi girl, what on earth are you doing here? You didn't phone. Oh my God, is someone sick, who is it?'

Laura didn't let her finish.

'Mary, there's no one ill. Well there is, I'm here with Violet, Robert's dying.'

'Well finally, the auld bugger is doing us all a favour. He should have died years ago, surely Violet's not feeling sorry for him. Where is he? I want to watch and make sure.'

Laura laughed.

'Mary you are incorrigible, have you no feelings for a dying man?'

'No, I have not, why have you?' she answered.

'No, I don't really but I agreed to come with Violet. She hasn't any feelings for him either but she felt she should be here. And guess what, the Reverend Whylie is the prison minister, we couldn't believe it when we saw him. He really has aged.'

'Well, it's great to see you anyway. Are you still coming here for the weekend? I have tickets for the Opera House, there's a great show on,' said Mary.

'Yes, I'm looking forward to it, I need to get some social life. There's not much happening in the village, except the guest tea and dance in the hall on Friday night. It's a fundraiser for the school so we have to go.'

'Well, aren't you living the high life. Do you see much of that brother of mine? What's this new girlfriend like? I haven't met her yet.'

'Yes, I saw her last Thursday night, Violet invited Peter and her to supper. She's lovely, he seems happy with her. She's an art teacher in a school in Armagh but she's from Londonderry,' answered Laura.

'I'm glad he's found someone. I hope he stays with this one, it's not right him living alone. My mother worries about her, you know. You would think he was still at school. She makes him a beef casserole every week, he says it lasts for days but he hasn't the heart to tell her he doesn't want it.'

'I know, last week when Alan came home he didn't want dinner. He said Peter gave him and Niall lovely stew and could he go back for more next day.'

Mary sighed.

'He loves them boys. I thought that him and his last girlfriend, Carol, would have made a go of it. They were together for nearly four years. He should be married and have his own children, he would make a great Dad.'

'Yes, I'm always telling him that but he said he's going to remain a bachelor as long as I'm a spinster,' laughed Laura. 'Now I've got to get back to Violet.'

Mary gave her friend a strange look. She came with her to see Violet. When they arrived, they could see something had happened. The doctor was in the room and the prison officer.

Reverend Whylie acknowledged them and told them that Robert had died a few minutes ago. Both women went over to Violet and held her. She looked visibly shaken. The prison officer asked her if she would sign some papers and make the funeral arrangements. He and Violet spoke for some time and finally the minister asked if she would like to see Robert one last time but she declined and asked Laura if they could leave. She signed the necessary papers and asked that the prison take care of the funeral, requesting that they cremate the remains. They told her that Robert had left some money but Violet told them she wanted nothing to do with it. Mary saw them out to the car and recommended a little tea shop where they could stop for a while and get something to eat before driving home.

Sitting in the little tea shop near the outskirts of the city, Violet told Laura what had taken place between the Reverend Whylie and herself.

'Robert begged him to contact me as all the letters he sent over the years had been returned unopened. He wanted to ask me to forgive him. The last five years he lived a life of fasting and prayer and helped to look after the sick in the hospital wing. The Reverend Whylie had remained in contact with Robert and when his wife and son left him, he returned to Belfast and got an unpaid job in the prison. They spent a lot of time together and he told me that Robert was full of remorse. He said Robert had written a letter to Winnie's parents to ask them for forgiveness and he asked me to deliver it.'

Violet said she had the letter in her bag and would bring it over to the McCanns herself tonight. Laura could see that the visit took a lot out of this kindly woman but she knew that Violet had done the right thing in making the journey. Laura looked across the table at her now and thought that it must be very difficult for her to do all this without feeling something for the man who was her husband for so long. She looked around the tea shop, it had that lovely old-world ambience, with silver cutlery and china. The food was delicious, tiny sandwiches and cream scones. Neither of them touched the wonderful iced cakes. Violet smiled.

'Isn't this nice and such variety. We don't have anything like this in Tullybeg.'

'Yes,' agreed Laura, 'I was just thinking the same.'

'Wouldn't it go down well in the village? There's plenty of passing trade, not even counting the locals. You know Laura, I was telling you the other day that I wanted to discuss something with you. When that letter arrived it just left my mind. Well, maybe this is the time now.'

'Listen Violet, why don't you let business sit for a while? You've had a lot to think about today and you have to watch your health, remember.'

'Och sure my health is fine, thank God, and I need to move on this now, it can't wait much longer,' said Violet.

'Is something wrong? Tell me you want to retire and do some travelling that you have always talked about.'

'No, no,' said Violet, 'I've no notion of retiring, far from it, no. But the petrol station people have been to see me. They want me to make room for a bigger forecourt and two more pumps but I don't want all that hassle, not now.'

'Well you have plenty of room for improvement if you wanted but it will mean a lot more work and taking on more staff,' said Laura.

'I know all that and I've thought of nothing else all last week and I've come to a decision. How would you feel if I offered the petrol business to the McCann family?'

'The McCanns?' said Laura, somehow taken aback. 'Why? You'll miss the business.'

'Maybe I will. Something I've seen today has really changed my mind but I need you to agree, you see the McCanns are running the garage so they could sell more petrol than ever I could, it makes sense, they have the room and the manpower. And I know that they will jump at the chance for I heard from the company they were enquiring about doing just that but the company will only allow one petrol station in the village. Now, what do you think?'

'Well, the way you put it makes good sense but won't you miss the revenue from it? It's a great wee earner, you know that,' Laura said.

'Well, of course they would have to agree to it and there would be some form of payment. I would have to talk it over with my solicitor but I need you with me on this too, for I've something else on my mind to take its place.'

'Now what? You know you never fail to amaze me,' laughed Laura. 'Come on tell me what you're thinking.'

Violet smiled.

'Look around you, this is what I've had on my mind. From Myrtle's cakes and bread started selling so well, I've been thinking wouldn't a little café go well. There's always some stranger asking where they could get a cup of tea, you know that.'

'Yes, I know but it means a lot of reconstruction at the shop and there's a lot of work attached to running a café. We would need to talk on extra help,' said Laura, with a worried look.

'Now,' said Violet, 'it won't be so much of a café as something like this. I've been looking at the menu, it's quite simple. Here,' she handed the menu to Laura.

'Take a look. It's all simple food, soups, sandwiches, cakes, scones. That lovely brown bread that Myrtle bakes would go down a treat, what do you think?'

'What do I think? I'm flabbergasted, that's what I am. When you should be taking things easy, here you are thinking of expanding the business.'

'Oh but will you help me get it going? You have a great business head. If you said no, I would abide by your decision, you know that.'

'I wouldn't say no, I'd help in any way but I suggest that you get someone from the Chamber of Commerce to talk it through with you and make sure it's viable. Do you agree?'

Violet smiled.

'Whatever you say.'

CHAPTER 40

CHRISTMAS WAS STARTING to show signs in the towns and villages. It was crisp frosty weather. Alan and Niall were busy making decorations – the kitchen table was covered with coloured paper and glue was everywhere. Alan held up his finished streamer.

'Well, what do you think of this one, Mum? It's taken me ages. I was going to give it to Aunt Violet to put up in the shop window, do you think she would like it?'

Laura took hold of his very delicate collection of coloured rings.

'This is lovely, Alan but I think it would look better in our sittingroom. With all the activity that goes on in the shop, this would get broken. You see, the ones we use there are a lot stronger, just make them for here instead. What about yours, Niall?'

She looked at his masterpiece.

'This is just great, your Mum will love it.'

Niall smiled up at her.

'It's not for my Mam. Our Sheila is making some for the house, and this one is for my Granny McCann They don't have any children to make theirs. Do you think she will like them?'

'She certainly will. It's very colourful and all those shiny stars, she will love it. Now,' said Laura, 'you will both have to start tidying up. I've got to make the tea, then I have to go down to the shop. You can make more tomorrow,'

'Oh, that's great,' said Alan, gathering up the leftover paper carefully, 'can Niall and I come too and look at some of the decorations you sell? Maybe we could get some new ideas, eh Niall?'

Niall nodded in agreement but Laura put her hand up.

'No boys, not tonight. I'm taking Niall home, then I am having a meeting at the shop with Peter and Auntie Violet. You can see the new decorations tomorrow after school. Now, I'm making burgers and beans, is that alright?'

Both boys agreed and quickly tidied up all the papers.

Later in Violet's warm sittingroom, Peter had laid the plans for the renovations on the table. He had asked a college friend, Eric Watters, who was now an architect, to draw them up. Violet wanted the character of the house left intact. A typical Georgian house with its distinct fantail window over the tall front door, and two large windows on either side. She produced some old photographs showing a garden with railings at the front of the house and a glass conservatory to the side that had since been taken down. She pointed to the people in the foreground.

'That's my father and grandfather with the coal cart and you can see my mother and aunt in the doorway. There's another one with Sam Woods holding the head of the horse, Sam was only young there. He's Lorna's grandfather, she was delighted when I showed her these.'

Peter and Laura looked over the collection of photos. Peter held up one that gave a good view of the whole front of the house.

'Eric loved this one, that's the one he drew up the outside plans on. You can see it here.'

He showed them the blueprints. Eric had copied the plans of the old conservatory in Violet's photograph and instead of a garden there was a paved courtyard with a couple of wrought-iron tables and chairs. The front was fenced with tall railings.

'What do you think Violet, is that olde-worlde enough for you? By the way, why did you remove the conservatory?'

Violet smiled, remembering.

'I was only a girl then and I remember sitting there with my grandparents. Grandma loved to take tea there in the afternoons. There was always a flowery smell in the conservatory with all the big plants. They needed more room to get bigger coal trucks in, so they demolished the conservatory to open up the side of the house. People used more coal in those days, especially during the war.'

Peter put the photographs back.

'These are great to have and hopefully the council in their wisdom will give you planning permission so you can ahead with the work. Did you see the interior plans, Laura?'

He unrolled another sheet from the plans. The shop itself was not going to change that much but the hall door opened directly into the new tea-shop. With the big hallway gone there was a lot more space. He showed them the counter, which fronted on to a little kitchen. An archway opened out from the sittingroom into the new conservatory. Eric had dotted the rooms with tables and the big fireplace completed the overall effect. Laura was amazed.

'This looks great! And the floor tiles, so in keeping with everything. Are you pleased, Violet?'

'Och, I'm delighted, sure I couldn't have done it better myself,' she laughed. 'And the way you are changing the back, new stairs as well, did you see this?' she said, handing the paper over to Laura.

Peter leaned over, explaining the changes to her. Violet would have a whole new self-contained apartment upstairs. She decided that when they were changing things, she wanted a new bathroom as well. Peter sketched out the new design and explained how easy it would be to manage. The original floors would be sanded and polished and the bathroom and kitchen tiled.

'Violet, you won't know yourself! It'll be great, very posh, won't it Peter?'

'Yes,' he agreed, 'and there's only the back extension to think about. Look here...'

Again he was very close to her as he leaned forward to point it out. She could smell his aftershave and it was nice but for some reason she felt uncomfortable. She lifted the plans off the table and brought them over to where Violet was sitting.

'Look, Violet, this is the new store room and here are the toilets. The old kitchen is part of the shop so you're going to have plenty of room.'

Peter began to pick up the plans and put them into the long tube.

'What did the health and safety man say, Violet? You said he called the other day.'

'Well, I don't think we will have bother from him,' she replied. 'He seemed well pleased and thought that we had everything right.'

'Well,' said Laura handing the last of the plans to Peter, 'that only leaves the planning permit from the council and I can't see that they should have a problem with this either, do you Peter?'

'No,' he answered, 'I think they will be all for it. After all it will be great for the village, especially in the summer. Did you see that contractor the other day? I heard they were good, they did some great work at that new hotel in Cookstown, the owners were well pleased.'

'Yes,' said Violet, 'he's Paddy McCluskey. He called last week and we had a great chat. His aunt used to live just outside the village near the bridge. She was Maggie, a sister of his father's. They were a lovely family. I told him that, if I got the go-ahead from the council, he had the job but I wanted a time-limit on it. I can't be doing with workmen hanging round the place for months.'

'Well, aren't you the perfect businesswoman, Violet?' said Laura. 'Did he agree?'

'He agreed. I'd like this up and running for Easter, if not before. Now, who's for some tea, or would you like something stronger? I've got a very good malt whiskey a traveller gave me. It's time to open it I think, don't you?'

Violet got up and left the room to get it from upstairs. Peter offered to go but she said she needed the bathroom anyway. He came over and sat down beside Laura on the settee. She told him about the boys making the decorations and the fun they had and he told her of the excitement at home when Violet had offered them the petrol station. It meant a lot to his father Paddy for they knew the income it provided.

'Violet knew exactly what she was doing, even though it gave cause for more gossip, especially with Robert dying at the same time. You know some people are so cruel. She was coming out of church last week and she overheard two auld biddies talking. They were calling the petrol station "more conscience money", saying that Robert owned the whole business and he gave it to your family because of what he did. Will they never stop?'

'I hate it when people say things like that to her, she is such a good-natured person and she doesn't deserve that,' said Peter.

'I know,' said Laura, 'but a lot of it is just begrudging. They don't like the fact that she didn't go under when he was convicted. And now she has given your family the petrol station, and them Catholics. It's just too much for them, bigots,' she persisted. 'Sure we have to listen to the same from our own crowd. A lot of them altar-eaters don't speak to us because Mickey and Jimmy got into trouble with the police. That's why the lads don't want to come home, they don't want the family getting hurt any more. Sometimes I feel like doing the same.'

'You mean move away from here?' said Laura, shocked. 'But... but... you can't! What about your work? Sure you're doing great, aren't you?'

'Och, I'm not doing too bad but there are times when I feel I'm going nowhere. I hate it when people cancel an order when they discover I'm a Catholic. Then they call and see if I will do the job at a cheap rate. You can imagine what I tell them,' he laughed

'Now,' said Violet, coming into the room with the whiskey, 'are we too early for a wee drop?'

CHAPTER 41

CHRISTMAS WAS CELEBRATED with the usual excitement, especially as Violet's plans had been approved. They were not officially notified till the New Year but the chairman of the planning board called himself to tell her. He was involved in the Chamber of Commerce and he commended Violet for her foresight in the new venture. They were sitting, enjoying the peace after the meal was over. Alan had gone with Niall to watch the skating on the lough, after a surprise invitation from Peter and his girlfriend Lisa. When Peter phoned to invite Alan, Laura was somehow excited. She expected him to ask her to come along like they did last year but he told her that Lisa was with him and asked could he bring her up next day for the usual Boxing Day tea.

'Of course,' she said, they would be welcome.

Alan was over the moon as he dressed in his warm clothes. He said he would go down the lane to meet them but his Granda decided to leave him down and maybe walk a little way with him. Then he reminded Alan to be home for milking and the feeding of his two new calves, which he gave him for Christmas.

After they left, Laura refilled Violet's glass and her own and settled down at the fire. They talked about the business and village gossip. Violet laughed.

'I wish you could have seen wee Willie Brown and the wife the other night. He was plastered, and could she get him home! He came out of Black's Pub carrying two bottles of stout. She was trying to take his arm but he took about three steps forward and four steps back, then leaned against the wall and slid down to the ground. She tried for ages to lift him. Then she got fed up and took the bottles from him and went home on her own.'

'Och the poor woman, I imagine them two had quite a head next morning,' laughed Laura,

'That's nothing,' said Violet. 'He was still there when I was locking up. The next day, there the two of them were, linking each other going into McKeever's pub at dinnertime. Sure they must spend a small fortune in drink. And I was thinking of asking her to make the new curtains I need for the house, do you think I'm mad?'

'Well, I don't think so. I've seen curtains that she's made, they're perfect. Someone told me it doesn't matter how much she drinks, it doesn't affect her sewing, she's an expert at curtains. What room are you thinking of?' asked Laura.

'I think I'll get all the upstairs done. I'm not sure if I'm going to curtain the new place for a while, I'd like to see how it turns out. So, if I get Mrs Brown in to measure up in the New Year, she should have them ready when the work is finished. After all, the size of the windows won't change.'

'I can't wait for all the work to start and finish, it will be great. Did anyone ask you about your plans?' asked Laura.

'Oh yes, quite a few were asking what I intended. I was telling some of them about the tea-shop – they all thought it was a good idea. I just wish it was finished and I didn't have to put up with all the dust and dirt.'

'Well there's only one answer to that,' said Laura. 'You will have to move up here till the work is finished, the dust will be very bad for your chest.'

Violet looked at her, amazed.

'I couldn't possibly do that! I mean, it's alright coming here for Christmas but I couldn't stay that long, it will take weeks. I don't think your father would agree to that.'

'What would I not agree to?' said William, coming into the room. 'Are you talking about me behind my back?' he laughed, 'I hope it's good. My goodness that's one cold day.'

He moved over to the fire and stood with his back to it, facing the two women.

'We were just talking about the renovations in Violet's place. I told her she couldn't stay there as there would be too much dust – it's not good for her chest – and that she should move up here till it's finished. What do you think, Father?'

'I think it's the only solution, sure all that dust would be very bad for anyone.'

'Are you sure, William? I wouldn't want to put any of you out.'

'You wouldn't be putting anyone out,' said Laura, 'there's plenty of room. Sure you know that we would be delighted to have you, now that's the end of it. Now who's for a wee refill? Here, Father, I'm sure you could do with it after the walk.'

It was well into January before the work got underway. Everyone was roped into helping with packing and storing stuff. They were lucky in having plenty of room in the old store beside Peter's workshop. Even her father offered and was accepted. Afterwards he moved Violet's stuff up to the farmhouse. Laura insisted that she go with them and she would see to the work at the shop. Alan and Niall worked like little Trojans, eventually Laura insisted that they had done enough for that day. So Myrtle and Jim took the boys home and Laura and Peter were left on their own.

It was nearly ten o'clock when she fell, exhausted, on to the couch in the storeroom. Peter fell down beside her. They sat there quietly, too tired to speak, and next thing Laura heard a slight snoring. She watched him for ages, afraid to move. She didn't want to disturb him, he looked so peaceful, very boyish, in his sleep. She had hardly seen him since Boxing Evening at the farm. It was a great party, even better than usual this year, as she had not been able to persuade the McCann family to join them. Mary, Yusef and his brother and sister; Myrtle and Jim; Pat, Mary, Niall's parents and his sisters Moira and Monice. And of course they all brought something, which meant there was far too much food and drink. The children of the party were upstairs playing with Alan's new train set, a present from Peter. He had come on Christmas Eve and set it up for him in one of the small rooms. Laura hadn't see him as she was working. Peter spent a good part of Boxing day playing with children who were full of excitement. Lisa seemed to enjoy their company too and got on well with everyone. At one stage she was in the kitchen helping. She told Laura that she was an only child and her parents were in Scotland for the holiday. She and Peter were going over for the New Year. Later, watching them dance together, Laura felt an awful pang of jealousy. When Peter asked her to dance she changed the music to a highland fling. She didn't want to dance close to him as she couldn't understand her feelings for him. She didn't know if she was just jealous of Lisa because she didn't have anyone, or did it run deeper? The whole evening was a great success and she was delighted that the McCanns came. At first she wasn't too sure how her father felt, he seemed a bit awkward but as the evening wore on he lightened up. He and Paddy McCann partnered in a game of Whist, and they won! She was glad her father was losing his bitterness against the Catholics, it made life a lot easier.

She sat on the settee half asleep, watching Peter's peaceful slumber. She would love to reach over and kiss him. This made her angry with herself. God what's wrong with me! What are these feelings? How would I feel if he suddenly upped and left with Lisa? He did hint at it, is he unhappy to? What will I do if he does leave? Is this going to be my life, single Mum, looking after an aged father? She shouldn't think like that, she had a great chance of happiness with Ian but she let him slip through her hands. Did she regret it? Yes, sometimes she did but it was of her own making, no one else was to blame. Now here she was, sitting watching Peter sleeping beside her and she knew he too was out of bounds. He had a fantastic young girlfriend and they would probably up and leave soon, she chastised herself. Oh, stop feeling sorry for yourself get on with your life! Yes, she thought, but what life?

Peter stirred beside her and then as he yawned and stretched, his eyes widened in amazement at seeing her there.

'Oh Laura, I'm so sorry. How long have I been asleep?' He looked at his watch. 'Oh my God, it's nearly eleven thirty! I can't believe I've slept so long, why didn't you wake me?'

'You looked so peaceful lying there I hadn't the heart and I expect you were very tired, you've been on the go all day, remember.'

He stretched and stood up.

'You should have left me here, I would have understood. Did you have a sleep too?'

'Yes,' she lied, 'just for a while. I couldn't go home – I gave my father the car to take Violet up.'

'Oh, I'm really sorry. Come on, I'll take you up now or will you come next door to my flat and I'll make you some coffee?'

'No, I don't want anything thanks, I just need a bath and bed. I'm really tired and coffee would only keep me awake.'

They checked that everything was locked up and he drove her up to the farm. He reversed the car on the street and looked over to her.

'You're very quiet, are you annoyed at me for keeping you? We really got a lot done today. We make a great pair, don't we?'

When he leaned over and put his arm around her she didn't pull away.

'Yes Peter, we do make a great pair, long may it continue. Now I'd better get in.'

Before she knew what was happening he took her face in his hands and kissed her. She didn't pull away, she let him kiss her again, this time with more passion and she could feel a longing deep inside her. They stayed that way for ages, neither of them speaking. They kissed again as Peter held her in his arms. She felt so at peace with him but this was wrong and she knew she would have to make the first move. Gently she pulled back and took his tired face in her hands.

'Thank you, Peter, I needed that. You are always there for me and I hope you always will be.'

Peter covered her hands with his own.

'I'll always be here for you, Laura, and this needn't end now, not if you don't want it too, you know that.'

'Yes, Peter, I know but not now we're both too confused. See you tomorrow.'

She kissed him once more, got out of the car and ran into the house.

CHAPTER 42

THE RENOVATIONS on the shop were going well. Violet was really pleased, the workers were getting things done. She settled in well at the farm and got on great with William and Alan. She was worried that she would be in the way – it was one thing staying for a few days, like she did at Christmas but actually living there indefinitely was a different matter.

Laura could see that she was trying to fit in as best she could and not be in the way. Indeed Laura was annoyed when she discovered that Violet would retire to her room shortly after the evening meal, especially the nights that Laura worked late. She mentioned it to her father, that maybe he would try and make her feel more at home.

'Well, I don't know if I can do anything to help her,' he replied. 'She's grand when you're here but then women can talk all night about nothing. Do you mind when her and your mother got together after the tea? Sure I took myself into the kitchen, I couldn't keep up with them. I don't know that I still would be any use, I think she feels a wee bit embarrassed.'

'Oh, I don't want her feeling like that. There must be something to make her feel at home. I don't want her moving back till everything is just right, she can't be near dust or her chest gets infected,' said Laura, with a worried look. It was young Alan that solved the situation. He came home from school next day and announced that his new school project was 'The Village Long Ago' and they had to ask all the older people for information.

'So,' he said, 'I don't have to worry do I? I have two of the oldest people right here in the house, don't I?'

Laura laughed.

'Don't be so cheeky, young man! There's no way your Granda and Auntie Violet are the oldest people. Don't let them hear you say that or they won't help with your project.'

'I'm sorry,' he said, 'I didn't mean it that way. They are the only two people I know well enough to ask, and Granda must be a good age, eh?'

So he asked them that evening and immediately they both began to tell him things. He was delighted and every evening they would spend ages remembering people and places. Violet had a box of old photographs, which they would set out on the table after tea. Alan loved looking at the way people were dressed, and the collection of animals, dogs, horses and cattle. There were some wonderful photos of the hunt – they were taken a the top of the village street outside Black's pub and staff could be seen offering the master of the hounds a drink in a tiny little cup. Violet and William were able to name many of the riders and onlookers.

Long after Alan had gone to bed, they would sit and remember the old times, people they knew and remembered. They would still be sitting there when Laura returned home and they got into the habit of having a wee hot whiskey before bedtime.

Two weeks flew by. The new tea-shop was almost complete – the next month would see the finishing touches being added. Laura and Violet had a great time shopping for china and silverware, and the soft furnishings. Peter had made the tables, chairs and outside railings. All the rubble was cleared away and that left only the outside painting to be done. Violet decided that the lovely Georgian door with the fanlight would suit a bright pillar-box red. The wisteria and ivy were trimmed and the stonework cleared – the whole place looked great. The design of the conservatory was very impressive. It boasted a magnificent domed ceiling with skylights. It was L-shaped, which meant that part of it almost reached the outside railings. The forecourt was crazy-paved and dotted with planters, which would be full of blooms in late spring and summer. Violet was overwhelmed with the result, now it only left her living apartments to be completed.

Alan and Niall were real little troopers – they fetched and carried tables and chairs all day and unpacked boxes of containers for the kitchen. Laura decided that she would leave the china and the glassware till the last.

That evening she made the boys their favourite tea – burgers and chips. They talked non-stop about all the things they had done.

'It was very hard work, Granda, nearly as hard as farming. I'm glad it's nearly finished. It's going to be great, isn't it? Auntie Violet, can Niall and me serve the tables when you are very busy?'

'Well,' said Violet, 'we'll have to wait and see, won't we? And hope we get plenty of customers in… but we have really needed all your help, you pair were great, weren't they Laura?'

'Yes,' she said, patting Alan's head. 'And as a little reward I'm taking you and Niall for a day out on Saturday to the zoo and a film. Aunt Mary and Yusef are still in Germany, so if you like we can stay in her flat, how does that sound?'

'Oh Mum, that's great, wait till I tell Niall! Can Peter come?' he asked.

'Well, I don't know, it may not be his idea of a day out,' she replied.

'Oh, it is, it is,' he said. 'We were just talking about it and he said when all the work was over he would take us, maybe at the Easter holidays, so I knew he'd love to come. Can I tell him tomorrow?'

'Well, seeing you have it all planned…' she said, 'why not.'

'I expect you will be needing pocket money for your day out. I'll treat you both, you've certainly earned it,' said Violet.

'Thanks Auntie Violet, I'll tell Niall tomorrow. We'll have a great time, won't we Mum?' he said, wrapping his arms around her.

Later on, that night, when Alan was in bed, she organised some clothes for him and her to wear for the outing. Alan asking to take Peter put her in a spot. She hadn't been alone in his company since that night he took her home. It wasn't that she didn't think about him – she did all the time – but she deliberately kept out of his way, she was grateful to be kept so busy. Her feelings were all mixed up and every time she saw Lisa and him together she couldn't help feeling jealous of her. She imagined them together and wished it was her. What was wrong with her, was she going through a mid life crises at almost thirty-eight, long before her time, or was she just plain frustrated, in need of sex? Oh, why didn't she say yes to Ian? He was out of her reach now too – the last she heard he was happily married with two children.

CHAPTER 43

THE OUTING TO THE ZOO and cinema was a great success – the boys were in their element and Alan took photographs everywhere they went. At one stage they were standing at the giraffe's cage, just herself and Peter, when Alan asked them to turn around and, quick as a flash, he photographed them. Peter had his arm around her, pointing to some of the antics in the monkey enclosure. It was the first time they had been close since that night, when he had given her that special smile of his and she had felt herself burning inside. Was she in love with him?

'Those two boys are dead to the world,' said Laura, returning to the lounge in time to see Peter about to pour wine into two glasses.

'No Peter, not for me,' she protested. 'I'm going to follow the boys' example and go to bed, I'm exhausted. Today took all my energy running after them.'

'Here,' he said, handing her a glass, 'didn't I do my share of running? Sit down here and relax, and enjoy a lovely evening to end an exhausting day.'

She took the glass and smiled at him.

'I suppose you're right as usual. One wee glass won't do any harm.'

They sat sipping the rich red wine and looking out at the river. It was just getting dark and the lights of the city reflected like diamonds on the slow-moving water.

'I think I deserve something too, for all my hard work today,' he leaned over and surprised her with a kiss. Laura sank back into the deep recesses of the big comfortable settee. She sighed, a deep, contented sound. Peter turned to face her, smiling.

'You sound like the cat that's got the cream.'

'Maybe I did,' she said, softly.

Slowly he put his glass down on the small table, took hers and did the same. Then he held her face in his hands and kissed her long and passionately. She responded with her hands, holding his head to hers. She didn't want to go. When they finally came up for air, he stared at her, his hands caressing her gently.

'Oh Laura, I never want this to end, do you know that I am very much in love with you? I think that I always have been.'

She shushed him to be quiet.

'Peter, let's not talk of how we'd like it to be. Just for now let it be, just us, the two of us, here and now.'

Gently he released her and went and stood over by the window, gazing out at the night. Puzzled, she followed him.

'Peter, don't be like this. How can I tell you how I really feel, have you forgotten about Lisa? You two have been together for a long time. Indeed I thought you would have got engaged at the New Year and I think she was expecting it too.'

Peter put his arms around her and pulled her close.

'Is that why you wouldn't commit yourself and tell me that you love me too? Well, let me put your mind at rest. Lisa is a lovely girl, we had some great times together and I hope that we will always be friends but she wanted something that I wasn't prepared to give, and that was me. She wanted me to be something I'm not, to wear the right clothes, be seen in the right places, drive a better car, even my job... She suggested that I stick to designing, get into management and leave the rough work to the boys in the shop. What she couldn't understand was that I love the work, welding is my life. So we began to drift apart.'

Laura looked at him.

'But she didn't just walk away, what happened?'

He smiled.

'Do you remember Eric Watters, the architect who designed Violet's place? Well, from the day she met him I could see that he was what she wanted me to be. He had a great lifestyle, dressed well and he used to look at her with a wee glint in his eye – the two of them got together with my blessing.'

'You really didn't mind?' said Laura, surprised.

'No, why should I? Lisa already knew where my feelings lay, right here.'

He kissed her again and suggested some music. He went over to the tape deck and checked out the titles. He turned and smiled.

'How about a dance? We haven't danced in a long time.'

He pulled her on to the floor to the sounds of Elvis. They rocked and sang to all their favourites and finally fell on to the settee, exhausted.

'Do you remember our Mary teaching us to dance in the kitchen? She was a great mover and singer, she knew them all. We were eager to learn the right steps before we would ask any of the girls out at the hops. We were always trying to get you to come with us.'

Laura laughed.

'Much as I wanted to, Father had other ideas and dancing wasn't one of them.'

Just then the tempo changed and he took her up to dance again, singing along with Elvis.

'Wise men say, only fools rush in, but I can't help, falling in love with you' – the words seemed to say it all.

Laura was dancing as if on a cloud. They danced as one. As the song continued, she could feel he was very aroused and she had a burning sensation deep in her groin. His hands were now gently caressing her and moving around her breasts, the nipples hardening to his touch. Before the song had ended, they were both on the settee, their clothes strewn around the room.

Laura was amazed at the feelings she had and how brazen she felt. She knew they were both excited by the thought of making love and he didn't need any guidance. It was long and erotic and Peter took her to new heights. She had never felt so passionate and she didn't want it to end. Peter was a wonderful lover and he knew how to excite her further. They explored each other until they both lay spent, the sweat gleaming on their entwined bodies. She felt so contented. After a minute he surprised her by swinging his long legs off the settee and kneeling in front of her as if in adoration. With butterfly kisses he touched her neck, her breasts and down into the very core of her being. She held his head in her hands, pulling him closer. This was the most erotic feeling she had ever experienced. Then he rose, his arms going round her as he tried to stand. He slipped, bringing her down on top of him. They lay there laughing on the carpet, then he cupped her face in his hands and told her how much he loved her. They made love again, this time it was slower and even more erotic, till they finally fell asleep with the first rays of the dawn spreading across the city skyline.

Laura awoke with a start. She sat up and looked at the state of the room, clothes everywhere. She disentangled herself from Peter's arms and legs and found a blanket to cover his nakedness. He moved and reached for her but she leaned over, kissed him quickly and got up. She picked up the clothes from around the room and left his in a neat pile beside him. She smiled at his sleeping form as she left and went into the bedroom. Slipping into bed, she was asleep in seconds. Alan woke her, jumping on the bed, and she pulled the sheet up to cover herself.

'Mum, Mum, it's time you were up, it's getting late. We're up for ages. We went out to the shops to buy stuff for breakfast. Come on, it's nearly ready.'

'Oh Alan, give me another few minutes, I'm tired. We did a lot of walking yesterday.

Alan laughed.

'Well at least you had a lovely soft bed to sleep in, poor Peter was sleeping on the floor, and Mum, he had no clothes on, and I took his picture, we had a great laugh.'

Laura nearly died.

'Alan, you didn't! You shouldn't have gone in to waken him. And to take his picture, that was awful!'

'No Mum, it was alright, he didn't have any clothes on but he had a blanket around him. He looked very funny and said that he must have fallen off the settee during the night.'

She smiled at him.

'You must be careful when you use your camera, you could offend someone. Now, off with you, I'll be out in a minute.'

She padded into the kitchen wearing a dressing gown of Mary's, bringing a smile to Peter's face.

'Hello there, sleepy-head, are you ready for your Ulster Fry and my culinary skills?'

He put a large plate in front of her. The smell alone was delicious. A well-presented breakfast of bacon, egg, sausage, bacon and black pudding, topped with fried soda farls. She looked in amazement at the amount of food on the plate.

'Peter, I couldn't eat half of this.'

He leaned over and placed a napkin beside her.

'Nonsense, of course you can. You need to keep your strength up, we have another full day planned, isn't that right boys?'

Laura looked at the boys for an answer but they just laughed, said it was a surprise. She looked to Peter, who smiled and said that when the food was all eaten and the place put back in shape he would tell them. Finally, after listening to all their questions, he agreed to tell them.

'I've decided that I need a day out to a place I've never been to so you all have to come with me. Will you come?'

They said they would and there were more questions from the boys but he held his hand up and motioned for them to stop.

'Alright, alright, I'll tell you – it's the Giant's Causeway and Dunluce castle.'

They jumped up and down in excitement. Laura asked:

'When did you decide all this? It's a great idea! I love that part of the country and it's a beautiful day for it. Come on boys, hurry up, you can help me clean the flat before we leave.'

It was a lovely drive up the Antrim road and not that much traffic so they made good time. When they got to the causeway there were quite a lot of visitors. They spent a long time climbing the rocks and exploring the little pools left by the outgoing tide. Then they had lunch in a café with a wonderful view of the coastline. Next stop was the castle. The boys loved it. They got talking to an old man who knew the history of the place and he had them enthralled with stories. At one stage, Laura and Peter were sitting on the rocks and a strand of her hair had blown around her face. Gently he removed it and whispered to her that he loved her. It was at this moment that Alan decided to photograph them. Laura laughed but made a mental note to take the films and get them developed herself before she showed them to her father.

The rest of the day went quickly. They enjoyed the wonderful beach for an hour, then spent some time at the famous Barry's Amusements before heading for home. Just ten minutes into the journey the boys were asleep so Peter pulled her closer and kissed her every chance he got.

She knew she loved him and wanted to be with him always but making plans was out of the question. She wondered how her father would react. As the saying goes, she was between the devil and the deep blue sea, she didn't know which way to turn.

CHAPTER 44

THE LUNCHTIME RUSH was over. The shop and the new tea rooms were both doing well. A surprising number of regulars came now, especially people working nearby, and the passing trade was good.

Laura was just about to check the outside tables when she stopped dead in her tracks. She couldn't believe her eyes, a familiar figure was striding across the road towards the courtyard. She inched backwards into the kitchen and watched as he chose a table near the gate. She stared at him, heart pumping.

There he was, bold as brass, that all-too-familiar lock of blond hair falling into his deep blue eyes, and the way he kept flicking it back with his fingers. He hadn't changed one bit.

He was smartly dressed as always, in a lightweight grey suit and white open-necked shirt. June, one of the young waitresses, rushed over to take his order. He gave her that heartrending smile of his and Laura could see that he was paying June a compliment, the way she blushed.

When June came into the kitchen, she told Mollie, the other waitress, about the handsome stranger.

'He's just to-die-for, Mollie, he has the loveliest eyes, and that hair! He has a queer accent though and he said I should be in the movies. Imagine, me a film star! Do ye think maybe he's someone important, Laura?'

Laura looked at June with her big brown eyes full of hope.

'Well, stranger things have happened but somehow I don't think that fellow out there has anything to do with the films. And if he asks any questions about me, say nothing, do you hear? Don't say one word, that's if you want to keep this job.'

Laura carried some delph to the sink, with June staring after her.

She stood in the kitchen, her hands gripping the rim of the sink, her knuckles white with anger, still reeling from the shock of seeing Andy again.

Were Belle and the girls with him. What was he doing here? She needed to know. She moved over near the shop window. He was sitting with the *Belfast Telegraph* propped up in front of him. As she watched, he took out his cigarettes, then to her amazement the little lighter – it was very distinct, in the shape of an MG racing car and it was pillar-box red. He flicked the miniature bonnet and the flame shot out of the bonnet. He lazily puffed his cigarette, enjoying the moment.

She remembered that lighter all too well. It was Christmas many years ago, they were all in the parlour after dinner, exchanging gifts. Andy had just got a new red Ford car a few weeks before, telling her that someday he would buy himself a brand new MG racer and be the envy of all his friends.

Everyone had exchanged presents when Belle surprised them all by giving Andy a large gaily-coloured box. He was so excited as he began to unwrap it. He kept finding smaller boxes inside. It reminded them of the game, 'Pass the Parcel', they played at the church socials. Finally they were all falling about laughing when the last box was left. It was very small, not much bigger than a matchbox, wrapped in gold paper with a tiny card and the words 'Something you always wanted, love Belle'.

Andy undid the wrapping to reveal a small elegant box and inside lay the little red lighter.

Laura remembered well the look that Andy gave Belle. Thinking back now, it said a thousand words. Little did she know then that it was the start of their affair. Her mother and father thought that young Belle was so witty and clever to think up such an unusual present. Laura, in her mind, could see him hugging Belle and telling her that he would always treasure it and it was the best present he had ever got, and even if he never got the real one he would always keep this one.

Well, she thought, it looks like he kept his word. Now here he was sitting outside the tea room, bold as brass, still holding Belle's present.

She was standing in a dream when she suddenly realised the time. Alan would be coming out of school soon – she couldn't let Andy see him and there was no way she could leave the shop. She began to panic.

Violet was at the hairdresser's and she couldn't tell the girls anything. She went back into the kitchen wondering what to do.

Just then she saw Peter crossing the yard. She tapped the window but he didn't hear, he was going to his car. She nearly fell out the back door in her haste to catch him. She called his name. He rushed over and grabbed her, laughing, trying to kiss her.

'I didn't know that you were *that* anxious to see me. You look like you've seen a ghost, are you alright?'

Laura told him what had happened.

'You mean the bugger's here? I don't believe it, how has he the nerve! I'll go up right now and beat the living daylights out of him.'

He made to turn away but she stopped him saying that getting Alan was more important and if Peter could take him down to Niall's house she would collect him later. Peter could see that she was really upset and he put his arms around her and told her not to worry, that he would get Alan.

'That bastard.' he thought, 'coming back now when everything was beginning to get better.'

He kissed away her tears and ran up the driveway without looking over towards the courtyard.

Laura dragged herself up the stairs and into the toilets – she needed to freshen up and compose herself. When she returned to the kitchen she could see him sitting there having coffee and scones.

June was full of chat and wouldn't stop talking about him. Then she asked Laura how she knew him.

'He wants to know if I know ye and if ye still work here, and what time ye'd be here, and if ye were married. Then what do ye think he asked?'

Both women looked at her, and waited. Mollie couldn't contain herself any longer.

'Well, are ye going to tell us or do we have to wait till the evening paper comes? What does he want?'

June flicking her hair back and with a smug smile said:

'He only wants to take me into town for a drink – he really fancies me. Imagine, he doesn't waste any time, does he?'

Mollie stared at her, open-mouthed.

'Jazus, he only had to smile at ye and ye'd lift yer petticoats for him, ye've no bloody shame! Have ye forgot about Victor?'

June laughed.

'Och, I'm not goin'. Sure Victor wouldn't agree to that, are ye mad?'

'Well I wouldn' put anythin' past ye,' said Mollie, putting some plates down, 'I thought yer eyes were goin' to pop out when ye looked at him.'

'Still, it's nice to be asked and I wouldn't mind making that Victor fella jealous,' June said, laughing, as she went to serve another customer.

Laura smiled at the two girls.

'Well, I am very glad that someone has brightened up your day. Now maybe we will get some work done here – those scone baskets need refilling. And less talking about the customers now, if you please.'

It was a good hour before Andy left. Having had several cups of coffee, chatting with a very happy June, he finally went. He gave her a very generous tip and really made her day by telling her that he would be back and that he would not take no for an answer.

June was on a high the rest of the day.

Laura watched his confident stride across the road. As she watched, there was another surprise in store for her as he took out his keys and jumped into a red MG, parked across the street at McCann's, switched on the engine and roared off at speed. She wasn't the only one staring after him – June was in the courtyard with a wistful look in her eyes.

CHAPTER 45

LATER THAT NIGHT when Alan was in bed, she decided to tell Violet and her father about the incident with Andy in the café. She was still shaking. Her father gave her a guilty look.

'I'm sorry, child, it's my fault, I should have said something earlier. I didn't think that he would turn up so soon.'

Laura stared at him. 'What do you mean turn up, what do you know? Is Belle here too?'

'I don't know but I heard the other day at the mart that auld Richard Carson had a bad heart attack and that he was in hospital. I should have said something when I came home but I didn't want to open up old wounds.'

'Did you know that Andy was back?' she asked.

Her father nodded

'Och, Joe Scott that lives beside them told me that the whole family had been sent for. Sure there was only the housekeeper looking after the place, and the daughter is abroad some place working in the missions. They don't know where the David fellow is. He was a bit on the wild side, wasn't he?'

'Well, he wasn't the only one, was he? And what about Belle?' She could see her father was getting upset. 'I'm sorry for jumping at you, Father,' full of remorse as she looked at him, 'but I got such a shock seeing that devil sitting there. I didn't know what to think.'

Violet looked concerned.

'It must have been awful, Laura, him turning up like that. Wasn't it great that Peter was there and able to get wee Alan for you. What are you going to do about it? Someone is bound to tell him about the child.'

Laura was really worried.

'I know I can't keep it a secret from him but I'm just worried what that devil will do. And worst of all, I'll have to talk to Alan now,' she gave a deep sigh. 'I don't know what to do for the best, or how he will react. I told him that his father left because he didn't want us but that was a lie. Alan really doesn't know anything much about him. Now what will I tell him?'

William was sorry for his bewildered daughter.

'Knowing you, you will find the right words. Wee Alan is a great child, he'll understand. Don't worry about him.'

Laura hoped her father was right but the problem was taken out of her hands the very next day, before she had a chance.

She had arranged for Alan to go to his friend Niall's house again after school. She was working the late shift at the shop but she would take him home for his tea before she went. She was out in the garden bringing in the washing when she heard the roar of a car engine coming up the lane. She ran around to the yard in time to see Andy in his fancy sports car doing a handbrake turn with gravel flying everywhere. The surprise that took her breath away was his passenger – Alan! The child was sitting in the front seat with a wide smile on his face and waved when he saw her.

'Look at me Mum, in a real racing car, isn't it just great! And Andy says he's my Dad.'

Andy sat there with a smug grin on his face. Right then Laura could have killed him, she was raging,

'Alan, get out of that car right now and go to your room!'

The child began to protest but the look on his mother's face changed his mind. She grabbed him as he got out of the car.

'What have I told you about talking to strangers, now go inside and don't come out again. I am really cross with you!'

'But Mum, he said he was my...' The rest was left unsaid.

As she pointed inside, he ran in and she could hear him crying. It was breaking her heart. She turned her anger on the grinning Andy, who had got out of the car and was just standing there beside it, grinning.

'How dare you upset my child like this! What gives you the right to come into our lives like this and pick up my son? If you ever try a stunt like this again I'll call the police, do you hear me? You are not welcome here.'

She made to take a swipe at him but he was to fast. As she raised her arm he grabbed her and pulled her close, pinning both her arms behind her.

'My God, Laura but you look fantastic when you're roused. Why didn't you ever show that spunk when we were together? I never would have left you. My God, you really are sexy, do you know that?'

She tried to pull away but he only tightened his grip and the next thing she knew he was kissing her passionately. He finally let her go but not before she slapped him hard and sent him reeling back from the force of it.

'Well, well, you're the right little spitfire. A big change from the little mouse that I used to know but from what I hear, maybe you have been taking lessons. I believe you like the Taigs but then you always did, didn't you?'

She made to hit him again but he was too fast. He caught her and pushed her against the car and kissed her again. She was dumbfounded. She tried to knee him in the groin but she couldn't, he was holding her too tight. He pushed her away at arm's length and was about to jump into the car when she kicked him hard in the shins. He yelled.

'You hateful bitch! And I thought I was doing you a favour, showing you how a real man acts.'

He began to nurse his injured ankles as he sat in the car. He looked at her.

'You really have got spunk, I like it. You have grown up, Laura, and maybe we'll continue this again soon.'

'Yes Andy, I have done a lot of growing up since we last met and I never want to see you near me or my son. You have no reason to come here again, do you hear? Now get out of my sight and don't come near my child again.'

He laughed at her.

'I wish you could hear yourself, "my child". You stupid bitch, do you think you created him all by yourself? Maybe now that you are a bit older your memory is playing tricks on you but I remember all too well just how and when he was conceived. You couldn't get enough, sure you had me wore out. We were lying up at the lake under a big full moon just like the gypsies. And I want to tell you now that I have as much right to him as you, isn't he my spittin' image?'

Laura was hurting at his words and his threats but she held her reserve and told him again to go. It had no effect on Andy. He stayed, mocking her with a leery smile, then he totally floored her with his next admission.

'Laura, I've been watching you and Alan for days without your knowledge. Last Sunday I saw you and you father coming out of church looking all saintly and holy. What did your fine church-going friends think when you produced a wee bastard, eh? I can't imagine many of them rushing to shake your hand. A crowd of auld hypocrites, that lot. You thought I didn't know about him, didn't you? Well, I've known for years, sure didn't my own father tell me.'

Laura stared at this excuse for a man, wondering how she could have loved him?

'You've known all this time and did nothing. What sort of being are you, how could you ignore your own son? Do you think that you can sail into his life just like that? What did you father have to say?'

'Well,' he replied, in that familiar lazy manner of his, 'my father saw the child with you and your father at a mart and he made a few discreet enquiries from friends of his. And cute enough, he got our David to take a few photos without you knowing. It was at the Omagh Agricultural Show. The wee fellow was only about four or so. Oh it was a lovely photo, I have it here.'

From his jacket he withdrew a leather wallet and removed some photos and handed them to her. One showed her father holding Alan up to view the prize-giving, the next was herself and the child sitting on a bench eating ice cream cones. She looked at them remembering well that day. She was wearing a new Moygashel suit in lemon and a matching straw hat. Alan was wearing a blue outfit, he looked really cute with ice cream on his nose. They were both laughing at something in the distance. She handed the photographs back without speaking.

He looked at them, grinning.

'A perfect picture of mother and son, eh? You looked great then too. But now I want more than just a few photos, I want to spend more time with my son and you can't stop me. Today he was playing on the green with his friends and I called him over. You see, we had already met. I was in my car at the petrol pumps and all the wee lads were asking me questions about it and how fast it went. Like all boys they were excited and I let some of them sit in it. Sure they thought they were in heaven and I told them that next time I would take them for a ride down the street.

Laura was annoyed

I still can't understand why Alan was in the car. He knows how much I have warned him about strangers. He won't do it again in a hurry.'

Andy smiled at her in a teasing manner.

'Och, don't go blaming the boy. He was with his friends and I called them over and asked if any of them knew of a William Steenson who lived near. Alan came running over, saying that was his Granda and he would show me and the next thing was we were racing out of the village and up here. You had no need to worry, sure he was safe with me.'

Laura could hardly contain her anger.

'Well, father and son won't be racing down the village street again, you have had your vindictive fun and we don't need to see you.'

'Laura, Laura, you can't stop me, I'll be around for some time. I sat outside that tea-shop the other day and watched you trying to avoid me, it was so futile,' he laughed. 'You can't keep him from seeing me and I know that he will want to.'

He looked at her with that awful mocking smile.

'Remember he knows now that I am his Dad, now try getting out of that. What fairy story did you concoct for him?'

With that, he draped his long legs over the side of the car and slid down into the driver's seat. He slowly switched on the ignition without taking his eyes from her frightened face, then he revved up the powerful engine, shouting,

'Tell my son he'll be seeing me soon.'

He drove away laughing, leaving her standing staring after him, her body now racked with sobbing. She rushed over to the grass and got sick at the very thought of his plans for Alan.

CHAPTER 46

ONLY THE TICKING of the big grandfather clock in the hall broke the silence. She sat at the kitchen table, her head in her hands, crying. Her whole body was exhausted. Then she felt two little arms tighten around her and a very wet face snuggle against her own.

'Mum, Mum, please don't cry, I'm so sorry, I will never do it again but when the man asked for Granda, I thought it would be alright. Then he told me he was my Dad. Is he?'

Laura pulled him unto her knee holding him close. She held him that way for ages without speaking, unable to find the right words, and finally she spoke.

'Alan, I didn't want you finding out like this. Do you remember what I told you about your father?'

Alan looked up at her, his face red from crying and his wee eyes all puffy.

'Yes Mum, I think you told me that he went away, that he didn't want you or me. One time I asked Granda and he said that my Dad had important business abroad some where and it didn't suit him to take me. But is he really my father, is that him?'

She looked at him, wondering what she should tell him. He was growing up fast and deep down she knew he deserved the truth.

Alan put is hands up to her wet face, looking at her with his innocent big blue eyes, his blond hair falling damp over his face.

'Mum, do you not want to talk about him, was he bad?'

Laura flinched, how she could answer that?

'No Alan, he wasn't bad, well he didn't think so. But he is your Dad and I didn't tell him about you because he went away with your Auntie Belle and I didn't know you were coming till he was long gone.'

The child stared at her, open mouthed.

'Auntie Belle, the pretty girl in the photo in Granda's room! Why did he go away with her and not you?'

She looked at her bewildered son.

'It's a long story but I suppose he just loved Belle more than he loved me, so the two of them went off.'

'That's sad isn't it, where is Auntie Belle now? Why isn't she here too?'

'Well, I don't know,' Laura answered, 'but we heard that Andy's father is sick in hospital and Andy had to come and see him.'

Alan looked very serious.

'Has Auntie Belle any children? I asked Granda but he didn't say much. Does she write to you, is she very far away?'

Laura waited for awhile before answering.

'No Alan, she doesn't write to me but she writes to Granda sometimes and she has two little girls.'

The child thought for a minute.

'Granda said she lives in Canada, does that mean that my Dad lives there too? Is he their Dad as well, do they look like me?'

She smiled at her son, and pushed the hair away from his eyes.

'We will tell Granda all about this when he comes home and maybe he will show you his photos. They might look a bit like you.'

Alan smiled.

'Oh, that's great. Are they my cousins, or what are they? I can't wait to tell Niall my father owns that great MG, he'll be dead jealous.'

Laura smiled at the child's logic. Here he was, just discovering he had a father and all he could think of was that he had new relations and his father owned an MG. Laura looked at him.

'But Alan, you have cousins. Have you forgotten Uncle Sam and Auntie Anne has two little girls and the lovely presents they send from New Zealand?'

'I know that but I will never see them, will I? It's so far away but one day soon I will see my father's other children, won't I?'

'Alan,' said Laura softly. 'they won't be your cousins, they are your half-sisters.'

The child was totally confused now.

'I thought that Auntie Belle was your sister, so her children are my cousins.'

'No, she said, 'they are your half-sisters because Andy is also their father, do you understand?

'Well I....'

He didn't finish what he was going to say as the door opened and her father came in. Alan rushed at him, shouting.

'Granda, Granda, guess what! I have a real Dad and he is very rich and has a super racing car and it's red, and only very rich people can own one and I have two half-sisters, what do you think of that?'

William looked at him, speechless.

CHAPTER 47

LAURA WAS GLAD that the shop was busy, she didn't want time to think, although she could not forget the fury on her father's face when he heard what had taken place between her and Andy. When they finished their dinner, which she hardly touched, she left for the shop.

Violet was away visiting a friend for a few days and she had no one to talk to. She needed to see Peter, as she had not seen him since that awful day when Andy came back into her life. She wondered if Peter was avoiding her. She missed Mary too but she was still in Germany on her course. She thought of phoning her but changed her mind, she didn't want to burden her at the minute and anyway she was due home soon. Laura was glad when it time to close up, she was exhausted.

She went around to Peter's flat but it was in darkness. Then she saw a light in the back of the workshop and called out but it was one of his workers that opened the door, Reggie Hall. He told her that Peter had had to go off on business and would not be back for a few days.

Laura left and went to her car feeling very dejected, she couldn't understand why Peter didn't tell her. She began to drive towards home but pulled into the side of the road and sat thinking. She wasn't ready for a whole lot of questions from her father, she needed more time to herself.

She turned the car and headed for town, she had no plans on where she would go. She reached the outskirts of the town and instead of driving in she turned right and drove out to the Black Lough, a favourite beauty spot. Tonight it lived up to its name. The water looked black as pitch. It was a great place for courting couples – she was glad there was only two other cars parked and she moved as far as she could from them.

She looked at the deep blackness of the lough. The lights from the town and the houses dotted around the banks reflected on the water. The stillness gave it an eerie appearance. She adjusted the car seat and lay back, thinking of all the awful things that Andy had said, and his threats, especially about taking Alan from her. She couldn't imagine her life without him or what it would do to her father. She let the tears come – this time there was no one to hear the awful sobs.

Finally she composed herself and got out of the car. The wind had risen and was blowing ripples on the water. It was also helping to clear her head and she was totally alone now as the other cars had left. She walked slowly to the water's edge, her mind still in confusion, not knowing what to do about this terrible situation.

She looked at this mysterious, wonderful lough and the joy it brought to so many people over the years. They came here on picnics and to watch the bird-life on the water with the ducks and the swans – hundreds of them flocked here all the year round and the little island in the middle was home to many va-rieties. Alan had done a project on the birds last year and they had spent a lot of time here. His Granda got him a book on birds and they spent hours trying to identify all the species. She remembered a few short years ago coming here with the child and her mother. The lough had frozen and people were skating and sliding on the ice. A friend gave her and Alan a sleigh-ride on to the frozen lake. It was great fun. They'd even had their photo taken for the *Tyrone Courier* but her mother stayed on the bank watching.

Now Laura gazed down into its dark depths and wondered about all the secrets it held. Suddenly the wind got stronger, and she nearly lost her balance. She turned and made her way back up to the car. It was as if the lough was telling her it was time to go home, tomorrow was another day.

It was late when she drove into the yard. She saw the kitchen light on and quietly made her way in. Her father was in his usual chair at the fire. His glasses had fallen to the end of his nose, giving him a comical look. She suddenly thought of Alan and his precious camera, he would have loved to take a picture of this and tease his Granda with it. She noticed that his Bible was still open on the table beside him and a photo of her mother and father with a young Alan between them – it was a happy smiling group.

She pushed the kettle over near the heat and in seconds it was boiling. The noise wakened her father, he removed his glasses and smiled at her.

'I'm glad your home, I was worried about you. Where did you get to?

Laura looked at his tired face.

'You should have gone to bed Father, I'm alright. I just felt like a drive, I needed time to think. Now I want a nice mug of hot tea, will you have some?' she asked, lifting the teapot.

'I will of course. And a wee slice of that fruit cake that Myrtle made, it's lovely, isn't it?'

Laura told him of the drive to the lough and how nice it was and then she asked him if Alan said anything after she left.

'Said anything? Sure he never stopped. He's over the moon about his new Dad. How on earth did you explain it all to him? It couldn't have been easy for you.'

'No it wasn't but it had to be done. I'll never get over the shock of seeing Alan in that bugger's car, the smug smile on Andy's face, like it was the most natural thing in the world. That devil has some nerve.'

Her father gave a deep sigh.

'Well, it looks like we will be seeing more of him whether we like it or not. Alan says that you don't mind if he sees his father, is that right?'

'Of course I mind but I don't have much choice, do I? Andy reminded me that he has rights and he's going to use them.'

'Rights,' said her father. 'What rights has he? Sure he didn't even know that Alan existed, he can't breeze in here after all these years and demand rights to him, you have your rights too.'

Laura sighed.

'Well, I thought I did but he has known about Alan since he was four. David saw us and took some pictures and their father saw us at a mart. That fellow was biding his time till it suited him.'

'Laura,' said her father, 'maybe you should see our solicitor, Mr McMullen. You'd need to take legal advice on this, what do you think?'

'I know I need advice from someone. I'll call him tomorrow and listen to what he has to say. It can't do any harm.'

Her father sighed.

'Well, it will ease your mind anyway. I still can't get over how quickly Alan accepted that man as his father. He must have some questions, eh?'

Laura smiled.

'I think that he was more excited by the fact that Andy owned a red MG, sure he never shut up about it, didn't he tell you all about it?'

'He did indeed, you could see his wee face light up when he described it in detail. Sure isn't he car mad. Him and Niall watch for all the special cars that stop for petrol or drive through the village. Didn't he see the driver of a silver Rolls Royce go into the tea-shop last week. He heard him ask directions for the McClean place and he raced home to get his camera to take pictures. He was up into the top field and down into the gardens in a flash. He was telling me all about it. I told him that he wouldn't go up after the cattle as quick but he laughed at me and said that the car was a lot better-looking than the cows. What do you think of that for cheek!'

'Indeed, it was cheeky of him, the wee brat. It was just as well he wasn't caught. Did you see all the new signs about trespassing? Myrtle was telling me about the new owners. She said they were very snooty and asked to see the whole staff. You should have heard her laughing at that.'

'The whole staff – her and Jim!' Her father laughed. 'Well, they won't get away with being snooty here. Where are they from, did you hear any more?

'No, not really, Myrtle and Jim are not too impressed with them. The new lady of the manor ran her gloved finger over the furniture to see if there was any dust but of course there wasn't. Then she tried to find fault with everything else. After the house, they went into the garden – they want to redesign the whole place. You should hear Jim, the final straw was when they told him that they wanted the rose-bed cleared as they intended to build a swimming pool. That rose garden is just beautiful. Jim created a masterpiece there and now they want to wipe it all away, isn't that awful?'

Her father shook his head.

'Well, they must be from a big city and know nothing about the work that goes into making a garden. It looks like they have more money than sense. Maybe they won't be buying at all. I saw the "for sale" sign still up at the end of the avenue, so they haven't bought it yet.'

'It's a lovely house. Myrtle gave me the grand tour last week. The size of the place! Wouldn't it make a great rehab house for Mary's burns unit? She has always dreamt of a place like that, it would be ideal.'

'Oh, it would be grand. Sure them poor people would be as right as rain in no time,' agreed her father, 'with all the fresh air and good food but I can't see the Health Board agreeing to the cost, can you?'

Laura sighed.

'What Mary needs is a miracle, and so do I, to stop that bastard annoying us.'

Her father stared at her.

'Now don't talk like that, what we should do is pray. That's what I'm doing and maybe you should do the same.'

'Och Father, you're right as usual but I know what miracle I'd like to see happen to him. Come on, it's time we were in bed. You lie on in the morning, you look very tired.'

Her father got up and put his Bible back on the shelf. As he turned, he patted her on the back, a very unusual gesture for him.

'Don't worry girl, things will work out for the best.'

CHAPTER 48

LAURA WAS SITTING enjoying a cup of tea in the new conservatory. The plants were thriving in the warm atmosphere and she made a mental note to put some smaller pots on the tables.

She had still not heard from Peter, she couldn't understand it. The only explanation she could arrive at was that he had gone to Scotland to see Lisa. She felt very down, thinking that maybe they had got back together again. She wondered if that evening had meant nothing to him was it all false, the words he spoke? Somehow she couldn't imagine him doing anything like that to her. She decided that she would visit his mother later, maybe she knew something.

It was nearly a week now and Andy had not appeared, Laura was glad. She could manage without seeing him at all, if it wasn't for Alan's questions. When did she think he would be here, did he phone last night? It was starting to get on her nerves but she didn't want to hurt his feelings.

She was lost in her reverie when she heard a familiar voice.

'Here, have you nothing else to do only sit over cups of tea and admire the scenery?'

She jumped up to hug her friend and burst into tears.

'Oh Mary, you don't know how glad I am to see you, I missed you so much!'

Mary laughed.

'Why the tears, I didn't know you cared that much,' but she realised that her friend was shaking. 'Laura, what's wrong? Has something happened, is Alan alright?'

She guided Laura back to her chair and sat opposite.

'Now, tell me what the problem is.'

Laura smiled.

'You don't know how good it is to see you. Have you got a bit of time to spare?'

Mary nodded.

'I've got all the time in the world for my best friend.'

Laura called June over and ordered more tea and cake for them both. While eating, she told Mary all that had happened with Andy.

Mary was speechless.

'Laura, it must have been like a waking nightmare for you! wee Alan must be very confused.'

Laura nodded.

'Well, he is but he's excited as well to discover that he has a Dad and that he is very rich but I think it was the car that did it. You should have seen his face. He hasn't seen him for days and he keeps asking about him. I don't know what to say to him.'

'What about your father, he must be in an awful state. Is there any news of Belle or the wee girls?'

'No,' said Laura, 'he just said that they were still in Canada. I didn't ask, he told me. I knew that Father would want to know – he hasn't heard from her since last Christmas and that was just a card.'

'Well,' said Mary, 'maybe the bugger has gone back to wherever he came from and done you all a favour. Wouldn't that be just great?'

'Och, it would,' she answered, 'but somehow I don't think he has gone too far. You should have seen his face when he looked at Alan, you could see that he was already planning his future.'

'Listen girl, you need good legal advice and I know just who you should talk to,' said Mary. 'Alice Quinn, she specialises in family law, a lovely girl. She's married to one of Yusef's doctor friends, Michael Scott. She keeps her own name for legal reasons, she'll put you right.'

'Thanks Mary but my father is planning to see Mr McMullen. You know him don't you?'

'Yes of course I know him. He's a nice old man but he's not living in the real world. You need a sharp one like Alice and I know she'll help you. Will I arrange a meeting for you?'

Laura looked perplexed.

'Maybe you should. Sure Father will understand, he knows we need the best. Now enough about me, how did you get on in Germany? You must be an expert now.'

Mary smiled, 'Well, hardly an expert but I did learn a lot. They're great scientists, the Germans. Their skin-grafting techniques are the best in the world but you don't want to know all that stuff, and I do have some news for you.'

Laura nearly screamed out.

'Oh Mary, you're pregnant, I'm so excited!'

'Hold on or you'll wet yourself. No, I'm not pregnant, are you joking, after all this time! Now that *would* be a miracle, wouldn't it?'

Laura looked sad.

'Oh, I'm so sorry, it's just that your face, you looked so happy.'

Mary laughed.

'So I am. Yusef and I both agree that it will never happen and we're resigned to the fact. He devotes so much time to his work as well as trying for a decent rehab unit. The wards we have are alright but we need a bigger place, away from the hospital, to let the patients really heal. And that's my news, now will you listen.'

'Och, go on then what is it? And don't tell me that you are moving to Germany,' said Laura.

'No, nothing like that, sure I wouldn't leave here but as you know, Yusef and his friends, have been begging the officials at the City Hall for help to fund the Rehab Unit. Well, finally they have agreed that it is a necessity and they'll help with funding if the premises are suitable, isn't that great?'

Laura was delighted for her friend's good news.

'I'm so glad for you all! And I just happen to know of a very suitable house,' she said, smugly. 'You remember the McClean place? Well it's on the market again. It's the right size and I know that Yusef would love it.'

Mary smiled.

'It sounds great but what about the price? I'm not sure what the budget is but it wouldn't do any harm to have a look. I'll phone Yusef tonight but I have a gut feeling that the money from the Health Board will not be enough for a place like that,' Mary sighed.

'It would just be perfect, Father and I were just saying the same. Isn't there any way you could meet the price?'

'I don't see how we could but I'm sure that Yusef would love it. Now, what's the rest of the gossip? Fill me in, I believe you all had a great weekend in the city – Niall was on the phone to me, he had a great time. And Peter went too, I hope you enjoyed the wine I left for you, which reminds me I have a few bottles of that German wine you like, they're in the car.' She looked at Laura. 'You're blushing, did something happen that I don't know about?'

Laura felt herself getting hot but now she only felt foolish.

'No, not really but we did have a good time, Peter was a great help.'

Mary looked at her and smiled.

'Come on, it's me remember, and we don't have any secrets. Did our Peter try anything? He did, didn't he? Oh the devil! I'll kill the wee bugger, I...'

Laura didn't let her finish.

'No, it wasn't like that, he didn't do anything wrong. Quite the opposite in fact, and I know that he enjoyed our day too.'

'Laura Steenson! You and our Peter! Your Da will kill you, that's for certain. You and a Catholic! Did you have sex? Come on tell me all the news.'

Laura laughed.

'Well, I'm not going to tell you, for there's nothing to tell.'

Mary looked at her with a cynical expression.

'Hello, it's me you are talking to. And you know that you never could tell a lie, not like me, I was an expert, remember?'

'There isn't anything to tell, we had a great time and I haven't seen him since. I don't know where he is, he went and got Alan that afternoon when Andy appeared and took off.'

Mary smiled.

'Well, I think I know where he is.'

'You do?' said Laura with an anxious look. 'Tell me then, what was so hush-hush about it that he couldn't even phone me?'

She looked at her friend for an answer and saw the sadness in her eyes.

'What is it, have I done something wrong?'

'No, no, it's nothing to do with you, it's just a family problem that he had to deal with.'

'I'm sorry, I just wondered. I mean, after the things he said I didn't expect him to keep anything from me but if it's confidential I understand.'

Mary reached for her hand again.

'You're part of this family, always have been but we got a shock last week. You see the twins were released from prison and Mickey is very sick. Peter and the rest of the family wanted to be there when they came out the gate but the shock of seeing him looking so weak was too much for my Ma. So Auntie Alice suggested that we all stay at her place, you remember her lovely big farm in Armagh? Her family has all gone now and there's plenty of room. It'll give them time to get to know each other again but Ma is causing us concern, her heart isn't good.'

Laura's eyes were filled with tears as she spoke.

'Your mother has been through so much in these last few years, no wonder her heart is giving up. But now that the boys are home, she will start to feel well again. It's great news about them, what about Mickey, is he alright?'

'Yes Mickey's fine, Laura. He just needs feeding up now but, I'm more worried about his mind. He's still very bitter about all the years they've been locked up and the beatings they endured. And, of course, they still maintain they were framed, that they didn't shoot that poor man. My God, Laura, if you could see them your heart would go out to the both of them!'

'What about Mickey? How is he?' asked Laura. 'I always remember Violet calling Jimmy "Mickey's shadow". He followed him everywhere, didn't he?'

'Aye, they were like peas in a pod and they looked so alike but Mickey was always the strong one. He made all the decisions, and Jimmy did everything he told him to.'

'Sure, at school he got slapped instead of Mickey! I remember the headmaster coming to our house complaining about all the things they got up to. They hated that man, indeed he was a cruel auld bugger. He left more welts on their hands than on anyone else in the class.'

'Oh, I remember him,' said Laura. 'Master Boyle, wasn't he? A tall man, he never smiled. Even in later years when he came into the shop, he was very dour. He always bought the *Irish Press* and a packet of imperial mints. He never missed a day. He used to park his bike outside, it had a basket on the front of it for all his books. Do you remember him?'

'Of course I do, very well. He didn't care who he hit with that long cane of his. I remember one day our wee Winnie, God rest her, went over with the twins' lunch – they had forgotten to take it with them. She went into the classroom without knocking the door, sure she was only a wee thing then. Well, Master Boyle gave her a whack on the legs with that cane. She ran across the road to my Ma, roaring and screaming. Well, my Da went over to him and only for another teacher pulling him off, Da would have killed him. But it didn't stop his cruelty and it made the boys hate him all the more.'

'Aye but did I not hear that they got the better of him one day?' laughed Laura.

'They certainly did,' said Mary. 'The pair of boys tied a rope to the saddle of his bike one day. He used to keep it at the corner of the shed near the toilets. They covered the rope with leaves and wrapped it round a tree. The Master came out and climbed on the bike and tried to cycle away – when it stopped dead, he went flying over the handlebars! They could have broken his neck. He was off school for weeks and when he started to tackle the twins again, our Pat warned him that he'd go straight to the bishop if he touched them again. After that they had no bother at all. And do you know something, their school-work was a lot better as well.'

'They were great fun when they were small. I used to love going to your house, there was always such craic. And Winnie, remember she always insisted on standing on a chair when she sang? She had a lovely voice, your mother used to say that she would be on the stage one day.'

Both girls began to cry at the memory of Winnie. Finally, Mary dried her eyes and stood up.

'Come on girl, that's enough reminiscence and tears for today. You and I have work to do and I see your son coming.'

Alan came bounding into the tea-room and straight into Mary's arms.

'Auntie Mary, it's great to see you! Thanks for the cards from Germany, they were lovely, Master Graham put them on the wall for our geography class. Are you staying for awhile, is Uncle Yusef with you?

Mary hugged him tight.

'No, not this time, and I'm here for another day,' she held him at arm's length. 'Let me look at you, are you on stilts? You've grown so tall.'

'I'm *not* wearing stilts,' he insisted. 'I'm just getting bigger, sure I'm going to be eleven soon. Did Mum tell you that my Dad's come back? Isn't it great? And he has this smashing red MG and he took me for a drive. All the boys were mad jealous!'

Mary smiled.

'Your Mum's just told me all the news, you must be very excited.'

'Oh I am and I can't wait till he comes back. He said he would take me out for the whole day. Did he phone yet, Mum?'

'No,' she replied, 'not yet. Now do you want some tea and scones now or just something to drink? We will be going home soon for dinner.'

'I'll just have a drink then,' he said, crestfallen. 'Is it alright if I call for Niall? I need to tell him something and can I bring him up for a drink?'

'Go on,' she said 'but don't be long.'

She watched her son flying out the door.

'My God, Laura but that fellow is going to break a lot of girls' hearts soon. He's growing up so fast and so handsome. What about Andy, has he still got his good looks?'

Laura sighed.

'Aye, and still playing the Romeo.'

Then she told Mary about him asking June out for a date and telling her he would make her a star and filling her head with nonsense.

'I'm telling you, she comes in here in the mornings with a ton of makeup on her face and her skirt up to her arse. She never leaves the window watching for him, God help her wit.'

Mary laughed.

'Sure it's not that long ago that we were doing the same, watching the boys and trying on makeup and you having to clean it all off before your Da saw you.'

'Oh, I remember alright. Our Belle told on me and he had me reading The Bible for an hour every night for a week. He told me that I was following in your corrupt footsteps. If he only knew the things we got up too, he wouldn't have let me out at all!'

'Do you mind when our wee Winnie found my new bright red lipstick and had it plastered all over her face and used Mickey's new white shirt to wipe it off? The only one he had! And him needing it for the school choir next morning. I'll never forget it, she was covered in it and her clothes as well, she was a comical sight.'

Laura laughed.

'Wasn't that the day she hid in the horse-box that was going to the Dublin Horse Show? Wasn't it lucky that the man had to put the horse in or she would have gone all the way to Dublin? And your mother crying her eyes out when they couldn't find her. God, it's just like it all happened yesterday.'

Mary hugged her friend.

'Isn't it good to have all these memories, especially the funny ones? When we were all at Auntie Alice's the family remembered more things and the antics she got up too. Mickey had us in fits with stories, it was good for all of us. In my mind it was the wake that was only then taking place... Now I've got to go but I will see you later.'

The two friends walked out to the courtyard gate. Most of the tables were filled and June and Mollie were busy. Mary looked around.

'I can't get over all the changes you have made. It's so good for the village. I tell all my friends about it – lots of them have tried it and were very impressed.'

Laura smiled.

'Yes, Violet had the right idea and she's very proud of the place but it was Peter's design and hard work that made it possible, he has great taste. I had your mother over for tea after we opened and she was bursting with pride when she saw his handiwork. We put his iron-craft on display in the courtyard and he's doing great.'

Mary had a big smile on her face as she said:

'Talk of the devil and here he is.'

Peter, came striding towards them, smiling.

'Well, haven't the women a great time chatting all day over cups of tea? How are you, Laura? I came over to say I'm sorry for rushing off like that but I suppose Mary's told you why.'

He moved closer to her and before she knew it he had her in his arms and was kissing her full on the lips.

'Well,' said Mary, astounded, 'is that the way it is, or do you greet all the women like that?'

Peter turned to his sister, and smiled.

'No, sister dear, only the one I'm madly in love with.'

Laura was still standing, speechless and now deeply embarrassed as well. Mary joined them, hugging them both.

'I couldn't be more pleased. You two were meant for each other, I can't wait to tell Ma, she'll be over the moon! I'm away.'

Laura and Peter didn't notice she had left. They just stood staring at each other and they were brought back to reality with the sound of Alan's voice – he had just come in with Niall.

'Are you two just going to stand here all day? What about them drinks? We're parched.'

The boys went inside, laughing. Laura felt her face redden.

'Do you think they saw us? Now he will say something to my father and all hell will break loose.'

Peter put his arms around her again and pulled her closer.

'Will you give your father credit? Sure he's not senile, he must have sussed long ago that you fancied me. Who else would take a Protestant spinster and her child, only a stupid auld Papish like me,' he laughed, and kissed her again.

They went in and joined the boys, who were sitting at the table laughing at some private joke.

'Well,' he said 'What's the craic, or are you pair laughing at us?'

The two boys went red and looked at each other for help. Alan stammered.

'W… w… we were just wondering if you were Mum's boy-friend and I think you are. I was showing Granda the photos that we took in Belfast and he was looking at the ones with the two of you in them and…'

Laura didn't let him finish.

'Oh my God, when did you get them out? The roll wasn't fin-ished, I was going to take them in, I asked you the other day.'

She was in a panic but Alan caught her arm.

'It's alright Mum, Niall's mum took them in for me. We took the rest in his garden and Granda got them for me yesterday when he went to town and he thinks that they are great.'

Laura and Peter, looked at each other, and he shrugged,

'Now he knows. Anyway, what are you worried about? After all, you have a life to live too,' he smiled, 'even if it is with me. Do you want me to come home with you and tell him?'

'No, I think this is something I must deal with myself but I will call you later. Come on Alan, finish up and put your school-bag in the car.'

She walked Peter out towards the back. He was going to his workshop and she was returning to clear the tables when she heard Alan shout.

'Mum, Mum! Dad's come back! Can I go for a drive, please, please, Mum?' he begged.

She turned. Andy was standing in the doorway, looking suave as ever, he was dressed in a navy blazer, grey slacks and blue open-necked shirt, for all the world like a film star, with a pair of sun glasses perched on his head.

She looked at this man she once loved and now loathed.

'I was hoping you had left the country,' she said, turning her back again.

'Not a hope, honey,' he replied, coming very close to her. 'You can't get rid of me that easy. My son and I are going to spend a lot of quality time together.'

He reached over and pulled Alan to him, the three of them now almost linked. She pushed him away and kept Alan beside her. She felt a burning hatred deep inside her and she stared up at him,

'For a start I'm not your *honey*, and I'm not letting you take my son anywhere. Now we're going home, and you can make an appointment before you call next time.' She pushed past him, still holding a protesting Alan, with June and Mollie standing open-mouthed watching them. They left him standing there, speechless.

Laura's father knew there was something wrong as soon as he came into the kitchen for dinner. He started telling Alan about the problems he was having with some of the cattle, when he noticed that the young fellow wasn't paying much attention. He looked at his daughter, hoping for an explanation but she just shrugged her shoulders. It was Alan who finally spoke.

'Granda, my Dad has come back and he wants me to go out for the day with him but Mum has said no, that's why she's cross.'

William looked at Laura.

'Well, what happened, did you give him his walking papers?'

'Yes I did' she said, with the anger still burning inside. 'How dare he drift in and out of our lives whenever he feels like it, he has some nerve! So I told him that he should make an appointment next time.'

'I don't blame you. He'll have to realise that he can't come here and go upsetting this wee lad,' said William patting Alan's arm. The child looked up at him.

'It's not my fault. Dad saw me putting my bag in the car. He called and asked if I wanted to go for a drive but Mum said no. It's not fair is it?'

'That's for your mother to decide,' said William. 'I can't get involved.'

The young lad sat at the table, put his head in his hands and didn't speak. Later, when his mother put his dinner in front of him, he hardly touched it. William asked him if he wanted to help him with the cattle. He said that he had a lot of homework to do. It was so unlike him – normally he would jump at the chance to help. He pushed his plate aside and asked to be excused, then took his bag and went upstairs.

She was just finishing up in the kitchen when the phone rang, it was Andy.

'Just calling to make an appointment to see my son. I want to pick him up from school tomorrow, that's if you have no objections.'

She held tightly to the handset, fury rising in her.

'Are you still there? Maybe you can't find your appointment book,' he said with a sarcastic tone.

'Don't be such a smart-alec,' she answered. 'Yes, you may take him but I want him home by seven o'clock'

She could tell he was raging.

'I'm not putting a time-limit on the first outing with my son. You can't do this. I'm not sure where we're going yet.'

'Tough, that's my terms, take it or leave it,' she said.

'If that's the way you want to play it, fine. But remember, soon I'll be calling the shots and taking him anywhere I please.' He paused. 'I wonder if he would like to live in Canada?'

'Don't try those games with me, Andy,' she said. 'I will fight you all the way. This is his home and he knows it.'

'Well, maybe you have your reasons, eh? After all, that farm is worth a fortune and he's your father's only grandson, isn't he? You wouldn't like him to lose it now, would you?' he sneered.

Laura could feel her blood boil but she tried to sound calm.

'This farm is our business and don't you even think of going down that road for you will never get your filthy hands on it,' she paused. 'Now, if you want to take Alan out for a few hours, fine but only when it suits me, do you hear?' she slammed the phone down. She didn't want to hear his voice again.

She went into the kitchen and sat down heavily on the settee, tears streaming down her face.

Oh, dear Lord, she prayed, don't let that bastard take my son. He mustn't, I couldn't live without him. Lord, help me, please! Laura fell into the cushions, crying her very heart out. She stayed that way until she heard Alan coming down the stairs. He came into the room looking very sheepish. She opened her arms to him and he flew into them, saying how sorry he was.

'No, it's not your fault. It's just that your father has come back into our lives and he knows he is upsetting me and he enjoys doing it. I know he has a fancy car and you love it but he'll go away again, I know it, and you're much too young to understand.'

She felt his arms go around her neck.

'Mum, it's alright, I won't go with him if you don't want me to. I'm a big boy now, I do understand.'

She loved this son of her's to bits and she was never more proud than at this moment.

'No Alan, you must see him, he is your father and he is picking you up after school tomorrow.'

She could see the sheer delight in his eyes.

'You and Granda don't mind?'

She smiled at him, and gave him a hug.

'No, you go and enjoy the drive but tell him not to drive too fast, he has a precious cargo on board. Now away and help your Granda.'

CHAPTER 49

LATER ON, with Alan ready for bed and watching television, Laura made light of the outing with his father the next day. She knew William was dying to know what had happened but she wasn't sure what to tell him. She didn't want to tell him what Andy had said about the farm, so when she heard Mary's car drive up she was delighted. She went out to meet her and they agreed that they would discuss this problem over a walk and a few drinks. Laura left her two men, telling Alan that one more hour of television was enough, and then bedtime. The two friends went off towards the lake. Mary parked the car and they walked up the lane that edged the water. There were quite a few people about – some were fishing from the banks and others were out in boats. The weather was lovely, everything looked so peaceful with the evening sun shining on the water. They made their way to the far side and sat on the rocks. Laura told Mary all about Andy's awful phone call, his subtlety and his remarks about Alan's inheritance of the farm.

'That devious bugger is up to something and the sooner you get legal advice the better. What did your father say?'

Laura told her that she hadn't mentioned it to him.

'I could see that he was annoyed and I didn't want to add any more worry.'

Mary shook her head.

'Not a bit of wonder he's upset. I'm going back to the city tomorrow and the first thing I'm going to do is contact Alice Quinn, that solicitor I was telling you about. You can't leave it any longer, you don't know what that fellow will do next. Now, what about our Peter? I know he's serious, what about you?'

Laura looked at her.

'Do you not think that I've got enough to worry about right now without more complications? Can you imagine how that would stand in Andy's favour, if he heard that I was seeing Peter.'

'Sure it's none of his business who you go out with, especially after his behaviour. He's one to talk, God knows how many girls he's seeing. You were well rid of him, I expect your Belle has her hands full with his carry-on,' Mary replied.

Laura laughed.

'Are you thick or what? Sure the fact that Peter is a Catholic is enough for him. You know how his mind works, I mean, he's never approved of our friendship, has he?'

Mary took her friend's hand.

'Don't let him get the better of you. Peter is crazy about you, always has been. You deserve a good life.'

Laura's eyes filled with tears.

'I don't think I'm meant to live my life with anyone, especially Peter. I love him Mary but if Andy uses my relationship with Peter to take Alan from me, I know who I would choose. I can't lose him, not to that vile bastard, you understand, don't you?'

Mary took out a clean tissue and dried her friend's eyes.

'I do understand but will Peter? He has waited a long time for you.'

'Did he say anything to you this evening?' asked Laura.

'Say anything? Sure he never stopped. He came over for his tea with the family and you were all we talked about. It's a wonder your ears were not burning. I had told Ma about you and him but she just laughed and said she had known for years that you were the only one for him but the pair of you were too stupid to do anything about it. Then the boys started slagging him. You know it's the first time I've heard my family laughing in a long time, they all looked so happy.'

Laura looked anxious.

'So they don't mind then?'

'Mind!' said Mary, laughing. 'Sure Peter has already got you walking up the aisle and he said he doesn't care what church it's in and none of our family would care anyway. Our Mickey joined the craic, suggesting that the wedding take place out on the green and my Da said why not the Forge, like they do in Scotland!'

'Oh my God, how am I going to face them all?' said Laura. 'Can you just picture it, Father Hughes and the Reverend Graham, side by side under the big oak tree with Peter and I, and everyone in the village looking on. Sure wouldn't they have something to talk about for years. Can you just imagine it!'

The pair of them fell about laughing at the idea. They stayed there chatting, watching the May evening sun turning the water of the lake red.

When the arrived back at the house, everything was quiet. Her father had gone to bed and Mary made herself at home by the fireside while Laura prepared two hot whiskeys, a perfect end to the evening.

CHAPTER 50

MICKEY MCCANN stood at his bedroom window gazing out at the familiar scene he had thought he would never see again. It had changed of course. Ah sure nothing stays the same, he thought. Even with most of the bigger trees gone, it was still a very welcome sight. He watched now as people he had forgotten about wandered about the village street on their business. Children he didn't recognise playing on the green in front of his home, looking across the wide street. He could see the new tea-shop and Wray's courtyard – there were quite a few people sitting at the tables enjoying the warm May sunshine.

When he thought of the Wrays he remembered that beast Robert. May he burn in hell for what he did to my wee sister, Winnie! His thoughts went back to the day that Mary and Pat were given a special permit to see him and Jimmy. He knew as soon as he saw their faces that something terrible had happened. Then when they told them, all he could remember now was someone screaming very loudly... it was himself!

They had felt so powerless, rotting away in prison, and there wasn't a hope in hell that the culprit would end up with them. Oh no, buggers like that got sent to mental hospitals and were treated like royalty, not like him and Jimmy. They were beaten and tortured like animals and left to rot. Even though they protested and claimed that they were innocent, it didn't make any difference.

He thought of his parents and the deadness in their eyes as they buried their child – no parent should have to do that – and how they had clung to them as they were taken out of their arms to go back to that hellhole the authorities called a prison.

Hearing that Robert Wray was the bastard that did it only made it worse. The thought of that dirty old paedophile touching his wee sister made him want to break out and kill the devil.

They begged that day for more time to be with their family but instead they were dragged away in front of their parents and thrown into the truck and had to listen to hateful jeers and filthy remarks from ignorant guards. The twins beat one or two of the guards up in the process and ended up in solitary confinement for two months. That part of the sentence nearly finished him, not a soul to talk to and light for only one hour a day. The cell was very damp. He made friends with the cockroaches – he actually talked to them for the sake of something to do. Another week and he would have been a screaming looney. When he was returned to the wing, he could barely walk and the light hurt his eyes but it was the constant headaches that plagued him. They were so severe he just wanted to die, go to sleep and never wake up but the memory of his parents' faces always kept him going. He couldn't put them through another useless death.

Now he was free, if you could call it that. The nightmares and the headaches just wouldn't go away. He was having treatment, it wasn't doing much good but to be able to walk through a door without keys clanging, to feel the rain, wind and sunshine on his face, was heaven. He loved to walk at night on his own and often had the urge to strip off all his clothes and run naked through the fields but he didn't risk that part of his freedom. He didn't want to end up in gaol for being a pervert.

Standing at the window now, his mind in a turmoil, he recalled the night of their arrest vividly.

He was leaving the house when Jimmy caught up with him.

'Where are you off to? Wait for me!'

Mickey turned to him.

'Not this time, Jimmy. This is an important job, you understand?'

He looked at the expression of disappointment on his brother's face and worried about him. When they were younger they had been inseparable. Mickey had always watched out for his brother but now they were grown up, things were different. Through some of his friends, Mickey had got involved with the IRA, just as a driver. Tonight they needed him to go on a job.

He had to obey orders and he couldn't take Jimmy with him. Jimmy pleaded:

'I know what you're up to, why can't I come? I heard you talking to yer man last night in the yard. I'm not stupid, you know.'

Mickey began to protest. Just then, a lorry pulled up on the street and someone called his name. He spoke to the man and then looked back at his brother and invited him to join them.

They had been driving for over an hour into the deep bog-lands at the foot of the Sperrins – a low range of mountains with a maze of laneways and grass tracks. The darkness of the November evening gave them great cover, there was no moon. Mickey was nervous, although he had done the journey many times, both at night and in daylight. This was his first major job and he didn't like the thought of having Jimmy with him. They were going to a fuel dump, well hidden in a hollow below the mountains, to relieve the B-Specials of some of their precious liquid. They picked up two more men on the way – they were going to work the pump. Their informer had said that there would be only one man on duty that night. His name was Eric Boyd and, as there was a big football match on, he would be listening to his wireless. They approached the old stone wall surrounding the disused farm – the dump was hidden in an old barn. The men worked fast while Mickey's job was to keep watch. Jimmy wanted to be useful so Mickey told him to go up on the wall near the gate and let him know if Boyd came out into the yard. He warned Jimmy to stay quiet.

Mickey heard a car approaching. He scrambled along the top of the ivy-clad wall towards the gate. Lying low, he saw Boyd let the driver of the car into the yard. Mickey could clearly hear the stranger asking Boyd if he had anything for him. Boyd shook his head and an argument took place, with him protesting that he had nothing more for the man and didn't want anything to do with him. As Boyd got to the door of the hut, he was grabbed from behind, pulled to the ground and pinned there by a heavy boot on his neck. The man kept swearing and shouting at Boyd that he needed the money tonight. He was gasping for breath when the man finally let him up and he made his way inside the hut saying:

'This is the last you're getting.'

Mickey could see the stranger take out his cigarettes and light one. He saw his face clearly now but didn't recognise him. Boyd came out of the hut, shouting:

'Are ye mad! This is a dangerous place to have a smoke – put that out – the whole place could go up!'

'Never mind that, where's my money?' said the stranger, as he played with his lighter, flicking it on and off.

Finally, Boyd handed him a package, which he opened, shouting:

'This is only half of what I want, where's the rest? You had better come up with the rest of the money if you know what's good for you!'

'I can't get any more, that's it. Do what you like, you bastard!'

'This is your last chance, do you hear me, ye fucking pervert!'

Boyd took a swing at the stranger but it didn't connect. The stranger lashed out and Boyd was flat on his back in seconds. He kicked Boyd viciously in the groin and bent over him.

'That hurts, doesn't it? It will hurt even more when your wife and mates hear you have a special liking for the wee boys in your Sunday school class.'

Boyd was crying now.

'I don't care any more, ye've taken all I've got. I'm going to tell the wife everything and take you down with me, ye evil shit!'

Slowly he got to his feet and went towards the hut, shouting:

'Do your worst, I've had enough! I'm going to tell all tonight and...'

He didn't reach the hut or finish what he was saying. Mickey watched in disbelief as the man pulled a revolver from his pocket. Recalling it now, it seemed to Mickey that everything had happened in slow motion. Without saying a word, the man fired a shot into Boyd's back. Boyd went down, tumbling forwards towards the hut, groaning in pain. Turning his head slowly towards the executioner standing over him, his eyes pleaded mercy. Without emotion, the man looked straight into Boyd's eyes, pressed the gun to his temple and fired.

Mickey lay on the wall, paralysed with fear. He knew the men would have heard the shots. He was unable to see where Jimmy was and worried that he might give their cover away. Everything had gone silent. Shocked, he watched as the stranger dragged the body across the yard and into the barn, picking up a newspaper that had dropped out of Boyd's jacket. Flicking on his lighter once more, he held it to the corner of the newspaper and tossed it into the barn. He ran to the car at the gate, opened the door, took out a cap and placed it firmly on his head. It was then that Mickey realised it was the cap of a B-Special uniform. He watched the stranger speeding away.

Finally, the power returned to Mickey's body and he jumped down from his hiding place on the wall. He saw Jimmy and motioned to him to do the same but Jimmy was frozen to the spot. Then suddenly the barn exploded. For the next few minutes, all hell was let loose. As Mickey ran around the wall to the lorry and drove it to where Jimmy was and dragged him off the wall. Two of the men got on the lorry, shouting:

'Move, move, get the fuck out of here!'

'Where's the other fella?' asked Mickey.

'Drive on, comrade. He's trapped in the flames, there's nothing we can do. For Christ's sake, move it!'

Mickey drove in silence, not wanting to talk to anyone. Jimmy sat like a zombie between Mickey and the other two men. They turned into the side lane that would take them far up the mountain to their safe house, when suddenly they saw lights move in the distance. Mickey braked and the two men jumped out. Disappearing into the bracken, they shouted for him to do the same but he couldn't get Jimmy out and he wouldn't leave him. In seconds, the brothers were surrounded by the dreaded B-Specials.

They were dragged on to the laneway and kicked and beaten by a group of men in uniform, shouting and swearing at them, until someone in charge ordered them to stop. Mickey thought the man's voice sounded familiar but couldn't place it. He was worried that he couldn't see his brother or what they were doing to him. He tried to get up and remembered feeling a hard blow and nothing more. Some time later lying in a cell he realised who the voice belonged to – it was the stranger who'd just shot Boyd. He tried telling someone in authority but of course they didn't believe him. The rest was a living nightmare for both of them.

Jimmy and himself were offered a chance to go to Canada, to their Uncle Paddy, a brother of his mother's. Jimmy was wild excited about it and he took it for granted that he felt the same but he didn't. He knew that there wasn't much work here for them, and anyway who would employ two ex-convicts? He always liked mechanics, tinkering with engines and stuff like that but now you needed qualifications to get anywhere and there wasn't much hope of getting them here. His Da wanted him to work in the garage and Jimmy was doing a stint as a petrol-pump attendant but there wasn't enough work for them all. They had a lot of Protestant customers that wouldn't be long leaving if two ex-IRA jailbirds started to work on their cars! It wouldn't be fair to the family either but the thought of going far away from them again was breaking his heart. He wanted to stay.

Mickey stood there watching the passing traffic. The design of the cars and the amount of them was astounding but to him the classics would always be the best. Like the one he could see now down at the petrol pumps, a bright red MG sports car. He smiled to himself. Ah, wouldn't I just love something like that! As he watched, the driver got out, a tall fair-haired man. As the man went around and removed the petrol cap, he saw his young brother, Joey, rushing to attend him. Mickey stared at him, there was something familiar about his stance. Did he see him some where before, was he a prison officer? No, he didn't think so.

The stranger moved over to the big oak tree and stood there, the branches partly shielding him. Joey was washing the car after filling it up and called something to the driver. Then Mickey nearly had a fit! As he watched, the man walked up and down, then stopped and took a packet of cigarettes from his pocket. He took one out, put the packet away and began to light up. It was when he saw him flick the lighter and toss it from hand to hand that it hit him. Mickey was sure it was *him*!

Laura lay in Peter's arms. They were in his flat. She felt so safe here and very much at home.

She had come over directly after closing the shop, and for the last hour they had devoured each other, their love-making very intense. Now they lay exhausted, just enjoying the moment. She knew she couldn't make any plans for the future because of Andy's threats to take Alan. She told Peter of her intended visit to the city to see Mary's friend, Alice, and he insisted that he would drive her. How lucky she was to have him, he was so thoughtful. Tonight was the first time she had been alone with him since the evening in his sister's flat. Somehow, every time they'd planned to meet, something had come up. She knew that she loved him and wondered what the future would bring. Now she must get dressed and leave him, she didn't have a choice.

She hadn't had a chance to talk to her father yet. She dreaded that but with the worry of Andy and his demands, she didn't have the heart to give her father any more bad news. She felt Peter touching her gently with his finger-tips, she knew that he was aroused again. Playfully she got on top of him, pulled his arms over his head and held them there.

'Now,' she laughed, 'you're my prisoner and you will do exactly as I say!'

CHAPTER 51

THE McCANN BROTHERS, Pat, Mickey and Jimmy, waited anxiously in the back room of a popular bar in the town. They ordered a drink and nodded to the barman. He showed them into the small back room, as they had arranged. It was lightly furnished with two long tables, a few chairs and a big roaring fire. The boys sat down and the barman returned with their creamy pints of Guinness. The barman told them they wouldn't have to wait long but that had been nearly half an hour ago. They finished their drinks and ordered more, this time a young boy delivered them. Jimmy was pacing the floor like a caged animal and Mickey was worried about him. His hands were shaking and he could hardly hold his glass. Suddenly, he slammed it down, spilling its contents all over the table, blurting out:

'Look, I'm away. We've been waiting here long enough and this room is making me feel like I'm back in prison again.'

Mickey tried to calm him but Jimmy pushed him away, saying:

'This fella, whoever he is, is making a fool of us! Are ye coming? Who the hell does he think he is? How do we know if he is the right man?'

A deliberate but quiet voice spoke from behind them.

'I'm the man that can answer all your questions.'

The three men turned, they never heard him or noticed the small sliding door in the corner of the room. He stood there, small and wily-looking with piercing black eyes. His long dark curly hair stuck out from beneath a black peaked cap. He had a dark scarf wrapped around his neck and wore a black, belted, leather coat that fell to his ankles. He stared at the boys.

'Now, I know who *you* are, you don't need to know who *I* am.' The wee man sat down at the table and nodded to Jimmy to do the same. 'I know what you're going through. This is a very small room, I've been there, it will pass.'

He spoke in a low, husky voice.

'Now, that man you've seen, he could be the same one we've been looking for. I need to know more details, times, car registration, and the rest...'

For the next hour they talked and went over the awful episode of that fateful night. The wee man filled in the gaps. Although the brothers hadn't known it at the time, he had also been there that night, watching from the hill above. He looked at Jimmy:

'I could see you up on that wall, paralyzed with fright – and remember, that's nothing to be ashamed of – when I saw yer man shoot Boyd. I was about to help you down but your brother got there first. When the barn exploded, I raced down and tried to get my comrade out but I was too late, the place was like an inferno. I saw his feet and tried to drag him out but I was driven back by the smoke and the flames. I couldn't help him, the fire was all around me. I could hear him screaming. That sound will live with me forever... Both my arms were on fire, I rolled on the ground to put it out. It took me ages to get to the wall but I made it. I moved as fast as I could to where my motorbike was hidden. Later that night I had to organize a minor house-fire to explain the third-degree burns on my arms and my neck. An ambulance brought me to the hospital and they kept me there for nearly six months. I could get no information from anyone about you fellas – it was weeks before I knew where you ended up.'

Jimmy was angry.

Why didn't ye get in touch? Ye *knew* where we were, ye *knew* we didn't shoot that poor man. Have ye any idea what we went through!'

Mickey took his brother's arm.

'Jimmy calm down, you don't understand. We took our orders, we knew what we were getting into and the rule was, if yer caught you know nothing or nobody. I told ye that but ye still wanted to come, didn't I try to stop ye?'

'That's right,' said the man. 'Rules are rules, there was a major cock-up that night as ye know, and that wasn't meant to happen.'

'He's right Mickey, that fella ye saw is the one to blame,' said Jimmy.

'He's the one,' said the wee man, 'in more ways than one – sure he was the informer. It was supposed to be quiet that night. The bugger planned it well. He knew my mate would go looking for him and he was ready for him. What he didn't know was that I was there to witness the whole thing.'

'But if that's what happened, why didn't some of yer other friends pick him up?' asked Mickey.

The wee man shook his head.

'That was the problem. You and my dead comrade, God rest his soul, were the only people ever to see him. We heard of your description but without you to finger him we hadn't a hope, and afterwards – well, you were sick, things changed.'

Jimmy looked over at him with a worried frown.

'Now what happens, what are you planning to do?'

The man stood up, removed his scarf and coat, and looked at the boys.

'Nothing ye have to concern yerselves with. We know he was high up in the B-Specials, maybe a captain, for he had a lot of information to sell. Now ye must not get involved. Just ignore him if ye do see him, right?'

Pat also stood up, reached out and shook the man's gloved hand.

'Thanks for your time, you've eased our minds. My wee brothers have been through enough and so has my family. I'm very grateful to you.'

The man shook his head.

'No need to thank me. As a matter of fact, I owe your family a big favour. Ye see it was yer sister that nursed me back to health, look.'

He rolled up his sleeve to show hideous scars all the way up his arms and shoulder.

'I'm sure you'll take my word for the rest, half my back, neck and my hands. She is a great wee nurse, she gave me back my life. At that time I couldn't care less if I lived or not but now I know I still have important work to do.'

He put his coat and scarf on again and said.

'It's time you left, the back door if you don't mind. You will never come here again and you won't know me if we ever meet, you understand.'

He directed them out the back way, to a side-entry that would take them to the car in the next street. Hardly a word was spoken till the boys reached the village and into Devlin's pub. Big Pat shivered.

'That wee man gave me the creeps, I don't ever want to meet him again. Now what about starting on that decorating job for my Da, eh?'

Mickey and Jimmy both laughed. Mickey asked:

'Will tomorrow be time enough for you, it's a bit late to-night?'

CHAPTER 52

LAURA WAS KEPT BUSY, there was a lot of passing traffic at this time of the year and trade was good. June and Mollie were rushed off their feet and she didn't notice him arrive until he spoke. June ran over to him but he said he needed to speak to Laura. The poor girl walked away looking crestfallen. Laura looked at his handsome but arrogant face.

'Andy, I'm very busy as you can see. June will only be too happy to attend you.'

'No,' he said, 'I need to talk to you, it's urgent.'

Annoyed, she stared at him and reluctantly she led the way down to the back of the café. She sat at a quiet table and rested her hands on it.

'Well, out with it, I don't have much time,' she said.

Slowly, he sat down and waved to where June was still watching them. She came quickly over and he asked for two coffees. Laura protested that she didn't have time for one but he just laughed in that lazy way of his and told her not to worry that he was not intending to poison her, he just wanted to be sociable.

June brought over the coffees and lingered, arranging them on the table, until Laura told her to go as she must have other customers to see to. She left in a sulk and Laura watched Andy's eyes follow her every move.

'Right,' she said, 'What's all this about and why could we not talk at the counter? You know I don't want to spend a second in your company, now what do you want?'

He smiled at her and took out his cigarettes, then his wee lighter, and lit up. She was getting angry now as he played with it, opening and closing the bonnet and laughing as the flame shot out.

'I'm surprised you still have it after all this time and it's in good working order. What about Belle, is she the same?' she said with a sarcastic tone.

He looked at her, surprised.

'Sarcasm doesn't suit you but yes, Belle is still the same, always there for me and stands time well, just like this lighter she gave me. She knows quality when she sees it.'

He tried to reach for her hand but she was too quick and pulled away. Annoyed, she asked him again what he wanted.

'Well,' he said, 'I expect our son has told you about the great day we had last week. He really enjoyed it all and he knows a lot about cars. A very intelligent boy, takes after me no doubt.'

'Yes, yes, of course he told us all about it, many times but life is not all about presents and outings, is it? You'll be off home soon I expect, so I want you to let him down gently. He's excited now but there is a lot of stuff he does not understand.'

'Maybe he's only ten,' he said, 'but he knows a lot more than you think. You deserve great credit for his upbringing and I know how proud you are of him. I know I am and I want him to get to know the rest of his family. My father is on the mend and getting out of hospital tomorrow. I want to bring Alan up to see him at the house the day after. It's time they met.'

Laura was worried as to what his intentions were but now she was furious.

'So, your father wants to see his only grandson in the flesh, so to speak? A photograph won't do this time, no? Look, if he was so anxious to meet him, why didn't he visit him when he found out about him all those years ago? I mean, he had to pass by our lane every time he went into the town, didn't he? But then I suppose a small child wouldn't interest him.'

'Och, don't be so stupid, he didn't know what sort of welcome he would get.'

'Oh,' she answered, 'is that right? Or maybe he was hoping that your wife would produce a son and he wouldn't have to recognise Alan as your bastard! It must be very embarrassing for him now that he has no choice. He'll need him to carry on the Carson name.'

Andy stared at her, surprised at her outburst.

'There's no doubt at all about that, after all the Carson name is very important to my father. Isn't he one of the most important landowners in the north of Ireland? Alan is very fortunate.'

Laura played with the sugar-lumps in the bowl, her coffee untouched.

'So, you have his future all planned. Well, let me tell you something, for a start his name is William Alan Steenson, do you hear? And that's on his birth certificate and where it says "father" I put "unknown". So where does that leave him, eh?'

Andy was gobsmacked. He stared at her, his mouth wide open.

'You vindictive bitch! Belle always said that's what you were and now I believe it. How could you not give him my name, knowing that he was my son? It's a name to be proud of.'

Laura laughed.

'A name to be proud of! A man that runs away, not only with my bitch of a sister but with all my savings, and Lord knows what else. You, a man who robbed poor farmers of their lands and laughed when they were homeless, a man called Carson! That's a name to be proud of alright. Listen one last time, Alan is my son and when he's twenty-one he can make up his own mind but until then neither you nor your father will get your filthy hands on him, do you hear?'

She stood up then, about to leave, when he caught her arm tightly and stared with hatred into her face.

'Listen to me, you bitch! *I'm* his father and no scrap of paper can change that. I was hoping that I could talk civil to you about his welfare but I can see now that I would be wasting my time. If I have to fight you in the courts I will and I promise you I'll win. Why can't you be civil just for once?'

She wrenched her arm free, hoping that none of the girls could see and turned to face him once more.

'I have listened to enough of your nonsense and now I would like you to leave.'

He moved as quick as lightening and stood before her.

'I'm not quite finished yet. You see I told Alan that I was going to ask your permission to take him to Canada for the summer holidays. I know he would love to come with me and the family are all looking forward to meeting him but maybe I should let him decide for himself, after all he knows his own mind.'

Laura's eyes blazed with anger.

'He is not leaving the country without my permission and I certainly won't give it and that's final! If you want to see him the odd evening after school, that's fine but now I have to get back to work.'

Andy raised his hand to her shoulder and gripped it tight. Facing each other they didn't see Peter and Violet arrive. Peter was totally taken by surprise for the scene looked very different from where he was standing. Violet was speechless. Suddenly Laura saw them, pushed his hand away and rushed over to Violet and hugged her.

'It's great to see you, did you have a good holiday?'

Violet saw tears in her eyes and asked if they had come at a bad time.

'No, No, not at all, he's leaving.'

She turned and saw that Andy had moved towards the door.

'I believe our business is finished and I'm very busy as you can see,' he said curtly, as he got up and casually flicked cigarette ash on to the floor. He smiled at her and said he would call his son tomorrow and make arrangements. He waved over to the waiting June, blew her a kiss and left.

Peter had gone ahead with Violet's bags and the two women followed. They went into the kitchen and Laura prepared tea for them. Afterwards she sat down to hear of Violet's holiday. Then it was time for Peter to leave as he had to see his brothers but he said he would be back later. She stood up to see him to the door and he surprised her by taking her face in his hands and kissing her and whispering that he loved her. She returned to the table to see Violet with a big smile on her face.

'Well, so you have finally got it together. And not before time! How does William feel about it?'

Laura sighed and looked at her friend.

'I haven't told him yet. There are more important things on my mind and that bastard Andy is driving me insane. Now he has just told me that he intends taking Alan to Canada for the summer and I know in my heart that he won't bring him back.'

It was too much for her and she cried bitterly. Violet came around the table and held her till she calmed down.

'Laura, you have had a lot to contend with these last few years but you are not to let that vile excuse for a man do this to you. We'll get you legal counsel, the best there is. You have rights as a mother after all. Now stop worrying and think positive, right?'

Laura shook her head.

'I know you're right, Violet, it's just that the very thought of losing him will kill Father and me. He's so excited about his Dad that I don't think he really understands what it's all about. He loves that fancy racing car Andy drives around in and he's over the moon with all the attention.'

Violet smiled.

'I wouldn't worry too much about wee Alan, he has his head screwed on. And sure he would never leave you or William, car or no car.'

'Now I want to hear your most important news, you and Peter, and don't leave anything out, do you hear?'

Laura blushed.

'I'm not telling you everything. Suffice to say that we love each other but we're keeping it quiet for a while till I tell Father and you know that won't be easy. I need to deal with this trouble that Andy's causing, then I'll explain everything to him but I know how he will react. Catholics are fine to have for friends but anything else is out of the question, sure you know that.'

Violet nodded.

'What's wrong with this part of the world? Too much is set on what church you attend but you know, your father has changed a lot these past few years and you might be surprised when you do have a wee chat with him... and don't leave it too late. You know the gossips, they'll have a story out before you know it.'

They chatted another while before Laura went back to the shop. She told Violet that she was going to the city next day with Peter to see Alice Quinn, the solicitor. She was delighted with the news and told Laura not to worry, reminding her that she had a lot in her favour. She was Alan's mother. Even when Andy had found out about him he never offered anything towards his keep and she should tell Alice this.

Laura felt a lot better after their chat as she watched for Alan returning from school. He would be delighted that Violet was back and to see what she had brought him. Laura smiled to herself, thinking how lucky she was to have Violet for a friend.

CHAPTER 53

PETER DROPPED LAURA off at Alice Quinn's office. It was easy to find, just behind the City Hall. She told him to meet her at the Europa Hotel in an hour. She was shown in almost immediately to a cluttered but elegant room, overlooking the busy street. A tall, leggy girl with long auburn hair rose from behind the big mahogany desk with her hand extended to greet Laura. 'Nice to meet you, Miss Steenson. I would have known you anyway from Mary's description.'

She had a lovely warm smile.

'Please, no formalities, it's plain Laura, and thank you for seeing me at such short notice.'

'Not at all, anything for a friend. Now begin at the start, how you met him, your relationship, the break up, his leaving and most important, your pregnancy. I need to know every small detail.'

She switched on a small Dictaphone and Laura began. Next the hour was up – she had opened her very soul and now she was crying.

'I'm sorry to carry on like this. Forgive me but it's the thought of losing my son... I just can't help it.'

Alice smiled.

'Don't worry, you have a good case and I will do my utmost to see that you don't lose your son. You have given me a good picture of the situation. Now I need to know about his father's life in Canada. I have some contacts there and they will be of great help. I would like to know more about his lifestyle and his financial status. This will take time but leave it with me for a few weeks. He can't take the child out of the country without an order from the courts, so please, try not to worry too much,'

Laura thanked her again as Alice showed her to the door and directed her to the hotel. She felt good about the meeting, she found Alice a very forthright person. Peter was waiting for her and she filled him in on what had taken place. He was very interested when she told him. Afterwards, he went to the bar to order some food for them. While she was alone she looked around the familiar surroundings and thought of the last time she had been here, with Ian.

'Penny for your thoughts, love, and I hope they're about me,' he leaned over and kissed her.

She blushed but it wasn't because of his kiss, she was remembering the last time she'd spent here. He smiled.

'Do you fancy staying here for the night? Do you really have to go home?'

'Yes,' she replied, 'I really would like to but I can't. Maybe soon we'll do something special.'

'I suppose I'll have to make do with that but I'll hold you to your promise.'

They finished their tea and decided to have a look at the shops. Peter stopped at the big jeweller's, he insisted that they go inside. She admired everything she saw. Peter showed her a little gold locket and held it up to her so she could see it properly. It was inscribed with both their names and a date. It was the day of the zoo outing. She was amazed. He put it round her neck.

'Well, do you like it? I know you wouldn't let me buy you a ring, so I had them do this when you were at your meeting.'

Laura was really touched.

'It's lovely Peter,' she said, as she examined it. 'I'll put your photo and mine in there. I must look through Alan's collection for some nice ones. He got them developed and didn't tell me. I wonder what Father thought, he never said a word.'

The coldness of the gold felt good against her warm skin. The remainder of the day was spent window shopping. She bought a few things for Alan and herself for the coming summer. They enjoyed spending time together and made plans to do it more often. When they arrived home, she got Peter to leave her off at the shop. Her car was there. Violet was anxious to know how the day had gone.

'I'll be interested to know what he got up to in Canada, especially his finances,' said Violet. Laura told her that Alice was going to have him investigated, as she had a lot of contacts in that country.

'I mean, not too long ago Belle was asking Father for a loan. Sure he knew that he'd never see it again.'

Violet looked surprised.

'Did you ask him anything about it when he said how well they were doing? I mean if they are so well-off you'd have thought that they would have returned it, wouldn't you? God, they have no shame!'

'Och, I've known that for years,' said Laura. 'That's why I think there's more behind all this stuff with Alan. That bugger has something else in his vile mind. Sure he was always devious but I was too blind to see it. When I think of all the things he used to do and say when he wanted to buy some poor soul's land. He would tell me that he had got a certain farm he was after for a song. I always thought that there was a more sinister side to him in the way he relished new property. He would laugh and say it was their own fault, the way they had let the place get so run-down, or the animals got sick and sometimes there was an unexplained fire. All that has been on my mind lately. That's why I don't want him to get his filthy hands on my son.' Violet patted her friend's shoulder.

'Well, at least you are now doing something about it, now get yourself away home. William will be anxious to know how you got on and I happen to know that Myrtle is cooking something for your dinner tonight.'

Laura gathered up her shopping and was putting it in the car when she saw the McCann twins, Mickey and Jimmy. They were painting the outside of the house. They both waved when they saw her. She smiled, it was great to see them home with the family again.

CHAPTER 54

LAURA WAS IN AND OUT of the doorway, getting very irritated – Alan should have been back hours ago. Andy really annoyed her. They'd had words the previous week because of his attitude to timekeeping, *and* this was a school night. Last week it had been nearly ten o'clock when he roared up the lane. She had warned him that if it happened again she would not allow him to take Alan out at all. He just laughed at her, saying that soon he would have him all the time. She stood watching him, anger building up inside her.

'You can't threaten me, Andy. You don't have any rights. You gave them up the day you walked out. I regret now that I let you see him at all.'

His face came close to hers.

'*You* let *me*? Who the hell do you think you are?' he sneered. 'Alan is my son and I'll see him when and where I damn well like. We're planning our holidays and he's very excited.'

Laura stepped back, not wanting to be near him.

'What do you mean, planning his holidays? You can't. He's going to Donegal with his friends, then we're going somewhere special, it's all arranged.'

'Well,' he said, 'you can just change it. I don't approve of him going off on camping holidays with a crowd of Catholics. I don't want him having anything to do with the likes of them – you don't know what sort of notions they put in his head. I don't want him growing up with them for friends. I'm not like you and I'm surprised your father allows it.'

Laura was furious.

'You know nothing about it! They're all children and they get on great. I don't want my son to grow up a bigot like you and that's the end of it, do you hear?'

Before she could move, Andy reached out and grabbed her roughly. He shook her, leaving her startled.

'No,' he said, 'it's not the end of it. I'm taking my son to Canada for his holidays and you can bloody well lump it. And what's more, he wants to come.'

She tried to twist away but his grip tightened. He pulled her closer:

'I'm getting to you, eh? Is a Prod not good enough for you now that you're jumping into bed with that Fenian papist?'

Laura felt the blood rush to her face.

'I'm right,' he snarled. 'I know all about your carry-on. Do you think that I would let my son have anything to do with that? No way, he's not going to grow up with a Catholic. He belongs to me, and the courts will say the same.'

He put his arms around her she could smell the whiskey on his breath. He tried to kiss her, she turned her head, he pushed her away laughing at her.

'Do you think that I would want the likes of you, now that you're with that papist? Sure you're only a slut, Laura. I know all about you and so does my lawyer. You're playing right into my hands.'

He turned and jumped into his car. He was almost at the end of the lane before she could move. She was shaking, he had really frightened her with his threats.

Here she was again, waiting. She had told him that Alan had to be home before seven. She walked to the top of the lane. It was a lovely May evening. At any other time she would have enjoyed the scene before her: It was almost dusk. There was a mist over the fields and it had rained earlier. Now the evening perfume of the shrubs and flowers were at their best. There were scented lilacs and the clematis was spiralling its way up into the trees.

She was just turning to come back when she heard the car. It roared to a stop beside her and a very red-faced Alan, his hair blown all over the place, jumped out. He reached into the car and brought out several parcels.

'Look Mum! We were shopping. Dad took me to Belfast and bought me loads of stuff! We had a great day and we got our photographs taken in a special room – it was like a wee wardrobe – wait till you see them.'

The child began to pull long strips of photos out of his pocket but she stopped him, saying:

'Why don't you bring them up to the house and I will look at them later, it's getting very late.'

Alan agreed and said goodbye to Andy, reminding him to phone tomorrow. She watched as her son carried his precious packages up the lane to the house. Then she turned to Andy, who was standing beside the car lighting up a cigarette and flicking his lighter, as was his habit. She looked at him.

'Andy it's late, where were you? I told you it was a school night, he should have been in bed. You can't see him any more during the week, just Saturdays.' She was about to turn away when he stopped her.

'Listen, you bitch, don't tell me what I can or cannot do. I've told you before I'm taking him whenever I damn well please. You weren't that worried about him last night when you were seeing your papist loverboy. Out till all hours, making a show of yourself. And you think you can tell me what to do!'

Laura was livid.

'What I do is none of your business, neither is who I see! You're not seeing Alan any more during the week. I can't get him up for school in the mornings and last week he didn't do any homework.'

'Och, give over,' he replied. 'You have him like a real mammy's boy. Anyway I've got some business to attend to so you'll be glad to know I'll be out of your hair all next week. Tell Alan I'll call him soon. Now I suppose you'll be off to see lover-boy,' he sneered, as he jumped into the car and reversed all the way down the lane.

When she returned to the house Alan had gone upstairs and her father was examining the contents of the parcels. There were tee-shirts, shorts, football boots and a new football. Lying in a box on the table was a remote-control racing car, an exact replica of the car Andy had just left in. Laura stared at them and then at her father. When she picked up the clothes, she noticed they were all top brands.

'These must have cost a fortune! What's his game? I'm worried sick Father, he's putting all sorts of ideas into the child's head and now he's threatening to take him away to Canada for the summer. I wish he'd just go away and give my head peace. I'm going upstairs to the child now.'

Alan was in bed when she went in so she climbed into the bed beside him. She noticed some schoolbooks under the covers. He gave her a worried look.

'Are you mad at me, Mum? I'm sorry but we were all over the city, it was great! Then we met some of Dad's friends and had tea in a big hotel. I was getting tired for they were talking business all the time. Did you see the photos? Aren't they great! Dad says I need one for my passport.'

Laura was shocked that he'd mentioned the passport.

'Your photos are very good. There are an awful lot of them. Did you show them to your Granda?'

'He thinks they're great but he was sad when I told them one was for a passport.'

Laura sighed deeply.

'Listen love, that's something we'll have to talk about. You're very young and I don't think that I'd like you going that far away from me for the whole summer. You're Granda and I would miss you something terrible.'

The child looked at her.

'I know you would, Mum, but Dad says that I'd love it and he says he's got horses and that I'm just the right age to learn to ride.'

Laura didn't know what to do for the best.

'Alan, all this has happened very fast. I would prefer that you'd wait till you're older before going. I can't explain it now but I know you will understand some time.'

She put her arms round him and held him.

'You're still my baby. You know, I don't know what I'd do if you weren't here and Granda would be lost without you.'

She felt her son's hand on her face.

'It's alright Mum. Maybe you and Dad should talk and then you could come to Canada as well. Wouldn't that be great?'

She smiled at him.

'I don't think that would work, Alan. I'd like you to go with your friends to Donegal as usual and maybe next year you could go with your Dad.'

She felt him give a very deep sigh.

'Mum,' he said, 'I'm worried. 'Dad said that I shouldn't go to Donegal because they are nearly all Catholics and I'm a staunch Protestant so I shouldn't be friends with them. I told him Niall was my best friend.'

'What did he say to that?' she asked. 'Sure you two have been friends since you were babies.'

'I know,' he sighed. 'Dad said that I was older now and that I should get my Granda to explain about our history. Mum what does "staunch Protestant" mean?'

Laura looked at his earnest little face.

'It means that you believe strongly in the Protestant faith and attend your church. Remember that we all love the same God and Catholics worship him too, in their own way. But that doesn't mean you can't be friends, the Lord wouldn't like that.'

The child looked up at her.

'Would he not? That's good for I wouldn't like to lose Niall as my friend, or Peter. When are we all going out for the day again? We had a great time, didn't we?'

She smiled.

'Yes we did, a great day. Maybe I'll organise something soon. Where would you like to go?'

Alan got excited.

'Can I really choose? I'll ask Niall tomorrow after school.'

She smiled at him and kissed him on the forehead.

'Now it's time you were sleeping'

She covered him up and removed his books.

CHAPTER 55

HER FATHER was sitting at the fireside, reading. He looked up from his Bible when he heard her come in.

'Well, is everything alright? Alan seemed very flushed when he came home.'

Laura moved the kettle over on the range to the heat and sat down at the table.

'He's fine, Father but it was much too late for him to be out. Andy just won't listen. He has to do things his way, as always.'

Her father put his Bible down and moved his glasses up on his nose.

'You're worried about him, I can see it in your eyes. Alan told me that his father is going to take him to Canada for the summer and he is getting him his own passport, is that right?'

She gave a deep sigh.

'I wish that he would take himself back there and leave us in peace. He is filling the child's head with all sorts of wild notions, he has him all mixed up. Him and I had a wee chat and I tried to explain to him that maybe when he is older he could go and he would enjoy it more.'

Her father shook his head.

'I don't expect he was too pleased. Sure he was telling me all about how much land the father had and that he would have his own horse because everybody rode horses in Canada. Laura, I'm worried too, for didn't he ask me how much land we owned and did we own all the fields next to McCleans, and would it all be his one day. What do you think of that?'

Laura was really annoyed.

'That man is really evil, the only God he knows is money and land. He'll never change and he's putting all these ideas into the child's head too. Maybe he thinks he can get his hands on this place through Alan, I wouldn't put anything past him. He's trying to change him. Now he's told him that he doesn't like his friendship with Niall as he is a Catholic and he reminded him that he was a staunch Protestant. You know, Father, in the middle of it all I had to laugh when he looked at me with those big eyes and asked me what a staunch Protestant was. I told Andy that I didn't like him talking to the child like that. He might be a bigot but there's no way that Alan is going down that road. I just want him to be a true Christian, and I told him that,' she sighed. 'Oh dear God, just let him understand.'

Her father shuffled his feet on the floor, looking very uncomfortable when he spoke.

'Laura, it's not that long ago that I was classed as a bigot for the way I behaved... and I was. It wasn't until I got to know the other side better that I knew I was wrong. Sure your friend Mary and her brother are two of the finest Christians there is. The way they looked after Violet that time, especially under the circumstances.'

Laura smiled, she didn't think that she would ever hear her father admit he was wrong about something like that. She nodded.

'As I told Alan tonight, we're all God's children. We just worship him in different ways, that's all.'

'Aye,' agreed her father.

'You're right, live and let live. That McCann family have been good friends to us all, eh? What about you and Peter, you and him have always been good friends you're seeing a lot more of him I notice. Alan was showing me the photos that he took on your day out. He says that he is your boyfriend, is that right?'

Laura felt herself getting hot from the neck up. How should she answer this, she thought. She looked over at her father and saw that he had a wee smile on his face. Well, she thought, the truth is always the best, so without any hesitation she answered:

'Yes father, Peter and I are very close. He says he loves me but that's as far as it goes. It's too early for us to make any plans, especially now.'

'Well, Laura, whatever you decide about your future is fine with me. I just want what any man wants for his daughter – that she finds a good man and she is happy with him. Your mother would have felt the same but as far as I'm concerned, Peter is the lucky one. Now, what about a wee drop of tea before I go to bed? I'll see to it.'

He got up and went towards the kitchen, leaving her staring open-mouthed after him.

CHAPTER 56

THE SHOP AND THE TEA-ROOM were doing great business and Violet was delighted. She enjoyed meeting the old and new customers and sometimes making the time to have a coffee with them.

Laura was interviewing a few girls, they needed extra staff for the summer. She came into the shop to speak to Violet when she noticed June standing staring into space, as if in a dream.

'Come on girl' she said. 'You're not paid to stand there doing nothing. I can see tables that need your attention. What's the matter with you these days, you're always half asleep and never on time for your shift? You're having too many late nights, girl, and it's not fair on Mollie. She had to work two of your late shifts this week already. Now move!'

June turned on her and with a vicious tone in her voice said:

'What's it to you? And Mollie doesn't mind the extra nights. Anyway I've got a life ye know, apart from this place, not that ye'd know anything about that. I thought that Violet was the owner, not you.'

Laura could hardly believe her ears.

'Listen Madam, first of all this is my business and it's Mrs Wray to you. A little more manners wouldn't go astray.'

She looked at the young girl – too much makeup and not enough skirt.

'You've changed, June. You used to have such a lovely disposition, what happened?'

June looked at her, eyes blazing:

'Ye know somethin', yer just jealous. Yer past yer best and ye can't accept it. That's why yer always findin' fault with me.'

Laura was finding it hard to control herself, she wanted to slap this pretty little face in front of her.

'June, what are you raving about? Why on earth would I be jealous of you? Don't act so childish. Now, do you want to continue working here or not? It's up to you.'

She left the girl standing there. She knew for some reason that June had more to say but she couldn't cope with her right now. She went into the tea-room where she found Violet, sat down at her table and told her what had taken place.

'Violet, I was so surprised. I mean, she was always very forward but never that cheeky. What's got into her?'

Violet sighed.

'Och, you're not the only one. Sure her Auntie Mavis told me only last week that she has her heart broke, staying out till all hours and sometimes not coming home at all. And when she tries to speak to her, she gets nowhere.'

'She's always been a bit flighty,' remarked Laura, 'but she's very young. I suppose her and that young fellow she's with want to get as much as they can out of life.'

'I don't know about young Victor Boyd, sure he's that sensible. He told me that he was saving hard to buy a field to build on and start his own business,' said Violet.

Laura laughed.

'Well, June must have changed his mind then for she has some very high falutin' ideas. Now, I'd better do some more work or you'll be giving me my walking papers.'

Violet smiled.

'I suppose you will be missing Peter – he told me that he had work at some big hotel in Monaghan. He's staying there all week, isn't he?'

'Yes,' she replied, 'I'm missing him already. He wants me to come and stay some night but the way that bugger Andy's behaving... I can't trust him, God knows what he'll do next. I must phone Peter later and tell him about Father.'

Violet looked worried.

'Your father, is he alright?'

Laura smiled.

'As a matter of fact, he's great. And guess what? He gave us his blessing and told me that he was very happy for Peter and I. You should have seen me, I was totally overcome with shock.'

Then she told Violet everything that had happened – her friend was delighted for her.

'I always knew that it would sort itself out. I think that William has a soft spot for Peter.'

Later on when she went out to the back steps for a breather, she found Mollie there having a smoke. She jumped up when she saw Laura.

'Sorry Laura, I know I shouldn' be out here but I needed a smoke. I was run off my feet there for a while, it was dead busy, wasn' it?'

'It certainly was. Stay where you are and enjoy your smoke, don't you deserve it?' She sat down beside her on the step but Mollie made to get up.

'I should get back in, June hates workin' on her own.'

'Stay where you are,' said Laura. 'It's time that she did a bit more. She hasn't done much lately, has she? Where does herself and Victor get to every night? It must be costing him a small fortune to keep her going.'

Mollie leaned over the railing and blew the smoke skywards.

'Oh, she hasn' been seein' Victor for weeks. She has a new boyfriend and she's crazy about him. He takes her everywhere. They were even at a fancy nightclub in Belfast,' Mollie sighed. 'I wish my Seán would take me out places like that. We only go to the pictures once a week, if I'm lucky.'

'Who is this new boyfriend? He must be well-off. He's not from around here anyway, or we'd know him.'

'But ye do know him,' said Mollie. 'I saw ye talkin' to him a few times, Andrew Carstairs, yer friend.'

Laura was speechless for a moment and then she spoke the name almost under her breath.

'Andrew Carstairs, so that's what the devil is calling himself now. He's much too old for her, what in the name of God is he thinking of?'

'Are ye mad at her?' said Mollie, timidly. 'Oh, I shouldn't have said anythin'... but you should hear how she goes on about him and what he's going to do.'

Laura was interested now.

'What sort of things did she tell you?'

'I suppose I'm the only one she can tell. She said he was buyin' a big house in the village and turnin' it into a country club and she was goin' to be a hostess. Sure I wouldn' believe the half of it, would you?'

'I don't know Mollie but I can tell you this, he's a great one for the stories. Tell June to catch herself on before it's too late.'

Mollie laughed.

'I have told her but she's daft about him and believes everythin' he says. I mean... a hostess! Sure everyone knows they only work on big airlines. He told her she'd be perfect for the job and top businessmen from the city would all be comin' here. Did he not tell ye himself?'

Laura got up from the cold step and smiled at her.

'No Mollie, he must have forgotten, just like the way he changed his name. Now, it's time we were getting back, before the Hostess comes looking for us,' she said, laughing.

She had just closed up when Mary phoned. They told each other all their news, and Mary was delighted at William's acceptance of her brother.

'So what's the next step, shopping for a special dress for the big day?'

'No Mary, that's a long way off yet. I need to deal with this problem with Andy first... and wait till you hear the latest!'

As repeated what Mollie had said she heard her friend gasp.

'Laura, the other thing I had to tell you was that the McClean property is on the market and the auction is in two weeks. We were the only interested party until yesterday, when our solicitor told us that someone else is interested, a local. Do you think it could be Andy? That's all we need! But where's he getting the money?'

Laura sighed.

'God knows. Sure he was always involved in dodgy deals and he's been up meeting business people in the city this week.'

'Well,' said Mary, 'this property is our only chance. If we lose it we're finished but to lose it to him is worse. I just wish he'd disappear, he's a blight on all our lives.'

'Well, nobody wishes it more than me. Call me if you hear anything more, won't you?'

They talked for another few minutes before hanging up. Laura stood by the table deep in thought. What was that bugger up to? She remembered all the questions that Alan asked about the land and the farm and how much they owned. She knew Andy had put him up to it, that man was getting more devious by the hour. From the day he'd returned he had disrupted them all. And now, when she had a chance of happiness, he was about to destroy that too. Dear Lord, I need a miracle, she prayed.

CHAPTER 57

THEY LAY CONTENT in each others' arms, she felt so fulfilled. They hadn't been together for over a week and now they were making up for lost time.

Laura sighed, her hands exploring Peter's broad chest. He smiled at her.

'What are you thinking? You have a very satisfied look about you.'

She laughed.

'Maybe I have. You know something, this has been the best day of my life since Alan was born.'

He moved up on his elbow to look at her and kissed her brow.

'Maybe I should be absent more often to make you feel like this?'

'No, I don't want you to be absent at all! Tonight was the icing on the cake but today I had a letter from Alice Quinn.'

'It must have been good news to make you feel like this.'

She smiled, reached over to her bag, pulled out a letter and gave it to him to read. He scanned the contents.

'I can't believe it, this is great news. He can't go near Alan unless you agree to terms and times,' he hugged her tightly. 'This will certainly ease your mind. But what about all this other stuff here?'

He pointed to the other page.

'It's great news, all of it. Alice had contacts in Canada and they sent her the information. He's being investigated by the police for fraud, among other things, and under several different names. Lord knows what else. He left his wife and children months ago and sold their house that wasn't his in the first place. He won't have a leg to stand on when it comes to claiming Alan.'

Peter looked at her and asked.

'Why didn't you show me this when you came in. Why so secretive, you wench?' he teased, pulling her on top of him.

'I wanted to but I wanted you more. Now we can both read it slowly together. See, I'm a sadist!' she joked. 'There's something else... Alice sent me a personal note, it's about Belle. She left him a year ago and took the girls with her. She has been having an affair with his wealthy boss – he gave her a place to live when Andy sold their home. Now Belle has filed for divorce. I had told Alice about the threats he made, so it's only a matter of time before he's arrested and finds himself up in court.'

'This is all great news. What about Alan though? He has grown fond of him, hasn't he?'

'I know,' she said, 'that's the only blot on the landscape. How do I tell him? When the letter came I showed it to Father and he said the same. I know he'll be upset. He thought his Dad was the tops, he could do no wrong. Now I don't know what to tell him.'

Peter shook his head and said it would be very difficult.

'Did your father mention Belle? He must be worried about her.'

'No, he surprised me by saying that she would be alright, she always knew what side her bread was buttered on! Anyway, he's more worried about Alan. Himself and Ernie Wilson had planned on going to a big fair over the border in Ballybay so he says he'll take Alan too. When Father told him he was over the moon, sure he loves the fairs. I know I'll have to sit him down and explain... but not yet.'

Peter tightened his arm around her.

'You know, I have the greatest respect for your Da, he knows how to handle a delicate situation. And I bet he'll be the answer to your prayers regarding Alan. Come and cuddle up closer – now that I have you where I want you, I'm not letting you go.'

CHAPTER 58

THE RED MG drove out of the McClean drive, Andy turned it towards home. He stopped the car in the driving rain and told the girl beside him to get out.

'What? Aren't you going to take me home? It's raining, I can't walk in these heels.'

'June, I'm not taking you home, what made you think I was? Now, get out!' He leaned across her to open the passenger door but she held on.

'What's wrong, what did I do? I thought you loved me.'

'Well, you thought wrong, didn't you? Now, hop it! I'm in a hurry.'

'Please Andrew, don't do this. How can you be so hurtful, after what we've been to each other?'

'For heaven's sake will you move, you're really getting on my nerves now.'

Still holding on to the car door, she looked at him. Filled with shame thinking of how they had spent the last hour. Earlier, the McClean's caretaker had given him the key of the big house. This was where he planned to open his new country club. He had told her that she would look well as a hostess, catering to the rich business people from the city. It really excited her. Then they had made passionate love again, on the magnificent drawingroom floor with a full moon shining through the open shutters on their sweating bodies. She had been like putty in his hands. He could persuade her to do things she had only read about before. They had downed a bottle of whiskey, now her head was spinning.

'Andrew,' she begged, 'what about our plans, my job as your hostess?'

He pushed her out of the car and looked at her. She was a mess. Her eye make-up had run and streaked down her face. She stood there pleading with him, her head filled with notions.

'You, a hostess! Will you catch yourself on, you stupid bitch. The girls that work for me will be rather more classy than you. Now move!'

He revved the car up again, slammed the door shut and drove off, leaving her standing in the rain.

A few miles up the road the rain had stopped so he pulled the car over, got out and put the top down. He loved the feeling of the open road and the wind in his hair. Tonight he was in great spirits – everything was finally falling into place.

Further up the road a watcher waited in a field under an overhanging hedge. From where he lay he had a good command of the oncoming traffic. This was also a well-known spot for accidents – after a long winding climb, the road dipped sharply towards the glen and drivers often approached it far too fast.

The watcher waited... He had great patience and had been there every evening for nearly a week. Tonight conditions were right. He had been keeping a close watch on his target and he knew that the waiting would soon be over. He lifted the high-powered rifle with the night-sights and positioned it on its tripod.

Andy drove at great speed, feeling elated – tomorrow he would be the owner of the McClean estates. Then he would claim his son and in a few years he would probably have the Steenson farm as well. Oh yes, life was good. He needed a drink, the remains of the whiskey was on the seat beside him. He put the bottle to his head and gulped, it felt great!

When he was almost at the hill, he put the engine in full throttle and sped ahead. He laughed, no one could stop him now. At the top of the hill he reached for his cigarettes, put one in his mouth and groped around till he found his lighter. He flicked it open and lit it, he only took his eyes off the road for a second... then it happened. The car spun out of control, the surface was wet and there was nothing he could do. He tried to bring it back on the road but he couldn't. He began to swerve when the huge oak tree loomed in front of him...he hit it head on.

At the farmhouse in the glen, the owner was out with his dogs and heard the crash and the screams. He knew it was something terrible and went inside to phone for help. By the time he reached the road it was too late, the car was a fireball against the tree and there was no saving the driver.

The watcher smiled... a good night's work. He saw the farmer arrive on the scene and stand hopelessly by, unable to do anything. A short time later he heard the police siren.

As silently as he came he went. At the top of the field he dismantled the rifle and packed it into a small holdall. He stood up and tied the belt of his long black leather coat, adjusted his scarf, and disappeared into the night.

The police, ambulance and fire brigade were on the scene, each man shocked at the sight of the burnt-out car and driver. Debris was scattered all over the road. They began to clear it away, stopping oncoming traffic. When the driver of one of the cars got out and approached one of the policemen.

'Excuse me, officer, I'm a priest, can I be of any help?'

He escorted the priest to the burnt-out wreckage.

'I'm not sure of what persuasion he is, Father but a prayer always helps at these times.'

He left the priest giving the last rites. As he walked away, he noticed something shining at the side of the road. He picked it up and brought it to his sergeant.

'What is it, a toy?' the sergeant asked. 'There's not a mark on it, it must have been thrown from the car. Well would ye look at that, it's a wee lighter.'

He flicked the bonnet open and the flame sprang up.

'It's a lovely thing, I'll give it to the next of kin for there's nothing else here,' he said, looking at the wreckage and shaking his head. 'When will these young bucks ever learn? Another young life lost to drunk-driving.'

Back at Peter's flat, Laura shivered in his arms as he pulled her closer.

'Are you cold?' he asked.

'No,' she said, 'But I think I have just walked on someone's grave.'